THE UNSEEN

The Guard Trilogy Book 2

N. L. Westaway

Original Cover Photo by Pier Francesco Grizi
Cover designed by Beach House Press

This book is a work of fiction. Names, characters, places, and incidents either are products of the author's imagination or are used fictitiously. Any resemblance to actual persons, living or dead, events, or locales is entirely coincidental.

N. L. Westaway
Visit my website at www.NLWestaway.com

Printed in the United States of America
ISBN: 978-1-7339442-4-3
Beach House Press

December 2018 Limited Edition Print Copies – Not for Resale.
First Publication: May 2019 Beach House Press

The Guard Trilogy

The Guard

The Unseen

The Believer

This book is dedicated to Luc, Mac, Vicki, Olivia, Spooky, and Shortcut, for allowing me to use their likenesses for this adventure.

You all know who you are. *wink-wink*.

"But what really matters is not what you believe but the faith and conviction with which you believe...."

~ Knut Hamsun, Mysteries

Anagram - An anagram is a type of word play, the result of rearranging the letters of a word or phrase to produce a new word or phrase, using all the original letters exactly once. *www.en.wikipedia.org*

    Resistance = Ancestries
    Conversation = Voices rant on
    The Hurricanes = These air churn

Chapter 1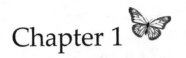

"*Well…,*" Uriel had said, "*…if the Watchers are no longer bound — do you know what this means?*" He'd grinned. "*Neither are we!*"

Acknowledging had softened Vretil's worried face. "*Clever, Arch of Peace, Harmony, and Balance. Very clever.*"

Uriel had known the leaders of the 200 would wait to see if the Charges would fail. He knew if they did, those leaders who watched over evil humans, might nudge *free will* in the wrong direction, create chaos on Earth, in hopes of showing *Him* that man was not worth *His* effort — that humanity was not worth sparing. Some of the fallen understood the atonement for their crimes, but the others — their anger festered over the generations of men, 70 generations to be precise, and now the proverbial *gloves* were off. And without proof that humanity — these women, were shown to be worthy in *His* eyes, no one would hold them back from destroying the human race. Uriel and his brethren had questioned the shift in the balance, questioned what could be done to set things straight, keep the evil from destroying the Earth. There would no longer be four daughters to carry forth the secret, keep the balance and safeguard humanity. Who or what would tip the scales in their favor, they didn't know, nor did they know what Gabriel had set in motion.

"*How can Gabriel be so sure?*" Michael had asked. They all knew why they had chosen whom they chose, but it had been 5000 years ago.

Gabriel had made his choice 35 years ago. *"What made his choice the right one, what made it so special?"* Michael had said in challenge.

"Trust me," Gabriel had told them. *"Be patient and trust your Charges,"* was all he had given them, all he'd felt he could share—for now.

Home of Olivia White and Family – Early September 2010, Current Day, Ottawa, Canada

What a week, hell—what a night!

I figured I'd crash hard after the adventures of the night, but instead I'd lain in bed staring at the ceiling. How could I sleep with all this stuff running around in my head? So many questions—too many questions and no answers. Not that I was complaining, I was thankful to be staying with my friend and her family, but this week had been a whirlwind of events and information I wasn't sure I had grasped. If I were to tell someone outside our little group what we'd found out— discovered, about our mothers, they'd think I was full of crap or living in a fantasy book or perhaps on the verge of losing my marbles. All this information, this talk of *the secret* and passing on the responsibility from mother to daughter was hard to grapple with despite being a witness to all the findings. And this threat of illness and even death, was for what? The *balance*? The balance of what… life and death… light and dark… water and earth… heaven and hell… seen and unseen… good and evil?

Mom's journal hadn't given us any answers, but the mere mention of it to Vicki's mom had sparked a series of events. The first being the discovery of the map in the old trunk, the one originally belonging to Vicki's grandmother. The map took us to our next clue, the old pencil box we'd found hidden under the remains of a historical site, an old wooden platform that still held up a large cast iron bell. In fact, it had been Derek, *Shortcut Jones*—as I call him or Shortcut for, well—short, who had helped us find the hidden compartment in the trunk, deciphered the symbols on the map and directed us on how to open the antique pencil box with its tricky lid. But neither the map nor the vintage box had been the real treasure. The real find had been the letter we'd found inside the box, the one Vicki's mom had written and addressed to her.

Vicki had known of my mom's journal before that day, and its mentions of *the secret* and *illness or death if passed on,* and the references to the *Sorceress, Healer, Scribe* and *Scholar,* and how it reflected the same as in that letter. Vicki had wanted to ambush her mom for answers, but I'd asked her to wait until we could go over everything, the journal, the list of weird, and the letter. Thankfully she'd agreed, because the following day when I'd spent time with Mac and her mother, we'd inadvertently found the next clue in this treasure hunt.

On that visit, Mac's mother had also reacted strangely at the mention of my mother's journal, more so it was the contents of the journal itself that had thrown her off. It was then she'd questioned Mac on her great-great-grandmother's cookbook. The letter we'd found from Vicki's mom had ended with, *She is the Sorceress, The Witch and she holds the Grimoire of Nature, the Tree of Life will be in plain sight,* and this grimoire, had been the cookbook Mac's mother had asked about, and it had been on Mac's shelf in her kitchen for years. And like Vicki's trunk, the cookbook had turned out to be something more than family recipes passed down.

The cookbook was full of rituals and spells every good *witch* should have. Yup, witch—*sorceress* as was written in the letter and journal. When we'd reread the letter and its description of the Sorceress—or Witch, we'd deduced it had to be Monica—Mac's mom. We'd found another description at the back of the cookbook, one describing *The Healer.* For a brief second, I'd assumed the description might have been of my mother, but too many of the pieces didn't fit.

I'd again asked Derek for his help, having him find out more on this *Tree of Life* and the snake and sword symbol we had found with the Healer's description. He'd come through in record speed, and despite being a skeptic, he'd even surprised himself, because what he'd found seemed plausible to him—but only because it was based in science he felt he could relate. He'd noted other secret societies in existence, *Freemasons* being the most famous. And he'd said, *"Who's saying you haven't stumbled upon another one—a matriarchal one."* Being that he was my IT guru, scientific geek, fact-or-nothing-friend, I'd chosen to wait in telling him the strange findings, then I'd eased him into the weirdness. But when I told him the whole *Cipher* thing, he'd fallen right into the role—liked it, he enjoyed puzzles and riddles. He loved solving anything, especially our little mysteries. The same night I'd told Derek of our latest finds, he'd proven his skill as the Cipher again when he'd helped Olivia and me with not one—but two puzzle-like tasks. Interestingly enough though, it had been Olivia who'd offered the answer to the first part of the quandary. I had sent Derek off to find information on the snake and sword, but when I mentioned the symbol to Liv—she'd known what it was and had told me it was a *Caduceus.*

Of course, that had started me all a tingle again, which led me to the realization that the description in Mac's cookbook was Liv's mom—she was the Healer, and the Caduceus being a medical symbol. We'd gone through all of her mother's boxes, but it wasn't until she mentioned her gran's old roll-top desk, that we'd found another piece of the puzzle. The old desk had presented its own challenges, a secret compartment. The only way in had been with the help of our Cipher.

Derek guided us in getting the first part open, but the challenge hadn't ended there. In it, we'd found an old-fashioned key, but found no place in the desk it would fit. Smarty-pants Shortcut suggested we move the desk away from the wall and voila—keyhole, in the side of the desk with another hidden compartment. Inside we'd found a caduceus-shaped puzzle box. I'd been excited about the find but had practically reached my wits end with all these puzzle elements. Thank goodness Derek loved this kind of challenge, and with help again we'd gotten the puzzle box open. In it was yet another letter.

This one was written by Olivia's mom, and mentioned similar things as written by the other mothers, only this one contained the description of the Storyteller, or Scribe whichever, and told how she *carries the Codex of Balance.* My heart had been pounding through my chest at that point, and it had also been pounding in my head with little pulses of clarity pushing to the forefront. Well, not clarity for the grand mystery, but more for who the Scribe was. Part of the description had sparked a memory, something I'd read; the obituary Alison had written for her mom. The words were not exact, but they'd been close enough not to be overlooked. After the comparison we knew it made Alison's mom the fourth, she was the Scribe. When I'd told Alison of our findings, she'd been shocked and thrilled, but it wasn't until she'd questioned her father about the book—this Codex, that we'd gotten clarification that she had had something resembling a big journal. The tricky part was that we needed to find it. Alison's dad had mentioned that after they'd moved out to Calgary, he'd never saw the big book again.

To our luck, the next day when we'd gone to *grill* Vicki's mom for more info, we'd found out more of what we'd needed. It wasn't so much an ambush, more of a sneak attack on Vicki's part. The charade of a friendly visit had changed quickly after we'd arrived as Vicki hadn't been able to hold back. This had been the first time we'd had one of the mothers right in front of us to answer questions. Unfortunately, we'd learned little about this *secret* and the *men* mentioned in the writings, but we had discovered Jeannette—Vicki's mom, had been visited by Alison's mother, and had had the elusive book in hand for it. And not only did she visit Vicki's mom, she'd later called her from Calgary. That had been four years ago we'd been told.

It had appeared as though the pieces were revealing themselves, but then we'd hit a roadblock. Claudette—Alison's mom, had told Vicki's mom on the call, that she'd hidden the book—near a monument of all things, but which one, Jeannette could not remember.

After our visit, we'd gone over to Mac's place. She and *her* mother were waiting for us. Monica had been ready to share what she knew, but she described things much the same as Jeannette had; about the *man* who'd visited her, and the *role* of mother and daughter. She had however, gone into more detail about the *balance*—a balance between good and evil, as she had depicted it.

We'd determined using the letters who the four mothers were; Monica being the Sorceress, Pamela being the Healer, Claudette being the Scribe, and Jeannette being the Scholar. Their daughters were now the recipients of the secret, the responsibilities, these corresponding roles having been handed down via mothers and grandmothers etc. prior. But what these responsibilities were exactly, we still weren't clear on, only that they were *theirs* now. Full circle we'd come it seemed, but new clarity or not, we were left with more questions regardless of speaking with the mothers.

Hoping to find more answers, I'd expanded Derek's by giving him more details and scanned copies of the grimoire to review. He'd firmed up the belief this was a kind of secret matriarchal thing, so I'd emailed him the names of the *men*; Uriel, Michael, Raphael, Gabriel and Shamsiel. Like everything else we'd given him prior, we hadn't had to wait long for his response. He'd come back stating that the grimoire pages we'd sent him were in the *Witch Alphabet* or *Witch Writing*, concluding these were spells—not recipes.

The following day, we'd returned to Mac's, where she'd run down the list of *do's* and *don'ts* and *how-tos* on her new vocation in witchcraft. After, she'd pulled off a spell for us—a genuine full-on protection spell. It'd freaked us all out, but even Olivia had enjoyed it. Alison had called right after the spell. It had been the information from her call that had sent us on our night's adventure. She'd told us about how her dad had taken her mom downtown *twice* before they moved. First to sell a writing desk and the second to see a monument, near to where she'd sold the desk. He said she'd been adamant about going to the *Human Rights* monument and that she'd had a bag with her, with something big and heavy in it, but when she'd returned to the car, the satchel appeared empty. With the monument being mentioned, we'd been confident we knew where we needed to go. But the real kicker, had come when Derek had emailed back the information on the names of these men.

I had breached the idea with Olivia first, but my idea had been further enhanced when Derek had come back with a long email stating how the names matched those of Archangels. Of the descriptions of each angel Derek had given us, three had matched with each of the letters. We had figured Alison would eventually be matched with one of the remaining two, Shamsiel or Gabriel, but that would leave us with one extra. The girls remained skeptical on the men being actual angels, figuring they'd merely been named after them.

We needed the codex more than ever and we believed the book had the answers to *everything*. Before any of us could change our minds, we'd all hopped into Olivia's car and had headed downtown to find its hiding place. We'd been successful thus far with clues and puzzles, but it had proved to be more difficult than we'd expected. It hadn't been at the monument; it had been hidden in the *Ottawa City Hall Heritage Building*. Derek had once again been invaluable in the discovery, and totally in his element, I might add.

Though we hadn't found the book exactly, we'd assumed we'd found it, but, what we'd recovered had been the lap desk Alison's mom had *supposedly* sold. She'd hidden it, and since she'd told Vicki's mom she'd hidden the book, our chances were more than decent that the book was inside. And we'd managed to sneak that sucker out of the building and without being seen... or so I'd thought. The creepy thing was my senses had shot off the chart as soon as I'd exited the building.

The surrounding temperature had dropped unnaturally, and a sick sense of foreboding and nausea had crept up my spine like a slow-moving spider with sharp needles for legs. Each prickle had invoked a new level of sickness leaving the back of my throat thick and wet with the taste of something wrong. Then I'd seen it—him, casting a shadow from the streetlamp. I'd panned the rest of the street, but when I'd glanced back to the figure under the streetlamp, he'd disappeared. It had taken us seconds to funnel into the car and we'd been off up the street, and thankfully the horrible sensations had lessened, changing to a warm soothing blanket of relief, hope and energy.

Someone or something had been watching us—me, as we left the building. But more specifically, after we'd gotten into the car, *four* someones, then a *fifth*, had watched us drive away. Why? Who, or should I say *what* as it felt more like, had been there—watching? I'd sat in the rear seat, glancing back through the window hoping for more clarity, but as we'd rounded the corner at the end of the street, things became more *unclear*. It seemed the farther we went with this hunt for knowledge, the less I knew or understood.

That *book of balance* had better damn well be in that desk, and it better have all the answers. If it's not, I might lose it. We assumed it was inside—*hoped* that is. This was the latest and hopefully the last piece of the puzzle, the crazy, unbelievable and rather mystical and still unclear-puzzle. But we still needed to figure out how to get into the desk. For now, the lap desk was safely nuzzled between other pieces of the mystery, in a big wicker basket stashed under the desk in Mac's office.

Mom's journal had started all this and yet still I didn't understand her involvement, or what it all meant. Both Vicki's mom and Mac's mom suggested that my Mom was a facilitator of a sort, and that I had facilitated bringing the four daughters together. Was I supposed to make sense of this? Was this our role—my role? Was that it—was I done now? Aside from these questions, I wondered now what sick group of individuals had started all this drama, and who were these men with angel names and why were mothers and daughters paying with their lives? What secret could be so important someone would risk illness or death to pass it on? Was it blackmail wrapped in a myth, or a form of brainwashing mixed with faith? Had my mother been brainwashed—had my friends' mothers been caught up in the same? Were we all slowly, methodically being brainwashed to put our lives on the line? And if so—for what? What was there to gain or lose, what was the payoff—was there a payoff, or was it all a sick joke? "Close your eyes, Westlake," I muttered, as I dozed off. There'd be no answers tonight.

Even with the lights out, in the wee hours of night, Gabriel used his full veil as he stood at the edge of the bed—*just in case*. His sense of bewilderment was mixed with pride though his mind replayed the accusations made earlier by his brethren. *"Did you see that? Gabriel's Charge—she looked right at us. How could she see us? She wasn't meant to see us—who revealed themselves? Gabriel was it you?"* Raphael had questioned him. The others had stood speechless, staring as the car drove away.

"She doesn't require a reveal to see!" he had exclaimed to the others. That's when they'd all turned and looked at him, mouths hanging open, including the ever-suspicious Shamsiel.

"What... in heaven's name—is that supposed to mean?" Michael had asked next.

He smiled. What *had* he meant when he'd uttered those words... what... indeed?

Chapter 2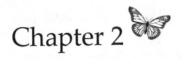

Olivia and I sat staring into space as we sipped away at our coffees as the usual song and dance blurred around us as the other family members once again readied themselves for the day. No one mentioned our late night.

Between sips of coffee, Olivia explained Mike hadn't even stirred when she'd climbed into bed. Both the girls' bedroom doors had been shut, making our sneaking in that much easier. Not that we had to sneak, but there'd been no need to deal with questions at that hour.

I checked the clock on the wall, and said, "Two hours until Alison arrives. You wanna come with me to get her? I'll drive this time... you can sleep on the way, then we'll head over to Mac's again. Alison won't want to wait a minute knowing her Mom's desk is there waiting for her to open it." I yawned. "She's gonna want to see all the other stuff too," I followed up, drawing out another yawn.

Olivia smiled and sipped her coffee as if pretending she wasn't just as eager to see what was inside the lap desk. She, like the rest of us, was hoping to find all the answers to the questions.

Slow on the get-up-and-go, an hour and a half later we were out the door with our to-go mugs full of wake-up brew. As we eased out of the driveway, I said, "This'll be a big day for all. And I'm thrilled you and the others finally get to meet Alison."

She took a big sip of coffee from her mug and grinned. "I'm sure she's dying to meet the rest of this motley crew." She grinned bigger this time. She had found a bond and new friendships with the others she hadn't expected to find.

"Guess I'm the hub connecting all the spokes, eh?" I said. "You guys being the spokes on this crazy ferris-wheel ride." I took a long swig from my travel mug. "This may have been the only way the four of you to have met—through me. What might have happened if I'd never reconnected with Mac and Alison?" I paused. "Or if Will and I had never reconnected, you and I wouldn't have met either." I let out a nervous laugh. "I'm thankful for those forces seen and unseen—I'm tell'n ya. Without whatever or whomever—this venture would never have taken place." A fast tickling shiver shimmied across my shoulder blades, vanishing just as quick.

"Hurts my head when I think about it too much. Just letting it be whatever," Olivia said, still sipping her brew. She was calmer than usual, but I figured it was the lack of sleep.

As we took the long road out to the airport, my thoughts shifted to how interesting it was that all airports—no matter the city, seemed to have this same long stretch when you entered *Airport Land*. The Ottawa airport was simple, you go up for departures—all of them, and down for arrivals—one entrance each. If you were lucky, you could hover outside the main doors to pick up your party or do a quick circle around to catch them as they came out. Parking was available, but you only used it if the flight was delayed or you were early or wanted to surprise a person inside. But since Alison was on a domestic flight, this would be a cinch, and no immigration line.

The time on the big digital clock outside the arrivals door showed 10:05 a.m.. The flight tracker app on my phone showed her plane arrived at 10:01. Alison would be out with her luggage in no time, and given she didn't know what car to expect on pick-up, I got out and went around to the passenger's side that faced the exit doors. I leaned against the front panel of the car and Olivia rolled down her window.

"How long has it been since you've seen her?" Olivia asked.

I did the math in my head. "Last time I saw her was when she and Ken were in Miami looking for investment properties. It's gotta be over three years now I figure." Too long.

One by one, we watched as people exited the arrivals area. A tall man with a cowboy hat came out and moseyed to the left to get into a waiting pickup truck. From Calgary—no doubt, no one around here wears a hat like that. I giggled a little as he passed by. Overhead, the sky got a little bluer, the sun shone a little brighter, and as the main doors to the airport slid open once again, out came my Spooky.

She was smiling so big you'd swear someone was pinching her cheeks for her, and I could hear her giggle already as she rolled her luggage over our way. Meeting her on the road divider, she dropped her hold on the suitcase. In unison, we wrapped our arms around each other and squeezed, hugging like we were holding on for dear life. When she loosened her grip and as we separated, my eyes followed the separation of our bodies. There, under a dark green pullover was a hint of baby-bump saying how-do-ya-do.

"Smuggling contraband again," I asked, trying to keep a straight face.

"You know me, I'll try to get away with anything I can these days," she said, grabbing me in her arms and squeezing again.

When she let go again, I turned and introduced her to my little Olivia, who waited patiently in the car. Olivia, akin to Alison, is an easy person to like, all smiles and giggles. The kindness oozes out of them, and you can't help but get it all over you. And what happens then, is, well—you're a goner and they've sucked you right into their enjoyment with life.

"Hiiiii, Olivia," Alison said as she eased into the backseat. I smiled and placed her suitcase in alongside her and shut the door.

Then I shivered as a cold, near icy breeze scraped across the side of my cheek. Queasiness hit me next. Sickness—nausea, rising from the depth of my toes, up through my thighs, to the hollows of my stomach. Swirling heat passed over my diaphragm up into my esophagus reaching the back of my throat. *Breathe*, I told myself—breathe. *Yer gonna puke if you don't take in some air*. I turned in the direction where the chilled wind had come. There near the entrance in the shadow of the arrivals sign was a tall dark… *familiar* figure.

He wore all black and his hair was dark as coal. A swipe of black facial hair marred his perfect chin. His eyes peered out from under the thick shadow of his brow, but I knew those eyes were as pitch dark as midnight. He was handsome, but the malevolence coming off him scraped away any possible appeal. His evil factor only intensified as his gaze fixed on us—on *me*.

Voices calling my name pulled my attention from the man and broke me from what I branded as a *death* stare. I turned my head towards the voices, my vision blurring as if in slow motion. Olivia's head was out through the open window, her lips moving, her hands reaching for me.

"Lynn!" she'd said for the umpteenth time, "What's going on—what are you staring at?" She grabbed my arm, and just like that, the sick sensation left.

In control of my senses, I turned my attention back towards the dark stranger, but he was gone. I took a quick sweep of the arrivals area noting all the cars lined up and newly arriving passengers, but I did not see *him*. "Nothing," I said, and patted her hand. She let go, and I circled around the car to get back into the driver's side.

"You okay, Spook?" Alison asked, leaning in-between the front seats.

"Oh, I'm good—something caught my eye. I was trying to get a fix on it—sorry, didn't mean to freak you guys out. Been seeing and feeling some unusual things lately, but it's nothing, I'm sure." I gave them both a big reassuring grin, but I knew something wasn't right.

They seemed to take my words with ease, but *I* wasn't so at ease. *Would they think I was nuts?* No, they wouldn't, because this was all nuts. I'd had this same dreadful vibe before, twice now. The first had been here at the airport when I'd arrived from Miami. The other had been outside the old town hall last night, but I hadn't been able to see who'd been watching us.

What were the chances it was this same guy? Why did his presence give me the sensation my guts were crawling up my digestive track? Had anyone else seen the figure in the shadows? Should I tell them what I'd seen last night—what I saw now, how it *felt*? No, there'd be time later to tell them. Besides it wasn't relevant to our current focus and most likely an offshoot of my stupid Lynnie-senses.

My reassurance must have passed their test, because as we drove, Alison said, "Where're we going to first? I'm dying to see all the things you've found." It made me smile for real this time.

Olivia turned to face the backseat. "Oh, it's been quite the treasure hunt. And the lap desk—we have to find a way to open it," she relayed, trying yet failing at keeping her anxiousness to a minimum.

"Man, we were up till midnight last night racking our brains," I said. "But the exhaustion of it all seemed to have shut our brains down. Besides, five clear heads are better than four sleepy ones. We'll get the thing open today," I added, glancing at Alison's face in the rearview mirror.

"Wow, things here sure have changed in the last fifteen years. Haven't been back much since my parents moved out Calgary-way." Alison sighed. "Feels like a hundred years since I was here." She was smiling ear to ear, glancing out the window, watching as all the familiar and unfamiliar things passed by.

When I turned down Mac's street, I spotted Cooper out front guarding his home. I liked seeing him out front, protecting his family, and I like him protecting us while we visited there. Vicki was here already. She'd parked her car on the road along the edge of the front lawn. I hoped she was brainstorming with Mac on how to get the damn box open because I had exhausted all my ideas.

"House is so cute," Alison peeped, when we pulled into the driveway, "You'd never know a witch lived here." She let out a witchy cackle.

"The inside is even cuter," I said, dragging my exhausted body from the car. An equally tired Olivia groaned as she exited the car. Once again, I was in the lead, but this was not my parade. With Alison and her luggage in tow, the two of them followed up the stairs behind me.

At the top of the stairs, I took a quick glance through the main door window where I saw Mac and Vicki in the kitchen. I pulled the screen door open and knocked on the main door only to push it open without waiting for a response. "What are you two cooks whipping up in here?" I asked, hoping it was something warm and delicious as they both had a talent for cooking and baking.

"Weeeeell, if it isn't the walking stomach," Mac tossed at me. "I see Cooper let you by again. Must like you — can't figure why." She walked over, and using her empty arm, she hugged me around the shoulder. Her other arm cradled a large plastic container of warm muffins topped with all sorts of goodness baked into them. "Hello Sleepy," Mac directed at Olivia. "Aaaaand you must be, *the Scribe.*" She gave Alison a big toothy Mac grin.

"Tis me, the humble Scribe... Storyteller extraordinaaaaaar," Alison responded, bowing to our witch.

Mac let go of me, and then the two of them giggled and embraced like old friends. I snatched two muffins from the bowl and headed into the living room to get comfortable and set up shop with my laptop again.

"Tea, anyone?" Vicki hollered from the kitchen. Vicki never drank coffee.

"I'm empty," Olivia responded from the couch, holding up her empty travel mug.

"Got any caffeine-free? I'll take some if you do," Alison asked, moving to the kitchen.

"Guess I'll have some too. Have to wash these terrible muffins down with something. Full caffeine for me, please," I teased. I was exhausted, and I would take whatever caffeine I could get my hands on at this point.

"Watch it, or I'll put a little eye-of-newt in yours," Mac said, pretending to give me the evil eye, half-laughing as she tried the eye-to-hand pointing gesture.

"If it will wake me up — giver!" I shot back, looking back down at the laptop as it made its familiar blips and beeps.

"How was your flight?" Mac asked Alison.

Alison was still standing in the hall between the living room and kitchen. "Oh, pretty standard; airport, lines, cabin-pressure, sore ears, landing, more lines, luggage — you know, the usual," she said laughing, giving everyone the full magnitude of her contagious giggle, and sending knowing giggles down the line.

"Any crazies on the plane or at the airport," Olivia asked, not being a fan of flying and its understandable non-perks.

"Not really, thank gawd. But there was this one guy in the boarding area who kept staring at me. When it was time to board the plane, he just stood there, to the side—still watching me. Never got on the plane. Totally weird," she recalled, giving a little shudder.

"Eeeshhh!" was all Olivia gave in response, her own little body-shudder apparent.

"It could be the hormones, but the totally weird thing wasn't the fact he was watching me. It was how his watching made me feel."

The word *feel* made me look up from the computer and I waited for her to continue. Alison made a face as if trying to find the right words. Mac and Vicki stood in the hall with her while Olivia leaned over the back of the couch to face her. The expression on Alison's face prompted the recall of those *feelings* from the night before, taking me to dark places in my head, the fear, the pain... and the *sorrow*.

"Don't get me wrong here. On the surface, this guy was hot. I mean model material, beautiful...," Alison said, pulling me from my memory, "... beautiful like a panther... evil, dark... like the villain in one of those romance novels. *Nasty* radiated from him." She shivered and then rubbed her belly. "Made you feel dirty—and not in a good way." She laughed as if trying to break the dark mood, but she couldn't hide her anxiety. "The guy wore black—head to toe, with jet-black hair, and a thin black pinch," she recalled, drawing a line from her lower lip down to the tip of her chin. She rubbed her tummy again. "Kid needs a muffin—slide me one of those would ya, Mac." Deflecting, Alison looked to Mac for sustenance, breaking us all once again from the doom and gloom, and into more giggles.

Mac smiled as if to break her own *ick* feeling and handed over the container of muffins to the giggling baby-mamma.

Vicki returned to the kitchen to get the brew.

I turned back to my computer, but I couldn't shake the image Alison had described. Evil. Two dark strangers—three? Downtown... in the Calgary airport, and outside the Ottawa airport—twice. Should I say something? Did we need more dark dialog? No... this was about the four coming together, and not about my weird feelings... but Alison had felt something. Maybe not as overpowering as the waves of malevolence I'd received, but it was something. For now, I'd keep the stuff to myself. There'd be a time to share later once we got the book out, and we got answers. I'd tell them then about the someones watching me—us—them.

Shake it off, Westlake, I told my brain, focusing back on my email. Perfect timing too, Derek had written back. "We got an update from Derek," I shared, "Something about a *skeleton key*."

"Skeletons? Must be a witch thing," Alison said, cackling, doing her best witch imitation, trying not to spill her tea as she laughed her way to the living room.

Mac responded with, "Hello, kitchen-witch here—not wicked-witch." Grimoire under her arm and with her own muffin and tea in hand, Mac nestled into her usual chair. Gesturing to Alison, Mac motioned for her to come sit near her in the chair adjacent, the one she'd dragged from the back-family room, its navy-blue fabric showing its blatant disparity to the warm tones of the rich dark chocolate furniture of the living room. Alison scooted by me to sit in the warn but comfortable blue chair. "Wait until you see the rest of the stuff we've found," Mac said, leaning into Alison.

Alison nodded then stared down at her mother's lap desk that rested on the coffee table

"Hold up there, Harry—let me read what it says," I said, poking fun at Mac's *Harry Potter'ish* attempt at opening the box from the other night. Summarizing the email, I said, "*A skeleton key or passing-key, is a key modified to bypass the sections inside the keyhole. You strip down a key to its essential parts or an object capable of opening any lock.* So we need to find something that will fit iiiin the keyhole, but also has an edge to turn the wards inside. Everyone follow?"

Vicki blocked the laptop screen with a mug of tea.

"Where's yours?" I asked, taking the mug she offered.

"Mug's right there." Vicki pointed at the big mug on the coffee table "Touch it—and you're dead. Got it just the way I like it," the tea-addict warned. She gave me a sideways glance, part joking—part dead serious.

"Like I'd sip from your cootie-cup anyway," I said, giving her my best-disgusted face.

Settling in next to Olivia, Vicki handed her the other mug. Then Vicki pulled Alison in with the first question. "Alison—what do you make of all this?" She waved a hand out as if she were one of the lovely ladies on the Price is Right.

Leaning in, Alison ran her hand over the decorative surface of the piece. "Didn't know it had an *inside*… figured the bottom was hollow, and it sat on your lap." Her words trailed off as her focus came back to the group, but she hadn't answered Vicki's question.

"Let me see the keyhole again," Olivia requested, turning the box such that the lock faced her.

"What are you thinking, Liv?" I asked. I could practically hear the gears turning in her head.

Panning the room, Olivia asked, "Where's the big basket? The one with all the treasures etc." As if remembering, she hopped off the couch and rushed up the stairs. "Boy-proof—just remembered," she said halfway up the stairs, caffeine kicking in.

Mac flipped through the grimoire but then slammed it shut. "Nothing! Not one thing on cracking locks in here," Mac said, handing it over to Alison for her perusal.

"It's not a handbook for thieves, Mac. It's for healing, conjuring, and communing with nature, not busting open locks," Vicki reminded our witch.

As if having no real response, Mac responded by sticking out her tongue. Vicki responded with an equal retort, her tongue extended with her face scrunched.

"Mature—both of you, very mature," I joked, shaking my head and laughing a little. In a simultaneous immature rebuttal, the two of them stuck their tongues out at me.

We all turned to the stairs as Olivia returned down the steps, basket secure in her arms. Then Alison gathered up her Mom's desk making more room for Olivia to set down the basket. Olivia undid the fastenings and flipped open the lid wide to let it flop on its hinges to the other side. Rummaging through the basket, she retrieved the caduceus box in which her mother's letter was found. Opening the box by removing the puzzle piece key, she palmed something from inside, something small that had before been left in its hold. Then she raised it up for us to see. "A key," Olivia said, panning our faces, "Thought it might fit. Similar era—similar lock. And like Derek's info, it's stripped down to its essential parts."

"Clever," Alison said, repositioning the wooden lap desk with the proper side forward, keyhole facing her.

Olivia beamed back at Alison. "Here," she said, handing her the key, giving our new arrival her first opportunity to be part of the discoveries.

"Ready?" Alison asked when no one made a sound. With no response, she tilted the edge of the desk up and placed the key in its waiting collaborator, key to keyhole. "Well, it fits," she confirmed, turning the key to the right. "Seems to work," she added, but then frowned when nothing opened.

"Wait—there's a trick to this Derek wrote," I said, remembering the extra instructions he'd written. Finding the email again, I scanned to the part I needed. "Here... he says, *pull the drawers out, push down... once you do, you can slide the bottom part forward... then pull out the whole front of the box.*" I took a quick glance at Alison to make sure she understood the instruction.

She had, but Mac leaned in to help. Together they manipulated the drawers and maneuvered the front piece out.

Needing to make room for the lower part of the lap desk and its contents, I put my laptop aside on the floor and then move the basket from the table. "Here, Spook—lots of room." I leaned forward again, gazing inside at its contents. There it was, the codex.

Outside, a roar of cheers only dogs could hear rang out. Cooper ran the length of the front yard, back and forth and back and forth again, then stopped alongside Uriel's flank.

Though the others smiled, a frown dragged down Vretil's face in concern. "Armaros was at the airport—watching her." His grimace deepened. "Where was Shamsiel?" he asked, directing his demand at Michael.

As did the others, Michael turned to look at Vretil. Vretil was the wisest of all the Archs, they all knew it, but why had he asked that which he already knew?

Ignoring the question, Michael instead stated the obvious. "I was with my Charge at her home, Raphael was with his Charge, and Uriel was here watching over his...."

Interrupting, Uriel said, "Shamsiel was here—with me, watching over the book." He gave his friend a smug look. "Where were you my exceptionally cautious friend? Checking the wings of the plane, making sure the airplane food was edible for your Charge, or were you checking the airstrip for bumps in the tarmac?" he questioned, relaying his friend's ways—his habits, his often over-attention to details and safety.

Vretil winced at the telling and all-knowing words, only then realizing where he *should* have been. "No," he whispered, "In the control tower."

All he received in response from his brethren, were headshakes.

Chapter 3

Alison placed the bottom of the desk on the coffee table. Then she leaned into gaze at the ancient looking text. We were all silent watching, as she reached in and wrapped both hands around the immense volume, and slowly lifted the weighty tome out of its harbor.

At first glimpse the codex resembled an oversized journal, but with measurement much grander than your average Britannica. It had fit snug in the box, being similar in height and width to the desk and roughly shy of 6 inches thick. A thin binding wound several times around the outside, most likely to hold the cover closed and its contents guarded within. Both the leather of the cover and the banding were of the same natural pale golden shade, worn from age and handling. The cover part itself wrapped around more than once, tied closed at the spine, the length more likely meant to accommodate future pages yet to be added.

"It's no wonder the wooden thing was so heavy," I stated, breaking the deafening silence. I scooted my ottoman closer to Alison. She smiled at me, the corners of her watery eyes crinkling.

"Wow," was all Vicki managed as she leaned forward. She loved books, any book, and this one was a doozy.

"Do you feel something?" Mac asked to no one in particular. "I know the protection spell is up, like it's... well, connected to me, a part of me... and I'm a part of it."

Vicki put her hands up like she'd done previous. "I don't feel anything more than before."

"Should we?" Alison asked, "What should I feel? I mean I wasn't here for the spell."

Vicki took her hand and raised it out to the edge of the circle Mac had created prior. "There—do you feel it?"

"A kind of static—I feel it!" Alison squealed.

"Shhhhhhhh!" Olivia said, putting her hands out to silence us. "Do you hear it?"

More silence.

"What do you hear?" I asked. I heard nothing. I looked to the others, and they shook their heads *no*.

"SHHHHHHHHHHH!" she said louder and then closed her eyes.

More silence again.

"I can hear... something like the sound of... heartbeats... five different rhythms—no six, one quicker," Olivia said, glancing down at Alison's little belly-bump.

"You can hear our hearts beating—hear the baby's heart beating?" Alison whispered.

"What the hell?" I said, staring at the book resting in Alison's lap.

No one else said a word.

We refocused on Alison as she undid the fine ties and unwrapped the cover. She held the edge of the leather back cover as it released, then rolled the length inward, revealing the persona of its true face.

No distinguishing marks or symbols had donned the cover, and although the outer side of the cover appeared sturdy, its inside was a much paler and suppler, a fresher-looking version of its warrioresque alter ego. The front or start of this cyclopedia of sorts appeared to be made of firm ancient wood. The wood, by its grain was the heartwood of whatever tree it had come from. It had a light subtle grain, a blond unstained colour, with rich golden undertone that appeared sanded, silken to the touch. Along the side were small perfectly aligned holes bored into the seamed edge. Through the holes ran the flush end of a strip of hard leather, stitched into it and representing the codex's spine. Stitched to the spine was the long length of softened leather that made up the full covering. The wooden part of the cover appeared to have no understandable words, only symbols—three of them. One I recognized being the same disjointed star-shape like on the letters from the mothers, the one that reminded me of a squished spider. With the words of the letters being the focus, I had paid little attention to it, but it obviously had an important meaning. The other symbols looked similar to the unusual writings found in Mac's grimoire and were more than likely another ancient script.

"Not sure what this symbol is," Vicki said, pointing to the symbol in question. "But it's old, not sure how old, just, well—that it is. The other two symbols are for *Mother* and *Daughter,* or at least the equivalence of the English words. It's Sumerian—ancient, 30th century BC," she explained. "Aaaaand I'm not sure how I know that—but I do. It's like I've always been able to read it." She gave me her WTF face, the one that rarely surfaced for her unless she was genuinely confused.

"Extremely old," I said. "Weird, Vicki." I couldn't manage much else to say at the moment.

"Super," Mac agreed.

"Major," Olivia shot out.

"Mega," Alison concluded, caressing the engraving. Then tenderly she turned back its firm wooden cover. Doing so unveiled a thick collection of varying paper formats and exposed the inner wooden cover itself as having writings or symbols on its inner surface.

"Gonna need Derek's help with this one," Vicki said, tilting her head to look at the script. Alison angled the book for Vicki to see better. "I'll need a different key to decipher it. No idea what this language is, but this here...," Vicki said, pointing to the first page past the wood entry, "... it's also Sumerian."

"Papyrus," Alison said. "The paper I mean." Turning more pages, she revealed more of the same. A few inches in, she said, "Parchment." She turned pages again. "Silk as writing materials? And look here, handmade papers with the same unusual writing found on the cover." She caressed the papers with a light touch. "Beautiful really. It has pressed flowers in it, right in the pulp of the paper—still holds the colours and everything." Flipping past, she lifted the book to show us what appeared to be regular paper, like artist sketch paper or watercolour, with lots of grain and texture. Furthest in, the pages became a more modern bond-style paper assembled into small page groupings sewn into the inner flap of the leather spine. Alison stopped flipping and glanced up at us. Her eyes were glassy. "This entry... is my Mom's handwriting," she said, turning a few pages back, "...and this must be my grandmother's, it's written in French." Moving forward in the codex again, she noted, "There are several more groupings of blank pages, sewn in after the last written pages."

We remained quiet, waiting as Alison took in a deep breath. Then she opened wide the pages revealing the decorative calligraphy-styled writing that presented itself on the last entry. Clearing her throat, and not waiting for permission or prompt, she read aloud,

Spring 2000
Dear Daughter,

I fear I may be too late in writing this down. My faculties are failing, verily you know I would hate to admit such a thing. Regretfully, I have done things that have caused me illness over the years and this I feel will shorten my life greatly. If you are reading this, it means you have found the book and I am infinitely grateful.

When my mother passed the codex on to me, I wrote all that was said to me, all she knew. You were very young when she died, but as instructed I wrote what I was told.

My mother mentioned an important name before her passing. The name was Vretil, he is the wisest of all. This name has been passed down through our generations. Vretil was the one who told the first of us to write down the knowledge and to pass it on to our daughters. Only once has our line broken, but it was swiftly carried on by another, a true friend, whose choice it was to carry the burden forth when one of our own could not. I am unaware of how the past Scribes knew the information about the three other lines now contained in these pages, or how my mother knew who the next Linguist would be. I knew not to question such things.

The codex had been kept hidden in the lap desk for years and had only been brought out and shown to me for the first time when I was pregnant with you. It was then my mother revealed the secret. The next time I took the book from its hiding was just before I fell ill. I had spoken to you about it in one of my medicated hazes. I thought for sure this incident had sealed my fate because shortly after came the diagnosis of my breast cancer. I knew then I should tell you the story of the four women, but with the treatments and medications I was very weak and could not recall things properly. Later, when I recovered from this illness, I understood it was not my time yet, nor your time to carry the burden.

Too many times my Daughter, I challenged fate, taking this book out to look through the past generations and the different languages I was unable to read. It was the role of The Linguist, not The Scribe's, to decipher the past and only if needed. I longed to know the reasons for all of this, the reasons why we need still carry the message forward to our daughters. I know why we do it, but not why it was started. The first pages of the codex contain the first story of the first four women as told by the first Scribe, though they do not contain the why of the beginning.

With regret, this entry will be my last. I share with you my feelings along with what I am about to do, and how these actions may well be what ultimately seals my fate.

I knew none of the others but found I could trace the lines through the few languages I could understand. In them, I found another whose generation had broken, but the other two lines remained intact. I plan to seek out The Linguist, to tell her who I am. After, I will hide the book, and at such time when I feel my memory may soon fall short, then and only then will I tell her the location. I feel the book must remain here, and cannot come with me out West, as the risk is too great.

This is what I know of her....

Stopping, Alison flipped back to the earlier entry her mother had mentioned. No one spoke a word. Amazed and mesmerized we sat still, allowing her to continue—to read what we all knew would be the description of the Linguist.

Taking another cleansing breath Alison read on,

Her generational line of women was broken halfway through the bonds of Those Who Watch. But the Linguist from that time found a way for it to move forward with another.

The current Linguist, is the English-speaking daughter of two French-speaking parents, furthering her amazing proficiency for languages. She is also the younger of two sisters. Her mother and Linguist before her, was a young widower who spent most of her life without a man to help her, a strong, but silent French woman, who did the things needed to be done without asking, without complaining.

In her youth, the current Linguist loved parties and social gatherings, never wanting to work hard at learning anything. She loved to cycle in the summer and ski in the winter. She attended college to become a secretary, but found it was not the role for her. Later she moved to a big city to work for a large bank, only to find her calling at the library near Parliament. Here she met interesting people from around the world who were visiting the capital. This allowed her to explore new languages without leaving the security of her city.

Now married with four children, two of them daughters, separated by brothers, one daughter being the eldest, and the other the youngest. She required the help of her own mother in rearing the children as her talents pointed elsewhere. Exceptional in the organization and administration of information and services relating to linguistic study. She is the Linguist, a translator, and she carries within her the Keys of Language.

All I have done and all I will do, I consider my sacrifice for the balance and my faith in the four, for those who have come before us and those who may come after. For you my daughter, I will risk everything. As it was with me, with my mother before me, the knowledge comes to you. Now you must write what you know and perhaps what you may find and learn. I feel the answers to all the questions will be found in the very first entry, not in the pages, but on the wooden cover itself, written by the hand of another. Find the key and you find the truth.

I love you. You are the future, you all are.

Alison looked at Vicki and smiled. It was Vicki's mother she'd read the description of. Alison flipped pages to that of her grandmother's handwriting. And though she could read French fluently, she said, "Vicki?" giving her the floor, and chose not to read further.

Vicki scanned our faces, and then in a soft clear voice she said, "I noticed the weird star-like symbol does not accompany this entry like the other letters." She smiled at Alison. "It could be an official stamp of sorts—linking the letters to the codex?"

"She mentions a man's name in the entry, but no personal visit from one like the others," Olivia pointed out, squirming a little in her seat.

Alison browsed through the rest of the codex, pausing to show us the countless entries. "There must be hundreds of different languages and writings in this thing," she noted. Then relinquishing the tie to her mother, Alison handed the book to Vicki. "This is clearly your mother, because we knew my mom had gone to see her—based on what your mother said. This entry confirmed it." Alison flipped the page, so Vicki could see the description for herself.

Vicki perused the entry, and it was clear by her smile that the description of her good'ol mom amused her. "There's lots of blank paper in here—for more entries. Would you like to write something in here?" she asked Alison. "Perhaps everything we know so far?" She handed Alison back the tome.

Resting the massive thing on her lap, Alison reached next to her chair for her purse. She took from it a standard pencil, and then without apprehension she turned to the first new page, then wrote today's date. She tilted her face up and to the side in my direction. "Okay Lynnie," she said, "you started this. Where is your famous notebook of weird?" She let out a little giggle, I'm sure for the sake of her sanity as much as it was for ours.

Giggling back in response, I pointed to the open mouth of the basket. Then I reached in and pulled out the modern notepad. "Doesn't have the latest stuff in it—the stuff on us finding the desk," I said.

"Guess we have a new name too. *Vretil*." Olivia said, "Must be your guy, Alison."

"How about we ask Derek to check him out for us?" Vicki suggested, giving me a little chin tilt in question. "May I?" Vicki requested, addressing Alison, seeking permission to continue reviewing the book, craving its knowledge and feeding her book addiction.

"Let's hope he wasn't the creepy guy you saw at the airport," Mac added, making a disgusted face.

I shivered at the mention of him, a hint of memorable nausea twinging my insides. Was now the time to tell them what I'd seen? I figured now was a good a time as any and took a deep breath to start....

"Oh man—the guy looked evil. Like he ate small children for breakfast and was looking to sample mine," Alison cut in. An equally disgusted expression spread across her face as she rubbed her belly once again.

"Nice visual," I said, despite knowing my sightings had been more menacing. Feeling my moment lost, I redirected my attempt to share our latest inquiry with The Cipher.

Chapter 4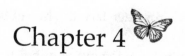

"Oh heavens! She didn't say—she couldn't possibly think… that I was the wretched being in the airport?" Vretil shouted.

"Calm down. You weren't right there with her—get over it," Uriel shot back, testing out a modern comeback.

Turning to the uproar, Shamsiel countered with, "Besides, how could she know who or what any of us would look like."

As if appalled, Vretil straightened the front of his white un-tucked dress shirt. "I certainly don't wear black and I have never acted like the villain from one of those romance novels…."

"She said the guy was—how did she put it, *totally hot*," Michael reminded, teasing his friend a little. "Beautiful, she called him." He tried to hide a smirk, and then he scowled. "Can't believe the hideous devil showed himself, and for what purpose—to scare her?"

"They are still not sure who we are, they're still trying to grasp what we might be and what we have to do with all this," Raphael said, moving in closer to peer through the front window.

In the same instant, Gabriel shifted from where he stood to ease his friend away from the window. "Keep in mind, although the others can't see you—she may," Gabriel said, giving the others a sideways glance, "But only if she's *trying* to see."

"Vicki you're gonna have to make time to read those entries—all the past writings. There'll be more info in there," I said, readying my email to send to Derek.

"My mom mentions that the reason for all this, is in there," Alison said, "and the first entry is from the original Scribe," she added, handing back the codex to Vicki, pointing to the first page and not the entry on the wood.

Caressing the cover, Vicki skimmed over the script on the inner wood cover. "Can't make out the stuff on the wood—the real first entry," she said. Skipping it she moved on to the papyrus pages. "The languages obviously go from oldest to newest. This first page is Sumerian, one of the first languages." Vicki stopped. Turning the pages to see the other languages, she said, "I feel something."

I glanced around at the others. Feeling stuff was usually my gig. "What do you mean?" I asked.

"It's not a feeling, more like a *knowing*." She paused. "I know how to read these pages—not because I can, but because I *know* I can." She shook her head as if struggling with her clarity. "I'm good with languages—really good, because I've studied the ones I know. But these.... I've never studied these—yet I'm confident I'll know them. And the ones I don't—like this one on the wood, I know I'll figure them out." She took in a long breath, exhaling it slowly. "Something is happening, I feel it—know it." Scanning the faces of the others, she said, "Anyone else feel different?"

As if in school, Mac sat up and raised her hand. "I feel it—felt it when Mom was here, telling us her side of things." She lifted the grimoire. "Hello—I can do spells. I don't just read it and do it. I know I can do magic, earth magic. It's like it's in me—mine." She slumped back down and put the spell book in her lap. "Is it weird?"

"No weirder than the fact I can feel the life-force of Alison's baby," Olivia blurted. "Sorry did I forget to mention that?" She gave me a timid grin. "Think it started when I helped deliver the baby a few days ago. I wasn't even in the room with her—was on the phone. You were there, Lynn—remember?"

I nodded.

"It's as if I know the health of things—nature, people. I concentrate, and I can see it, like chakras directing me to the unwell parts. And somehow, I know how to redirect the bad stuff—out of the body. Heal it," Olivia finished.

"Liv, why didn't you tell me?" I asked.

"Oh, I know. Lynn, you know best about feeling freaky stuff—I should have told you. Guess I didn't want you to think I was nuts," she added.

I was taken aback by what they were all saying. For years I struggled to get them to understand what strange things I often sensed. I'd been scared they would think I was off my rocker. Hell, I thought I was off my rocker a lot of the times. Alison was aware, but Mac had been listening to my accounts of bizarreness the longest. Mac tended to laugh and call me silly names, but Alison loved hearing about my premonitions and such. And here they all were with their own weirdness to deal with. Maybe they could understand me better, or maybe now with their newfound gifts, they wouldn't be interested in what I saw or sensed. Still stunned, I made myself blink and turn to look at Alison. "Spook?" I said.

She stared back at me. "Ya, Spook?" she questioned.

"Feeling—ya know, different?" I clarified, raising my eyebrows in query.

"Uhm... well...." She paused then grinned. "Not sure what it means, but I feel this overwhelming need to *write*. Not just write—but *tell*. I just got here—haven't been here with the rest of you, but I feel like I know the full story of what has happened—like I can see the past few days in my head, describe things I wasn't here for." She reached out and touched my arm. "Like your shirt—the one you're wearing, I know it's the same one you were wearing when you found your mom's journal."

She was right.

Alison turned to Vicki. "Lynn told me about the visit to your Mom's house—about the tea you guys had. I know what the teacups look like, what the chair looks like you sat in—and the one your mother sat in." Alison giggled. "Like you said, Vicki... you just know it." She examined the lead tip of her pencil. "I can see the story clear in my mind and I neeeed to write it out. I probably don't even need your notes, Lynn, but best I review them as not to leave anything out... until I feel confident in my mind's eye, you could say."

"And you guys call me weird," I said—had to say it.

"I like *gifted* better," Alison said, letting out one of her infectious giggles. They all laughed.

"Lynn can you type this—these languages in the order I give them, send them to Derek?" Vicki asked, turning a few more pages. "I'm curious about the timelines for each. Dates entered seem to only be in the latter half of the book. I can read the others, just don't want to guess on the dates—you know."

"Sure-sure," I said, "I'm just putting down the information on our new guy—Vretil, first." I hit the return on the keypad to start Vicki's part of the email. "Okay, gimme what you got," I prompted, wiggling all my fingers over my keyboard.

"Right," Vick countered, "For starters, *Sumerian*, the language of the first Scribe." Going on she said, "*Egyptian, Akkadian, Canaanite,* uuuhhhmm *Ancient Greek, Aramaic,* and *Hebrew*." She continued to look deeper into the book, but said, "That's good for now."

"Done," I said and hit send on the email. I glanced around at the others. All of them were staring at Vicki for more.

Realizing the focus was still on her, Vicki continued, "*Old Persian*. Says here the Scribe's name was *Mitra*."

"Mitra?" I cut in. "That's the same name as the old woman who lives next door. It's in my notes," I added, turning to Alison who was still perusing the scribbles in my notebook of weird.

Alison flipped over the pages of the steno pad, then stopped at the entry I had referred to. "Blue eyes—right, Spook?" Alison said.

"Yup." I grinned at her. Mitra had amazing blue eyes—beautiful for a woman of her years.

Alison winked at me, then looked down at the page. "Reference, neighbor, Mitra..." Clearing her throat, she read, "*Old Persian name meaning, Angel's Name. The name refers to people who have excellent skills at analyzing, understanding, and learning, often mystics, philosophers, scholars, and teachers... often introverts, as told by the granddaughter, Dunya.* You quoted her as saying, '*her grandmother tends to see the larger picture, her analysis of people and world events make her seem melancholy to their plight'.* After the 9/11 events, Mitra had said, *'they are watching... the balance will be kept'."*

"Uhm—wow," Mac said. She had only flipped through the notepad after I had told her about things originally.

"Wow is right," Olivia added. "Keep going, Vicki. Maybe there's other info like it in the codex—stuff matching what we've found."

We've? You mean ME, don't you? But I didn't say it out loud.

On the next turn of the page, Vicki said, "*Latin,*" but stopped short.

"What, Vic?" Alison asked, worry showing on her normally cheerful face.

Without looking up, Vicki said, "This entry mentions the generational line for The Linguist broke during this time. That's my line."

Without saying a word, I search the web and found *Latin.* Feeling good about my slick search skills I broke in before anyone else could speak, and read aloud, "*The language of Latin first appeared around 440 BCE.*" Doing a little quick math, I said, "That's thirty-five generations ago." Derek had told me prior that a generation calculates into 70-year increments. "Keep going, Vick, what else does it say?"

Vicki's expression was that of annoyance for my interruption, but she adjusted the codex in her lap, and then went on. "It mentions the *Priestess of Demeter* along with her maidens—or Virgins, who were allowed to sit and watch the Olympic Games." She paused. "Hmmm must be the first games if we are going back that many years." Refocusing again, she read, "Says these women were not permitted to engage in sex and therefore could not have children. A descendant of this line—one maiden in particular, was brought into the fold, and it was she who carried the secret. It had been handed down to her by her mother. It mentions something here that she refers to as her *salvation.* On one occasion at the games, she witnessed a woman named, Cynisca, who was the Greek princess of Sparta. She was the first woman to win in the Olympic Games. Well, she—Melissa, requested an audience with Cynisca. With Cynisca being so strong and well placed, Melissa took the chance to ask her the favor of carrying forth her secret. It says Cynisca understood—felt the urgency of the situation, felt a strong feeling of kinship for this woman, and bravely agreed. Melissa gave her the description and location of the Sorceress—or *witch*, then told her that she must pass this knowledge on to her future daughter." Vicki stopped and lifted her face up to look at us.

Grinning at Vicki I said, "So you're a descendant to the first female Olympian? Explains a lot." I gave her a poke in her ribcage, acknowledging her need for speed on that bicycle of hers. "What else?" I prompted.

Giving me a big prideful smile back this time she continued. "Later in the entry, the Scribe writes of the changing of hands and how Melissa, now an elder Priestess of Demeter, had been pestered by the other priestesses. They tried to make her tell them about the secret conversation she had had with Cynisca, but she remained silent." Vicki's eyebrows pinched together. "Hmmm the handwriting changes here," she said, and a sickly expression crossed her face. "Oh God... in anger, the women attacked her—tore her to pieces because she wouldn't tell them. But the secret was safe with Cynisca."

"Niiice—not," Mac said, her revulsion showing. All of us a little grossed-out over the entry, we all made our own revolted expression.

Moving on and changing the tone, Vicki said, "Look, *Sanskrit*, it's another symbol-styled language. And that squashed spider—it's a Sanskrit symbol—I know it now, translates into... *Glean*."

"Glean? What the hell?" I threw at her. "Doesn't glean mean gather or harvest or something like that? What does it have to do with the letters?" I looked to the others. "Am I missing something here? You sure you got the word right, Vic?"

Shaking her head, she said, "Oh I don't know—give me a break— suddenly I know over 100 different languages and you expect me not to get anything wrong?"

At first, I was afraid she was mad. Then in light of the situation she stuck her tongue out at me. "I'll go back to it later, figure it out," she said, extending her tongue a second time.

"Sorry," I said, and laughed. "That stupid star-squished-bug has been bugging me—no pun intended." My dumb accidental pun made the others laugh again, and we needed it after the eeewww factor of the earlier entry.

Turning a few more pages, Vicki continued again. "This one is *Common Germanic* or *Proto-Norse*, I think it's called." She appeared intrigued while the rest of us sat lost waiting for way more clarity. "Mentions a splitting off of the race, one side good—one side evil." More eyebrow scrunching. "Hey, send it to Derek, Lynn, would you? He may find something on it, could be useful."

I set up for another email for the clever Cipher just as one arrived back from him labeled *Sumerian*. "Just got one back from Derek, it's on Sumerian," I informed them.

"Perfect—what does he have for us?" Vicki demanded.

"Uhm, here we go," I announced and read the entry,

> *Sumerian, meaning 'native tongue'. The language of ancient Sumer, southern Mesopotamia. It's modern Iraq to us. Been around since at least 4000 BC, but during the 3rd millennium, 3000 BC, the people of the area developed what was referred to as a very devoted cultural collaboration between the Sumerians and the Akkadians, it's the second language you asked about. This also included widespread bilingualism. Scholars note this as a sprachbund.*

"Sprachbund?" I repeated, confused on this one. Not that I understood any of this.

"It means language crossroads or linguistic area—get it?" Vicki confirmed, tongue sticking out at me again.

I ignored her smarti-pantsness and finished with the remaining part of the email,

> *Somewhere around the turn of the 3rd and the 2nd millennium BC, Akkadian gradually replaced Sumerian, but the dates are debatable. Sumerian was still used in Mesopotamia until the 1st century AD for sacred or ceremonial, and for literary and scientific languages.*

"Bet he liked the part on the scientific stuff," Olivia tossed out.

"No doubt," I agreed, "But he's been sorta coming over to our mystical side of things." The others nodded in agreement then turned back to Vicki for more.

"This first record is from the 3rd millennium, somewhere after 3000 BC," Vicki clarified. "These entries keep going—language change to language change. *Primitive Irish, Arabic, Old English, Japanese*—I'd begun learning that one before—but now I can read it fluently."

"It must have something to do with the book and the coming together of the four," Mac said as a guess.

It had to be something along those lines I assumed too, but still found it comical how things could appear to be clearer yet still make no sense.

Continuing through the codex deeper, Vicki said, "*Old Norse, Old French, Bengali, Italian, Russian, Hungarian, Danish.* Always on the move—the women changing cities, regions, countries. *Portuguese, Polish, Thai,*" she added with a hit of exhaustion, as if sympathizing with all the moving.

I knew that feeling.

"So many languages—so many places, how did they do it—and why?" Olivia asked.

Vicki, quick to respond said, "I get the impression from their writings, it was all part of keeping things secret—keeping their daughters protected, keeping the book of balance protected." Vicki flipped gingerly back and forth to various spots in the book. "There are symbols throughout the book too. Sanskrit ones. Perhaps the symbols have something to do with magic, protection for the words like in the grimoire," she mused. "I see a repeat of symbols and words in the different language, mentioned over an over—the meanings a repeat of the same. Friendship, Fate, Death, Life, Mother, and Daughter." Appearing puzzled, she said, "And this word again, *Glean.*" She shook her head. "I'll work with Derek on this one too—can't hurt," she added, laughing a little.

"You know he loves a challenge," I assured her, glancing back to my laptop, checking for other responses from Derek. Nothing yet.

"Didn't your mom mention in her earlier entry that your line broke, Alison?" Olivia asked as she sipped another cup of tea.

Alison glanced up from feverishly making notes in the remaining pages of my steno-of-strange. "Ya, about that, Vicki. Did you find mine anywhere—my line?" Alison asked.

Going back to the codex, Vic said, "Not yet... hmmm, let me see... *Early Modern English...* uhmmm, here—*Romanian.* It mentions the line breaking for the Scribe as well." Before continuing with the generational break, Vicki said. "Oh, make a note of *Cherokee* and *Modern French* too, looks as though the French part starts with your great-grandmother, Alison, then it leads into your grandmother's and then your mom's entries in Modern English."

Alison smiled bigger, knowing Vicki was getting close. "Go on," she prompted again, waiting.

Flipping back and forth through the last few pages, Vicki said, "The break looks like it was five generations back, the entry is dated 1592. Mentions the name *Esther*, whose husband was a Jewish merchant. She oversaw all relations—including commercial, between the wives in the current Sultan's royal harem and the outside world. Known as a *Chiera*, the title given to a person who performed this service. She was friends with a woman named Safiyeh, who was the *favorite wife*. This friendship caused jealousy with the others employed by the Sultan, and as a result, the Sultan had Esther and her son executed and then he took all her assets, all their possessions and property." Stopping her translating Vicki added, "Haaaaaaaarsh," finishing yet another violent entry.

We nodded and adding a few "Yups" making similar disturbed faces to that of Vicki's line break.

Following up with a deep exhalation, Vicki continued, "But… not before Esther shared the story and secrets with Safiyeh, who later passed the story on to a lesser wife. This wife was later dismissed of her duties due to an unknown illness—faked of course. The illness was a pregnancy, resulting from one of the many visits with foreigners. With the book in her possession, she left with her growing belly and the secret."

"See," Uriel said, "our four did whatever they had to back then. It must count for something. And the new four are all together, like in the beginning."

Peaceful and smiling, Vretil said, "They are a resourceful bunch, aren't they?" He rocked back and forth on his heels, clasping his hand behind his back. Enthusiasm showing through, he added, "Oh look, here comes my part."

All heads except Michael's turned towards the faint sound from inside the house. Michael continued to glare at Gabriel, mulling over his fellow Glean's last comment of, *'But only if she's trying to see.'*.

Chapter 5

A "*Bing,*" sounded a new email arrival.

"Got another one from Derek—it's labeled *Angel of Karma*," I announced, glancing up from the email to see Alison's cherub face grinning at me. Winking at her, I asked, "Ready?"

"Ready, Spook," she said and winked back at me, twice.

"Vretil," I pronounced, straightening up in my seat to read more,

> *...is known as the Divine Scribe, his official title being the Archangel keeper of the treasury of Sacred Books. As noted in the Book of Enoch, he dictated 366 books to the guy in 30 days, the contents on every form and type of knowledge. Many references say he is the wisest of all the angels. Some religions refer to him as the Angel of Karma, and he's the one you speak to when you have questions on the Karmic cycles. It also says he is often associated with the Archangel Uriel.*

"They must be friends," I said guessing, looking from Alison to Vicki, pausing for a second,

> *Karma is the universal law of cause and effect. It's his job to remind us that our paths and the way we travel along them, has impact both on ourselves and the surrounding environment, even the energy surrounding us. Obstacles and challenges we encounter on our journey help to teach us lessons of compassion and love. Vretil helps guide and instruct us that 'what we give, eventually we receive', if we*

want positive loving energies directed towards us, then we need to give it out first.

As if I'd spotted a hot guy, I gave Alison a few eyebrow-raises.

She actually blushed. "How about my guy!" Alison said, beaming, "Not bad—not bad at all. How appropriate he's a Scribe too, we have so much in common." She giggled, going with my hot guy—perfect match routine.

Interrupting the match-making, Vicki cleared her throat glancing up from the big book of balance. "Anyone else see a theme here?" she asked. But before I could say, *Angels*, Vick said, "Books." She pointed at Alison and back to herself, repeating the motion with more intent. "Books," she said again, pointing at Mac who was holding the grimoire, then back at Alison again echoing the motion for them and once again with herself and Mac.

"Hmmmm," was all I got out, annoyed, but still interested in her observation. Not what I would have said, but before I could add more, she spoke again.

"Healing," Vicki said, doing the back and forth again but this time with Mac and Olivia, repeating the word *"Healing,"* then the words *"Natural... Karma... Magic...,"* and then, *"Books,"* again, making a circle for the four of them with both hands. "The same stuff is repeating and repeated throughout the codex too. I know we're supposed to be a quartet, but I didn't realize the tight conjoin."

"Cool, right?" Olivia said.

"Very cool!" came from Alison.

"Weirdly so," Mac added.

From out of left field, Alison asked, "Vicki, I take it you're my billet?" Looking over to her suitcase that sat near the front door, she added, "Anyone hungry? My inner creature needs to be fed—literally. Ideas on food?"

"I'll go out and get food if you guys want." I grinned. Although none of it directed my way, I could still feel the love in the air, and I wanted to feed it even though I wasn't one of the Book-Karma-Magic people. But my offer was ignored and quashed when Vicki announced hers.

"That would be me—Hotel Quinn, at your service." Vicki faked a bow. "How about I take you and your suitcase to my place? I'll grab a few pre-made goodies from my fridge and freezer while you throw your stuff in the guest room." Sounding confident, and assuming this was the route they would take, Vicki got up and headed for the front door.

And in continuance with discounting of my offer, Mac added, "I have a few things here I can whip-up too. You guys do what you gotta do, then meet back here for eats." Mac got up then from the big chair and headed to the kitchen to *whip-up*. Olivia followed her to the kitchen presumably to help. At the door, Vicki gathered up Alison's suitcase, and with Baby-mamma hot on her heels, the two of them took off out the door.

Everyone had gotten up but me.

With my offer still hanging in the air, I did my best impression of someone who didn't care. Frustrated, I turned back to my email just as another email popped in from Derek. *Myyyyyyyyy friend, Derek,* I noted to myself. The label of this one was, *Herbalism*. I read through it, figuring I'd paraphrase later if someone noticed I was still sitting here. The email contained points on *botanical medicine* or medical *herbalism*, normally used to cure animal ailments. It was a traditional medicinal practice or folk medicine, dating back to the beginnings of human history. Moving down the email it read,

> It's based on using plants and plant extracts including fungi, bee products, minerals, shells, and certain animal parts, like in Chinese medicines. Plants synthesize substances like phenols and tannins for example, useful for maintenance in the health of humans and animals. In medical treatment, herbs have three basic functions: detoxification, regeneration, and self-healing. Can be taken as: teas, elixirs, ointments, pill form, as an inhalation or as an herbal bath.
>
> The World Health Organization (WHO), approximates 80% of the world's population uses herbal medicine for some facet of primary health care. It included hundreds to thousands of indigenous plants for treatment of ailments since prehistoric times, and across all continents. The Old Testament mentions herbal medicines. It's the oldest therapy practiced, and was illustrated in cave paintings found in France, radiocarbon-dated at somewhere between 25,000 and

13,000 BC. But in written records, it dated back over 5000 years to the Sumerians.

"Again with the 5000 years," I muttered to myself, noting another repeat of facts. Derek also wrote,

Since the 19th Century, herbal healing has significantly declined because of the introduction of active chemical drugs such as arsenic, copper sulphate, iron, mercury, and sulphur, followed by swift development of chemistry and other physical sciences. This leading chemical medicine as the dominant mainstream system of the 20th Century.

He'd noted how herbalism and natural remedies have had a reappearance in recent years, and that the tonics and preparation used vary from the recipes found the most ancient texts, and more blah blah blah... but it was the earlier email on Sumerians being over 5000 years ago, that I found interesting. The other details didn't resonate with me, but they may for the others depending on what else Vicki finds. I calculated that 5000 equaled 70 generations, but I couldn't recall why it was important, only that I'd read it somewhere else.

I checked the time, it was past 2 p.m.. No wonder Alison was hungry, it was 12 noon for her Calgary-body. My stomach hadn't been joking with me either—I was starving. Willing the girls to come back faster, I leaned over to get a look at the codex. But Vicki had closed it up and placed it back in the lap desk's bottom half for safekeeping.

Safe from who, me? Leaning closer, I ran my hand over the outer cover. Out the corner of my vision something caught my attention, something moving from outside the window. But when I turned my head in the direction, there was nothing. Hoping it might be the girls returning, I got up and walked to the window. Still nothing—no one was there, well no one other than Cooper.

With Mac and Olivia busy in the kitchen *and* paying no attention, I closed my eyes and put my hands against the window. I could feel the wards Mac had put up the night before, the prickling of energy like static electricity, its power pushing back on me. I wasn't sure what the others felt, other than how good it felt to be inside. *Safe.* Not that outside was bad—it was just different... *a sense*. At the sound of a car pulling into the drive I opened my eyes. It was the girls returning— thank goodness.

Through the door they came with Vicki announcing they had a big tray of veggie lasagna and fresh whole-wheat buns. Mac had helped Olivia whip-up her famous Caesar salad, a perfect complement to Vicki's healthy Italian she'd brought back with her. Whatever, it all sounded good, I was famished, and due to my lack of sustenance, I had forgotten about being... *forgotten.*

The spread of food was out on the kitchen counter making it easier to serve. We all filled our plates and then resumed our seats in the living room to eat.

Bellies filling, it was time to get back to business. They got back to their business, I should say. Vicki read pieces of the book aloud and Alison made meticulous notes. Mac and Olivia moved themselves back into the kitchen, this time to review spells. And me, I sat listening to their shared information, not specifically shared with me, but with each other.

"Derek sent information on herbalism...," I called out to anyone who'd listen, taking a turn in the conversation. "Goes back to 25,000 BC. The first written recordings were in 5000 BC, and in Sumerian...."

Alison and Vicki just nodded and continued with their work.

When I turned to look at the other two in the kitchen, Mac and Olivia seemed more annoyed than interested at *my* shared information, as if I'd interrupted them.

Fine. I'll sit here, waiting... for something... *again.*

In my silence, I watched Alison record everything we had discovered, the new facts on the desk, codex, and the missing information Vicki was translating from the codex.

"You okay with me writing in the notepad, Spook?" Alison asked, noting my expression.

I guess I was feeling a little possessive of my steno pad *and* the earlier writings I'd put in it. Realizing I'd transposed those feelings across my face, perhaps looking as though I'd caught her eating my last potato chip or something, I morphed the mess into a cheery face. "No-No," I said, covering up, smiling my best happy smile. She was the Scribe, she should use it.

"I'm going to expand on all this once Vicki's done with her translations, write it with in more vivid detail in the codex. I want to keep all the facts together, cool?" Alison added, flipping to see how much paper the steno still had.

"All good, Spook. You can just toss it my way when you're done," I said, attempting to sound carefree. What the hell was I going to use it for, anyway? They were on the case.

"Okay, you guys have to come and hear this," Vicki announced. "It's the information on the *first* four… and these men."

Mac and Olivia stopped what they were doing and hustled into the living room. Her words had gotten their attention, but she had also interrupted the little conversation Alison and I had going. And to my dismay, despite the interruption, Alison sat ready with her pencil. Me... I did nothing... again, because Alison was here now, and the recording of things was now off my to-do list.

Ears ready and eyes on her, Vicki read again. "The first entry is written in Sumerian script—as I told you. We can comfortably say they must have all been from the area, yes?"

There were nods all around though she didn't look to me for one.

"Well," she began again, "the first Scribe documented everything, well—almost everything. I still need to figure out who these guys are. Their names are mentioned—same ones as the letters, they could be descendants like us, but I'm not sure."

"Or angels!" I spouted out. Vicki gave me that look, the one you give a child interrupting the adult conversation. I grinned at her, not a happy grin but still a grin. It held back the not nice words I wanted to say. Instead of saying anything I turned back to my laptop. But *Hello*, I'm the person who A—found all your missing crap, B—got you all together, and C—provided you with my personal fact specialist— Derek, but noooo, go ahead discount anything I might offer. I'll keep my opinions to myself.

At my disinterest, Vicki continued. "The entry talks about four men coming down from the *Mountain of Chief*—not sure where this is, but I'm sure Derek can find details on it for me."

For me, she'd said. Annoyed, I pretended to be engrossed in something on my computer, and didn't bother to say, *I'll email him for you*, then continued to eavesdrop on the new information. If she wanted my help again, she could ask me, *nicely*.

But she didn't—didn't ask I mean, but she did go on. "The first Scribe was chosen by Vretil. Her name was *Nin*, and she was considered the storyteller, record keeper, and historian of her people, as was her mother before her. She described herself as having long wavy brown hair with strands of honey-colour around her face, high round cheekbones, and large bright eyes. Vretil taught her how to write, and record her stories and history on parchment, and how to bind them into a book form."

Vicki looked at Alison as were the others, including me. We couldn't ignore the obvious, how the description, despite the break in generations, closely resembled Alison.

"Your line broke, but that sounds like you, Spook," I said, needing to share my thoughts. I looked into her big blue eyes and gave her my best *love you* smile. It must have felt good for her to have the connection, see it written in the words of the *first*. I kept smiling though my connection to this was slipping away. I hoped my connection to them wouldn't do the same.

Alison glanced back at me, and then to Vicki for more.

Taking the cue from Alison, Vicki continued her rundown of the translation, and said, "Next she wrote about Michael, who chose the first Linguist. Her name was *Pau*. It says she often translated for the neighboring communities of the southern area like the Akkadians. She could also read the Sumerian language. At the time it was only given to men to read and write. She's described as having fine shoulder-length tawny coloured hair, with beautiful brown eyes. He taught her the language of the...." Vicki stopped and let out a big breath. "There's that ridiculous word again," she said, rereading the last line again, "language of the *gleans*... and the key to all language." She paused. "Alison, please make a note of these words—the ones I'm finding that don't seem to make sense. The first one being glean—or gleans. This entry, it translates as, *the four guards* but makes little sense in the paragraph. This one too, *na newcomers forgo houseful*." Vicki looked up at Alison, possibly checking to see she'd got them all, then she glanced over at me "What?" she said, "You think this is simple?"

Putting my hands up in defense, I said, "Whoa there. I'm just listening. Don't get pissed at me because you have a few questionable words and phrases—sheesh!" Still obviously bothered, Vicki said nothing else to me, then turned back to Alison.

What was that about? Why was I the target of her frustration, just because she couldn't figure out the words? What, like I impact her translating ability—*not*—impatient much? "Gah!" I let out, but no one seemed to care about me being berated for no reason.

"Aaaand, *harbored four guest*," Vicki ended, completing her problematic list, further ignoring me, irritation clear in her tone. Refocusing, she went on with the original four. "Uriel chose a woman named, *Ashu*, who had an affinity for the earth and nature and who had already been cooking using the earth's herbs while others ate bare food. She described her as short and shapely, with long chestnut coloured hair, dark almond-shaped eyes, and a bright alluring smile. He taught her magic and healing using the earth."

We all looked at Mac, who was now fluffing her long chestnut coloured hair, fluttering the lashes of her dark almond-shaped eyes, and giving us her usual toothy grin in reflect of Ashu's similar appearance to hers.

Vicki smirked at Mac's performance, then shook her head and continued. "Raphael chose *Ena*, who the others sought when someone in the area fell ill or injured. She was close with Ashu and spent a great deal of time with her, learning herbs for healing of the sick and calming pain. She also functioned much like a doula for the other women in their village and neighboring areas. She was petite, with kind eyes and her hair was cut short while the other women wore their hair long. He taught her healing and midwifery."

"Interesting," Olivia muttered, running a hand through her short hair. Then she started that head-nodding thing of hers again.

Cutting in, Vicki said, "Get this, it says Nin assisted Pau with her Scribe duties, teaching her how to write both Akkadian and variations of Sumerian for writing her stories, along with keeping the accuracy in recording the names of the newborns for Ena, and the documenting of herbs for Ashu."

"Cool—what a team," Alison said, stopping now from her own scribing.

Cool, what a team, and no need for a fifth member either. When no one questioned the obvious, I asked, "Does it say who the men were, other than just their names?"

"Nope, just says who they had chosen to keep the balance and there's no mention of the other two, Shamsiel and Gabriel." Then Vicki asked, politely I might add, for me to pass on the info about this mountain to Derek, to see if he could come up with anything.

And I did.

Mac and Olivia returned to the kitchen, and Alison followed to get more to eat. Vicki went back to busily reading and ignoring me again.

I picked up my steno pad to read Alison's notes, and found lots of words like *gorgeous, handsome, breathtaking, beautiful,* and *divine,* also *magnificent, exquisite, radiant* and *otherworldly,* to describe these men, but it was nothing I hadn't already read or heard. I put down the notes as she returned. Then I took my turn at getting more of the fantastic food.

Trying not to impede Mac and Olivia as they worked, I refilled my plate and grabbed another warm roll. Standing in the doorway to the kitchen I ate plate number two and watched them do their thing.

At the corner of the counter was a mortar and pestle. Mac had been using it to grind certain herbs and then she'd bag'n tag them. Their dialog sounded as though they were trying to define healing potions for different parts of the body. Olivia was pointing out the different chakras and their associated organs as Mac identified the homeopathic herbs, making notes on them in the grimoire. When Mac stopped what she was doing to grab herself a bun, I asked, "Can I see the stuff you've written?"

Mac glanced at Olivia and then they both looked at me.

"Uhm sure... here, not sure you'll get much out of it, just magic—healing'n stuff," Mac said, handing me the grimoire.

"Right—nothing to do with me," I responded, but I still accepted the book for my unimportant viewing. God forbid I take them away from their charm-fest, find any clues or helpful things to lead them anywhere, nooooo.

Scanning the pages, I searched for anything that might jump out at me. One section was labeled *The Elements of Spell Making*, with sub-labels like *Purpose, Sequence, Sacred Space, Supplies*, and *Timing*. Farther down she'd written stuff on the days of the week and their corresponding magical herb info and its *Timing with the Moon*. There were words like *Charm* and *Pocket charm, Simple* and *Simpling*. At the top of the next page was a list labeled *Candle Colours*, outlining different colours for different magic. At the bottom was a note on *Fabrics* and *Ribbons*. Seemingly, the types and colours of them had an impact. I made a little mental note on the colour purple, not that it was my favorite—blue was, but purple was for psychic powers, spirituality, and to increase personal power. I remembered hearing this forever-ago when I'd visited that fortuneteller in my teens. Done, I smiled and handed back the book. I said nothing, then continued on my merry way to the living room to my friend the computer.

Sitting again, I stared at the empty inbox of my email, pondering the speed and strength at which everyone's abilities were changing. Stronger by the minute it seemed, yet they remained calm with the whole unfolding of things. Vicki's talent with her linguistics was obvious. Alison documented the past and recent events with supreme detail as if she'd lived them all herself. Mac's knowledge and skills were becoming more intuitive with the magic, while Olivia's healing ability to sense chakras and issues within were making leaps and bounds. She and Mac were finding ways to make them *all* stronger, working hard to create potions and herbal remedies to strengthen them and the surrounding protections. But I was the one who brought them all together... no biggy, right?

"Mac, are you going up to the cottage tomorrow?" I called out from my tiny spot in their big world. Whispers came from the kitchen.

I turned to look in their direction just as Mac called back. "Noooo, called Don earlier. Told him I would hang here with the ladies and talk jewelry-smack since the other gig got cancelled," she said, holding up her hands making finger quotes for word *cancelled*. "They'll be back Sunday night," she added.

I had no response, but I understood the need to hang with your friends when you didn't get to see them much. In fact, it sounded painfully familiar. I glanced back down at my computer screen. The clock in the right-hand corner showed 7 p.m.. Again, the time had whizzed by and I hadn't noticed its passing. I glanced up again to survey the view out the window. Outside had gotten dark and the modest streetlights on the houses were all coming on like tiny beacons to safe havens. *"Bing,"* came another quiet notification, redirecting me back to my email. It was from *Louise*.

She'd written;

> Hi Lynn,
> How are you? I'm doing well considering. I'm home all day tomorrow, interested in stopping by, having tea with me?
> Would love to see you,
> Louise

Eeeesh, more tea? But I'd drink mushroom tea if it meant I could spend more time with her. This was saying a lot considering I hated mushrooms more than anything. Apparently, there was a food I'd met that I didn't like.

I typed out a quick response saying I was *free all day* and for her to let me know what time would be good and hit send. I figured I'd be free, not like I'd be needed around here, other than to send emails back and forth to the Cipher. But I could give Derek's email address to Vicki. She would have her computer handy *working from home,* and therefore she could send him any new troubleshooting requirements they had.

As the next 30 minutes ticked by, I periodically checked my email for… *anything.* Then my cell phone rang. Saved by the bell, it was Will with his morning call. Not that I cared who I interrupted, but I got up and headed to go outside to take the call. I just needed some air.

Chapter 6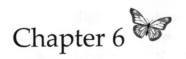

Letting the screen door slam behind me, I stood on the porch and answered the call. "Hi, morning," I said, a little happier, laughing a bit at the fact it was the morning where he was.

"Hi there," he responded, followed by a yawn and stretching sounds. "Whatcha do'n?"

"Nut'n much," I countered, feeling the distance creep in. "What do you have on your plate today, beside strange and exotic new foods?"

Will's laugh vibrated through the phone. "Oh, you know me—I'll try anything once," he said, then he went on to tell me about his day ahead. "Going to see one of the tallest buildings in the world, Taipei 101." He took a breath. "Then I'm off to the National Palace Museum. It has one of the most important art collections, originally housed in Beijing's Forbidden City. Today the museum holds over 700,000 items, including jade, bronze, porcelain and lacquer pieces, and tapestry and embroidery," he informed me. He continued with stuff on how in 1931 when the Japanese invaded, the collection was moved around a lot—to places like Nanjing and Shanghai.

I gave him a "ya" here and an "oh" there as he talked, but I tended to fade out when he mentioned *war* stuff, or until I heard something I could comprehend.

"The place I visited yesterday was amazing," he said, "Sun Moon Lake. It's this beautiful alpine lake, the largest in Taiwan. It's divided by the tiny Lalu island. Has the shape of the sun in the eastern part and the shape of the moon in the western, hence the name," he pointed out. "But the coolest part is the constant changes of mists and atmosphere on the lake, makes it impossible to appreciate just a single look. It's remarkable, you'll have to see it someday, Lynn."

"Ya, someday," I said, knowing someday was a long way off, if ever. I always tried to sound excited for him, but I rarely said much on the calls as I had nothing equal to contribute.

"Where are you?" he asked.

"Just hanging with the girls," I told him. It would be enough to make him happy, hearing I was where and with whom I needed to be with, even if he didn't know what was unfolding, or perhaps crumbling around me.

After a few more minutes describing his day ahead, he wrapped up the call. "Okay, I gotta go—need to meet my guide and the tour operator downstairs for strange meal number one—then we're off."

"Gotcha," I answered, reluctant to end the call. "Love you—have a fun day."

"Love you too. I'll send you more photos later." He ended the call.

Putting the phone in my side pant pocket. I stayed on the front porch, studying the area again, this time from the outside.

There was *something*... something in the air. The surrounding view seemed to shimmer, like I was seeing a reflection in calm water. The colours reminded me of the acrylic paints I'd used back in a long-ago art class. The night's colouring was deep purple—aubergine, as the dusk was turning to night. If it weren't for the tiny property lights, it would have been a dreadfully dark street.

To the right, at the corner near the side of the house I spotted Cooper sitting next to a weathered wooden Adirondack chair. It was as though he were resting next to where his loving master would have sat if she'd been out there with him. He turned his head towards the chair as if acknowledging something... or *someone*.

Instead of going back inside, I headed down the front steps and crossed the front lawn in the direction to where Cooper sat. He didn't move or get up as I approached, only turned his head again, watching as I moved to stand in front of the old-fashioned lawn chair.

"We have a visitor," Michael said from the unseen, stepping in closer. "Get up, Gabriel," he said, nudging his shoulder and coaxing him out of the old chair.

"She was talking to the water-bearer," Gabriel disclosed. Timing was everything Gabriel thought as he lifted himself up and out of the way. "She's always far away from those she loves. Sad, really," Gabriel said, moving to stand, turning to face the old chair. The others came closer, gathering around the chair.

Raphael came to a stop, standing behind it.

Uriel came to stand behind Cooper on the right, with Vretil peering from behind.

Gabriel remained out in front. His gaze dropped, as did the gazes of his friends.

They all watched as Michael knelt on the left side. Facing the arm of the chair, he leaned in. "She looks familiar… do I know her mother?" Michael asked.

"No," Gabriel replied, his tone soft.

Looking deeper this time, he gave a slight tilt of his head to see her eye colour. "Grey-blue," Michael noted. "Her father perhaps?" Leaning in again a little closer, he said, "She smells different from the other, like something sweet, ambrosial... no, empyrean." Michael glanced up now at the other three. They all had their brows pinched as if deep in silent deliberation. Glancing over at Gabriel again, Michael noticed that his eyes were closed, and his arms were crossed tight over his chest.

It was then that Shamsiel appeared, stepping up behind Gabriel. He leaned in close enough to speak into his ear. "Is it time yet?" he whispered, peering around Gabriel's shoulder and directly at the now *empty* chair.

Not meaning to, I let the screen door slam shut again as I came back into the house. Through the opening to the kitchen I saw Mac's head snap up. "When did you go outside?" she asked.

I checked my watch, it read 8:30 p.m.. "An hour ago," I noted. Whooah time-warp, black hole, gap, crack, fissure—whatever, just lost an hour, and no one had noticed me leave, or that I'd been gone a whole hour.

Mac said nothing in response.

Shaking it off I resumed my seat. Waking up my sleeping computer, it showed I'd received another email, this one from Derek. "Got an update from Derek," I called out in a not so quiet voice, not caring who I disturbed.

I guess a message from Derek warranted their attention even if I didn't because Olivia and Mac stopped what they were doing in the kitchen and came back out to hear the latest. That's when I noticed Alison had the codex now, most likely to enter her own writings. Vicki had made her own notes on another pad of paper, perhaps discrepancies for Derek to work through. "It's the Mountain stuff," I added. I tried to hide my lack of enthusiasm, but I was sure it showed. And as they all regained their usual spots, I read his email out for them. "*Cipher strikes again...,*" I read, pausing to enjoy his enthusiasm. Then I continued,

> I researched 'Mountain of the Chief' and came across a few different references. One was on Mount Hermon, a mountain in the Anti-Lebanon mountain range. Its summit spans the border between Lebanon and Syria. This is near Sumer, and translated it means 'land of the civilized lords'. This civilization started agricultural practices around 5000 BC.
>
> There was another reference on the 'Mountains of Media', mentioned in the Book of Enoch. The Watchers are said to have come down from this mountain area as well in the time of 5000 BC.

"That's it," I said, "The rest is for me—buddy stuff." I put a little emphasis on the *buddy* part though no one seemed to care. "Still skeptical?" I said, prodding, and remembering now where I'd read the stuff on 5000. "That Enoch guy wrote about it. And since more and more information seemed to link back to those Watchers—the angels," I added. "Even Derek thinks it's related, or he wouldn't have made a note. When no sarcastic comments follow his facts, it usually means he believes what he wrote." But they should know that about him.

"Sooo, you think the same guys whom the first four met—are the same guys our mothers were talking about... that they're angels?" Vicki responded, mocking my deductions.

"It's a great story Lynn," Alison commented, using a much gentler tone. "But it has to be something else—something like us—descendants, possibly. Like what Vicki said, right?"

"Something like it I'm sure," Mac agreed, likely sensing the unnecessary tension growing.

But I wasn't ready to concede. "Okay, you can read a million languages now. Alison is documenting like a computer gifted with the creative writing talents of a Pulitzer Prize winner. Olivia literally sees life and illness in the human body and Mac's doing, well—*magic*. And you can't let your mind wrap around the concept of angels? Okey-doke." Enduring, I said, "Look it's...," I glanced at my watch yet again. "...10 p.m. and I'm tired, been an extremely tiring week for all of us." I didn't want a long discussion on this. "Olivia, are you ready to head out?"

Guilty-faced, she said, "Uhm, I'm staying... here with Mac." She glanced at Mac as if to avoid seeing the frustration on my face. "I called Mike earlier—guess you were outside." Again confirming no one had noticed I'd left. "He told me he's taking the girls up to his mom's place by the lake, so I told him I'd be hanging with the ladies here," she added.

"We're heading out. Baby's tired—and that's my first priority, sorry... Vicki?" Alison said, changing gears and diverting the attention to her ride and billet in a proposal to leave.

"Ya, I'm ready too," Vicki responded. "Have to be up for work early even though I'll be at home." This was Vicki's way of avoiding more confrontation, avoiding me and stepping on my toes.

"Wait!" Mac said, her intent more as a command. "I need to reinforce the wards. That way they encircle each of you whether you are in here or out there." She pointed towards the big living room window, waving a hand at everything and nothing in particular. We all looked towards the window as if there was something to see. "Didn't know how to do it yesterday, but it's almost ready—give me a sec," she said, hurrying back to the kitchen.

We'd all been standing, but with reluctance everyone settled to their seats for Sorceress Mackenzie to do her thing. Either way, the dialog I'd started was over and I was being further ignored.

Mac returned to the living room with a medium sized basket filled with more items I assumed were for spell casting.

"Okay... I need four blue candles, one white and one black," Mac said, picking out the first six items she needed. She placed the single white candle in the center of a small tray she'd also brought with her. Then she placed the four blue ones at the corners representing as before, North, South, East, and West. Reaching in the basket again, she pulled out a piece of blank paper and handed it to Olivia. "Each of you, write your full official names on this paper—three times each." She handed Olivia a black pen for her to write first. As Olivia wrote, Mac returned to the basket a third time, extracting a small clear pouch filled with what resembled toasted coconut. "This is angelica root," she informed us, kyboshing my observation. After Olivia, Vicki wrote her name, and Alison followed with hers. Then Alison handed Mac the paper for her to take her turn writing. Mac scribbled her name down the allotted three times and placed it next to the white candle.

Hey what about my name? I wanted to say, but Mac had already begun the spell by sprinkling the angelica root on both the candle and the paper. My mouth hung open wordless as she continued.

"Protect this house, protect the souls within it, while here and away from this safe harbor." She repeated it three times and lit the white candle. Then she picked up the blue candle for West. Using a small pocketknife, she carved the symbol of what I'd seen in the grimoire, 'O' for Water. Continuing in a circle, she did the same with the North candle for Earth, 'Θ', East for Air, 'Π', and ended with South for Fire, 'N'.

Those same four symbols also represented the four Archangels. Coincidence? I think not, but frankly I was done with coincidences at this point. Derek had included those elements in his summaries, but I kept my observations about it to myself. I could consider it fact if Derek could.

As Mac carved, she chanted. "Powers four and powers bright, protect us now with all your might." She repeated it for each candle, replacing each in its spot around the white candle, and lighting each one. Taking the paper with the names, she folded it, making it smaller and smaller, folding in the direction away from herself. When she couldn't fold it anymore, she stopped and then lit the black candle.

It was a fact you can only ever fold a piece of paper 12 times, no matter the size of the paper. Derek had told me that. Was one of the many little interesting facts he'd shared with me, making me full of *useless* information.

"Keep Safe!" Mac called out, bringing me back from my thoughts. She repeated the phrase three more times as she lit the folder paper on flame. She let go of it to burn in the hollowed top of the candle. The paper turned to ash. Then she blew out the black candle, leaving the other five to burn. "You're supposed to keep the others burning to strengthen the protection," Mac informed us. "The longer they burn the stronger the protection." Then she stood. "You're safe to get up now. Blessed Be." Turning to Alison, she asked, "Do you prefer to take the codex with you or leave it here?"

Alison glanced down at the protection setup. "It's safer here. I'll just put'er back in the lap desk for added safeguard," she said, reaching for the book. With a gentle touch, she picked it up and placed it in the open mouth of the lap desk, then shut it in. "You're the keeper," she told Olivia, handing her back the key.

Olivia took the key and then she and Mac returned to standing in the kitchen doorway closest to the front door.

I grabbed up my tote, following close behind Alison and Vicki as they headed towards the exit. But before they could go out the door, Mac stepped forward and held out a small satchel to Alison.

"It's a *Simple*. A little something extra... protection for the baby," Mac explained, placing the charm in Alison's hand.

"I made it," Olivia beamed, grinning wider, glancing over to Mac.

I recalled the term Simple from reading the grimoire notes earlier. A Simple; basic element, charm or spell that has only one ingredient, making it quick and well, *simple*.

"Later," I said, omitting my seeing the description, and choosing to be the first to leave. I didn't wait for a response, didn't look back, only proceeded down the steps and straight to my car.

As Vicki's car pulled away, I sat in the car a moment to sooth the hurt. *How could Mac, how could they all have left me out of the protection ward?* I took in a few deep breaths to calm my angry nerves before the drive back to the house... Olivia's house, *alone.*

"Wait—I thought they believed now," Michael said, his words more a question than a statement.

Uriel stood on the porch and watched as Vicki and Alison drove up the street. "They do but won't admit it to each other... or even themselves," Uriel said, as Vretil joined him on the porch.

"It's important they believe for this to work," Vretil followed up, watching as the girls drove away. "It's not a game or mystery to solve."

Standing on the grass in front of the porch, Raphael too watched as the car headed away up the street. "They believe in themselves—it's a start," he said trying to sound encouraging, but still doing a poor job of it.

"She's the only one who believes, and they are keeping her out of things now," Michael said, as he approached the rental car. Bending down, he peered through the passenger side door. "She feels left out... it was she who commissioned this to happen."

"Give them time," Gabriel said, moving to stand beside Michael near the car.

"Time—how much time?" Shamsiel demanded from the sidelines. He'd wholly expected some semblance of a response... but none came.

Chapter 7

Saturday morning and I woke late. Well, late for me when I was used to getting up with Will for his 5 a.m. swim practice.

Rolling over in bed, I checked the small clock on the low dresser, it was 9:30 a.m.. I could have slept for another ten hours with the way I was feeling. This past week was one crazy ride after another, and yesterday with its change in group dynamic pretty much beat the crap out of me. This stuff, this new world my friends were in, all of it, I suppose I'll get used to it. It was a lot for anyone to take in, and now that they had this common goal and each other, they were complete in the focus. It's what I wanted, for them to work together. I just didn't know I'd be left out.

Louise had requested I come over late morning just before lunch, so I guess my body clock had done its job. Had to admit though, it was nice to sleep in. I took my time getting up and ready, showering and dressing in peace.

Downstairs, with the kitchen table all to myself, I enjoyed a large cup of coffee, and set up for non-mystery-solving time with my computer.

Before leaving, I tucked my laptop back upstairs and then made a quick call. By the fourth ring, I'd almost hung up, but on the fifth, it picked up. "Yeeees, hello?" Mac's voice came through the phone.

"Hey, it's me, Lynn."

"Hey, Lynnie, what's up?" she responded, giving me nothing.

"How goes the hocus-pocus?" Was all I could come up with since I had nothing specific I could ask.

With a huff she said, "Oooh fine—kind of busy here—what's up?" she asked again.

Feeling the push-off, I said, "Nothing, just checking in—I'm heading out. I'll let you go."

"Okay—have a good day," she said in a less annoyed tone, then she hung up.

Great. They all couldn't wait for me to get home to Ottawa, but now I was an annoyance, perfect. There was no way I was calling Alison and Vicki if this was the response I'd get. I wanted to be in a positive state of mind when I visited with Louise. "Positive energy—positive energy, good air in—sickness out," I said as I grabbed my tote and left.

Pulling up, I parked the car alongside my father-in-law's front lawn. Since Louise and Will's father were neighbors, I could get two visits in for the price of one. I got out of the car just as David came out the front door of his place.

"Hi Lynn. I'm heading over to...," he said, the name or place muffled as the garage door opened. "Louise told me you'd be over for a visit. I'll be over in a while, once I get back," he added. He liked to keep an eye on his neighbors—and they on him. I scrambled up the steep driveway and met him at the opening to the garage for a quick hug. Then I scooted around the right side between their houses to the back gate of Louise's garden oasis.

Cranking the gate open, I scooted around a large flowering shrub just before reaching the patio. There she sat, *Wonder Woman*. She was decked out in a matching navy-blue and purple, yoga pants and hoodie outfit, her fake hair peeking out from under a purple and navy kerchief.

"It's a good day, I'm up!" Louise called out, spotting me as I spotted her. Surprisingly full of energy, she stood to give me a big hug as she continued. "Funny thing, I'm always full of vim'n vigor the day after my chemo. They say it's the anti-nausea meds, but who knows." She gave me a little boxer move, junior prizefighter fists pumping, feet shuffling. Made me laugh, and laughter was the best medicine. The absolute best.

"Okay there, Rocky, quit show'n off—you're making me look bad," I said reaching for another hug. Releasing her, I wiggled in around the far side to the padded bench and my usual seat at the patio table. Louise had our tea set up... *goody.*

"Don't worry," she said laughing, "I'll be sick as a dog tomorrow— when it finally hits me." Chuckling, she slid into her seat at the end of the table. "How about a cookie?" She tempted. She was another one of those food-pushers and she knew I was an addict, but I loved her for it. Good food, good wine, great stories, and bone crushing love all came from this house. It was a beacon for a hungry soul like mine.

I watched as she filled our cups with hot tea, decaffeinated and a good thing too, she was wired enough already. Then she passed me three—no four, homemade cookies. Bless her heart. Taking a quick breath in she said, "Sooo, what have you been up to since you got home." She stirred her tea, waiting for my answer, stirring, waiting, stirring... and waiting some more.

That was a big question. Normally I would have been quick on my feet and coming up with a witty response, but all I got out was, "Oh just me and the girls, hang'n—you know—same'old stuff," But she wasn't buying it.

"Hanging... with the girls... that's it?" She asked, pushing another warm gooey cookie my way like it was a bribe and I had what she needed.

Stalling for a better answer, I took a huge bite of the contraband and came up with an answer just shy of a lie. Swallowing first I said, "Well... we have been checking out old antiques, found a few old letters too—they're pretty cool. Found an old key that unlocks an old desk and an old book full of different foreign languages. Been like our own little treasure hunt." I shoved the rest of the cookie in my mouth, making it impossible to keep going.

"Really? How exciting. Sounds intriguing, I have to say." She took another sip of her not-so-piping-hot tea, then nibbled the edge of a cookie, waiting... for more.

"Not so intriguing, it all belongs to their moms and their moms' moms. No real mystery," I added, hiding the real truth, wrapping it up and topping it off with a dull grey bow.

Laughing again, she patted my arm. "Oh sure, ruin it for me. I had it all playing out in my mind. It sounded like a great mystery unfolding. Yer such a tease." She slouched back in her seat. Reaching a hand to her head, she brushed a curl of artificial hair out of her eyes.

"Nice outfit," I said, pushing away the latter.

Playing the model with all the moves, she posed in her seat giving me her best Madonna-Vogue poses. "Oh, well—thank you very much. It's the latest in post-chemo activewear. A girl's gotta look good you know." We both laughed, cutting through the reality of the situation.

The rest of our visit trotted along much the same way. Her deflecting how extremely crappy cancer was, and me pretending to agree life was all about the clothing. She's amazing. Tackling this nasty enemy as though it were *Hitler*, *Stalin*, and *Bin Laden*, cornered in a room with an assault rifle, guns'a blazing.

Her energy fizzled out two hours into the visit, and I helped carry in the empty cookie plate and teacups. It was my cue to skedaddle and let her rest. At the gate she hugged me again, only releasing me when I convinced her it was time for her to put her feet up.

When I rounded the corner, it was obvious David had not come home yet. No car in the drive. I'm sure he figured I'd be over longer, underestimating my chat time with the superhero.

On the short drive back to Olivia's, it felt strange. Not the drive, but how strange it was not to be going over to see my mom, not going over to *her house*. Since the sale of the house in the spring, my brother James had moved out to a quaint little place in the country. I'd never lived in this house, but I still considered it home. I considered Ottawa home, but it was feeling more like a stranger every day, every hour, every minute.

Back at Olivia's house, I noted she'd been back in my absence, but was gone again. She'd been home to shower and change, her clothes from the day before were lying strewn across her bed. But no call, no note... no nothing meant... nothing.

I dragged my laptop back downstairs and set up shop. Figured I'd make a late lunch and check my emails, again. I found leftover salad and half a piece of grilled chicken in the fridge. It'll do for now, but I'd order myself a pizza later should Olivia fail to show up again.

Surprise—surprise, there was an email from Derek, asking if *we* needed more help. I had no idea what *they* needed, but I wrote him back anyhow,

> Hey Shortcut,
> They're working on their own. Just got back from visiting another friend. I'm hanging at Olivia's by myself.
> L.

Send.

I got up and tidied my mess from my lunch prep. When I sat back down, there was a new longer email from Derek, this one telling me what he had planned for the weekend, and thankfully no mention of the other stuff. Excellent.

We emailed back and forth for the better part of the afternoon. I'd considered calling over to Alison, but I figured she and Vicki would either be over at Mac's, or she'd be just too engrossed to talk. Besides, they could always call me if they needed me.

Okay, I admit it—I was pissed. It'd been over three years since I'd seen Alison and all I'd gotten was a few hours with her, and no one-on-one. I had anticipated us talking about all the baby stuff and such. She was the last of my friends to have a baby, and with no babies in sight for Will and me, I was hoping for a little play-by-play on the whole experience. Guess it too would have to wait. We had time, she wasn't due until spring, and we still had months to talk about weight-gain, bloating and other discomfort funness, I figured.

At 7:30 p.m. I sent my last and final email of the day to Derek and shut down my computer. I still hadn't gotten a call from Will. No biggy, he couldn't call every night. I was sure he'd call tomorrow considering what day it was and how tough it would be for me. And since there was still no sign of Olivia, it was time for me to order from the best pizza joint in town, *Georgie's Pizza and Subs*.

One call and thirty minutes later, a medium hot steaming pizza was at the door. After giving the delivery guy a generous tip, I hurried back to the kitchen. I got a large dinner plate out of the cupboard and maneuvered three big pieces of pizza from the box to the plate. I left the last three pieces in the box on the counter for later... breakfast, maybe.

It was nice being in the house alone. Even their doggie was up at the lake with Mike and the girls. With no one around, I got myself comfortable in the family room on the couch, plate and napkin in hand, and then I surfed the TV channels.

What the...? Either I was going crazy, or it had to be another crazy strange fluke, because in the TV menu there were five—yes five, different movies playing, all of which were at different stages of play. But that wasn't the crazy part, the craziness was that these movies were all the same theme. *Angels.*

Michael and Vretil found the perfect vantage point in the park behind Vicki's apartment, keeping watch on the building itself and its surrounding areas, keeping safe their Charges. Raphael and Uriel had remained out front of the tiny home while *their* Charges busied themselves in the kitchen, still working on magic and healings together.

Placing themselves halfway between the house and the apartment, Shamsiel and Gabriel sat atop the roof of the Tim Horton's coffee shop, not that the location mattered, but Gabriel liked it here.

Leaning forward, looking over the edge of the roof and down at the big Tim Horton's sign, Shamsiel asked, "Who is *Tim Horton* and what does it have to do with coffee and donuts?"

"Seriously?" Gabriel responded.

"Seriously—what's the deal?"

"Only one of the greatest hockey players. Not to mention the man who started a business that has become a prominent fixture in the Canadian landscape—over 3,000 restaurants across Canada alone. Largest quick-service restaurant chain in Canada—and more recently, there's over 600 locations in the United States."

"Must be good coffee," Shamsiel joked.

"Darn good, and thirty-five different varieties of donuts with that darn-good-coffee."

"Thirty-five? No wonder the place is so popular." Shamsiel watched as the people came and went, all of them carrying their cardboard trays of coffee and boxes of donuts.

"It's not the variety—it's the quality." Gabriel said, continuing his dialog and giving his friend the facts. "They used to only have two in the beginning, the *Apple Fritter* and the *Dutchie*. Still two of the most popular, I might add." He licked his lips reminiscing.

"You're telling me you eat donuts and drink coffee?"

"Coffee nooo—never touch the stuff, but I've sampled a donut or two, but I'm a traditionalist. I like the *Old Fashion*, the plain style. It's the cake-donuts they make. Nothing fancy for me."

Shamsiel said nothing, only stared at him, surprised amusement spreading across his beautiful sun-kissed face.

"What?" Gabriel questioned, glancing back at the skeptic.

"I take it you like this hockey stuff too?" he asked, grinning back at Gabriel.

"Can't say I've ever watched a full game, but I hear what they say about Tim. Things like, *steadiest defenseman on the blue-line for 22 years in the National Hockey League*. Not sure what a blue-line is—but he played in 1,446 regular season games, four Stanley Cups, was an All-Star player six times. Some claim he invented the slap-shot. Again—not sure what it is, but it sounds important."

"The slap-what?"

Ignoring him, Gabriel continued, "Off the rink he was sharp too they say, investing his salary in this business."

"Guy must be rich."

Gabriel sighed. "Sadly, he didn't live to witness his business's enormous success. He died in an automobile accident back in 1974."

They both sighed, and then they continued to rattle on, exchanging ideas on food and sports, more or less like regular men.

Breaking the banter, Shamsiel said, "So, we're just supposed to sit here and wait for what exactly? The others are watching their Charges—and we're to do what?"

Gabriel said nothing, only stood up from his perch atop the roof to survey south of the city. Then he took a step forward.

"Where are you going?" Shamsiel asked, standing to meet his friend.

Without turning to look back at him, Gabriel said, "Where do you think?" Then disappeared.

Chapter 8

Comfy on the big couch and remote in hand, the most amazing and wonderful sense of clarity washed over me, and for the first time all day the knotted tension in my shoulders released. Those earlier pangs of gloomy emotion, segregation, and sadness were now gone. Replacing them was a delightful enthusiasm for the future, for all our futures. A heightened sense of compassion wrapped around me, giving me an irresistible urge to send those feelings back out into the universe, to my friends, to these remarkable women in my life.

I wasn't a part of things anymore, but I respected their courage to keep looking for answers. My four friends—the *Four*, have been given an unfathomable destiny to solve. And Louise, my dear Louise, her plight was unfathomable. Fighting the battle of her life, she more than anyone, needed all the positive energy the world had to offer. Cancer was evil incarnate. End of story.

Based on how I was feeling now, I guess I needed this little *me-time* to readjust my thoughts, my emotions. I had no other explanation for the shift in my emotional grid. I'm used to strange, but this was a different kind of strange. *What had changed?* Why the lightness, this sense of freedom suddenly? But here I was, blanketed in feelings of peace and patience, along with power and strength—not to fight, but to surrender, release, to transform.

Yielding to the truth and the synthesis of everything all around me, to the solitude in this room, I leaned into it. Calmness and warmth, like the feeling you get when your mother puts your favorite blanket around you. Like when you have your hands on a bowl of her homemade chicken-noodle soup coupled with another of your favorites like a grilled cheese sandwich. Perfect comfort.

I was grateful for the change, only wished I understood why or at least how it had come. Would be a nice thing to tap into if I could, *when I needed it*. My heightened senses were never anything I could control. I often felt like they controlled me. But this was different, I was alone, yet the feelings of joy and harmony were almost palpable. Simply from the tiny task of resting right where I was. I'd had a similar wonderful yet lesser sensation when I'd seen those five figures emerge from the shadows downtown. It was much like the sensation the other night when I'd sat out front of Mac's house with Cooper. Tenderness. Peace. Love.

Gabriel took up residence at the end of the couch, using the last third of it. This was the part he loved the most about sharing his presence, witnessing their calmness. Smiles stretching across faces out to the cheeks and up into the eyes. Happiness and pure contentment envelopes, and he truly adored witnessing the change, especially with one so torn, suffering with their internal struggle and confusion. He wanted to sit closer, look into those eyes, see into the mind behind those oh-so-familiar eyes, but he remained where he was, just *watching*.

"It's a Wonderful Life," I said aloud to nobody.

Gabriel pretended she was speaking to him.

"It's a classic—one of my favorites, but right at the end," I added.

"Oh, I love this part," Gabriel said, though no one could hear. It was the part with Jimmy Stewart, where the little girl who plays his daughter says that famous line, *'Every time a bell rings, an angel gets its wings,'*. "

"I wondered if the little actress ever played in any other roles," I said aloud again, then changed the channel.

The next movie choice was a much darker story, *Constantine*. Keanu Reeves plays a cynical chain-smoking detective whose role it was to send demons back to hell. It's a good flick, but I opted out on this one too as I'd seen it too many times, and it was past due for a Part 2 at this point. "I hated the girly gender-bending angel," I said, "who for whatever reason, was jealous of Constantine." Angels aren't supposed to look like that or be played by women unless the angel is supposed to be a female. I let out a big *"Groan"* of disappointment, concluding my thoughts on the movie.

"The woman is a good actress," Gabriel responded, "but why does she have to play me—why a female actor? I'm clearly male in appearance. And why am I portrayed as such a jerk?" He shook his head. "Change the channel," he said in an inaudible request.

Changing the channel a third time, I hit on another favorite of mine, *City of Angels*. "Seen it," I said to the peaceful room. "I'm sort of sick of Nickolas Cage anyway—but love Meg Ryan, and her hair in this one."

Gabriel, now rather comfortable with this milieu, said, "Guy's no Angel, married Elvis Presley's daughter—and thought he was *The King*. Good thing she divorced that wanna-be." Gabriel laughed at his colloquial use of the words despite being the only one who could hear his comments.

Next on the list was *Prophesy*, with Christopher Walken. Awesome actor. "I love this one too, but... it's half over already," I spouted in frustration.

"Sure, they finally get a good male actor to portray me, but then they make me seem like... an asshole. I hate this one. And what's with the nasty black hair?" Gabriel tossed out, enjoying the banter. Why he hadn't done this sooner, he didn't know.

With reluctance I went to my last option, *Wings of Desire*. "Never seen this one."

"Me either," Gabriel responded.

I clicked the info button for more of the description and read, *"Most romantic movie ever filmed about angels. An angel watches over the world, falls in love with a trapeze performer and likes the idea of being human. Peter Falk is in it."* Interesting, but he would always be detective Colombo to me.

"Sounds a lot like City of Angels, but eclectic and more poetic," Gabriel added, hoping it would be the one chosen.

"Okay, Wings of Desire it is," I said, giving in to the last choice.

Comfortable in his spot at the end of the couch, Gabriel crossed his arms over his chest with resolve, and deciding he would most certainly do this more often in the future.

A little over two hours later the movie ended, and I dragged myself upstairs to my bed. It was a wonderful realization when you'd had a day full of brain-smashing thoughts and anxiety, that when your face touched the soft cool pillow, you'd be out. Exhausted and overwhelmed from everything, I'd by-passed the usual washing of face and brushing of teeth, and took a header into the bed, my mind full of foggy scenes from the movie. Despite leaving the hall light on, my cognitive light faded out.

Images of two angels as they roamed the city watching and listening, filled my dreams… a pregnant woman in an ambulance, the distant screeching of the siren… a painter struggling for inspiration… and an old man dreaming of peace yet restless….

Gabriel stood beside the bed, watching his movie companion drift off and enter sleep. Her long lashes cast shadows on her cheeks, and he leaned over to listen to her soft breathing.

…images in both rich sepia-toned black and white and vivid colour all blurred in my unconsciousness. I opened my eyes, shifting from my chaotic dream-filled sleep. My fuzzy vision clearing… as I stared up… into the… most alarmingly breathtaking… *peaceful* face. "I'm still dreaming," I said, and shut my eyes. Refocusing, I jumpstarted my brain, because I knew I must have been dreaming. When I opened them a second time, the face was gone. *Nothing.*

Nothing remained but the feeling of wonder and fascination, and a tiny bit of *insanity*. Had to be that movie messing with my brain, with all its wild film footage and back and forth from black and white to colour scenes. Hell, Peter Falk plays himself in the movie, but in Berlin's Nazi past. On the flip side the character used to be an angel who had grown tired of always watching and never experiencing. He'd given up his immortality to become human. How weird was that? Normal imagery, right? *Nope.*

Rubbing my eyes, I remembered how annoying it was that the movie ended with the message 'To be continued'. Who does that unless they actually do a part 2? This one hadn't because it'd been made back in 1987. If it'd been done, I'd never heard of it, but then I hadn't known this one had existed either, so what did I know. What I *did* know, was I had left the hall light on *and* I hadn't brushed my teeth. My mouth tasted like pepperoni pizza—and not in a good way.

On my way to the bathroom I peeked in to see if my friend was in her bed, but found the covers were still in place, and still no Olivia. Face washed, and teeth brushed, I shut off the hall light this time and returned to my bed.

Lying in the dark, I ran over what I'd seen... what I thought I'd saw... what I'd dreamt.

That face.

Those eyes.

A perfect face surrounded by gold and flaxen hair. Though it had been only a split second, the image was now burned into my retinas, my brain—into my memory. Then I sat up in bed... *I'd seen that face before.*

Gabriel positioned himself out in the hall around the corner from the bedroom, flattened thin as a silk drape against the wall, panting as though he'd run up the highest mountain. In fear of being discovered, he covered his mouth to conceal any sounds, hiding for the first time *ever* in his whole existence. He didn't dare move until he was sure she was safe in her bed, *and* fast asleep. *Get a grip Gabriel* were his thoughts as he disappeared.

"What are you doing back?" Shamsiel asked when Gabriel's frazzled essence appeared next to him on the rooftop.

"She saw me!" he exclaimed, running his hands over his face hoping to shake off the reality of the situation.

"How?" Shamsiel asked. Then he took a big bite of a massive *Honey Cruller*. The donut split into two warm halves of goodness, some of the glaze sticking to the side of his face. Didn't matter though, Gabriel wasn't looking at him, instead he stared at his shaking hands.

"Thought she was asleep—let my veil down for a second," Gabriel confessed.

"Wha hapn?" Shamsiel asked, his mouth full of donut. Gabriel must have noted the fault in his speech because he turned to look at him.

Staring at his friend, Gabriel discerned the mess on his face and the fact he also held not one, but two donuts, one in each hand, a half-eaten Cruller in his right and a Chocolate Glazed in his left. Gabriel flinched and made that face, the one you see on a parent who has just realized their once tidy child has spaghetti all over them. He shook his head. Collecting himself, Gabriel said, "Nothing—she figured it was a dream. I hid around the corner to make sure."

Chewing and then swallowing, Shamsiel asked, "You know what today is, don't you?"

"Yes, of course. I hope to see her again up at Kelly's, but I'll be more careful this time."

"Kelly's?"

"Kelly's Funeral Home—the memorial wall, remember?" Gabriel said, his mind easing just a bit. For now, what he hoped might ease his mind, perhaps even make his anxious feelings over tonight's events a little less *telling*, would be to get *his* hands on one of those nice big fresh donuts himself.

Chapter 9

That face.

I knew it now, it was the same face from the photo at the Fairchild Gardens, the same face I'd seen across the street from my house. All this information about angels, talk of angels, and the movies with angels, it's no wonder I dreamt about them, *him*.

It had to be a dream, it was… wasn't it? After two hours of tossing and turning, and loads of hypothesizing later, I'd finally gotten back to sleep. At least I think I had. When I woke it felt as if I'd barely slept a minute. And though the clock on the dresser read 10 a.m., another major sleep-in by my clock standards, not much sleeping had occurred. It was too much. Way too much on the list for one person's mind to handle, and today would be one more emotional ride to add to that list.

Today, is one year since Mom passed, and I wasn't sure if any of my friends realized it. I figured Olivia would remember, with her mom's one year being next month. But then again, what she was doing now was all about her mom, all their moms, and all of them.

The clock wasn't the only thing telling me the morning was half over, my stomach was yelling at me to get up and get at making something to eat. Luckily, I had wonderful pieces of pizza waiting for me in the fridge, making breakfast prep-time minimal, so I headed downstairs.

A plate and 45 seconds in the microwave later, I had the breakfast of champions. Two minutes later I finished up with a coffee chaser and my day was officially underway.

I'd skipped the shower today and opted for the Sunday-shower-thing by doing a quick ponytail and donning my favorite *Life is Good* baseball cap, and then I was good to go.

Olivia's home was at the same end of town as Kelly's, only a short drive, and ideal for the emotional day I had ahead of me. I'd called James to see if he wanted to meet me at the memorial out at the funeral home, but when I'd rung the house, there had been no answer. I assumed he didn't want to talk to anyone today, and normally how he deals with stuff, *alone*. Taking a page from his book, I went with the option of spending the day alone and not bother the girls with my grief. Though, I had the overwhelming need to call my Aunt Kay, *wished* I could, was more like it, but she was gone too. "I miss you both so much," I whispered to the air as I drove away from the house.

On the approach, I could see the sprawling tan facade with its forest green roofs. When I got to the entrance, I pulled into the grounds, but instead of parking near the main facility, I parked to the right in the public parking for the memorial walk. I wasn't sure I could handle the sad faces of potential funeral goers, and I wanted to avoid the main area and any person or groups attending a service.

From where I parked, I spotted two of the memorial walls near the entrance to the arbor walkway. From the photos James had sent me, I knew neither were the correct ones. Since I hadn't been able to be there for the unveiling, he had taken photos and emailed them such I could share in the unveiling. I'd been the one who had received the offer to have their names memorialized on the wall, and James and I had shared the idea with my cousins. The memorial unveiling was another thing I'd missed. I hadn't been home when my mom or my aunt had passed away, but I was here now.

Once under the arbor, the path wound around to the left. Following it, I found the specific wall I had been looking for.

It stood at least 7 feet tall and 10 feet wide, in black granite a foot thick. Its top and side edges were rough cut in waves shapes rounded at the corners. The front was polished smooth and shiny like deep waters, but the names themselves had been cut into the stone and shone white in contrast. For ease of locating a loved one, the names had been put in alphabetical order. Just names—no dates, since it was about remembering *them* and not the day they left us. It was a shame Mom and Aunt Kay's names couldn't be together, but *they* were together now, weren't they.

Standing in front of the wall, I scanned for the first name, *Ross*. There she was, Kathleen Ross, but she would always be Aunt Kay—or Annie-K the way we'd pronounced it growing up. Taking a breath, I kissed the fingertips of my right hand and passed them across the etching of her name. Then continuing through the list, locating W, for *Westlake*. Down near the end of the list I found her, Sarah Westlake. But to everyone who knew her she would always be *Sally, Mom* or *Aunt Sal*.

Forcing a smile, I traced her letters with my fingers. Feeling the coarseness of each cut in the stone, I noted the pronunciation of each letter in my head as I passed over them. There were hundreds of names on this wall, but my eyes saw only two. I couldn't bear to glimpse any others for fear of recognizing the names. There were already too many names for me to handle, too many already carved into the inner space of my skull and imprinted on my brain. Stepping back from the wall and out of its shadow, I tilted my face up to feel the sun.

It was a beautiful day; the air was cool and still. Taking a few more steps back, I took up residence on the bench facing the memorial. Perfect spot for viewing and reflecting, and more than likely why it was placed here. As I sat in this place of solitude, the names of all my friends who had lost their mothers ran through my brain. Some of them were cancer survivors, but for many the battle continued.

A faint chill tickled the air as a single cloud passed in front of the bright sun. I was glad I'd put my favorite sweatshirt on before heading out. It was one of Will's he'd rarely worn, a thick white cotton oversized one from the company he worked for. It had a small company logo in the upper left-hand corner. The backside had a stylized jet-ski image, followed by the words *'Get out there!'*, meaning get out and have fun. It was high contrast to the non-fun I was having at the monument, but still the pullover made me feel warm and comfortable.

As the sun hid, the cold of the stone bench pressed up under my legs. I tucked the sweatshirt under my bum. With the clouds not moving on, and the warmth of the sun lost, the chill grew stronger. The quiet comfort I'd been savoring now vanished into the shadow.

Shivers.

Nausea.

Dread.

Those sensations were back. The same ones I'd had seeing the dark figure under the streetlight, and at the airport.

Anguish.

Pain, and sorrow... darkness... *death.* I wrapped my arms around myself in an attempt to warm my outside *and* my insides. Through a wave of nausea, I glanced across the expanse of the property.

There, just right of the main gardeners' shed stood a figure, *watching me.* The man was too far for me to make out his face, but I could see he wore all black and his hair was dark, same as the man from the airport. With my focus set in his direction, the fixation held me as though bolted to the bench. *Why are you here—why are you watching— watching me? Who are you—what are you?* The questions ran through my brain. I couldn't move my legs, but where would I have gone, if I could? To the car? To the main building, disturbing someone's service? No way. Instead, I closed my eyes tight and focused on willing the horrific feelings away. I'd been able to do it in the past with lesser feelings. Concentrating on the warmth within my heart I pulled it into my lungs, expanding the sensation outward through my limbs, my head and my mind, spreading warmth, and light... and *solace.* I breathed in deep, then out... repeating a few more similar breaths. Then, a new sensation filled me, the sense that something... *someone...* was next to me. I opened my eyes.

Nothing.

There was no one, nothing near me I could see. When I drew my attention across the property again, the man was gone, and so were the clouds... *and* those horrid feelings.

Shamsiel stood with his back to the memorial wall facing the bench, watching as Gabriel sat down in its open space.

"He was here," Gabriel said, staring at her profile as she gazed up at the wall.

Stepping forward, Shamsiel knelt right in front of her.

"Did you see that—sense it... she did it, she literally willed him away. Granted, he may not have fought back... but it was *she* who compelled him on his way. It wasn't our arrival... and now... only the slightest essence of his evil remains. He left seconds before we arrived—it wasn't us, Gabriel."

Gabriel still staring at the side of her face, said, "I am displeased she is still separated from the others."

"Do they still need her? She has united the four and they have the Cipher to help now." Shamsiel reached forward, placing his hands palms down on the stone bench, on either side of her. He leaned in closer. Taking a deep sniff in, he said, "Michael was right, she smells different from the others. Why is it?" he asked. "And look at her eyes— the colour, grey with hints of pale blue, and those lashes—long and thick... like feathers."

"It's hereditary—the lashes, the length and thickness are recessive genes in fact, both parents have to have the genes for it to show," Gabriel said, explaining the tiny fact. He turned away, his stare fixating on nothing in particular.

"You'd think it was a dominant gene set—seems backwards," Shamsiel remarked.

"Yes," was all Gabriel said, as he continued staring into the distance.

The dreadful feelings gone, I stood and stepped up to the wall again. I kissed the fingertips of both my hands, then in unison I placed them on the names of my mother and my aunt, pressing the transferred kisses to the stone.

I slouched in the seat of the rental car not wanting to drive or even start up the thing. I didn't know where I was going. And not that I was trying to avoid the four, but no one had called looking for me either. I'd contemplated on calling, but figured I'd wait until Monday to try another visit with them. I was fine with continuing this solo routine for the rest of the weekend.

"Screw that," I said, squashing that idea. Taking the leap, I started the car and then headed over to Mac's house to see how things were going.

Pulling up alongside the front lawn of the safe-haven, I spotted Mac coming out from the front door with her youngest in tow.

When I got out of the car, Mac said, "Hey Lynnie!" Her son flashed me a big grin. He was clearly heading somewhere fun with Mommy. "We're heading out for a play date—no pre-school for him today. What are you up to?" Her voice was cheerful as was her mindset for the time with her son.

"Just came back from running errands, but thought I'd check in with you guys," I said, still standing by my car. I didn't want to dampen her day by telling her where I'd really been.

"Things are great. Olivia's coming back here after dinner to get me and we're heading over to Vicki's—to work. Wink-wink," she said, giving me a real wink-wink. "What are your plans?"

"None really. You guys gonna need my help with anything?" I figured I knew the answer already, a big NO.

"Ya—you should head over with Liv. Alison mentioned she had questions for you, and Vicki needs Derek's contact info," Mac responded as she slid the side panel of the minivan shut.

Surprised at her response, I said, "Oh... sure-sure. I'll bring Olivia over later. You need anything before—just call me."

"Great! See you then," she called out through the van window. She backed out and the two of them waved as she drove away. I waved back, still in shock over the fact they needed me again. For what, I wasn't sure other than Derek's contact info, but it was something.

The clock on the car's dash read 12:15 p.m.. Olivia wouldn't be off work until at least 3 p.m., but I set forward driving back towards her area of town, anyway. It was mainly because the lunch grumbles were creeping in and I needed to find some food relief. The small plaza near her place had an amazing Vietnamese restaurant, and when my stomach remembered that fact too, I pointed the car in that direction.

Restaurant sign in view, I pulled in and found a spot near the entrance. Starving, I couldn't get out of the car fast enough, and was through the front door in record time. I knew what I wanted, and unless the menu had changed, it was item 410 with a side of summer-rolls. I used to live out here too, once-upon-a-time-ago, and Liv and I have eaten here a few bazillion times, but who was counting. After ordering, and in its usual prompt manner, the food hit the table, and I dug in.

The massive bowl came piled with vermicelli noodles, Asian julienne veggies, tiny spring rolls, and shrimp and chicken, scattered throughout. I topped it with the special fish sauce, adding dabs of Hoisin and Sriracha, then I mixed it all together. It didn't get any better than this for feeding happiness to your lonely stomach.

I smiled. I didn't care who was watching this lonely girl eat her lunch. Content, I ate and watched the other happy satisfied customers come and go, many of them Asian. Besides the fact the food was amazing, the cultural reference of people eating there was a pretty good indicator you were in a great restaurant. I mean if the local Vietnamese families liked it, how could you go wrong?

Less than forty-five minutes into my self-assigned lunch hour, my lonesome mood shifted, and I was blissful again. Considering my recent discontent, I was somewhat encouraged and optimistic about my upcoming visit with the girls. I smiled again. Then... *queasiness.*

Waves.

Nausea.

More waves—and more queasiness. *Again? Oh—please no—don't let it be the food, not one of my favorite haunts,* "Pleeeeeease," I said in a whisper, hunching over in my seat.

Through another wave I glanced up over my almost finished bowl-of-goodness to see the front door to the restaurant swing open. The sunlight coming from outside was so bright I couldn't make out the faces of those who were entering. Their silhouettes cast in shadows were the only things visible. Thunder clapped deafening the sounds of the restaurant and the brilliant sunlight disappeared replaced by grey nebulous skies. The no longer clear blue skies were now filled with ashen coloured squalls opening with a deluge of rain crashing down. The gusting air carried a dim scent in my direction, an aroma filling with dark spices and incense. Then the door to my safe-haven shut, revealing those who had come through.

At the doorway stood four men. Four remarkably huge men, making me think perhaps the *World Wrestling Federation* must be in town. The tallest of the four, his head reaching the doorframe, stood furthest to the back of the group. And based on the doorway, it made him close to 7 feet tall, the others measured close to the same.

Another wave of sickness hit me, but I forced myself to keep my eyes on this quartet. The two titans up front appeared so much alike they could have passed for twins if it weren't for their hair. One had thick straight jet-black hair falling in one length to his shoulders, while the other had short waves of deep russet hair. The other two were pale haired, the tallest man's hair was blond, more platinum than gold and cut short. The other had a brilliant white mane of hair pulled into a long braid that hung over his left shoulder. Going grey or white early perhaps because they all appeared to be in their mid-thirties.

Stranger still, they all had the same complexion, tanned skin covered with what seemed like a dusting of light grey ash, flawless but dull. They stood waiting like a force not to be reckoned with, a wall of shadow dressed in black from lofty head to giant toe. Mockingly, what carried those cryptic stone expressions were mysterious beautiful faces with heavy lashed eyes seeming to shimmer and glow as if backlit.

Discreetly, though hunched over due to my cramping stomach, I watched as the taller one in back scanned the room. The restaurant owner's son came forward to greet them. His nerves and apprehension showed in his stilted gait as he approached, trembling hands held the menus. But when the young man came within greeting distance, the massive man with the black hair raised a massive right hand, palm facing out, halting the young man dead in his tracks. There were no words exchanged, but the son swiftly returned to his place at the counter, then he continued to stack the lunch receipts on a small peg just as he'd been doing before their arrival.

I averted my gaze then and peered down into my bowl continuing to rub my stomach in hopes to evade throwing up. Using my other hand, I picked up my chopsticks and played with the few beansprouts left from my meal. Moving the wilted veggies around the bowl, I tried to appear as though I were busy eating my lunch and paying them no notice. But when I peered up again from my ruse, the tallest one, the man with the *Billy Idol* hair, was staring right at me.

His lurid expression with those laser eyes, bore a hole right into me... into my soul. My nausea escalated, and I dropped the chopsticks. The revulsion grew as sweat turned to beads on my forehead. I reached for my napkin and the room spun. I grabbed my napkin and then closed my eyes.

I held my stomach wrapping both arms across it, curling my hands around my sides. It wasn't the food I told myself, it was something else... it had to be. And this monster of a man's targeted stare was making it worse. *Why the hell was he looking at me?* I'd had aversion premonitions before—but not like this. It'd been years since I'd had one and never one this forceful or feverish. I knew the best way to cope was not let my fear or anxiety get the best of me, and to pull in clear thoughts, happy thoughts, strong brave thoughts, and regain balance, remain undaunted. Keeping my eyes shut tight, I continued to pull in every cleansing thought and positive bit of energy I could.

As my thoughts crested, a white light beamed through my closed lids with such intensity it made me flinch. It's strength so bright as if someone shown a flashlight inches from my face. Then my antipathy faded, and I let my tensed eyelids relax. Patting away the wetness from my forehead with my napkin, I gradually... and calmly... opened my eyes.

Gone.

All of them, gone.

In their place, the front door hung open, revealing streams of sunshine piercing white feathery clouds. It reminded me of those tacky idealistic paintings you sometimes see portraying the heavens opening. But now I understood where the inspirations came from.

Everything around the restaurant was back to normal as if nothing had happened. The owner and his son were laughing and talking with patrons, and the remnants of the lunch crowed still lingering had happy content faces. Outside, the rain that had thundered down, now felt like a bad dream from two nights past, because there wasn't a dark cloud in the sky.

What the hell just happened? Did I have a seizure or was it a hallucination? Was I the only one who saw the storm and its dark clouds... the only one who saw these men? The owner's son had seen them, had approached them, but you'd never have known it by his cheery demeanor. A few minutes ago, he'd been scared out of his wits by their presence, but now his face beamed with joy and amusement as if nothing unusual had transpired.

Collecting myself, I drew in a few cleansing breaths. I threw down some colourful Canadian bills to cover my check, and then I got up and left through the still open door.

I stood in the sunlight and studied the landscape, the sky, and the people who mulled around the parking area. I half expected to see four custom *Harley Davidsons* parked out front, or a few large black window-tinted *Escalades*, but there was nothing of the sort and none of those herculean men to be found either. I shook my head, then I crossed the short distance to my rental car and got in.

Shamsiel stood near the rental car. "How did you do that?" he asked, though he knew she couldn't hear him. He'd seen what had happened, but she was barely rattled. When he'd arrived at this spot, the location where the power of *Dark* and *Light* seemed to emanate the strongest, he knew who would be here. With these four comprising both powers, he knew well this four had arrived, and who had entered this place. He'd sensed it—sensed them, and their arrival. *The arrival much too soon* he mused. He had always been able to sense both the *Dark* and *Light* of his brethren since before his fall. They had been and still were fellow leaders, leaders among the 20, but he had not expected to find... *her* here.

He'd remained outside, watching through the restaurant's window, watching her and what she did. She hadn't known who or what they were, and she hadn't known what she was doing. But she was doing it, doing what her instincts told her to do. In with the good, out with the bad. "Does Gabriel know?" he questioned, in what was the silence to her. "He must—he has to, he must have known, but perhaps not the full extent."

He continued to watch her now from the passenger seat of the car, still hidden as she drove to the home of Raphael's Charge. "Or perhaps he did," he said into the silence again, then he disappeared.

"Okay, think I've had enough with the waves of dark, dank and dingy for a while," I said as I drove. It's not as if I control the stuff, but that was besides the fact. "I much prefer the blissful grouping of feelings I'd had the other night while watching the movie," I added, speaking the words under my breath, as though saying them aloud would have an impact.

Though I'd been done with my job for some time, I still had the habit of checking my watch, and it showed 2:30 p.m.. I'd been in the restaurant for two hours, but it had been 1:30 p.m. when I'd finished my lunch. To top things off, during the time between when *whatever* had happened and now, I'd lost another hour. *Really?* This pissed me off, left a bad taste in my mouth—literally, and not what I wanted after eating one of my favorite meals. It wasn't as though I had a schedule or any place to be, but c'mon. *Had I been hunched over my bowl for an hour while those guys stood at the door?* "How the hell did that happen?" I said, whispering under my breath again. "How had I lost time?"

I was hoping more for mental clarity rather than mental illness and tried not to think about it on the quick drive back to the house. *Was I losing it?* Did I need to get my head checked when I got back to Miami? Could it be something neurological, occlusions or delirium?

I was through the door and waiting for the elusive Olivia when the house phone rang. When I picked up, Olivia's voice announced, "Oh good, yer home. Can you do me a big favor?"

"Sure," I said. Again, no *hi, how are you*, from my friend, just straight to the point.

Her voice sounded breathless as she continued. "Mike was asked to stay late and I'm heading over to Mac's—can you drop the girls at the barn? Mike will pick them up—they're having a pizza-party for the riders. You don't have to worry about feeding them."

"Sure—what time?" Guess I was on my own again for dinner, and alone to head to Vicki's.

"Just after four. Thanks—you're a doll," she said, hanging up before I could ask what time we were meeting.

At four o'clock the girls arrived, changed clothes, and were raring to head to the barn, and like I always was, they were thrilled at the prospect of pizza. To them it made going to the barn that much better.

Two hugs and two kisses later, I gave them their instruction to meet their Dad 'right here' after they were finished. They both nodded in acknowledgement, then turned and ran, disappearing into the closest barn.

My turn. I wouldn't call first, I was just going to show up. I wasn't getting left out this time. Mac said both Alison and Vicki wanted to talk to me, anyway. No problem, right? They'd be expecting me if Mac had told them she'd seen me.

Agreeing with myself, I pulled off the gravel road from the barn and merged onto regular pavement, and then continued on my way.

Chapter 10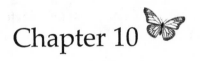

Shamsiel arrived in back of Vicki's building and traversed the spans of the tennis court to join the others, but then noted *no Gabriel* when he moved in next to the four. "Where is he?" he asked, not addressing anyone in particular. They all knew who he meant.

"No idea. Thought he was with you," Michael responded, taking his watch from the building. He scanned his surroundings and then returned his attention to the lit window on the third floor.

"How are they making out?" Shamsiel questioned, again addressing no one specific, but both Uriel and Michael turned at the question.

Going first, Uriel said, "I'd have to say rather well. Both mine and Raphael's Charge have made great strides. They are more than halfway through the grimoire and have created a successful charm or two." Uriel's pride was unmistakable in his expression.

"I'd like to say mine is making strides," Michael added, "but too many pieces are still missing—from the codex I mean, words and phrases she still does not understand. Some of these languages are ancient and without the key for the divine script, she may never find the answers they seek." Michael scowled, worry showing as he turned to Vretil for comment.

Vretil cleared his throat as if not prepared to speak. "Yes, the scribing of events is going well, but as Michael stated—pieces are missing. Well, the pieces are there, but they are unclear and confusing to his Charge, and therefore *my* Charge is unable to convey the information completely or coherently." He crossed his arms over his chest.

"Where have you been?" Raphael asked, finally saying something.

"I was with Gabriel most of last night and part of today, but he keeps disappearing. Never says where he's headed."

"Watching *her* I assume," Michael responded.

"Mostly," Shamsiel answered. As he contemplated on how to finish his response, Gabriel appeared at his side, and using him as a buffer between the others he noticed, as if hoping their focus remained on the Charges in the apartment—and not on his absence. Turning to Gabriel, Shamsiel whispered, "We need to talk."

Parking on the side street near the tennis courts, I got out and hustled it across the street, down around the back and across the lawn between the brick walk-ups. At the front door to Vicki's building I hit the call number for her apartment.

A second later Vicki's voice came. "That you, Lynnie?"

It was an unexpected happy greeting, and surprised as I was, I greeted her back equally cheerful. "You bet!" I said, putting my hand on the handle of the main door.

"C'mon up!" she responded. Her voice held more enthusiasm this time and was followed by the familiar buzzing sound stating the way was open.

I yanked the door wide and then climbed the three flights of stairs to her apartment. The door was generally unlocked for me when I came to visit, but I knocked nonetheless.

"Get in here," came a muffled voice from the other side of the door.

I pushed it open and found Alison standing in the front hall, arms spread wide for our standard greeting. Her face was lit, and her cheeks pinched in a huge smile. Pregnancy made her glow brighter than usual.

"Hug me!" demanded the now clear voice of my serial hugger. "Spooookyyyy," Alison bellowed adding to the welcome.

Surprised and thrilled at the welcome, I threw my arms wide and stepped in for the embrace. Her energy rushed through me and wrapped around me as did her arms. The joy soaked deep inside, into my soul and I sent it back out and around her and her growing baby.

"Hey Spook," I squeaked through squished face and a baby-bear hug.

Vicki winked at me as I peeked over Alison's shoulder still wrapped within the embrace. I spied Mac and Olivia to the right, they appeared to be sorting through the items in the big basket. The basket had housed all the treasures we'd found and right now it had its lid wide open for easy access. They both had smiles for me, and Mac added a peace-sign. Alison released me, and I moved to sit at the dining room table with Vicki.

Her computer was up, and a large white legal-size pad of lined paper sat to the side. The visible page was jammed full of writing, on top of several more pages of writing showing separation from the lower tight cushion of unused pages. Alison claimed the chair next to me. She too had a pad full of writing and question marks.

"Ready for a brain storming session, Lynn?" Vicki shot out.

"Always," I threw back at her, at all of them.

Things had changed, *again*. They needed me for something. I'd do my best not to question their motives, but I wasn't sure what I could give. "Not sure how I can help," I said, letting the statement mirror my feelings.

"Well," Alison said, "I have a ton of questions for you—let's start there." She wiggled in her seat with excitement. With her smile big beaming, she gathered up her notes and her favorite pencil. "Ready?"

"Ready-ready," I said and giggled a little, and so did she.

"Okay, let's go back to the first items in the journal," she said, checking her notes and reaching out for Mom's journal. "Your birthmother—what can you tell me about her?"

"Not much. Think you know everything I know," I said. A little stunned at the question, I leant down beside my chair and pulled my laptop from my bag and joined Vicki in the cyber-vapor. "I got more from the PI, but I told you about that too," I added. My computer hummed into action. "Let me find the emails for you."

"Great idea," Alison confirmed. "Has he written you anything else?"

"I checked my emails on Saturday, but nothing from him since those first few. He'd written about following up with some guy, but still nothing." Finding the saved email, I said, "Here... let me reread it, see if I left anything out from my notes." Paraphrasing I said, "Met with birthmother's best friend... told her to keep the pregnancy a secret. Wouldn't tell her who the father was—said he was unaware of the pregnancy, and she wanted to keep it that way."

"Got it," Alison said, waiting for more while she checked her notes.

"Mentioned something to her about a fortuneteller—woman told her to take the pregnancy full term." A little envious, I put a hand on Alison's belly. She smiled at me, the corners of her eyes crinkling.

"What else?" she asked, giggling like I was telling her a secret.

Giggling back at her, I said, "Says the best friend didn't believe the whole fortuneteller thing, meaning it didn't happen—a cover, for whatever reason she had for going full term." I skimmed down to find the family reference. "She thought it was strange how my birthmother was looking for a specific type of family—very specific, like she knew them."

"Maybe she did," Alison suggested, "Go on."

"Uhhm... they lost track after the friend left out East to university."

Hunger sensation growls escaped the confines of my pullover and I rubbed my stomach. And as if linked, Alison rubbed her belly.

"Oh, I'm hungry too—anyone else? Eating for two here," Alison said.

Before the two on the couch could respond, Vicki said, "Have no fear Vicki's here!" She laughed, adding to the giggle-fest at the table. "Just threw a healthy mac'n cheese casserole into the oven 20 minutes ago—should be ready in 10."

At that info I glanced over to Mac. She grinned back at me knowing how well *Mac* and *cheese* went together, being the cheese lover that she was. Hell, we all were. What a contradiction in terms it was, *healthy* and *mac'n cheese*, but if anyone could make an old bad-for-you classic healthy, it was Vicki. Not to mention making it still taste good. It made my stomach growl again in anticipation, but until the buzzer went off, I'd continue through the email for Alison's fact-finding mission.

"Nothing more in the emails," I told her, "but he met up with her after the call, and I'd talked to him over the phone about it."

"You made notes on the meeting. Let me see if we have everything," Alison said, flipping the pages from my old note pad.

As she flipped, I recapped what I could remember. "When he met with the friend, she had nothing more on the father—but told him more on my birthmother. She referred to a sort of psychic thing she had—how she always knew stuff... had interests in Wicca, spiritual stuff, the Earth, stars, natural healing." Looking down at Alison's belly I said, "She also talked a lot about angel stuff after she got pregnant, and she'd had an exceptionally strong insight during this time too. The friend thought it was *spooky*." I lingered on the word spooky for a second and smiled.

"It's all here too," Alison confirmed, "*Spooky*." A tiny giggle squeaked out when she said the word this time.

I rubbed my temples like it might help and searched my memory banks for any tidbit I may have missed. Then I said, "They hadn't talked in years, only met up after her diagnosis—the friend worked at the cancer center. Talked about the baby—first time since the birth." Then remembering the kicker in the info, I took my fingers from my temples and clapped my hands together in triumph. "Didn't think much of it then, but it must mean something. It fits with the theme of things we've discovered," I said. "They talked about how *the daughter was on the right path*—that the *balance was being kept*. The friend had been confused by the comments—assumed it was the cancer meds, but the friend also knew she always, well—knew stuff. Had considered possibly she'd been keeping an eye on her—*me*. My birthmother told her friend she was the only one who knew about the baby, but also shared with her that she always spent the day alone—on my birthday."

"Can't believe she said nothing about the father," Alison said.

Like a spark shot off I remembered something else. "He said she wrote stuff down—my birthmother that is. The friend said when she'd asked her about the birthfather, her response was, '*I've written it all down and the information is safe*'."

Alison skimmed the page. "That's not here—your notes end with the stuff on her going to see your Mom on your 27th birthday." Alison flipped to a new page. "Spook, oh... my... gaaawd."

"She may have written more things about you—secret things," Vicki said, giving me a few eyebrow-raises.

I said nothing, only speculated to myself why I hadn't made a note of it. But then again, I hadn't known secret-hidden-keep-safe-messages were a thing at that time.

"You should email him—Anthony. He could have more," Vicki added.

Nodding, I sparked up a fresh new email window. Making the message short and to the point, I wrote,

> Saint Anthony, Any more news?
> Lynn

...and then hit send.

The timer on the oven buzzed, and then Vicki's, Alison's, and my chair all squeaked in chorus as we pushed away from the table. As if hypnotized and nothing on the brain but food, Alison and I followed Vicki into the kitchen. The others followed in hot pursuit.

When Vicki pulled the family-size dish from the oven, the aroma of the melty-goodness just about made me faint. I swooned in ecstasy as she cut into it to serve it. Vicki grinned at me as she gave the first piece to Mama-bear, who at that moment was more like a grizzly bear with her hunger and hormones taking over. But I was next.

With my oowey-gooey cheese-pasta-heaven in my bowl, I beat tracks back to the dining room trailing close behind Alison to the table. And as we ate, Alison moved on to the next item on her list.

"Okay," Alison said. "These are the ones about Gabriel... and his appearances in stories from the religious texts *and* from those stories closer to home." She flipped the page. "Let me work backwards here. Your buddy, Luc aaaand Derek both gave you the references on this guy-slash-angel." She paused. "Hmmm, he's a kind of messenger—an Archangel, carries a trumpet?" she questioned.

"Yup," was all I had in response, hoping they might be on board with the *angel* thing.

"Aaaaand his name is mentioned in not one, but two personal stories?" Alison continued.

"Yup—the story about Will's Mom, the one she told Louise—who then told me. And Mom's journal, telling the story told to her by my birthmom," I said, pointing out the transference.

Alison nodded and said, "Still bizarre though, wouldn't you say? The stories themselves have similar threads—man visiting, keeping the balance, staying on the right path, the name *Gabriel*."

"Could still be lots of missing pieces there on both accounts. And both women were sick when they'd delivered these stories too," I reminded her. It reminded me of the broken telephone game we played as kids. Where a bunch of you sit in a circle and one kid starts by whispering a phrase like, *the cat is black*, into the ear of the kid next to them and so on, and by the time it gets back around the group it's morphed into *three sacks on my back*, or something equally stupid or just way wrong.

"You said you saw someone—at the garden, and outside your house? Thought it was the same guy?" Alison questioned.

"I didn't see the guy at the garden. He was in the photo taken at the garden—I sent it to you. It was after that I saw the guy on the street near my house—but only for a few seconds. He looked like the guy from the photo... but I don't know." I brought the photo up on my screen and turned my laptop to show it to her again.

"Pffff—not sure how you could've forgotten someone like him. The guy's positively pulchritudinous," she giggled out. "I mean *Hot*—for you non-scribes. Sorry, I've been waiting for an opportunity to use that one." Pffffing again she giggled harder.

"Until Derek told me, I hadn't noticed the trumpet in his hand." Enlarging the photo, I pointed out the horn. "The photo is where Luc got the idea on Gabriel and told me the whole horn-messenger thing."

"Luc tells you about an angel named Gabriel, Louise tells you about a man named Gabriel, and your mom transcribes the story about a man with the same name. It's all speculation don't you think?" Alison questioned again, yet still ignoring the obvious.

I was becoming more frustrated with the whole *angel* reference thing again and felt a rant coming on. Weren't they even going to consider it? Stretch or not, there were too many bizarre things, and connections to angels to be ignored.

"Both women describe the guy like he was something other or greater than a man?" Alison added.

Aaaaand rant, "Nowhere does it say this guy in the photo is Gabriel or he's the man who talked to Joan, or my birthmother, oooorr he's this messenger Luc told me about. All I know is the name Gabriel is mentioned—a lot, and this guy appeared in my photo and outside my house." And it was the same face I saw when I woke up the other morning... *dreaming*—I was dreaming. Giving my head a shake, I switched gears. "Both Vicki's and Mac's moms said they thought my birthmother—through my Mother—through me, were conduits to getting you four together. What do you want me to tell you?"

Before I could finish, Vicki cut in. "How and for what reason? And what does Gabriel and this Shamsiel guy have to do with all this? Where do they fit in?" she asked.

"When you think about it though, it sort of makes sense," Olivia's little voice peeped. We all turned to look her way. "Joan's story mentions you and Will had to get back together, possibly so you could meet me—so I could meet the others."

"You forget we worked at the same company yet never crossed paths—we could have met there. Will wasn't back in my life then," I pointed out, still wanting to finish my rant.

"Something's not right," Vicki said. "The timing, it's wrong...."

"Whattaya mean?" Alison asked, flipping through her papers as if worried about her note taking.

"Look." Vicki pointed to the men's names and dates. "Our mothers were visited and told to write the information down shortly after 9/11, but Joan's visit was before that. And Lynn's birthmom, she was visited before Lynn was born. Maybe this Gabriel person differs from the others—has a different role."

Outside, all eyes were on Gabriel.

"Gabriel?" Michael started. "Would you like to explain how you were able to visit with her mother-in-law before the 70 generations had passed... hmmm?"

"Yes, Gabriel, how was it you could visit with Lynn's birthmother as well, when all others had their hands tied—figuratively of course?" Shamsiel asked, using this moment to his advantage, putting his own question out there.

Gabriel's head whipped left to where Shamsiel stood. His laser stare aimed right at his questioning friend. *He already knew too much and saw too much* Gabriel thought. Lucky for him, the others to his right were oblivious to his enraged stare.

"Yes Gabriel, do tell, but more importantly *why* did you visit them?" Vretil asked, smirking and crossing his arms over his chest, *waiting*.

The others turned their attentions back to the gathering in the apartment.

Taking a deep breath, summoning up all my courage, I continued my rant, "Well, I know what I think about all of this. I know what I know—and I know what I see and feel, but you all have your own ideas... and this is not a right-fight." Pausing, I took in another breath of bravery. "All I know is you guys are together now—doesn't matter how it happened, it just did. Doesn't matter why it happened—it just is." Letting out the held breath I coupled it with a sigh. "I thought the answer to this or at least the answer to your destinies would be in that big book." I concluded my rant by pointing a critical finger at the codex, I had nothing more to add.

"So did we... but pieces are missing," Mac said, speaking out.

"Pieces?" I questioned.

Vicki shuffled in her seat. "Not pieces, more like words and phrases. They read or translate oddly, blurring the information in a way. And the writing on the wooden cover—I can't read it at all. The same writing repeats a second time later in the book, right before Alison's mother's first entry." Vicki pointed to the list of words she'd made, then flipped open the codex to show me the inside cover of the book.

I glanced down at the top of her list on the pad of paper. The first phrase read *70 rage tension*. What the...?

Shamsiel shifted his interest to Michael. "What does she mean *a second entry*? Didn't you make only the one—the first, on the pomegranate wood?" Shamsiel asked. "Who made the second?"

All but Gabriel look to Vretil.

"Tell him, Vretil?" Michael pushed, knowing he was the divine scribe and readily had access to the book via his Charge. And they all knew the only time he'd not had access was during its time of hiding, a time fashioned by the mother of his current Charge.

"Why Me?" Vretil rejected. "Why—because it was my Charge who always had the book?" He held his hands out in front of him, palms up, revealing nothing hidden like a magician. "I swear to you, it was not I who put in a second entry."

"Can we please stop using the word *Charge*, and use their actual names for Heaven's sake?" Shamsiel said, sick of all the pretense.

"*Heaven's sake*, really?" Michael scrutinized.

"The timeframe, Vretil, the entry must have been made just before your Charge's—I mean Alison's mother was told of her role by Alison's grandmother," Shamsiel noted. "You should know who added the entry—and what was written, yes?"

"Yes, you'd think, but it's been some time—many years, since I've looked inside the codex," Vretil said, guilt clear in his subtle grimace. "Perhaps I was—and wrongly so, overconfident the book was safe." He bowed his head avoiding the looks from the others.

Throwing up his arms in frustration, Shamsiel shouted, "Well, by all calculations, to me—it's clear as day." Shamsiel had done the math, reviewed the facts, and turned to look at Gabriel. "Isn't it obvious who put the entry down in the book... Gabriel?" He left his name on the air as a question *and* an answer.

"How about you tell them why you visited her at her home in Miami?" Gabriel lashed back in defense. Fury heightening, he turned a smug face towards the others, hoping to heavens he'd deflected the attention and questions off himself.

Shamsiel let out an exhaustive air-filled "*Huff,*" at both the situation and the diversion, then gave his answer. "You know very well I've watched Mitra's family since the beginning. She comes from a line of powerful Seers and Oracles and she is a descendant of mine. It was her *sensing*, which led me to Lynn, and you know if I can find her—so can the *others*." Waving his arms, he said, "The old woman needed to know what she sensed, was—and is real, and it was the reason I passed on the message. Her daughter does not have the gift, but the granddaughter, Dunya—she does. Mitra's sense regarding Lynn alerts me to what both she and her granddaughter are detecting, but it also may act like a beacon for the others." They all stared back at him as though not grasping his point. Shamsiel assumed he'd been clear in his explanation, but still rolled his eyes. "Working like an ADT security system. When anything harmful crosses the threshold or gets too close—I'll know it," he clarified, keeping with the current dialog and now non-pretentious rhythm of the conversation.

"Sounds like a job for the Cipher," I announced, relieved it wasn't another treasure hunt.

"Maybe there's something in that second entry about your birthmom and what she wrote," Alison suggested, always hopeful.

"Maybe," I said, trying to appease her, but I wouldn't hold my breath. I had nothing more for them and I knew it. And it was time for me to head home, back to Miami. It was a little earlier than I'd expected, but it was time.

"I'll have to take the codex to Mac's for scanning. I don't have a scanner here at home and I'm not taking it to work to do so either," Vicki said.

With resolve, I took Vicki's pad of paper and flipped to the next unused page. I wrote out Derek's contact information and then handed the pad back to her. And keeping my feelings about wanting to go home to myself, I took my well-licked dinner bowl into the kitchen to rinse.

When I returned, I sat watching the others work as a unit, four quarters of a whole. I watched as Olivia handed Vicki Chakra symbols to solve. Vicki translated them from ancient Sanskrit to English, aiding Mac and Olivia with their healings and charms. Olivia seemed to notice my despondence but appeared too afraid to ask me what was up, hiding her concern with a quick smile. I didn't have the heart to say anything about what was on my mind, nor in the mood to mention

Mom's anniversary, but did feel it was the right moment to set out on my own quest… and let my friends continue with theirs. "Okay gang, this treasure-hunter is done—feeling worn down," I said, working my excuse, setting the stage for my exit.

Alison handed me back my original steno pad and Mom's journal. "I have everything I need," she said, summing up what I already knew.

Officially done, I gathered up my computer and put everything in my tote. "Carry on, all. I'll talk to you tomorrow," I said, faking a yawn and waving a sleepy hand. It was late though, time had escaped our little mystery-solving bubble. My words of flight were greeted with smiles and busied waves as I headed out.

Down the back stairs and across to the parking lot I went. I had to finish my quest. First things I needed to do when I got back to Olivia's, was transfer my flight home, change it from the end of next week, to Monday—tomorrow. The car rental was also for two weeks, but I'd pay the penalty to shorten the loan-out. Come morning I'd fake being still asleep, then be on my way after everyone left for the day. I'd leave a note for the family—for Olivia, for all of them, but the time had come for me to leave.

"Look," Uriel called out. "She's leaving. Lynn—she's leaving again."

"Shamsiel—can you go watch over her," Gabriel asked, pleading, gripping Shamsiel's forearms.

"Of course," Shamsiel said, but not before giving his friend a look, one that said, *tread carefully*. And before the others could question his helping Gabriel, he disappeared.

"Gabriel?" Michael demanded, "Is there something you'd like to share with the rest of us?"

Chapter 11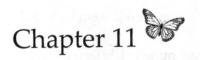

"What do you mean she's gone?" Gabriel snapped, as he approached Shamsiel, knowing full well he had no right to judge. She was ultimately his responsibility.

Shamsiel rested on the front step to Olivia's house. "This morning when the house was full, she still slept," Shamsiel tried to explain. "I took advantage of the situation to search out answers to other questions—ones I know you are fully cognizant of. And where the hell have you been?" he said, as a poor try to deflect.

Relaxing, Gabriel allowed his freshly shared honesty he'd given to the others to calm the surrounding air. "I was with the others at the apartment—explaining my actions. It was time." He stepped forward and properly greeted his comrade. Extending both hands palms up, he spoke softly. "Please forgive me for my deceptions, and for my outrage."

"Tell me... please," Shamsiel said. Standing now he placed his hands palms down atop of Gabriel's. Then he held him firm, so he wouldn't disappear on him again. "Please."

There was no need to hide it any longer. Gabriel looked Shamsiel in the face, right in the eyes. "It was I, who put the entry in the book as you suspected. It was part of what I'd been granted... document the change and the Chosen. It's all in there." He paused and took a deep breath. "As well, I'd been allowed two visits, as opposed to one like the others were granted. The first visit was to my Chosen and a second visit was for another—anyone, at any time I wished, to aid the outcome—this outcome."

Saying nothing, Shamsiel pulled Gabriel with him to sit back down on the front steps of the house.

Gabriel sat, bowed his head and continued. "So many moments in time—so many I could have picked, ones which would have altered things. But I needed to choose the right moment and the right human to assist me... when I could not assist the outcome myself. When it was done, there was no going back." Lifting his head to look at his friend he said, "I could only watch and wait, while the second visit—the person I'd chosen... did the best she could. Later I watched as she became ill. Her sickness was not the result of the choice she made to help, but verily, in the end it was her choice to pass on my words to another which shortened her life considerably. It did however shorten the time she would suffer from that horrible painful disease." His head bowed again, lower, mourning the loss—the loss of such a brave soul.

In concern for his friend, Shamsiel spoke his next words to sooth, "The Chosen... who was it?"

Gabriel looked up and into his friend's eyes once again. Delivering his words with complete and present clarity, said, "A descendant of Watchers."

"Mine?" Shamsiel asked, alarmed. When Gabriel shook his head, Shamsiel sighed in relief.

Locking eyes with Shamsiel, Gabriel released a shaky breath, letting the name escape his lips. "Zaqiel's," he said, lowering his head, again.

A shuddered gasp escaped Shamsiel's lungs. "That explains it," Shamsiel concluded. Explains the sudden appearance of the *others*—the other four.

Chapter 12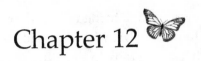

The flight back to Miami was fast as was the taxi from the airport, and I was grateful for the swiftness of the journey back, such that I had no chance to change my mind.

When I walked into the house, there was an immediate sense of peace. The peace and quiet that was ever present when I was home alone, as if the house had its arms open, welcoming me back. Perhaps it was all my little protection and guardian tchotchkes I had around the place. The house had a vibe I loved, and it made me feel peaceful, protected, *safe*.

I dumped my bags in the bedroom, but before jumping in the shower to wash off the air-travel germs and all-around ick of too many people in a small confined space, I headed through the sliding glass doors off the master bedroom to the backyard. I stopped mid-step through onto the patio.

The yard was flooded with orange and black butterflies. *Monarchs*. I hadn't missed the migration after all. Witnessing the migration was all about timing, and what perfect timing this was. I had missed it in Ottawa, and had I come home when originally planned I would have missed this stage of their journey as well. Breathtaking was the scene as I walked towards a collection of Jasmine bushes. A fluttering cluster mingled from branch to branch. The air was warm, not hot, and the normal high humidity for September was seemingly somewhere else today.

Tears welled in my eyes, and I turned in a slow circle as the overwhelming sentiment took me. "Hi Mom," I said in a soft voice. Tears traveled down my cheeks as I took in the gift.

The butterflies and weightless sunshine lingered for the rest of the afternoon. And as the evening crept in and the sunlight left, so did the assembly of merry-makers, moving on to the next part of their journey.

"See you next year," I called out as the last pair floated away on the night's air. It would be wonderful if they returned next year and every year after as part of their annual journey. It was unlikely, but one could hope.

Tomorrow I could ask Dunya if she'd seen them in the past, plus I needed to check with her to see if anything transpired with that Shamsiel guy. But tonight, was just for me... oh-errr and dealing with the disappointment from my friends. As the last hint of the sun dipped beyond the trees, I went back inside.

When my laptop purred and whirled to life, I reluctantly checked my emails. I had a good excuse for going home—fake, but good. Knowing the others would be pissed at my leaving the way I did, I prepared my reasoning in a brief, yet to the point email.

I wrote in the email that the alarm system had gone off and with Will out of town, I was the only one they could reach. Reassuring them, I explained it had been a false alarm, but they wanted a service man to come in and check out the *how* and *why*. And as a result, I needed to be back asap. It was lame I know, but good enough to get me off the hook with my friends and keep my real reasons to myself. Hated lying, even delivering the harmless ones, but it was easier this way.

After sending the explanation, I emailed Will letting him know I had come home early, and that the girls were too busy for a lengthy visit this time. I wrote I'd gotten to see Alison, that she'd made the journey home to see more of her friends too, and that I was lucky to have the time we had.

Will responded with a quick message back, saying it would be great I'd be home when he got back tomorrow night. It was nice of him, but I knew tomorrow would be a wash, him being in the air most of the day and the next day being all about recovery from jetlag.

Other than junk mail, the only other emails that sat in my inbox were from Derek. He'd replied to Vicki's first contact email, and he'd cc'd me. Vicki hadn't kept me in the loop by copying me on her email, but that was fine. He'd also sent a second email on information labeled *Enoch*, which I assumed was about that book everyone has heard of but me. I could always learn more I guess and be one of the many *in the know*.

Picking the first email, I started with reading the original part from Vicki's email she'd sent him, labeled *Strange Words*,

> *Hey Derek – Cipher*
>
> *I received your contact info from Lynn. I'm Vicki, The Linguist.*
>
> *Lynn figured you could help me with a few translation issues I'm having. I know languages aren't your forte, but puzzles are, and we may have a puzzle or perhaps a riddle here.*
>
> *As you know we have the book, the codex and I've translated many of the entries, but the problem I'm having isn't in the translation, it's the words themselves. The reason we feel they may be a kind of riddle is that the same words are repeated in multiple entries, but when translated they don't seem to make sense. I thought at first it might be culture specific, but they repeat in completely different languages like Sanskrit, Old Persian, Old Irish and even in Japanese. We don't think it's a coincidence, but words are my thing, not riddles. I've outlined the list of words and phrases giving me the most problems;*
>
> *the guard (every entry so far)*
>
> *guards the four (appears in the first entry and the two entries where the generations break and restart)*
>
> *glean (this one appears in almost all the entries so far)*
>
> *70 rage tension (symbols for '7 groups of 10', is followed by the words 'rage tension' but is only mentioned in the first entry)*
>
> *I also have another unusual symbol style language I'll need help with, but I need to have the entries scanned for you first. It's like the other language you found the key for, but I am unable to translate using the same key.*
>
> *If I find any other words or phrases of concern, I'll forward them.*
>
> *Thank you for your help*
>
> *Vicki*

"Okay, let's see what Shortcut Jones had to say about these puzzles," I said aloud, scrolling up the email to his response.

> Vicki, pleased to meet you.
> I am at your service and will try to help with whatever you send. Thus far I have been successful, and I hope to continue in providing the band of you with what you need on your quest.
> Unfortunately, the words alone are not aiding me in solving the riddle. Could you possible send me samples of the complete sentences that these words and phrases appear?
> I await your next correspondence and instructions.
> Regards,
> The Cipher

It was written so proper, it made me laugh *and* because I knew he was thoroughly enjoying this. I moved to his next email, again scrolling to Vicki's part first to see the sentences she'd forwarded.

"Yeesh," I said as I read the examples she'd sent at his request. I may not be a reader, but even in English they were all confusing. Scrolling back up, I went to Derek's response hoping for clarity,

> Vicki, thank you again, these few sample sentences did help considerably.
> At first, I dissected them as though they were riddles, but it gave me nothing. Nothing but a headache, just kidding. Then I took a different approach and tried to think of what words would make sense in their place. Then I realized, it wasn't word replacement, it was the shuffling of the actual letters that was needed.
> These are all Anagrams. In this type of letter scramble, you use a real word or words to create different words, but you have to use ALL the letters from the original. I'm sure you understand the concept.
> For example, in using the words you sent me, THE GUARD, it becomes the word DAUGHTER and although other anagrams can be created with those letters, I find under the circumstances, daughter fits the sentences best.
> You may find the others easier to do yourself, but I have provided my best solutions for your sentences.
> the guard = daughter
> guards the four = four daughters

Made total sense now. I didn't think the others could argue these solutions either, but the next line struck me hard. But I'd known this all along—not the word, but the truth,

>*glean = angel*

Angels must be part of this. Let's see them dispute and rationalize their way out of this one. For sure I would hear something from them after this. I'd tell them Old Lynnie wasn't nuts after all.

Feeling somewhat vindicated, I focused on the last words in the list, *70 rage tension,* and found that Derek had written a long explanation on it,

>*The last phrase on your list had me doing more research, but I'm sure you'll find it all useful. This one was a bit trickier with having numbers involved, but again, I found what fits the theme.*
>
>*70 rage tension = 70 generations*
>
>*You said it appeared in the first entry, the one written by the first scribe. Those words sparked a memory of something I'd read on the fallen angels, the watchers. In The Book of Enoch, it mentions The Fallen were punished for 70 generations. How they were punished, I'm not sure. Interpretations of the writings differ a great deal, but it's something about their involvement on the earth and how they weren't allowed to interact with humans but could only 'watch' for the next 70 generations.*

I didn't like the whole punishing Angels reference here, but I read on,

>*I'll explain my reasoning behind this and its interpretation for you.*
>
>*The first homosapiens originated 200,000 years ago, then after were the Paleo-Indians from 45,000 to 12,000 BC. In references on The Watchers, it mentions them arriving in 5000 BC, and the arrival being on a mountain near Sumer and its first people. Your first Scribe was Sumerian if I recall correctly.*
>
>*Enoch was supposedly born around 3100 BC, give or take, references on this are also varied. Following, we have the first*

recorded language being Sumerian, emerging in approximately 2900 BC.

Bear with me, here is the solution to the puzzle;

One generation equals 70 years and if you calculate 70 generations, you get 4900 years.

If you forward those 4900 years from when The Watchers were noted by Enoch as being punished, 2900 BC, coincidently the same year as the Sumerian language began, it brings you up to the year 2000 AD, the next millennia. And this being the year when The Fallen would supposedly be free, to do whatever they wanted I suspect. It's not an exact math, but I'm sure you understand why I feel this fits.

The questions I have for you are as follows;

There was mention of your mother, Vicki, who said she was visited by another's mother, early in 2000, and there was something said about how she was 'worried', is this correct?

The other question I have is on the letters, the messages to the daughters. When were the mothers instructed to write them, at the same time or different? These dates may help you fill in any other questions with this mystery.

I await your next instructions.

Regards, The Cipher

He's good, but I wondered what he was getting at with the *when*. We'd only made notes on the *what* about the things the mothers wrote.

No other email responses from Derek had come in yet, so I figured they were trying to find out the *when* — or they already knew and were trying to figure things out themselves. It made me proud to think they might be, and it made me realize I'd done what I was supposed to do, bring all the elements together, and right now I was where I needed to be. But then why did I feel so... *undone?*

* * *

Tuesday night.

Will called to say he landed, but before I could ask how things had gone, he told me he had to go into the office sooner rather than later. He explained that he needed to get things finalized for his upcoming week.

Ah yes, *The FCCA, Florida Caribbean Cruise Association* event during the last week of September, was being held in Puerto Rico this year. He would be gone a week, and knowing these events all too well, I knew I would not hear much from him. He'd be busy with meetings, speaking engagements and meet'n greets with other members, the usual drill. I also know it wouldn't be much of a visit for us between his trips, but I was fine with it. It would give me time alone again after the crazy time I'd had up in Ottawa. And I wouldn't be telling him about what had happened, I'd had my fill of skepticism, thank you very much.

Will's shuttle arrived, and he was through the door in his normally cheery mood, but something was *off*. I told myself the foreboding feeling was just tension over this next trip, but the strange feeling seemed to linger.

The feeling remained after our usual welcome home hug. It remained through his cheerful recall of all his adventures, the show'n tell of all the interesting trinkets he'd purchased, through the showing of all the swag he had gotten from the tour operators, and it remained even after he'd given me my usual country related gift. I always requested a guardian style trinket, carving or charm, something small representing the country he visited.

The foreboding feeling remained still even after I'd placed my gift at the front door. It was a wooden carving, one meant for protection, and Will told me it was meant to be placed at your front entrance. I was hoping it might help dissipate the *icy* sensation still hovering around me, but I was aware it was mostly wishful thinking for something that was only a piece of wood.

* * *

The next few days and the weekend that followed, sped by too fast and with the early Monday morning flight, Will was gone again off to the airport for yet another work event. And as par for the course, I was left again with that shortness of breath feeling I experienced each time he flew, and back to taking in a tight breath every second draw until he landed. This flight was under two hours. I'd be able to breathe again soon, but then I'd be back at it with the short draws in by the end of the week for his return flight.

Maybe I needed to be medicated or something. My anxiety over his flying would have to be fixed someway, because his traveling was not going to stop. These local trips weren't as bad, and if I needed him, he could be back much sooner than a race home from Asia or Australia. The anxiety was frustrating, but what bothered me the most about his travels, was that it *never* seemed to faze him. When he was away—he was away, not missing things back here, but who could blame him. He had an amazing job seeing the world from the perspective of a potential vacationer, not like the average business traveler who only saw the inside of a hotel or meeting room, because it was his job to see and feel what the cruise line passengers would experience. But for me, it was deep breath in... deep breath out.

When his call came this time, I let out my breath.

Chapter 13

Tuesday again, and the last week of September.

Despite not sleeping well, I was up bright and early with the morning sun, but only because I'd forgotten to shut the blinds the night before. And with a yawn, a stretch, and a couple eye rubs, I was out of bed and wandering off to the kitchen. As I passed through the living room, commotion boomed from out front of the house. Stopping, I peered out through the blinds of the big front window in the living room.

Dunya stood next to her family's SUV parked alongside the front lawn, and she appeared to be having a not-so-nice conversation with her mother. She leaned in through the passenger side window as her mother got into the vehicle from the driver's side. I couldn't understand what they were saying, it being mostly in Arabic, but I could tell it *wasn't* about the nice weather. In most languages you can pretty much detect anger or swear words, and there were definitely a few of those going back and forth. Then the exchange was abruptly over, followed up by a slamming car door and Dunya's mother driving off.

"Yikes—what a wrath," I said to no one.

My words were followed by another, "*SLAM*," this one from the front door at Dunya's after she'd marched back into her house.

I was eager to talk with her, but under the circumstances it could wait, and I continued my wander to the kitchen.

I cranked up the coffeemaker and then fixed myself breakfast. It was nice having no work, no agenda, and little to no responsibility to deal with for now, but I could see it getting old fast not having other people to talk with during the day. Email only gets you so far, and definitely not far enough away from lonely insanity. But for now, I was good, *content*.

"*Knock-knock,*" came from the front door startling me right out of my contentment.

Still in my oversized t-shirt, pajama-bottoms and mussed-up hair, I strode to the door. Checking myself in the mirror near the front door, I let out a small giggle, I attempted to flatten down my hair with one hand while reaching out for the door handle with the other. Whoever was on the other side, better be ready for what was coming. Better safe than sorry, I paused to peer through the peephole.

Pleasantly surprised, I let out a breath of relief, turned the handle and swung the door wide. "Dunya," I said with a sheepish grin, but still happy to see her.

"Did I wake you?" she asked, checking out my attire as if worried but still smiling.

My appearance was comical, and I smiled even bigger. "C'mon in," I said, throwing a lazy arm out to point the way. "Just made coffee—would you like some?" I widened my grin as she stepped in.

"Love some," she said, laughing.

"Excellent." I shut the door, then Dunya and I proceeded to the kitchen.

Dunya popped herself up on one of the barstools around the outer side of the counter while I got out the coffee mugs.

"He's back you know, Shamsiel," Dunya said, before I could even get the coffee poured.

"Did you see him? Did he come to your house?" I almost spilled the coffee as I handed her the cup.

Dunya glanced over her shoulder. Turning back, she gave a little side-to-side with her eyes as if checking the coast was clear. "I didn't see him—but Jadda did," she said, following up with more side-to-side. "But I *felt* him."

My mouth dropped open, and all I could do was stare at her. I couldn't help it.

Then, she asked, "How was your trip?" as though her previous comment was about how the *sky was blue and the grass was green*.

"You're kidding me here, right?" I said, mouth hanging open, again. But those big doe-eyes of hers stared back at me, telling me all I needed to know. *She knew*. She knew what I knew... what I saw—or sometimes see, and sometimes felt, because... so did she. It's what her comment had meant at the end of our first visit when she'd said, "*I believe we—you and I, will be great friends... and I believe someone, or something watches over us.*"

"When did it first start for you?" Dunya asked, then she took her first sip from the mug of coffee.

So much for beating around the bush. Mirroring, I took a sip of coffee. Then, with no bushes to beat, I threw it out there. "I'm not sure when it started, but there were things that would happen." I paused and sipped. "As a child—about five or six, I would know things. I'm able to remember things, events, conversations from when I was very young—as early as two years old. My mother couldn't comprehend how I knew these things when I would retell them to her. I don't understand it myself, but the memories were clear. I never gave it much thought—it was just how I was."

Dunya nodded her acknowledgement.

Smiling, I leaned on the counter, and said, "Sometimes I would be in the back seat of our car with one or both of my parents up front... and as I watched out the window, I'd get this strange impression like everything around me was speeding up—going faster and faster, but at the same time, I was moving in what felt like slow motion. Like moving underwater, but the world was whizzing by me." I took another pause and another sip of my coffee. "I would tell my mind to slow down and stop racing, but my body was the only thing that felt like it was going slow. I thought I was going crazy, but then the sensation would be gone just as quickly as it started." I paused again. "But past my adolescence, I never experienced that sensation again— well, not until recent," I added, remembering the incident leaving Mac's house in the car. "But I have what others would consider premonitions, or precognitions—knowing feelings, in dreams and in waking images." I took a long sip of coffee, staring at Dunya over the rim.

She stared back, continuing to sit silent, watching and listening for more.

Cat out of the bag, I kept going. "And sometimes it comes in a form of a compulsion to do—or not do things. When I act in opposition to the feeling's direction—or whatever, I feel nausea and sometimes extreme heat when trying to reject it. But when I give into it—the nausea goes away."

Dunya continued to say nothing, but gave me a nod and a knowing smile, waiting for me to go on.

So, I did. "Sometimes, I'll say something—out of nowhere, statements, words just coming—I don't know where the words come from. There's no internal thought before I speak... but sometimes—the words I say, are often profound to the person I'm speaking them to. Some people get a kick out of it—but for others... it creeps them out." I paused for breath. "I used to fight the feelings and try to ignore the images—thinking no one would understand what was happening. Hell, I didn't understand what was happening." I paused again and still Dunya said nothing, but I knew she knew there was more. "You ready to hear about my visit home?" I said, giving her a grin.

"Ready," she laughed out, anticipating a whirlwind.

Pulling up another barstool, I said, "Okay, Fasten your seatbelt. It's going to be a bumpy ride."

Three hours, a pot of coffee and two rows of Oreo cookies from-a-package-hidden-in-the-back-of-the-cupboard later, we had covered all aspects of the bizarre happenings in my life and recent trip. It was amazing to be able to unburden and share all the strange sensations I'd had, the things I'd seen and didn't see—just *sensed*. I'd even included the experiences from my day at the memorial wall and from the restaurant. I did however leave out the other things, the stuff about my four friends. Wasn't sure it was my stuff to tell. Instead, I told her I'd helped my friends find a few lost items, which in turn brought them all together. I figured that was strange enough. I'd gotten the sense she knew there was still more, but I'd save those details for another chat.

Then it was Dunya's turn.

She straightened up on the stool and began. "Jadda, told me she'd sensed it when you'd first moved in. Her clairvoyance is strong—but only I listen to her. Most think she is an old fool, but I know better," she said, splitting open another Oreo, dipping half into her coffee. Before she bit into it, she said, "My mother doesn't have what we have. She feels left out—but acts more like she doesn't believe in the *nonsense*— as she calls it."

It was my turn to nod. I had experienced many a skeptic in my life. "It's nice you have Mitra to share this with," I said.

Dunya gave me a smirk and then ate the cookie-halves, finishing them in two polite bites. Then she continued on with more stories, telling me about the first time she felt *it* and then the many times since. She recalled the time when her grandmother first came to her and told her of such things. She'd been scolded once for telling a lie to her mother—something that was in fact a truth, being that her mother didn't believe in these things. "Jadda, had told me to keep *those* types of things between the two of us. She'd said, '*your mother never believes me either*'. It got easier when Jadda came to live with us. It is better now that I'm an adult and have a home of my own—even with all of us living together." She rolled her eyes. "I should get going—let you get back to your day. Looks like you still need to get dressed," she said, giving me another look-over, smiling at the fact I was still in my pajamas. "I'll be sure to tell Mitra all you have shared." Done with her history, Dunya got up from our mess of cookie crumbs, and ventured to the sink to rinse out her coffee cup.

I left mine on the counter next to the cookie bag. "I hate that Mitra and I can't communicate," I said, following behind her as she headed for the front door. We stopped at the door and I opened it for her.

Turning to face me, she said, "You do... in a way—communicate." She tilted her head and smiled. "Thank you, Lynn. Enjoy the rest of your day."

"If you need me—you know where I am," I said as she turned back and descended the short stack of steps.

"And you know where we are," she called out as she hustled across to her lawn.

"Thanks, Dunya," I called back. Before shutting the door, I spotted Mitra at Dunya's front door, waving her little hand at me. I smiled and waved back at her, then continued to close the door.

Dunya's visit had been enjoyable and enlightening. Knowing I wasn't the only one like this was a relief. I wasn't *crazy*, but was I a *Seer* like Dunya said, like Mitra and she were? Crazy or not, I needed to make a doctor's appointment to talk brainstem, see if there was something going on there—or not. "Damn it!" I shot out to the silent house. I *was* losing it. I'd forgotten to ask Dunya what the deal was with Mitra seeing Shamsiel. We'd gotten off track with stories from our pasts and all the similarities, so much so I'd overlooked getting the details of what she'd meant. I mean I'd seen him too, so did Luc and Raven, but she'd said she *felt* him. What had that meant and who the hell was he?

Turning back to the kitchen, I caught my reflection in the hallway mirror. Dunya was right, I needed to get my act together and clean up. Especially since Luc and Raven would be coming over.

Luc had texted last night saying that after work today, he would pack a bag and come stay until Will got back, then go to and from work from here. It was why Raven was coming too, plus Luc knew I needed a little doggie time. I would work on getting my own four-footed-friend soon. With me being done work and Will traveling, I would need someone to talk to, but for now, it would just be me, Raven, and my two-legged friend, Luc.

Shaking off the morning's mystifications, I showered and dressed. Then I took a trip back and forth from the grocery store to stock up for the visit. As the homemade cookies I'd made cooled, and the dinner prep I'd done lingered on the counter, I moved myself into the living room, then fired up my laptop to keep me company.

Nothing but junk email arrived in my inbox. I was surprised there wasn't another exchange between Derek and Vicki to review. That was fine, because once Luc got here, I needed to show him what Derek had come up with. But before that, Luc would need the full picture, so I'd have to go through all the other stuff first. "*Sigh.*" I wasn't thrilled at unloading all this on him. He liked talking about freaky stuff, but this last visit home had put some serious *freak* in freaky. At the thought, I abandoned my laptop and sunk back into the big couch, then turned on the TV.

After flipping through the typical weekday afternoon television shows, I settled on an afternoon movie, and one of my favorites, *Steel Magnolias*. It was super-sappy, but the actresses in it were brilliant and I love the theme of all those strong women being there for each other. I've seen it 100 times, but when Dolly Parton says the line about Annelle's husband, '*doesn't know whether to scratch his watch or wind his butt*,' it kills me every time. I opted to watch it again and make it 101 times. And there it was again... that *feeling*, complete and utter relaxation and contentment... flowing over me.

"You're right, Gabriel. This is nice," Shamsiel said, sitting down on the couch to the right. Gabriel was already on the left.

"I can't tell. Do you think she has any idea she's not alone?" Gabriel asked, glancing to his right.

"Perhaps not, but those two next door are more than likely bouncing off the walls sensing I'm around," he said, following with a raise of his dark silky eyebrows.

"I like this movie," Gabriel redirected, "Tough women."

"Soft hearts," Shamsiel added.

Gabriel nodded. Together they sat for the next couple hours watching the rest of the movie in silence, right until the phone rang. "The Theologian," Gabriel guessed. He and Shamsiel disappeared a second later.

"Hi!" I said, on the second ring. "You and Raven on your way?"

Chapter 14

At 6 p.m. on the dot I heard Luc's car pull into the driveway.

When I opened the front door, Luc was out of the car and circling around to the rear of it. He popped the hatch and then helped the big guy out from the back of the car. Big doggie, small car. Raven comfortably out of the car, Luc grabbed a large bag of what looked like dog food, and then the two of them rambled up the drive.

"Hey, Lynn!" Luc said, seeing me.

Raven's attention shifted at his master's words, his slow gait changing to fast forward allowing him to beat Luc to the front steps and up to the doorway to meet me.

"Hello, my best-boy," I said, bending down for my greeting. Playing with his ears, I rubbed my face into his. "Did you miss me? I missed you."

"Hey Luc," I said, pretending I'd only just seen him.

"I see Raven has forgotten all about the guy who feeds—walks and bathes him." He gave me a big grin, passing by us into the house.

"What can I say—he loves me," I said, letting Raven in, then shutting the door behind us.

Raven did his usual scoped-the-place-out routine while Luc went to drop off his gear to his usual room at Hotel Lockridge.

"First time he's been back since we fixed the place up," I called out to Luc, as I watched the big doggie go from room to room, checking the safe-haven.

"You've added more stuff around the house too, so he'll need to check... every... single... thing!" Luc called, on his way back down the hall to the living room.

We both chuckled, watching Raven as he continued his rounds.

"Whattaya got to eat," Luc said, rubbing his palms together.

"And people think *I'm* a walking stomach," I responded, heading for the kitchen.

Naturally Luc followed. "It's your fault. Always bribing me with food," Luc said, opening and shutting the cupboards on his hunt for nourishment.

He'd miss the food prep and cookies on the island, so I said, "I could share a little of this healthy casserole I made." Vicki had sent me the recipe for the healthy mac'n cheesy-goodness.

Smiling big he said, "Bring it!" then pulled a stool out from under the island. Sitting, his smile spread in eagerness of being fed.

Raven walked in then, his doggie grin telling us there was another stomach needing to be fed.

"Okay, feed him first and it's a deal," I said, pointing a thumb back in Raven's direction.

"Deal," Luc said, then he was up off the stool before I could continue with the deal part.

A second later Raven was munching away on his dinner and Luc was perched back up on the stool. Grinning again.

I grinned back and moved to stand in front of the fridge. "Right. I'll share myyyyyy yummy food with you, but you have to sit quietly and eat while I tell you all about my trip. Deal?"

"Deal," he shot out again with no hesitation, and definitely past hungry.

"We still have to wait for it to cook," I told him.

"What? Awww," he said, disappointed, slumping in his seat.

While the casserole of mac'n cheese ala Vicki cooked away, Luc went first in the telling, bringing me up to speed on the gossip from work. I didn't miss the place, but it was enjoyable hearing the gossip. After a few stomach grumbles and a painfully long thirty minutes later, the timer *"Dinged"*.

When I opened the oven door, the aroma of melted cheese wafted through the kitchen, causing Luc to let out a *"Groan."* Then digging in as fast as I could, I handed the first large plate of goodness to my ravenous friend.

Before taking my place at the island, I left to retrieve Mom's journal and my steno pad from the living room. Returning, I placed them next to my laptop on the kitchen counter. Luc didn't look at them, or me.

His eyes were closed as he delighted in the steamy goodness. Letting out a long-contented sigh, Luc said, "Go ahead... lay it on me." Then he spooned in another appreciative mouthful, savoring it as though it were his last.

I took in a breath and let out my own sigh... though mine was a lot less contented. Taking a serving for myself, and a spot at the island, I began my spiel by first recapping the things he already knew. As I relayed the stories and discoveries, Luc ate, not uttering a single word as he'd agreed. Mind you, his eyes bulged enough at times to convey his feelings on the topics, while giving me the occasional head-nod.

To my relief, I'd relayed all the information in just under an hour, faster than I had expected, mainly because I had expected interruptions of which there were none. Finishing up the list of facts and the last of my meal, I read aloud the two emails Derek and Vicki had exchanged.

When Luc said nothing, I shrugged, took his empty bowl and got up. Then I refilled his dish with more of the mac'n cheese and placed it in the microwave reheating the serving for the long 90 seconds in the microwave. That's when he finally spoke. "Yes, thank you, I will have some more," he said even though the bowl of heaven was already heating. He grinned.

Not sure what reaction I had expected from him after the deluge of information, but I said, "What—can't process weird stuff on a partially full stomach?" I smiled back at him, then checked the last few seconds on the microwave.

"Ding!" went the microwave, and, *"Bing,"* went an email notice on my computer. We both turned to look at my laptop.

I handed Luc his second plate, then leaned in closer to the laptop screen. Clicking on the new email, I saw it was from Vicki to Derek. She'd cc'd me this time, and I read it quick to myself;

Hey Derek,

Still working with the solutions you provided, and yes it helped to reveal much more. As for your inquiries on the letters, both Mac's mom and my mother were told to write things out in the fall of 2001, shortly after 9/11 of all things.

Correct, it was my mother who was visited by Alison's. She told us that Alison's mom appeared to be worried, and she'd mentioned something had changed, but didn't say what. Evidently Alison's mom hid the codex shortly following that visit because she'd moved out West soon after. Although, it wasn't until four years later that she called my mother and told her she had hidden it and where. My mother didn't remember its location, but it's irrelevant now since we have the book.

We are unsure of any relevancy in the dates, but we can see the concurrence of them. Do the dates spark any ideas with you?

Regards,

The Guards

Nice play on the signature, I noted. They're seeing their roles I assumed, and perhaps believing in them deeper, accepting the truth in the words from my angel rant. I had accepted the possibility of the original four *men* being angels, well, I was trying to at least, but I still wondered if the men who visited the mothers were just like my girlfriends, part of the generational passing of the secrets, etc. I'm supposed to be the one who sees the unseen or whatever, but I was still struggling with the idea that these visitors could be angels too. I shouldn't judge the others for their disbelief if I couldn't commit to the idea. My reluctance may be more about *if* I conceded, said I believed... that it made everything a little *too* real.

I reread the email aloud as Luc devoured his second plate of food. I was used to the weirdness in my little world, but it kind of freaked *me* out to think this had something to do with things outside the earthly realm. I liked mysteries—loved them, but the information on this one had come fast and still confused me, especially the meaning of it *or* if it meant anything. My mind raced. *Just stories perhaps?* This mystery—the stories the mothers told us, all the things my mom wrote in her journal—I wanted to believe it—should believe it, but what if it was all crap? Not crap—no, but something else? How could I ignore the book we found—all those entries, those languages? And Dunya... what about Dunya and Mitra, how was I supposed to explain them away? It was easy to get caught up in all this reality/fantasy, but what did it mean? And what the hell were the four—or even I, supposed to do with it?

I had nothing else to add after reading Luc the latest email, and all I could do was stare at him. These questions raced around in my head. I may never find resolution... but... I couldn't let it go. Real and without answers to my questions it was a scary thing.

Luc reached in under his t-shirt and took out his Scapular, then kiss them. Then he said, "It's like I told you in the beginning, when I gave you the deal on Gabriel. This is something *big*, Lynn. They are involved in something monumental." He paused and kissed them again. "And I think they're together for a reason—a *big* one," he finished, lots of emphasis on *big*. He tucked the religious pendants back into his shirt.

Frustrated with all this *and* myself, I said, "All they have is the vague words from their mothers, and only because the mothers know little themselves. Alison's mom is gone, therefore they can't ask her what her reasoning was. This old book itself is just a repetition of the same information over and over, about how the four have to keep the balance. These guys chose the first four—but we don't know for what purpose? What's the purpose of me bringing them together—and why now?" I covered my face with my hands. The questions were getting the best of me, and I spread my fingers over my head in an attempt to keep it from exploding.

"These aren't just stories anymore—these are facts," Luc tossed out. "God sent down angels to watch over men—they pissed him off and were punished for 5000 years. Could it be these four men—whom I'm assuming aren't just men, could it be something *they* did to piss him off? Maybe their contact with these four women set something in motion and now that the 70 generations are done...." he said, running out a short question list of his own. "They were cut off from interaction remember—and now they're not. Maybe this alone is the reason your friends—the descendants of the original four, are all back together."

I lowered my head, putting the thought-heavy thing down over my crossed arms on the counter. Gazing through them down at the floor I said, "What do you want me to tell you? I don't have any answers... all I have is a few facts and one mammoth mystery."

Another email, "*Bing,*" sounded from the laptop.

Looking up at the email, I read the first couple lines. "It's nothing—just Vicki. She sent Derek scans of the book. The pages she couldn't read." *Whatever.* I put my head back down again. "Oh... I forgot to tell you about the neighbor," I muffled through my folded arms, letting out a breath-filled extended "*Groan.*"

"Dunya?" he asked, with a little too much enthusiasm.

Dishes in the dishwasher and leftovers in the fridge, I moved our discussion to the living room. Then I laid out the details from Dunya that added to the freaky stuff from my minuscule world. Luc, shared in my frustration, trying to keep me from slipping off the deep-end into a pool of my irrational thoughts.

With all the information out for our perusal, we still had no answers, nothing to contribute other than our useless feelings or thoughts on it. We agreed that all we could do was sit back and watch things unfold, if they unfolded. At the end of our deliberations, and when the clock showed 10 p.m., Raven came and sat on the floor by me while his master left the living room to go iron a shirt for work.

In the silence, I stroked a palm over the top of Raven's head and down the smooth fur of his back. I'd read—had felt it too, that petting an animal was soothing. It's part of why they have therapy dogs in hospitals, helps aid in patient recovery and sooth the souls of those who may be terminal. I found it calming and therapeutic as well, and I was thankful he was at my side even if he didn't understand all the craziness.

Finished, Luc came back out to the living room. "You gonna be okay?" he asked me. "Let's go Raven," he said, trying to coax Raven to come down the way to his bedroom. But the doggie wouldn't budge. He was glued to my leg it seemed, and I liked it. "C'mon Raven, bedtime!" Luc said, but still no budge. He smiled then. "Looks like you have someone to watch over you after all."

"Yup." I mirrored his smile.

"Good night you two," he said, then he turned and strolled back down the hall to his bedroom.

"Night," I said, continuing to stroke Raven's head. When I heard Luc's door shut, I forced myself off the couch, then proceeded down the hall in the opposite direction to my room, my guardian trailing alongside.

Chapter 15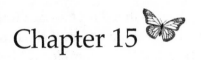

I'd slept well, exceptionally well, and was up early before Luc.

Getting things ready for Will in the morning had become a standard for me, so I ran the usual course whipping together breakfast and a lunch for Luc while he took Raven out for his morning walk.

When they came through the front door, I said, "Raven I'll be taking you out again later, for a just-for-fun walk."

Raven seemed to understand and like the idea because he, "Woofed," and wagged his tail.

When Luc was done with breakfast, he grabbed up his lunch bag and proceeded to the door.

I followed behind him and Raven followed me.

Out on the front step, Luc asked me again, "You gonna be okay?"

Giving him an enthusiastic smile, I said, "Got my trusty doggie to keep me safe and happy." Raven leaned into my thigh. "It's all good, seeeee," I said, patting Raven on the head. I gave Luc the peace-sign before he turned and continued to his car. He hopped in the car, peace-signed me back, and then drove off to work. I closed the door and went back to the kitchen, and Raven followed me.

I grabbed my laptop off the island and moseyed into the living room, and Raven followed again. I put the laptop down on the coffee table and hit the on-button to spark it up, and Raven found a spot next to me, stretching out on the cool tile floor with his head near my feet.

Email up, the first thing I see is that darn message from Vicki. The one she'd sent to Derek last night about the stuff she couldn't read. I hadn't bothered to review the full thing. "Dare I look?" I said out loud. It wasn't like I had anything else to do at 10 a.m. on a weekday.

Raven's head came up off the floor, his wet nose tickling my leg, giving me a little shiver.

Then the real shivers came.

Nausea.

More shivers.

Then a blast of *heat*. I bent forward clutching my stomach as sweat blistered over my skin. A bead of sweat dripped down off my forehead and hit the tile floor right next to where Raven had been.

Raven was up now, pacing in front of me, his backside to me as if keeping a watch out the front living room window. Back and forth he patrolled, back and forth... then a low growl boiled up from deep in his chest.

Another wave of nausea hit, and I dropped my gaze. At the sound of Raven's guttural snarl, I forced my head up.

Raven snarled again, his upper lip peeling back from his gums to expose his canines.

"*What big teeth you have, Grandmother,*" sounded in my head, surfacing from the recesses of long-ago childhood fairytales. Barely able to get enough air to speak, I whispered, "What is it Raven?" My breath hitched. Raven turned back to lick the side of my face, then he returned swiftly to his sentry, more pacing, and more low growling.

"You shouldn't be here!" Shamsiel shouted across the lawn to the *dark* Angel. "You have no part in this." Following his words, a gathering of lesser-angels filled the street behind him.

"This is not another war, Shamsiel. Tell your legions to back off," Armaros defended.

Shamsiel raised his hands to slow the torrent of his flock, keeping them back, yet still near enough. "Where are the others?" Shamsiel demanded.

"The four? They are watching the *other* four, who watch over *their* four," Armaros responded, his words much like a riddle. He gave a sinister grin like the narcissistic menace he was. "I've spent most of my existence trying to find those women—sabotage their lines. Did it twice—but, they recovered. And now, they're all together in one place."

Standing his ground, Shamsiel spoke again, "You did what—how?" His eyes narrowed. "If you seek them—why are you here? Is it not the *Book of Balance* you want?"

"I don't need that ridiculous tome. The answers needed aren't in there." Armaros gave an overconfident smirk. "The mother hid the information long ago—my doing."

"Hid what? Where? And how were you able to do such things—you were bound as we all were," Shamsiel questioned, biding his time, yet still curious. Shamsiel could feel the winds from the West building and churning. He smiled a little at what was coming—at *who*, was coming.

"How else, *Magic*. Hidden where—right here!" he spewed, arrogance covering him in a hateful shadow. Lowering his voice to a throaty grumble, and revealing nothing more, he asked, "Why may I ask are you here—instead of him?"

"I'm right here, Armaros!" Boomed a voice crashing down like thunder from behind Armaros.

Armaros grimaced, not from the sound but more as if hit across the back by something solid and weighty. Gabriel's arrival. Recovering, Armaros spun around to meet the Archangel's enraged stare.

Gabriel stood strong, face all a fire with anger and protective wrath. "It was you who persuaded her to hide the truth from her daughter." The West winds circled around Gabriel in a show of power.

Armaros turned back to glance over his shoulder towards his fellow fallen leader.

Shamsiel smiled at Armaros fully now because he saw the anticipated fear in the dark Angel's eyes. He opened his mouth to speak, but before another word was said, Armaros disappeared.

Gabriel panned the street, watching as the legions dissipated and moved off. Shifting his attention, he moved to stand on the front lawn of the house.

Meeting him on the lawn, Shamsiel asked, "How did you know he was here?"

"I didn't," he said, moving up the lawn to in front of the big window. Staring in at Raven, who now had his nosed pressed to the window, Gabriel said, "I came to tell you they have the key… to the divine language."

Shamsiel stepped up to the window next to his fellow Angel and peered in past Raven's cheerful wagging body. "She's safe, Gabriel."

Closing his eyes, Gabriel put his palm against the window at the level of Raven's muzzle, then whispered, "But for how long."

When Raven's tail wagging started, my nausea subsided. He had stopped pacing and left my side to look out the window. In sweet relief, cool air swept over me, and though I'd broken out in a full-body sweat, I wasn't chilled. My core and the surrounding temperature settled in close to perfect. A delicate scent lingered in the air, like the Jasmine flowers that surrounded my house… but those bushes weren't currently in bloom.

After joyfully peeking out the window, Raven resumed his place next to my feet on the floor. Any semblance of the nauseating sensations was now just a memory, and I straightened to sit up.

"Okay, what the… hell, was that?" I asked my canine companion. What is it with these bouts of sweaty-pukieness that keep coming over me?

I didn't want to admit it, but these fits were akin to my *repulsion* premonitions. I'd never—*ever*, had them this bad, and *never* while I'd been alone. In the past when I'd had one, it was in warning about a person I was standing near or perhaps speaking with. But these—at the airport, the memorial wall, the restaurant, and now sitting in my living room—these were different… and they'd been frequent. What the hell was the commonality? Were they connected somehow? Or were these bouts of sickness, just that—sickness… and coming more often?

Another email, "*Bing*," came from my computer.

Sigh. Did I *really* need to read the email exchange from Vicki and Derek? Had Derek replied? *Did I want to know?* I was tiring of being freaked out, on the verge of chucking my cookies, or just plain confused, but I figure it couldn't get any weirder or more confusing. I took in a few cleansing breaths... and then reviewed the emails.

First in this exchange was from Vicki, explaining to Derek that the attached was the scan of the inner-cover of the codex. Vicki had written it was the first entry of two which had the same script. The attachment she'd sent, the scan of the entries, reminded me of the ones we'd found in Mac's grimoire, but the symbols were different. It was definitely a task for Derek and not something I could help with, and still nothing to do with me. *Good.*

Moving to Derek's response, I checked out the attachment he'd sent, before reading his response. It was a copy of an alphabet much like the other he'd found for use with Mac's spell stuff. And like the other, it too had symbols representing more than one letter from the English alphabet, though it was still just a bunch of symbols I couldn't read.

Next, I read Derek's response;

> Hello All,
> When I received the scan of the entries, I thought I would have trouble locating any references to help, but to my surprise there were many, both in fact and fiction. The language is called the Divine Language. I attached the Angelic Alphabet, also known as the 'language of angels or God' in Abrahamic traditions.

"Oh... my... Gawd!" I smacked my forehead with the palm of my hand and dragged it down the front of my face. "I knew I shouldn't have looked at this," I said aloud again to no one. Then against my better judgment, I continued to read on;

> There were many references on a person known as John Dee, who called it the magic alphabet or Enochian letters. How he came into the possession of this, I'm unsure, but his reference is supposedly the first associated to the finding of this alphabet.
> This Enochian script is written not left to right like English, but from right to left. There are English equivalents to the Enochian letters, but different references have vaguely different forms. In addition, the pronunciation of the letters is like those of English, but some letters have different inflections, like an accent. Also, if you

haven't already put it together, the word Enochian refers to angels just like with Enoch.

The Book of Enoch, and the Enochian writings along with many others, were excluded or lost from the Bible. They are known as 'apocryphal' writings, stemming from a Greek word, meaning 'hidden' or 'secret'. The term itself is a bit messed up, because other references also say it means 'questionable' or 'fake', and other accounts say the contents was just too superior for the eyes of regular people.

I can translate for you if you want, but I didn't want to ruin your own fun of discovery. Should you have any difficulty, let me know. I do love a challenge.

Regards, The Cipher

Okay, it's just more of the same theme. No biggy, right? *Wrong.*

I'd been trying to go with the idea of angels since Luc put me on the path, but now, reading about the existence of an *angel* language, the idea was pushing me into the deep-end.

"All right, Lynn—get a grip," I said. "If it is angels, does this mean there's a supreme-being in charge of them—of us? Does it mean there is a heaven of some kind?" I loved the idea, it meant Mom and Aunt Kay were somewhere amazing, if that's what heaven is. It could be just a big ball of light that absorbs all the energy from the body when it ceases to function. "Could be a different dimension or universe, eh Raven?" I said, including my companion this time. "Oh man, I'm starting to sound like Derek." Raven lay there watching me as I rambled on. Watching as I lost my whole box of crackers right in front of him. Good doggie.

I made myself reread Derek's words and considered the idea again of reading up on this *Book of Enoch*, which meant more than the quick references I'd seen in my Google searches. My religion expert Luc—my *Theologian*, had never referred to the book in our discussions. I'd looked up the word theologian when I'd come across it in my Google search efforts to learn about Enoch. It was possible Luc had not mentioned it because it was a *questionable* religious text as Derek's email had stated. Maybe Luc and I could read about it together, and I could get his religious take on it.

As I skimmed my inbox for more emails from The Guards and The Cipher, a stray email popped in from my Theologian. It read;

> *Hey Freak-girl,*
> *How goes the first half of your day? I'm a bit afraid to ask, but anything fun and exciting happen this morning?*
> *BTW, thanks for packing me a lunch, just about to go eat it now.*
> *Chat with you later, Luc*

Lunchtime? But it's early...10'sh, he must be hungry. I checked the little digital clock on my laptop, and it seemed to show the wrong time. It happens sometime if there's a memory-drain issue on a computer, but mine had never experienced it. Could be time for a new laptop I supposed, then glanced over at the big clock on the wall.

The time showed... 12:35. *What the hell?* "Awww Lynn, yer seriously losing it," I said, jumping up and dashing to the bedroom.

I grabbed my watch from the bedside table, and again the time read 12:35. "How the...?" I questioned, looking to the bedroom doorway as Raven's head peered through the opening. Poor guy probably thinks I've lost it—crackers and everything. "No worries, Raven—just losing time... life whizzing by on me... brainstem." I pointed to my head like he might understand. "Hungry?" I asked, following up, realizing my body clock was also screaming *lunchtime*.

Although it felt like my grey-matter was oozing out my ears, Raven and I went to the kitchen to get nourishment. After pouring out kibble into the big bowl for my furry friend, I hunted for food through the cupboards and the fridge for myself.

I ended up in the lower half freezer, and there it was. "Frozen cookie dough—perfect!" I called out. Weird morning, why not weird lunch? Without a shred of guilt whatsoever, I sliced off a section of the frozen role, plated the beige and chocolate speckled sweet goop and then returned to my time-warp couch in front of my laptop.

Best to just give in, let the freak wash over me I figured. And what do you know, there, waiting in my inbox, was another email from Vicki to Derek. Perfectly weird timing and perfectly weird reading to add to my *perfectly* weird lunch. I clicked on the email.

She'd written,

> *Cipher,*
> *You guessed it, struggling a bit here and getting lots of weird word combinations again. Here is an example of what I'm dealing with;*
>> *na newcomers forgo houseful*
>> *Got time to help?*
>> *Vicki*

Short and to the point. *Help.* She must be struggling. Would be much easier if they were in the same place to work on this stuff, but Derek was in South Carolina, not exactly a hop, skip, or a jump. "Thank goodness for the internet and email," I spouted out to Raven, who'd resumed his spot next to my feet.

While I waited to see if there would be a speedy reply from Derek, I struggled with writing my response to Luc's email. I'd make mine short and sweet too... and would explain the real *funness* to him when he came home later.

> *Hey there,*
> *Just me and my pal Raven hanging out and surfing the web. I'm surfing the web—Raven is just hanging out. Ha!*
> *Hope you enjoy your lunch*
> *Lynn*

I hit send on my simple reply.

Raven was up again, this time doing his room to room surveillance like he'd done when he'd first arrived. When he'd finished with my bedroom side of the house, he returned to the living room holding a rubber chew-ring. Then he came back over and sat down facing me. He did the doggie head-tilt and gave me the look. I assumed it was one of pride, for his surveillance work. "Uhm, good boy, Raven—good boy," I gave him, still unsure what to make of his performance.

"He's quite handy you know. He knows when stuff is happening—even before she does," Shamsiel confirmed. "Knows when we're here—knows when one of *them* is here too."

"Kind of like a seeing-eye-dog," Gabriel joked, peering down at the laptop screen. "Anything from The Cipher yet?"

"Just the fact he found the type of script yours and Michael's entries were." Shamsiel said, "but Vicki is having a rough time with the translation. Too many variations in the alphabets available, plus the scrambled letters and words, it being part of its secrecy." Shamsiel paused and then said, "How come Michael was the one who wrote it out and not Vretil—he's the Divine Scribe."

Looking up from the computer, Gabriel said, "Well, therein lies your answer. *Divine Scribe*, he transcribes the word of the Divine, not those of *our* minor actions. Michael may have carved the words, but all of them contributed to the entry."

"*Bing*," came the sound of a new email arriving.

Chapter 16

"Got a new one, Raven—ready?" I was sure he couldn't give a *woof* about some stupid email, especially when he had a chew toy to rip apart. Even so, I clicked on the email from Derek, and read it out loud;

> My Friends,
> We have more anagrams here. No wonder the phrases were not coming clear. The phase you referenced, 'na newcomers forgo houseful' should be 'four angels chose four women'. To help, instead of doing a word-for-word translation, I summarized the overall entry, fixing the anagrams. I'll let you and The Scribe do the translation to have the full English record for the codex.
> What I found interesting about this entry is it tells of a similar story to what is found referenced in the Book of Enoch, about the 200 angels and its 20 leaders.

"Okay, Raven, your master and I definitely need to read more about this book." But for now, Derek's version would have to be my *Cliffs Notes* on this topic, and I read on;

> In this entry it tells the event much like the Enoch reference where they were sent to watch over the human race. Says over time the angels became entranced by the daughters of men, and going against their original command to 'watch over', they found they wanted to be more than observers. As a result, they each chose a woman to teach their skills to, one who would further teach their offspring. This involvement angered whomever gave the original

command to ' only observe'. No name is ever mentioned; they refer to this higher being as He or Him. In Enoch's account it's said to be God.

Here's where the story deviates from that of Enoch's. The entry say all were punished for their involvement, not just the 200, but all angels. None were allowed to help nor hinder the survival of humans. It says this 'He' favored both angels and humans, but after the recklessness of the 200, He became outraged at both. As a result, some angels from the original 200 lost faith in each other, in humans, and with Him.

It goes on to says that four Archangels (not part of the fallen) approached this 'He', asking for a favor. A favor where they could prove to Him the human race was worth saving. The four vowed it would take the strength and faith of only four women and their offspring, daughters—not sons, to show Him the full worth of the human race. I'm assuming their big boss still had a spark of hope because he granted them the favor.

The Archangels were each to choose one woman, and then they were to teach them valuable skills to pass on to their descendants. But there was one condition. It wasn't enough they'd be granted these skills to pass through the generations, that would have been too simple. In addition, they were told the women could tell no one about what they knew, nor could they go directly to the daughter with the knowledge. They would only be permitted to pass on the skills when and only when, the daughters came to them. Also, there must always be one daughter from each generation of the four to carry it forth, and if such a time the mother cannot fulfill this condition, she must find a way or find someone to whom they could pass the secret and the responsibilities.

"This confirms the stuff we had from the moms. Well, not you, Raven—but us—the girls, and Luc. We all knew that part."

Ears-up and a head-tilt, Raven gave me his doggie equivalent of recognition.

"Well then... perhaps you do know—or whatever," I said. Then I read on;

This is the nasty part. If any of the mothers spoke of or passed on this information to another, or went directly to the daughter with it, they would sacrifice their health and possibly their lives. So, what I've surmised, is that if the daughter doesn't come to them, they must be willing to make the sacrifice of passing forward the secret, even if it means causing their own demise. Faith and Balance.

"Aaaand again, more stuff we already knew... and definitely nasty," I said.

Raven, "*Woofed,*" in response, then rested his head down on his paws.

"I can stop there if you like?" I added, eyeballing him like I expected him to respond.

And he did, sort of. He gave me another "*Woof,*" and a grumble, ears popping up again.

"Okay, I'll keep going," I said, clearing my throat to read more;

The last part of the entry references the future and their purpose, how someday they may be called forth to prove the daughters of mothers can help keep the balance. It refers to the balance of good and evil, it talks about the evil offspring and the good offspring and how the four will know when they are needed, when the world appears to be in pain, when weather kills, and the wars and devastation of men are at an extreme.

"Sounds a little too much like the current condition of our world — don't you think?" I said.

Ears were up again from my companion, followed by another head lift and tilt.

"Glad to see you and I are on the same page here," I said, laughing at myself for deliberating with a dog. I reread everything, this time to myself. Buy in reviewing the information again, all I felt was more frustration. I assumed my four friends would be frustrated as well. This first entry gave us *why* the guys chose the original women, but... now what? Was that it, a history lesson? Ancient words from an ancient time? It was internet search time again.

Kneeling next to Raven, the two Angels peered around at the laptop, watching the Google search happening on the screen.

"What of your entry, Gabriel?" Shamsiel asked. "It should help, no?"

"Yes, I hope," Gabriel said, patting Raven's head.

"But what about what Armaros claims? About the answers being hidden — about his influence?" Shamsiel questioned again.

"I don't know—not exactly. I had watched over the mother when she'd documented everything in a letter. She had also known of a gathering—the coming together, but this was from her own gift of insight, not from me, and she'd made a note of that as well."

Gabriel knew she'd gone to Miami, had thought perhaps to celebrate her recovery, but when she'd returned, the papers she'd written on were gone. He'd explained everything to her in the beginning, on the visit he was granted, but she'd since added her insights on what was needed to keep the balance. He assumed she'd hidden these insights in Miami, but why—he hadn't known? All he'd known back then was that he needed for her to bring the letter back to Ottawa. But regrettably, before he could do anything to influence that, she was gone, deceased. The cancer had come back and fast. He'd tried to retrace her steps, years of going over things, hovering near her friends in hopes one of them had known something or had a copy of what she'd written, had it to pass on for her, but she'd been good at covering her trail. He'd questioned whether he should have waited to use his second visit to speak with one of the many people close to her. He'd told her to keep the information available for when her daughter needed it, so why had she taken it so far away? But he knew now... *Armaros*.

"I wasn't there when Armaros fooled her into hiding the truth of things—I hadn't known then," Gabriel said. The only other option was getting the daughter to Miami, so she could find what was needed. But how to do it? *William*, he'd thought. He'd moved to Florida back when she was still in high school and was still living there. That had been the answer, he needed to get Lynn and Will together, to help her find the answers in Miami.

It was a long-shot, he'd known it, but he'd found no other options. When it was time for him to use the second visit, he'd gone to speak to Will's mother. She'd been successful with keeping the two in touch in the past, and he'd felt she could help again. He'd known the two had drifted apart, hadn't spoken in a few years, but he'd believed if anyone could get them in touch, it was Joan. He'd used his last visit to influence her to help. She'd tried... but her illness had gotten in the way. It had been Lynn's insight, her reaching out to Will that Christmas, that had brought them together. Now Lynn was in Miami, and closer to finding the answers.

Shamsiel turned a shocked face towards Gabriel. "You know where the gathering will take place?"

"No, just that one would be needed." He'd known *who* needed to be the fifth, because he'd chosen her, Lynn's birthmother, and he'd known what her role was to be, or had been. It wasn't until last year when Lynn found her adoptive mother's journal, that he'd understood why the cancer had taken his Chosen so soon. It's also when he'd discovered she'd spoken to her doctor-friend *and* that she'd gone to see Lynn's mother, Sally. These visits, these violations, had been the reason his Chosen had died. But… where the crucial gathering would take place, he had yet to find out.

Never had he imagined the information would be out of his reach. He'd known there would be a need for a gathering, he'd been told it was a condition added to his request to add a fifth. He'd expected no interference since his interactions were kept secret in the book of balance. At least his Chosen had documented things as he'd instructed, wrote out the details of the gathering for her daughter. Reading the letter wasn't something he thought to do. The information was still out there, hidden, *somewhere*. "It should just be a matter of time I would think," Gabriel said, hopeful. "Lynn, she's brought them all together, including The Cipher."

"That makes five," Shamsiel added.

Gabriel "Sighed."

And Raven *"Chuffed"*.

"Good boy," Gabriel said, scratching Raven's upturned belly.

"Bing."

"Another email from Derek, Raven," I tossed out.

But there was no *ears-up* acknowledgement from Raven this time. Instead he lay on his back, exposing his belly as if waiting for someone to scratch his furry tummy.

Luc was through the door at 5:30 p.m., but I had my head buried in multiple web pages, all on the same topic, *Angels*.

Angels in religion, in spirituality, good and bad, heaven and hell, and even in-between. Angels referenced in different religious text, *Book of Revelation*, the *Seventh Seal*, and the questionable text of The Book of Enoch, to name a few.

"Hey, Angel Girl—Ghost Rider is home," he laughed out as he proceeded to the kitchen to drop off his lunch bag. Circling back out of the kitchen in void of my response, he called out again. "Helleeew, earth to Lynn—this is your brain calling."

"You ride home on the joke bus or something? Sheesh!" I laughed back at him, making my best *you're an idiot* face.

"Fine—be that way. Just for that, I'm not going to share the spectacular sushi I picked up on the way home." He waved a big white bag, swinging it in the opening to the kitchen.

Food always got my attention, and with hunger as my enemy, it got me again. "Okay, I'll let you share your sushi," I responded, smiling big.

"Forget it!"

"Aaawwwhh c'mon—I'll be yer best friend."

"Not good enough." He chuckled, walking over to where I sat, then tapped me in the head with the bag.

Changing my approach, I said, "If you doooon't—I won't tell about all the wild and wacky things I found out today."

Still smiling, he said, "Not sure if that's a bribe or a deterrent." He laughed again heading back into the kitchen.

Raven followed him into the kitchen this time. It was dinner time for him too. I could hear dog kibble hitting the big tin bowl, followed by the sound of munching. Then Luc left the kitchen and went to his room.

In the time he took to change out of his work clothes and into casual ones, I'd been up and back from the kitchen. Two plates, paper napkins, the sushi trays, and two beers, were now all set up out on the coffee table. Alongside the plates I had real chopsticks, courtesy of Will and his many trips.

Luc stopped short noticing my setup. Shaking his head, he crossed over to where I was on the couch with the mini-buffet. With a *"Huff"* he lowered himself to sit cross-legged on the floor across from me. "I guess I'll go with bribe," he said, picking up the chopsticks, then he poked my knee with them.

Raven found a comfortable place at my feet once again as Luc and I powwowed as we ate. We went over the emails sent between the Cipher and the Linguist first. Then I told him about all the references I'd found during my little internet searches while I'd been educating myself on the story of that Enoch book. And apparently, I wasn't the only one this book had alluded to because Luc had said he was only *vaguely* familiar with it. This time it was my turn to give *him* the religious scoop.

"Sooooo, from what I could find on the more detailed sites, the story goes like this," I said, clearing my throat. "God sent down 200 angels to watch over man. Among them were 20 leaders—this part we know. But the kicker wasn't about how they stopped being observers, it was the fact that they had become *more* than observers." I gave him an exaggerated wink-wink.

He shrugged like he didn't know what I was getting at.

"Duh. They took the daughters of men to be theirs." I winked again but didn't wait for a response. "Along with teaching them many things—things they wouldn't have learned on their own, the rumor is that they slept with these women. And if that wasn't enough to make God angry, their actions created offspring, called *Nephilim*. Half angel—half human." I'd seen the word before but hadn't known what it was then.

"I guess I had it wrong—thought it was the four archangels who made God angry. What else did you find?" Luc asked, anxious this time. He did a little kimchi dip with his sushi.

"Well, there was excellent info on one of these *apocryphal* text reference sites," I said, fumbling the unfamiliar word. I clicked on the link I'd saved, but instead of reading it to him, I summarized what I'd read earlier. "In the *Dead Sea Scrolls*, there's a story on Noah's father...."

Stopping me mid-sentence, Luc said, "That guy I know. Noah— big flood." He pointed his chopsticks at me, and he gave me an *I'm with ya* nod.

I gave him my *you interrupted me* face, and said, "May I go on?"

"Sure, giv'r!" he conceded, displaying a smartass grin and waving his chopstick for me to keep going.

Deep breath. "Well, the guy's father—Noah's father, accused his own wife of having sex with one of these angels. Get this, his reason was because little Noah was too handsome—amazingly so."

"Sounds a little *Jerry Springer*," Luc joked.

Laughing with him, I said, "Well, this story also supports the Genesis story about the *Sons of God* existing on the earth during Noah's time. Aaaand how they found the daughters of man tempting—same stuff, just like what Derek wrote about the codex's entry. But, I found no references to the four women, this other story on the archangels, or this *favor* they'd asked for."

"What did you do—spend all day researching this?"

"Yup—pretty much," I admitted. "Also read up on the 20 leaders of these Watchers—their names, their descriptions and all the things they'd taught their offspring. Wanna hear the list I made?" Eyebrow raise.

"You made a list?" Luc grinned again.

"Shut up—just added it to my current steno of weird." Holding it up to show him, I flipped to the list. "Here—listen. They taught magic, both poisonous and medicinal potions made from plants. The signs of the earth, sun, clouds, and constellations. Introduced them to and how to make weapons, such as knives, swords, and shields. Also, how to create ornaments and cosmetics. And taught them astrology too—how about that?"

"Great—I always wanted to know about cosmetics," he said, mimicking the gestures like he was putting on mascara and applying lipstick.

"Betcha did—ya big girl," I threw back at him, smacking his arm, causing him to poke himself in the face.

"Yer just jealous I know how—and you don't." He pretended to fluff his nonexistent hair on his shaved head.

Chapter 17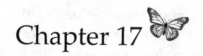

Up North, on the top floor of the three-story walkup apartment in *Mintoland*, sat four brave women, the descendants of those equally brave original four Chosen. Conversations mingled on topics such as magic and balance, coupled with deliberations over the direction of their roles, their lives, and the road their destiny would take.

"Damn it!" Vicki shot out. "Damn it! Damn it! Damn it!" she continued, adding to her brilliant and helpful statement.

"You need to take a break," Alison said. "You've been at that translation for hours. Why don't you go back to the codex entry that you found on the spells—the ones for communicating with the host?"

"Ya, maybe," Vicki said. Reluctantly Vicki flipped back to the entry. That frustrating entry was the one Vicki had found written in Old Irish, and had brought earlier confusion about the term *host*, normally reserved for a grouping of birds. Originally, she'd thought it might have been something on communicating with nature, but she was still unsure. She'd hoped perhaps someone else would have an idea on it because she'd exhausted all of hers. She'd referenced that dated as 700 AD in her notes after Derek had sent the listing on the languages and their dates of origin. She read the entry again, this time aloud for all to hear. "Okay," she began;

Prince of Summer cherished dream of new life. The fourth in this host may keep all from straying from the path. Light and Fire of Him.

Speak to the host and Ruler of Libra, find the way through the Goddess.

Vicki stopped, her expression of confusion was clear.

"Feels like a riddle," Olivia said. "Who is *Him*? We have too many *hims* at the moment."

"Well," Alison said, "I've read about how with ancient Irish bards, their outfits often comprised feathers, and the poets were portrayed as bird-men or angels. There was mention of angels as Muses, you know—to help you write. I even remember the mention of a White Goddess." She grinned at Mac.

Vicki skimmed the page again, and said, "Well, Libra is the sign for September—and I know that because I'm a Libra... but not sure if it's relevant. But this, *cherished dream, fourth in this host*... I don't understand."

"Wait!" Alison shot out, "I remember something." Flipping, she skimmed through her old notes. "There—in the references Derek sent us. I made notes on each of our guys." More skimming. "Here, his name means Light or Fire of God, his element is Earth, his season is Summer. That entry has to be about Uriel." She paused. "Doesn't the entry say something about a goddess? Uriel is Mac's guy, and she's the witch and Wicca involves the goddess. And it's not a host of birds like we thought or communicating with nature—it's a host of angels." She surveyed the room grinning, but the others sat as if stunned. Rolling her eyes, she added, "This same word is used to describe a grouping of angels. Vicki, you read *the fourth*—and there are four of them, he must be considered the fourth in their group."

"The entry sounds like we're supposed to communicate with him—to stay on our path," Mac said. "If we can contact his spirit—or the goddess—whatever, maybe we can find out what we're supposed to do—now that we have the codex."

Olivia picked up Mac's grimoire and turned through the pages. "Didn't Derek also say one of these secret spells was for conjuring spirits and angels?"

"Ya—you're right," Mac said. "We've been so focused on the codex and its content, we never went back to do the full translation of that spell. Derek told us what it was about—but not the full translation."

"Mac and I have been working on protection, strength, and healing," Olivia added, "but we've done nothing on communicating with spirits, not even calls to the goddess."

"You have to work on this translation, Vicki," Mac said then as a plea, placing the grimoire next to her and opening it to the conjuring spell.

"I will—I promise," Vicki assured them, "But first I need Derek's help on this damn translation from the second Enochian entry. It's the only one I couldn't put a date reference to. There are several parts stumping me, starting with this part about, *descendant of Watchers revealed.*"

Pacing back and forth in the parking lot for the one millionth time, Vretil came to a stop in front of Uriel. He said nothing, simply gazed at his friend, pain and anguish making itself clear in his eyes. Letting out a *sigh*, he turned and searched the faces of the others.

"I know, Vretil. They are losing ground," Uriel said, recognizing the pain in his friend's silent face. "With Lynn gone this battle may be over before it starts."

Speaking up, Raphael said, "Gabriel's entry states that there needs to be a gathering. Do they need her to solve this? What other purpose could she serve? It's not as though she knows where the gathering is to be."

"We've seen no sign of the dark one. Armaros has not been spying on them since she left—that has to be a good sign," Michael said.

Appearing next to the host of four, Shamsiel said, "But he was outside Lynn's home in Miami."

Like a flock of startled starlings, the others scattered, turning in unison to face and stare at their friend, the *Watcher*.

"She brought them together—remember," Shamsiel said, his gaze steady and pointed skyward to the lit window on the 3rd floor. But before the others could reply, he was gone as swiftly as he'd arrived.

Staring up to the same 3rd floor window and resuming his original position, Vretil said, "Could it be enough? Is Lynn's role over? The

Cipher makes five, and Gabriel stated in the entry that five were needed for the gathering." Unsure, Vretil rocked back and forth on his heels. "Mayhap they don't need her anymore."

"Were you looking for me?" Armaros shouted, appearing just out of reach of the others.

The four turned again, moving this time as *one* towards the dark angel.

Armaros held up his hands in a reluctant sign of peace. "I have done nothing—and I have stayed away from your four," he reminded them, lying. "But my feelings have not changed. These women—these humans, they are feeble and will not make the sacrifice for that which they do not understand, and the balance on earth *will* be lost."

Together the four took one powerful pace forward.

Armaros took a pace back. "*He* will not step in. These four women mean nothing to Him, and they have proven nothing about their humanity." Armaros took a quick glance around the open space of the parking area. "The other leaders know this, and they are waiting. And after all this time… He just… doesn't… care."

Michael took another stride forward. "You will bear witness to them!" he roared, using the full command of his voice. "To the sacrifices of those women who have come before them, of those who have kept the secret—stood by and waited to pass on the burden to their daughters. These four will show *Him*. With their ultimate show of unity—at the gathering."

In solidarity, sharing in Michael's words, the other three stepped up to meet him.

"They fail—Gabriel has failed. The *other* Four… they are already here," Armaros threw at them, before disappearing out of their reach again.

"We received what I needed from Derek on the Norse entry," The Linguist said, tapping a finger on her computer screen.

Alison leaned into Vicki's laptop. "It reads as though it's some kind of helper—the guardian it says—like us, the Guards," Alison responded, always the optimist. "Well, I know it means, daughter—but still."

"More protection—suits me fine," Olivia said, knowing she was often a tad skittish.

"It sounds similar to parts of the entry—the one giving me all the problems," Vicki recalled. "Let me check it again." Vicki took the codex and opened it to the right spot. Turning the book, she showed all of them the page.

"It's in that Enochian writing—what does it say?" Mac asked.

Translating, Vicki said, "When the four descendants of the original four are named, and the descendant of Watchers comes forth, the guard the fifth will be revealed."

"The... guard the fifth, what? It sounds a little... uhm... patchy— you sure you got it right?" Mac asked.

Shaking her head, Vicki said, "Aaahhhh, I have quite a few like that—need the Cipher again. Let me send him a quick email—clear it up." Before starting the email, she said, "Wait, I'll attach the scan of this entry too, since I'm struggling with it." Then she typed,

> *Derek – Cipher, Need your aid again.*
>
> *We found a similar reference to the watcher being revealed in the other Enochian entry, but the phrase has me stumped. I might be getting the two alphabets mixed up in my head, been at this too long.*
>
> *I've also attached a scan of the second Enochian entry and my attempts at translating. Below are the words/phrases I'm currently struggling with. The entry appears between the writings of Alison's grandmother and Alison's mother's entries, somewhere between 1900 and 1968, but unlike those two, this one has no date associated. Entries are normally from each generation, but this one might be an exception. It is written by someone else, not the same hand as either woman, and not the same hand as the first Enochian entry.*
>
> *Solacer*
>
> *Bar the fifth*
>
> *I thought Solacer made sense at first, it means sympathizer, friend or consoler, but it doesn't define the 'who'.*
>
> *Your help is much appreciated. We are close to a breakthrough on this I believe.*
>
> *Thanks, Vicki and All*

She hit send.

Michael now paced back and forth in the area behind the walkup. "They will translate the entry Gabriel put in the codex—I'm sure of it," Michael said, "My Charge—I mean Vicki, has deciphered everything thus far—mostly everything."

"Thanks to the Cipher's help," Raphael said, folding his arms across his chest.

"If they can't figure out *who* the fifth is, how can they create the gathering," Uriel exclaimed.

There was more than a hint of worry to his words. His Charge would be the one casting or conjuring. Mac's abilities would be useless without the answers—without the *who*.

"Gabriel changed things. His message had better be clear," Vretil said. Being the Divine Scribe, he knew Gabriel had to use this special form of writing to protect the words. And though Gabriel may have given them more time with his actions, his friend's mockery in using the frequency of anagrams, may have sabotaged their chance for balance.

They all knew *now* about the entry which Gabriel had made over 40 years ago. Gabriel had told them himself, and that the one he'd chosen, was *Descendant of Watchers*, from one of the leaders. Gabriel had kept his cards close to his chest—but this wasn't a card game. Still, he keeps his motives secret, revealing small details as things unfolded with their Charges. Why had he chosen this person—this descendant?

"The Cipher will figure it out, he has thus far," Raphael said. "They're like riddles, and he's superb at solving those. The words are used this way such that if the codex were ever to fall into the wrong hands, the messages could not be revealed so easily," he added. He made a magician-style hand gesture, emphasizing the statement. Then he returned to crossing his arms over his chest and glancing up to the third-floor window where their four Charges continued to work.

Elsewhere, in a small home office in South Carolina, surrounded by techie paraphernalia, monitors to the left, and sound equipment to the right, an email notification, "*Chimed,*" news of its arrival.

Derek glanced over to see another email from Vicki waiting in the inbox. He rubbed his hands together, and said out loud, "Cipher to the rescue. Whatcha got for me now ladies?"

He read the brief email first, then reviewed the translation Vicki had provided. Following that, he pulled out a sheet of paper with a copy of the Enochian alphabet on it.

Vicki's first item read, *Solacer*. He too looked up the definition of the word and found it had multiple synonyms. "*Solacer... friend, consoler, comforter, protector*," he said aloud again. Continuing in silence he read the rest, *safeguard, shield, defender, sentinel, sentry, nexus... the core or center.*

Scratching his head, he focused then on the sentences in question from Vicki's email,

> This is from the undated entry: When the four descendants of the original four are named and the descendant of Watchers comes forth, the guard the fifth will be revealed.

Further down the email still, was another sentence with question marks beside it, and it read,

> The fifth will aid the final four. These four will stand with the guard the fifth who is one of the Solacer.

Still uncertain and hoping for more clarity, he reread the translation out loud. "When the four descendants of the original four are named... and the descendant of Watchers comes forth... the *guard the fifth* will be revealed." He paused, wondering if Vicki was getting a little sloppy in her translating. "Hmmmm... The fifth... wait—fifth what?" He paused. "... The fifth will aid the final four.... These four will stand with the... *guard the fifth*... who is one of the...... *Solacer*?"

Chapter 18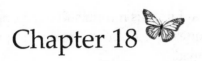

"Hey, let me read you this last email I got from Derek," I said, ignoring his pretend primping. "It's his response to a much earlier email I'd sent him on languages, when I was still in Ottawa."

"Let's hear it," Luc said. He took a swig of his beer and followed up with a satisfying "*Gasp*".

Opening the email, I said, "It's titled *Common Germanic* or *Proto-Norse*."

"Wait—what? You wanted to know about germ—and pronto-what?" he interrupted.

I held up a finger to halt him and continued to read,

> The differences between the two are rather small, although as several hundred years separate these language stages, inscriptions found in Scandinavia are considered Proto-Norse.
>
> Norse clans or the Scandinavian clan was a social group based on family or by formal acceptance into the group. Since there were no police forces, the clan was the primary security force for Norse society and was an honor thing they did to avenge one another.
>
> The Norse immigration of the Americas began in the early 10th century. Norse sailors or Vikings explored and settled in the North Atlantic, including the northeast periphery of North America. The colony in Greenland lasted for almost 500 years, although the North American settlements being small, did not become permanent colonies.

I paused and glanced at Luc. His mouth still hung open as if stuck from the last word of his question. Then as if realizing it was hanging open, he closed it and grinned.

And I read on,

> The term Viking is normally used to refer to the Scandinavian explorers, warriors, merchants, but also pirates who pilfered and settled in vast areas of Europe, Asia and North Atlantic islands within the late 8th to mid-11th century. They used vessels called Longships to travel far east to Constantinople and the Volga River in Russia, and far west to Iceland, Greenland, and Newfoundland, and as far south as Al-Andalus.

"Al-Andalus—No idea," I added, before Luc could ask. "Gonna have to look up that one."

"Sounds Latin, maybe it's Spain," he suggested. And although just as geographically challenged as I was, it was a guess—a good one possibly but still a guess.

"Here—the part I wanted," I said moving on,

> This growth, known as the Viking Age, created a major part of the medieval history and included not just Scandinavia, but Britain, Ireland and Europe in general. Lots of tales, sagas and stories sometimes fantastic or romanticized about 'tales of worthy men'.
>
> Norse mythology refers to myths, legends, and beliefs of supernatural beings during the pre-Christian times of Scandinavia, during the early Middle Ages. It became Nordic folklore, some facets surviving to current day, influencing modern literature and pop culture.

"This next part, he wrote it under the subheading, *Supernatural beings*," I informed him, raising my eyebrows, then I continued with more of Derek's treasures,

> There are several clans of nature spirits, referred to as gods, or Giants, Elves and Dwarfs, all believing to have souls. Most popular is Odin who is a major god. He has the two ravens known as 'Thought' and 'Memory' who keep him apprised of what is happening on earth since he gave up an eye in his quest for wisdom. In Norse mythology, the comparable of angels, are the Valkyries. They were originally known as evil spirits of massacre, dark angels of death. They soared

over the battlefields like vultures, killing warriors in honor of Odin. Choosing the heroes from battle and taking them to Valhalla, considered the heavenly home of honor for Odin's sprit army. Later they were romanticized as Odin's Shield-Maidens who soared over the battlefields as swan-like maidens or beautiful horse-mounted Amazons, then serving those heroes in Valhalla. This was portrayed in the 13th century Icelandic saga where the heroine was a beautiful fallen Valkyrie.

Stopping, I said, "Looks like everyone from East to West and North to South has mention of fallen angels or angel type beings."

"*Bing,*" came another email notification.

"Email from Vicki," I said before he could ask. "It's her response to the other email I read to you earlier."

Luc nodded and waited while I skimmed the response. I think he was still trying to process this current info from Derek, or perhaps why I was even interested in this information.

Moving forward, I paraphrased the rest of her email for him. "Says she needs Derek's help again with this second Enochian entry, and other possible anagrams she's found. Something about *descendants of Watchers*, how to watch for the signs, and how to know they are being revealed."

"Cool," Luc tossed out.

I shrugged. *Whatever.* Skimming, I said, "Says something about using the angel alphabet to do it. That the *Proto-Norse entry in the codex mentioned similar details about identifying a descendant,* but it uses the words... *a trained hug.* More than likely another anagram," I said.

"No kidding, not sure these Watcher dudes would be all about training humans to hug," Luc said, laughing. "They're looking at Norse stuff too?"

"Ya, Vicki had me send him an email on it when we first found the reference in the codex."

"Bing."

"Man—Derek is getting faster and faster with these riddles—check it," I said, turning the laptop and pointing to the screen.

Luc shifted my way to see the email. "The solution is... hmmm... sounds like another big guy we know," he said, glancing up at me.

"What—who?" I said, turning the laptop back my way. He'd read past where I had. So I read aloud what he'd just seen,

> *a trained hug = the guardian*
> *The translation for the description of the Norse descendant goes as such: He will be strong of arm and heart. Towering over the average man, pale complexion, and fair hair. Though large in stature, he hides his strength and his speed. He will be a trained hug (the guardian) and must choose his path, good or evil.*

"Sounds like Darius," Luc said, sitting back on the other couch.

"Seriously?" I asked, staring at him with uncertainty. "You think that's Darius—he's a descendant of the Watchers?"

"Whatever," he said, turning away in a mock pout.

I shook my head. "And how the hell would this help my friends in Ottawa with him in Miami?" I asked skeptical, my eyes wide in inquiry. "I'm gonna send Derek back a quick note—tell him he doesn't need to copy me on any new emails. The girls can tell me—if they want, considering I told them my stuff. But I guess when you look at it—it's their stuff."

"Okay," Luc said, "Tell him I say *hi* and the beers are waiting for him." He was smiling, clearly remembering their last fun-filled visit. It was great how they'd hit it off in the past, and that they had music and guitars in common too.

Composing my email, I read out as I typed,

> *Hey Shortcut, thanks for the update. Glad everything is coming clear for them. I'm sure they will let me know how things unfold. No need to copy me on any future emails. They own you now. Ha ha!*
> *Also, being done with work is great, and I'm enjoying the new house and time to myself.*
> *Luc says Hi, btw, told me to tell you the beers are waiting for ya.*
> *I'm waiting for ya too, come visit soon.*
> *Lynn*

Send.

When I glanced up, Luc was staring at me. He said nothing, but his dark bushy eyebrows where pinched together in a scowl.

"What?" I asked.

He gave me more scowl.

"Seriously, what?" I asked again.

His eyebrows relaxed, and he said, "Norse stuff aside—tell me you aren't the least bit curious still."

"About?" There was plenty to be curious about, plenty to be frustrated about too, but what did he want from me?

"About how or why, both your Mom and birthmom were involved in this," he said, referring to the earlier information I'd shared with him. "And what about the whole comment, *I've written it all down, and the information is safe* stuff from your birthmom? What's written and where the hell is it? Aren't you curious?" he asked, scowl returning.

I guess I knew the answer, but I didn't want to admit what I was truly thinking or feeling about all this. Instead, staring him straight in the face I went with, "Curious—no." From the information Derek had sent about angels, my girlfriends couldn't deny it anymore. Deny what I'd deduced about these guys being angels, and *not* men. Have they sent me an email admitting it—no. Looking away, I said, "Okay my Theologian, my turn to change the topic. Tell me what you know about the four horsemen."

"What's a theologian?" he asked.

"Really? Figured you'd know that one. It's someone who's versed in theology—God stuff—like you, now spill."

"Gah," Luc gave me. He took the last sip of his beer. Then he was off the couch heading to the kitchen. Exclaiming as he went, he said, "You want to hear my take on The Horsemen?"

What I wanted besides information, was a distraction, a change of direction from thinking about and questioning the reasons for all of this, for my role, my mother's role, my birthmother's role, *and* the miserable feelings I had about being left out by the girls. *Why did it matter?* It mattered because it was bigger than me, bigger than the weird stuff I'd felt my whole life… and I wasn't part of it, *not anymore.* How was I supposed to find and process information like this, gather the famous yet secret four, bring them together with the Cipher making them five-strong, and what? Just walk away, go back to *normal* life again? It's like being privy to a secret to the universe, the balance or whatever. Still, I had to let go. *But how?*

Taking a deep breath and shaking it off, I got up and followed after Luc into the kitchen.

He had cracked open another cold beer. I got one for myself in hopes to force my thoughts into the change in direction. "Yer the religion guy, you were raised on this—not me," I said, scratching my head. "All I know is what I've read, and that's the internet's interpretations of things. I want to hear yours." I needed a real person to tell me the real-deal, someone I trusted, and not a bunch of random religious folks from the internet.

He swigged, grinned, and then nodded. Beers in hand, we returned to the living room. I sat back in my spot as he took his on the adjacent couch.

Luc took in a long deep breath. "Now, I'm not an expert on this," he started, "I know what I know and believe what I choose to believe—okay?" He sounded like his own defense lawyer, deflection a version of *I cannot be held accountable for the actions of my client*. And he'd added a serious face as the chaser.

I smiled. I'd get it out of him one way or another. He might as well give in. Worst-case scenario, I'd pull out the homemade chocolate chip cookies I'd made yesterday. Figured if I couldn't get any answers about my mom or birthmom from anyone—the ones I truly wanted, I'd get answers to all the other stuff I was curious about.

And just when I thought I'd have to resort to cookie-bribery, Luc took another deep breath, and began. "Once upon a time," he said with a grin.

Like his fellow archangels, Gabriel also paced, but he was outside Lynn's home, and thousands of miles from the others, listening in as The Theologian discussed the *other* four... The Horsemen.

So close he thought, she was so close to seeing the truth. Maybe she wouldn't need to find what was hidden—maybe it would be enough. But her friends would need to know where the gathering would be. Maybe the answers to the gathering are with the *truth*, but what if Armaros also made her write lies—lies about everything? What then?

Joining Gabriel outside the house, Shamsiel said, "We have to tell the others."

"Now what?" he questioned yet knowing fair well what the angel meant.

"I was there—just now with them. They question the need for Lynn's involvement," Shamsiel shared. "I left them soon after hearing their complaints... but I lingered out of sight on the air to hear their discussions. It was a good thing too, because Armaros showed up—told them the *four* were here—well, not here-here," he said, waving his arms in a circle, "In Ottawa."

Visibly annoyed, Gabriel turned and asked, "How does Armaros know if they are here or not? For that matter, how do you know?" He crossed his arms, waiting.

"I can feel them you know," Shamsiel said. "Watcher—leader, remember?"

"And?" Gabriel added, arms still crossed.

In a surge of smugness, Shamsiel crossed his arms over his own chest, then in a little louder tone, he said, "I felt them—then I saw them." Giving a hint more of his smugness, he tapped his foot and said, "And so did *she*."

At this news, the anger in Gabriel's face dropped, as did his jaw, followed by the weight of his arms which fell and now hung at his sides.

When Gabriel said nothing, merely stared, Shamsiel followed up with, "That's what I've been trying to talk to you about."

Still Gabriel said nothing, mouth still gaping.

Swift and absent of Gabriel's response, Shamsiel recalled the event at the restaurant, describing in detail what he'd witnessed. In ending he said, "She was amazing." Then he turned and walked towards the window to peer in.

"Wait—back up," I said to Luc, "The apocalypse is an event, not a place?"

Shaking his head in frustration Luc said, "No, you're thinking of the *Acropolis*, that's a place in Greece." Backing up again for me he said, "The *term* does come from Greek, meaning *revelation*, and it means a discovery of something hidden. Generally hidden from a major populous, often most of the human race. It's about revealing something most of mankind considered *false*, but which is in fact *true*."

"It's the big reveal," I summed up. "When did this happen?"

Shifting in his seat he said, "Well that's the thing—it hasn't. It's another way of saying *the end of the world*."

At the mention of *the end*, something deep in the grey-matter of my brain sparked like a teeny tiny little stick of dynamite. Inconsistent with the brain implosion, I was still blank-faced because I had nothing to add—nothing but a gathering of drool settling in the corner of my now open mouth. I managed to pull a breath in before Luc continued.

"Some people thought it would be the year 2000—the millennia, and others believe it's 2012, as on the Mayan calendar—the date December 21, 2012, but there are tons of theories and speculations on this."

"Oh great," I said, with a hint of sarcasm. "Where do these four horseback riders come in?"

I could see he was trying to keep a straight face and not laugh at my reference. Then he said, "The four horseback riders as you call them—normally referred to as the *Four Horsemen of the Apocalypse*, represent the forces of destruction."

"Right... are they symbolic or real?" I questioned. Oh, like I wanted to know if these bad-asses were real—*not*.

He rubbed his shaved head and drew a hand over his goatee, then came back with, "Real? Hmmm that's a good question." Redirecting he asked, "Did you come across anything on the *Seventh Seal* in your searching?"

Recognizing the term, I said, "Ya—Book of Revelation and the Seventh Seal. Lots of references to these, and why I'm asking you all this, it's majorly confusing." I gave him my best confused face, and added bulging eyes for emphasis, my brief coma drool carefully avoided this time.

He appeared scared at first, sizing up my expression, but then laughed. "Nice face," he said, and gave another head shake. "Okay, it's all in the Bible, but let me give you the quick and painless version."

"That's what I was hoping for," I confirmed. Clarity would bring me calmness, I hoped.

He took another deep breath in as if readying himself., then began again. "There's supposed to be—yes you got it, an angel who has a book or scroll covered on both sides with writing." He paused for a second. I think he thought I was going to freak out, but when I sat listening like a good girl, he continued. "But, the book is sealed with seven seals, and it was given to God to hold. The first four seals are about the Horsemen, and when each seal is opened, they each in turn arrive on earth."

"Tell me about them," I asked when he paused. I was like a little kid hearing a story though I felt the weight of the discussion as Luc's face grew more serious.

Rubbing his chin again he said, "First is *Conquest*, the white horse. Its rider holds a bow. Second is *War*, the red horse. Its rider holds a sword. Third is *Famine*, the black horse. Its rider holds a pair of scales, and the fourth is *Death*, the pale horse, whose rider is followed by Hell."

He paused again, but I said nothing. I didn't like hearing the reference to *hell*, but who would? This story was giving me the serious heebs, and it made the fine hairs at the back of my neck prickle.

"Each are given authority to wipe out one fourth of the Earth," he said, and ending with a bang. He must have recognized my unease and frustration or perhaps my confusion in my expression, because he said, "What—not clear enough?"

"Yup," I gave in response, but something he said pulled at the back of my brain, again the teeny tiny explosions.

"Then what's with the face?"

It was my turn to do the head shaking. "I don't know—maybe I've just read too much, it's all sort of mashed in together." Grabbing my notes, I said, "But those four horsemen, they remind me of something... something else I read—not on the seal stuff, but... uhmm... here it is."

"They saw her—he saw her?" Gabriel all but gasped out the words as he stepped up to meet Shamsiel at the window. Lowering his head, he ran his hands from front to back through his thick blond hair, then drew his palms forward and down over his face. Then through his hands he said, "Zaqiel—he knows... and now... they all do."

"But it was in Ottawa," Shamsiel reassured him. "She's safe here." He paused. "But Michael and the others—they need to know." Sensing Gabriel's anguish, he wrapped a comforting arm around the broad shoulders of his new comrade. "I can help—you know that. With my little watcher-descendant-seers next door, I'll know if any of the *others* come this way."

Lifting his head, Gabriel said, "But Armaros—he knows where she is—he'll tell the *other* four."

"But he won't be coming back here any time soon," Shamsiel said, trying again to reassure him. He continued to watch through the window. "And like *our* four friends, he doesn't know everything."

"Right here," I said, finding the place in my notes, locating the names of the four I sought. "The leaders of the Watchers," I continued, flipping back again to the notes I'd jotted down from my recent search.

"Weren't there twenty leaders?" Luc questioned.

"Ya-Ya—there are, but these four—this little group here, they sound an awful lot like these horse guys." I flipped the pages back again eager to share. "Let me read you what I have."

"Shoot," Luc said, giving me the go-ahead with a quick royal styled hand gesture.

Scanning to the bottom of the page I found the last four leaders. I had grouped them together because I'd found a few more references on them and they'd been described as a group of four. "Kokabiel," I said, trying to pronounce the first odd name, "he's described as having long white hair, his name means *star of God* and he carries a bow. Next is Azazel, and he has short red hair—no name reference, but he taught men how to make weapons and he carries a sword. Third, is Baraqel, he has black shoulder-length hair, his name means *lightening of God*, and he carries a pair of scales." I gave Luc an eyebrow raise before sharing the last of the group because the likenesses were obvious. "Aaaand fourth, is Zaqiel, his name means *God has hidden....*"

Cutting me off, Luc said, "And don't tell me, he has pale hair." He gave me a look I'd not expected nor ever seen from him... *smugness*, as if he considered my assumptions foolish.

Scowling back at him I said, "As a matter of fact, pale *blond* hair."
I finished by crossing my arms over my chest and shooting smugness
right back at him.

"What's going on in that head of yours, Lynnie?"

"Don't tell me you don't see the similarity, that those four watchers
don't sound just like those horse guys!" I said.

"Yer serious?"

"Serious," I responded. Come to think of it, they reminded me a
lot of those four from the Vietnamese restaurant—handsome, yet big
and scary with the same hair I'd just described, but I kept that notion
to myself. He already considered my idea that the horse guys and the
four fallen guys being the same was ridiculous. Smirking I said, "Under
the information I found, it says these four Watchers are waiting on a
fifth... something about the fifth being revealed." I stopped. He was
blank-faced this time, staring at me as if waiting for more—but I didn't
have more. "Fifth what, do you suppose—could it be the fifth seal?" I
asked.

Luc's expression shifted, changing to one of puzzlement, perhaps
coming around to my thinking and not his earlier skepticism. Giving
me a tiny nod, he uncrossed his arms, and with the tiniest flicker of
fear, he said, "Only the worthy can open the seals and when they are
opened... judgment occurs."

It was my turn to stare waiting for more and I raised my eyebrows
up again, this time in anticipation.

Luc shifted in his seat. Having more to share he cleared his throat,
and said, "The Fifth seal—when opened, the souls of those willing to
die for their belief in God, cry out and are considered martyrs." He
paused but only briefly, continuing with, "*Sixth*, is earthquakes, the sun
goes black and the moon goes red like blood, and the stars fall to the
earth. *Seventh*, the heavens become silent, then seven angels sound
seven trumpets, releasing devastation on man and earth." His words
came out as if he'd memorized it, but then possibly he had.

I was sick to my stomach, a little gag reflex tickled the back of my
throat, and light beads of sweat warmed my forehead. "Okay," I said.
What else could I say?

"What do we do?" he asked, "Tell the others about this?"

"We do nothing," I said, swallowing my nausea, deflecting. "Not involved—remember." In further rejection, I gathered up our dinner remnants and proceeded to the kitchen to dispose of the not-so-fancy meal we'd just had. Simple yes, delicious most definitely, but my stomach wasn't thrilled with the current wave of queasiness running through it.

Putting the takeout containers in the trash my wave of nausea changed to a wave of anger, recalling the many fancy authentic Asian meals Will had described from his copious overseas trips. I was often envious of the amazing food he'd had the privilege to sample, but the envy had grown into a resentment of late. Resentment not from missing out, but because his work life away seemed better than his home life. At least it had seemed that way based on his enthusiasm and his lack thereof upon his returns. Hard to fault a guy for loving his job, but wasn't he supposed to love his life and me as much?

"Will back tomorrow?" Luc asked, shaking me from my thoughts.

I still had the tied garbage bag in my hand, having stopped mid-thought at the kitchen side door. It's not quite the topic of distraction my mind needed either, but my guess is Luc know I was done with the topic. He took the bag from me and pushed passed me out to toss the load in the big garbage bin next to the house.

"Yup," I said, mindlessly replacing the empty garbage can with a new bag. I turned. Raven was staring at me, his head cocked to one side. "What? You're looking for answers too?"

Raven, "*Chuffed*," and wagged his tail.

"Well, I have none—how about you?" I asked him back just as Luc came back through the door.

"Hey boy—come on Raven, bedtime," he said passing by both of us.

Without answering me, not that I expected one, Raven followed Luc, but then stopped before exiting the kitchen. He turned his head to look back at me.

"What?" I said to him again like a fool.

He, "*Chuffed*" again, turned back and padded off through the kitchen opening and out of sight.

A minute later, Luc came around the corner with the glass he kept on the bedside table in hand. "Need a refill," he said holding up the empty cup. "You staying up?"

"Uhm...," was all I got out. I was confused by the dog, confused by everything.

"Almost midnight," he added, filling up his cup.

"Midnight? Didn't realize how late it was," I said, as I meandered back to the living room.

"You okay, Lynn? You seem not yourself." He leaned a shoulder against the wall of the kitchen's opening, then took a sip of his fresh water.

"Ya-ya—I'm good. Fatigue catching up to me I guess." I smiled hoping to give him the sense I was okay, but I knew it wasn't fatigue, it was something else.

"Okay... see you in the AM... Night," he said, then moseyed off towards his bedroom.

"Sleep tight," I called out to him, pushing through the feelings, the foreboding, another premonition perhaps... of something changing.

Chapter 19

Thursday, and although Will wasn't scheduled to arrive until 10 a.m., the first one of us up was *Raven*. He'd made sure I was up early too by giving me a warm wet nuzzle in the ear.

In the kitchen, Luc and his cheerful grin arrived just as the pot of coffee I'd made finished brewing. Like me, not happy to be up, but thrilled for the coffee that was brewing. I poured the *just black* hot and ready coffee into Luc's mug. The creamer already in my cup, I then poured mine, watching as the dark and light swirled together, finishing to a mocha coloured marvel of delight.

After our first coffees, I sat on the couch in my PJs with my second mug of morning coffee, watching as Luc scrambled around making sure he had everything, all his and Raven's things. Raven's toys had been scattered from room to room like markers. I think he assumed this was his new place, toy marking and protecting it like it was. But I liked it even if it was only temporary.

I hadn't brought up the topic of the horsemen and neither had Luc. Luc had to head home first, drop off Raven, then he had to head into work, so we didn't really have time to chat this morning, anyway.

"Find a new apartment yet," I asked. Luc's rental place was up for sale and pending an offer which meant Luc would need to find a new place and vacate shortly.

"Not yet, but I'll be calling a few places today on my lunch,' He said, finding another doggie toy. Ever since meeting my neighbor—the lovely Dunya, Luc had been procrastinating on where he should move. He'd said he might like to be closer to mine—slash—Dunya's end of town, even if the drive to work was slightly longer. He'd tried to play it off as if it was the neighborhood and not the neighbor that appealed to him, but I knew the true motivation.

"You should move in here—we've got lots of room," I joked. Part of me wasn't joking. "It would be nice to have another person around with Will traveling so much." It would be nice to have Luc around even when Will wasn't traveling since they got on so well. Though it wasn't like Will was really home when he *was* here, it was more like *work from home*.

Work, work, work. I'd hoped that after everything was settled in the house, Will and I would have time to have fun, but even with me being off work, there never seemed to be much time for fun or us. This wasn't something new, it had just been my assumption we'd have more time. It was more hope than anything. I'd wanted a big house, so friends could visit, both the ones from up North and my local friends, but I'd take what I could get, and Luc was a quality friend.

Passing through the living room on a quest to find the last of the toys, Luc stopped to peek out the front window, then carried on his search down the hall. On his return up the hall, he passed through the living room one last time, only to peek out the window, again.

"Looking for someone?" I asked, finishing the last of my coffee.

"Toys," he said, as he zipped up his knapsack. He slung it over his shoulder and then picked up Raven's leash from the small table at the entrance.

"Right," I tossed back, though I knew Luc hadn't seen Dunya since before I'd gone to Ottawa. I hadn't seen her since I'd told her *everything*, but I had received a quick text from her.

He peeked out the window again, then glanced back at me and grinned. "Well, I was hoping to say *hi* to Dunya before heading out, but I don't see her car in the drive."

"Visiting her daughter up North for the weekend," I shared. His smile drooped a little. It's what she'd mentioned to me in her text, but she hadn't elaborated. I hadn't asked her about Mitra's seeing Mr. tall dark and handsome in our text exchange either. I had thought better done in person considering the context.

My laptop on the coffee table let out a, *"Bing."*

I glanced over to see who had written me. "An email from my favorite PI—Anthony," I said, reading further. "Hmmm…. it's info on how my birthmother had gone to Miami before she passed." Continuing I said, "The friend had mentioned something about a trip my birthmother took, but Anthony hadn't found much with further investigation and had been given only vague information from his informant, the one he'd mentioned before—Gabriel." Saying the name out loud had me shooting a quick glance at Luc.

His eyebrows were raised halfway up his forehead.

Trying to ignore the obvious, I read on, "The guy found she'd been to and from Miami in less than 48 hours—but the trail ended there. The guy had no clue where she'd gone while here." I glanced up again in time to see Luc shrug.

"Not much help, but weird—ironic, that she'd come here of all places," Luc said, crossing the distance from the front door. He reread the email over my shoulder. "How about the mention of the name *Gabriel* again, and in a messenger role?"

Shifting the laptop so he couldn't read anymore, I said, "I'll email Alison and cc Derek on the details. I'd emailed Anthony before I'd left—only fair I share the response, helpful or not." Was it helpful? I didn't think so, but it wasn't for me to figure out, it wasn't my mystery.

"Why don't you want to be involved anymore—why did you tell Derek to stop cc'ing you on the email?" Luc questioned.

Scrunching up my face, I said, "Maybe I don't want to know— maybe I'm tired of weird, maybe I want normalcy for once." I shrugged. "Maybe I want my husband to come home and for us to finally enjoy this house." But I knew the *real* whys to all this. I wasn't needed, not anymore, and I didn't like the off-putting responses I'd gotten when I'd tried to contribute. Each time I'd tried to stay connected, the others had made me feel like I'd been intruding. They didn't so much as say it, but it was the brush-offs and the guilty expressions on their faces that had conveyed it. It had been why I left. "It's their quest—their adventure, their history," I said. "Maybe Alison will write about their findings in a book or something. Like those stories people write about Christ having had children and how descendants of his are out there—something like that, ya know."

"But aren't you curious to know more?" Luc pushed.

Saying nothing, I stood and headed for the front door. Luc followed me. Then he leashed Raven, and I opened the door. "If you're curious, you can always email Derek—let him know I've given you all the dirt. Sorry for the rant," I said smiling at him. "Feeling a little off, sorry—can't put my finger on it, just off."

"Okay," he said, following with a nod. "Tell Dunya I said *hi* would ya?" Then he gave me a one-arm hug.

"I will."

In the next breath he and Raven were gone, and I was left to wait 30 minutes until Will's arrival call came.

Strange though, this time I wasn't feeling the usual pressure from waiting for the airplane arrival call. I usually felt as though I couldn't breathe until I got his call. Instead of feeling the need to gulp air, in its place was that foreboding feeling. The same feeling I'd experienced after his last trip, and now again, it swirled around me. Something was about to change.

Will's call came, but that feeling didn't leave. When he arrived home an additional 30 minutes later, and had come through the door, the feeling remained, and it remained still. There'd been no welcome home hug, no cheerful recall of all his adventures, no shown'n tell of all the interesting trinkets he'd purchased, no showing all the swag he had gotten from the tour operators, *and* no country related gift for me.

Even as night fell, after a long day of unpacking, laundry and only minor catch-ups, that foreboding feeling still spun around me. As we climbed into bed, the uneasy apprehension lingered, and as I closed my eyes, a hint of it still hovered as I drifted off to sleep.

* * *

Friday, and back less than a day, Will headed into the office to take care of the new issues with the Asian accounts.

He'd told me last night right before bed he'd have to fly to Tokyo Monday to meet with the company reps there. He'd be gone for 3 weeks this time he'd said. It also meant he wouldn't be home for Thanksgiving—Canadian Thanksgiving that is, which was always the second Monday in October. It was the first Thanksgiving in our new place, and I'd be doing it solo.

Before Will was out the door, I'd told him I'd be calling Luc to tell him he was welcome to come back. *"That's a great idea,"* Will had said, having no thoughts on the matter. My thoughts had been with the timing of another trip that it might make me feel better, but for whatever reason, that stupid uneasy feeling remained, still swirling around me.

I'd thought the plan was that once we moved, and I was done work, that we be spending more time together—not less, and I thought we'd be traveling together more as well. Considering Will's increase in work and his travel schedule of late, I'd wondered if the move to the new house had been just to pacify me, give me something else to occupy my time while he dove deeper into work. I loved being in the new house and having more free time, but the point was for us to be together. When had the plan changed?

As it was, my call to Luc was perfect timing, because he'd been informed that the house had closed, and he only had a few days to vacate the premises. He'd expected at least two weeks' notice, but it was his fault for not being better prepared. He'd known they could close the deal at any minute, and they had. But he was thrilled to have a place to go, though I'm sure he was more excited about the opportunity to see Dunya again than hanging with me. I didn't care. I liked seeing him all googly-eyed over someone, especially someone as nice as Dunya.

*   *   *

Monday, 3:00 a.m. and Will was gone, again.

The whole idea of not being able to breathe when he flew had become unbearable until... *now.* I tried not to read anything into it. On past trips I'd been nervous that something might happen to him, but this time it was different. There was still the relief when he called to say he'd landed, especially after this long flight, but something had changed, he was different. Or perhaps I was.

After calling in sick at work, Luc and Raven trudged back over to my house, this time with a small moving van. He had little, just his clothes, a TV, a laptop, kitchen dishes, pots and pans, plus other kitchen gear. He liked to cook. He also had four guitars, an amp, and a shit load of books. Oh and a few dog toys that accompanied Raven's food and water dishes.

He'd assured me he would find a new place before Will got back, but I wasn't worried. There was plenty of space for him to store the stuff. Luc was like family and Will liked him as much as I did. I knew Will would feel better knowing I had someone in the house with me, plus a big German Shepherd like Raven to protect me while he was gone.

Once the move-in and set-up of Luc's stuff was completed, Raven assumed his usual place next to me in the living room. After dropping off the truck and then cleaning up, my other new roommate had sashayed over to the neighbor's for dinner. Dunya had spotted Luc coming and going, and during one of his back-and-forth runs from the house to the truck she had offered to have *us* over for dinner. I'd expressed via Luc, that I was feeling under the weather—not completely a lie but it made way for Luc to have time with her on his own. *How could he say no?*

I was content to sit here in my living room with my furry date, reading my emails. I'd received one from Alison in response to mine regarding Anthony's email I'd sent. I'd assumed, she—they, would ignore my involvement once again, and I'd been correct. All she'd written on the subject was, *'Thanks for the info'*. Her email also mentioned that she had gone home. She'd been away from Ken too long and was due for a baby check with the doctor. I was happy to read that part and was looking forward to more on that topic.

As I scrolled through my other emails, a new one popped in from Will, the subject line read, *Great Opportunity*. I assumed he'd written it on his layover to Tokyo. The message read;

Calling tonight, 10 p.m. your time. Have big news! I've been
offered a great opportunity and I want to talk to you about it.
Let me know if you will be awake.
Will

I responded with just '*yes*' and hit send. Then that foreboding feeling returned.

His call came at 10:01 p.m.. He should have been tired, I was, but his enthusiasm pushed through the phone.

Apparently, his company had offered him this amazing opportunity, a position that would have him working in Japan, double his current salary. He was told that they would also pay for his accommodations while there. "They can get you a spousal visa to go with me, but you couldn't work," he said, "I'd still be traveling, but around Asia specifically." Before I could get a comment out, he added, "They'll pay out our mortgage there too, so we won't lose anything." We'd put a hefty sum down when we bought it, so mortgage payments were super low. We had less than a quarter left to pay off. "It would be great not to have to pay it ourselves," he added, when I had nothing in response.

I had pretty much predicted what he was going to tell me, considering all the extra Asian travel and meeting with bosses. But what I had not predicted, was how I would respond. He sounded more than overjoyed about the whole idea, about the opportunity to move to a new place. Me, not so much. "I'm not going," I told him. I understood why he thought this was a great opportunity for him, but it was not the same for me. I couldn't force him to let this opportunity go, but I knew I wouldn't be happy in a foreign place with him gone all the time. I'd had a hard-enough time going from Canada to the US. I'd sold my house in Ottawa, left my secure job, left my family and friends, all to start a life down here with him.

Nevertheless, instead of it being a wonderful adventure for both of us, he'd been the one on the wonderful adventures, and I'd been left at home, and mostly alone. Even when he was home, it had been like his mind was on work, and it had been. He'd admitted as much, and I'd let it slide for a long time, too long. I also couldn't make him stay here, with me. He would, if I asked. I loved him. He loved me too, but not as much as his job. He'd said on the call that he'd wanted me to see the world, see what Japan had to offer. But he understood why this offer was one I didn't want or need. I'd made the leap to come here, but he realized, the more we talked about it, that Japan was too much of a leap to ask of me this time.

We'd been friends a long time—a really long time, but we had fallen off being husband and wife when we hadn't been watching. I'd felt it... but hadn't wanted to admit it... I was too scared to... was too angry to. He knew I was right about our marriage and the direction it had gone. I think we had both been holding on to the romanticized version of our relationship, one that was now barely a friendship. He'd cried. I'd cried more, but by the end of the call... we both knew what we had to do.

* * *

Tuesday. I didn't get up to make Luc coffee.

I'd heard him come in late last night, but I'd chosen not to face him then with my news. Instead I'd sat on my side of the bed, staring out passed the empty spot next to me and out through the patio doors to the backyard. I'd stayed like that the whole night. It wasn't until I heard the front door shut and Luc's car start up this morning, that I finally pushed myself up and off the bed.

Walking through my home, I reflected on the soon to be empty spaces in the house, on how much time Will spent with work, his efforts with tending to the yard, *and...* how what a shame it was he hadn't put the same efforts into our marriage. You can't make someone else want the same things. All you can do is want them to be happy, and he was happiest when he was traveling. The regular day to day of home was not for him. I knew it, didn't want to see it... me the big *seer* and all. I miss my friends and family, but I loved this house, I would not be displaced again. But I guess what I would be... is *divorced*.

After a few coffees later, I was ready to send Alison an email on my not-so-wonderful-call from Will. She hated for me to be hurting on any level, even from a papercut, but I knew she'd also be proud of me.

Proud I was going with what *I needed* for a change, even if it meant being in this big house alone.

The only light in this whole thing with this split, would be this house. The offer still stood for the company to pay off our mortgage. I'd just wouldn't be going with the visa offer and the move. With the major increase in his salary, Will had offered to pay the taxes and the home insurance for as long as I needed, but the house would be mine. He'd said, "*It was always yours,*" and that he loved how happy it made me to be in it, and how happy it would make me to have my friends and family visit. He'd done that for me at least and I was grateful. Though, it wasn't *having* a house I'd missed when I moved here, it was feeling *home* I'd longed for, and I felt that here.

Before writing any emails, I remembered I needed to make an important call, this one to my doctor. I would sort out this nausea and blanking out of time thing once and for all.

With relief, 15 minutes later I had an appointment made for this Friday. I was actually due for my yearly exam, and she'd had a cancellation, so I grabbed the opening and was booked in. Getting in wasn't ever this easy, and I took it as a sign—what kind of sign I didn't know, but a sign none the less. First task done, it was now time for me to share the details of my night with my girlfriends.

I was still a bit bitter for being pushed out of the loop and I didn't currently have the emotional energy to write out separate emails. Instead, I opted for one email outlining the conversation and my thoughts on how things had unraveled. I made sure they knew it wasn't a complete shock despite my heavy heart. I let them know I wasn't alone either, and that Luc was hanging with me until he got a new place. I finished the email with a little lightness, letting them in on Luc and Dunya's potential new romance, how much I liked her, and how it made me happy to see them together. I hit send on the email.

With their busy lives and this quest stuff and all, I wasn't sure how fast any of them would respond. But within the hour, their emails started popping in.

Mac was pissed and hated I was so far away. She'd written, *We needed a night of reminiscing over past boyfriends, coupled with a few good bottles of wine.*

Vicki, being single herself, wrote, *I don't want you to wallow too long.* And tried to get me thinking about the possibility of finding, *someone who wanted to be in a relationship and not just on a ship.* Funny girl.

Olivia, she was the most shocked and the most disappointed, because of she and Mike being such good friends of ours. I wrote her back and did my best to explain what had happened, and how, *I'd not wanted to see if for myself,* and that, *the friendships wouldn't disappear for any of us just because Will was far away.* His friendships with them had always been hit and miss, where he was up for a quick visit, or an update here and there, but he never really invested in the lives of others. It wouldn't be much different, he'd just be farther away this time.

Alison, there'd been no email response from her, she'd gotten on the phone the minute she'd read my email, wanting to check on my heart, make sure it wasn't irreversible damage. The call had lasted 2 hours, and it had been great, although I'd cried through the first hour.

My tears finally dried up when she'd told me all about her doctor's appointment and had sent me the ultrasound picture of the baby. "*My new boyfriend,*" she'd called him, and I was happy to go with it. But, when she'd told me about the baby's room, it hit with a pang of sadness, though I'd said nothing. I'd realized my opportunity to have children with Will was now also gone, not just him. She'd told me that she would try to Skype soon, to show me how much her belly had grown. There'd been no mention of the work on codex and this time I was glad for it. Near the end of the call, we'd laughed over something silly Ken had said. He'd been in the background for the last part of the call and had made a joke about how *he* was having cravings for pizza now that *they* were in the second trimester. "*Any excuse for pizza—was a good excuse in my book,*" I'd told her.

"*Don't encourage him,*" Alison had replied, before ending our call with more laughter and an "*I love you*".

With the information out there now, I sat on the couch staring at my laptop. Then I turned to look at Raven. He'd sat stoic next to me through all the waves of emotions, all the tears and the laughter, just watching me. "Wanna go outside, buddy?"

"*Woof,*" was his answer, and I took it as a *yes*.

The next hour passed with us playing fetch in my backyard and him doing the occasional chase of squirrels up the oak trees. Then back inside after water and kibble, Raven decided it was time for more resting on the floor next to my feet.

My biggest effort of the day came with sending my brother and my other friends the crappy news. I knew James would be sad for me, but he was single and liked it, he wouldn't dwell on it long. As for Will's family and friends, he would have to inform them himself, I was done with pouring out my heart and keeping everyone else in the loop. Telling Louise, I guess would be my job, but I wasn't ready for it. She didn't need more bad news, not in her condition. I didn't know how I would break it to her, but I knew it could wait until a time when she was feeling better.

That aside, the other thing I knew, was I hadn't eaten all day. I went with ordering in delivery, just in time for Luc's arrival home after work.

I heard Luc's car arriving in the driveway, just as an email response from Derek arrived in my inbox. He hadn't written much,

Sorry, Lynn. Shitty.
Tell Luc to get the beers ready and I'll see what I can arrange.
Time for another visit.
~Shortcut

That worked just fine for me, I had plenty of room for visitors.

The second Luc came through the door, he knew something wasn't right. It could have been the packing boxes I had in the middle of the room, those leftover boxes from the move I'd pulled from the garage. I'd left them out to pack up Will's stuff. Or, it could have been the fact I was still in my pajamas, the fact I had two open beers in my hands, and that he was now sharing the front entrance with the pizza guy.

"Pizza," I tossed out.

Luc panned the surroundings as if looking for clues to what the hell was going on. Just then, Raven came from the kitchen with his metal bowl in his mouth. As if in anticipation of dinner, he quickly let it drop and clang to the floor, then let out a, "*BARK.*"

"Uhm, sure," Luc said, taking another glance at the pizza guy. "Everything okay, Lynn?"

"Money's on the front table," I said, setting the beers down on the coffee table. Luc paid the guy as I went to get napkins and plates. "We'll talk while we eat," I called back to him over my shoulder.

Chapter 20

The morning sun stung my eyes. Being I was three sheets to the wind when I'd gone to bed, I'd left the stupid blinds open again. There'd been six beers in the fridge, and I'd drank two before opening not one but two bottles of wine.

I'd opened the expensive ones Will had brought back from one of his trips. Figured I'd enjoy the wine even if I hadn't been able to enjoy the trip. Luc had drunk the beers while I'd poured out the wine and my news to him. I'd tried to give it a happy twist with the fact he didn't need to find a place to live now, *and* how Derek would be planning a trip down to see us as soon as he could arrange it, but Luc had seen through me.

Recalling now that he'd put me to bed, I covered my face with a pillow. *He'd* been the one who'd forgotten to close the blinds, *and* most likely on purpose to smarten me up. Nothing was made better by drinking, we both knew it. But he had let me get it out of my system — or into, so to speak, and had stayed up with me talking over everything. I'd asked him how his night with Dunya had gone, but he'd been hesitant to elaborate on the fun, considering my current condition.

Nice guy. Well, except for the fact he'd allowed for the screaming sunlight that now threatened to burn holes in my skull, or was it the wine headache doing that? Whatever, I needed water... and food. Lucky for me there was still pizza left in the extra-large box of deliciousness I'd ordered. It would make for a splendid hangover breakfast, along with a water and Advil chaser.

Ready now for food, I moved to get out of the bed. That's when my headache sandbagged, shifting from one side of my skull to the other. Raven rounded the bed just in time to steady me as I swayed and reached for the dresser. "Thanks, buddy." Pat, pat, pat. "Let's go get us some water—whataya think?"

"*Grumble—Woof*," he responded, and then the two of us moved gingerly from the bed… through the bedroom door… across the living room… and on to the kitchen to my hangover remedy.

Out of sheer kindness, I filled his water bowl first. He'd saved me from a potential stumble and crack to the skull. The bending over to get the bowl, and then back down to put in on the floor was no easy feat, but I managed. Then it was my turn for water.

I filled the biggest glass I could find, grabbed the headache pills from the vitamin cabinet and then chugged two of the miracle-workers back with the water. Swallowing the last mouthful of water, I glanced back to the living room.

Luc had cleaned up our dinner and drinks from last night. *Good guy.* But the best, was when I opened the fridge, there was a note that read; *Feel better*, atop three pieces of yummy pizza plastic wrapped on a plate. *Great guy.*

After eating all the pizza and drinking a few more glasses of water, I was feeling better, and I was glad to be home alone.

* * *

As the next days followed, I was left alone again. Not exactly alone, Raven was at my side wherever I went, following me from room to room. But I liked it.

Luc seemed to be adjusting well. He'd been over to Dunya's place, helping with *minor repairs,* as he'd called it. Ya right, repairs my ass. I didn't care, I liked Dunya, and they were cute together. And I was happy someone was having a romance even if it wasn't me.

Apparently, Dunya's mother had moved to Vegas shortly after that quarrel they had out front. She'd told Dunya she'd met a wealthy man and was out there to be with him before you could say *seven-card stud*. Dunya didn't mind it, her mother was gone most of the time, anyway. She loved her time with her grandmother, and now they no longer had to keep their dialog quiet to avoid the ridicule from her mother.

Luc had told me that Dunya's ex-husband had been a real piece of work. He had tried to take their daughter back to his home country without permission. Now he was banned from seeing her or ever coming back to the US. I'd wondered, but I had never asked her about the father of her child. I figured she'd tell me when she was ready. I'd also never thought to ask what she did for a living, as we'd never exchanged words on the topic. She'd known Luc and I had worked together and that I wasn't working now. Luc said, Dunya had been left a bunch of cash from family on her father's side, and her mother hadn't gotten a thing when her husband—ex-husband, had passed. She'd been living with Dunya, freeloading and it was why she'd taken off when she'd landed the rich guy. *Good riddance*, I say.

Luc had given me all the info the same night I'd shared my not-so-good news. After that, I hadn't felt much like going over things with anyone or talking to anyone for that matter. No one bothered with me and I didn't bother with them.

There wasn't much more I could say or explain, I just wanted life to go back to normal. But my life hadn't exactly been normal before. Now it was Friday, and also the day for my doctor appointment. I checked my watch, it was also nearly time for me to head out.

When I arrived, the nurse put me in one of the room and gave me the lovely light-blue paper gown-thingy to put on for my exam.

Changed, I sat on the exam table with my legs dangling over the side, trying to keep the backdoor to my paper dress closed. The room was cold like always, but I was sweating. The waiting was killing me though I knew it had only been a few minutes. *Was I sick?* Or was it all in my head? Maybe it was in my head—a brain tumor, or stomach cancer causing the bouts of nausea. *Was this from my telling the secret?* Telling couldn't hurt the four if they were the source—could it? I was the closest to the source—to them. Had it been the reason my mother's telling had caused her death, my aunt's death and my birthmother's? Louise was sick. Was it for telling what she knew? Could *I* be sick now for telling? "Oh my gosh—I told Derek," I said out loud. But wasn't he also part of this, the Cipher, it couldn't affect him, could it? "I told Luc." He had nothing to do with this, an innocent bystander. But he was safe if he told no one. Who would he tell? Who would believe him anyway?

I still struggled to believe all we'd discovered. If I was sick, I had no one to blame but myself. I'd read the journal, read about the implications of sharing it, yet I'd discredit the warning and told my closest friends. I had to believe the girls were safe, and Derek. They were the source—the five. The mothers would have said something, I'm sure. But Luc. I'd have to make sure he told no one, just in case. "Come on now, Lynnie, telling the girls couldn't be the reason for the sick feelings and those weird time lapses," I whispered to myself. But telling Luc, it might be why I'm sick. Perhaps I was only a *little* sick for sharing and nothing major. I let out a long-winded sigh, just as the door to the exam room opened.

"Well, look what the cat dragged in," my doctor said, giving me a welcoming grin. She crossed the threshold to where I waited on the paper lined table.

"Hey," I said, wiping my sweaty palms on the edge of my paper dress.

Dr. Melanie Harris is a tall, dark haired, fit woman around my age, with a light and cheery disposition. I'd been seeing her ever since I'd moved to Miami, and she'd been a welcome addition to my small circle. I had recommended her to a few people for both the fact she was an excellent doctor and had a comforting bedside manner. We weren't friends outside this office, but we always chatted like girlfriends when I had my appointments. Had we met out in the non-medical world, we would have been good friends I figured. "You're here for your annual?" she asked, flipping open the folder that donned my name in the upper left-hand corner. She must have sense something more from my expression, because she said, "Or is something else bothering you? You look tired, Lynn."

I took a deep breath, then summed up what I'd been experiencing. Told her about the stomach pains, the nausea, the sweats, and what I'd assumed were possibly blackouts that I'd been dealing with. I tried my best not to make it sound too *weird*, and merely a show of concern.

She gave me nothing but a, "Hmmm," as she continued with her usual set of palpations and the standard ears, eyes, mouth, and breathing checks. Then she said, "Let's get your blood work done and see if we can find the problem—if any."

After I got dressed again, we conversed about the other stuff going on in my life. Like a good doctor and a true girlfriend, she responded with kind and supportive words, expressing, "It's no wonder you look exhausted."

On the way out, I picked up my order for the blood work and then traveled down the main hall to the onsite lab. A poke and five vials later it was over, and I was out the door.

In an attempt to comfort myself, I repeated in my head that I was overreacting and that there would be a simple explanation *and* an easy fix for it all.

Before I drove away, I checked my phone and found there was a phone message from Luc. He'd said he'd seen the full boxes at the front door this morning, the ones with Will's name on them, and had offered to help move them wherever they need to go. Will never did empty those boxes of his from the move. He'd had them stashed in his office and hadn't bothered finishing them due to all his traveling.

It was nice of Luc to offer, but they were being picked up. Will's company had assigned a shipper to send them to him in Japan. All I had to do was pack the list of things he'd asked for and mark his name and company on the boxes.

The last part of Luc's message was him telling me that he and Dunya were heading up to see her daughter, 'Time to meet the boyfriend,' he'd said. He'd be home after work to get his bags but would be gone again right away. He added that Mitra would be going with them and they'd all be back Sunday night.

I was happy he had plans. I was wounded, but not for obvious reasons. I rubbed my arm. I didn't bother to call him back. Instead I hit the grocery store on the way home for a few items to get me through the weekend, like potato chips, which I loved but rarely let myself eat. I had no plans to leave the house and if I was to spend any time in front of the TV binge-watching movies, I'd need proper crunchy treats. I also made sure I had *real* food too, one cannot live on chips alone—well, I could, but I couldn't be that cruel to my body. The headache that still lingered reminded me of that.

I had myself propped up on the couch, legs outstretched on the matching ottoman, watching *Back to the Future Part II*, when Luc got home from work. The chips aaaaaaand the grilled chicken wrap I'd made myself, were out on the coffee table in front of me.

He was in and gone so fast that we only exchanged a few words. I'd forgotten to tell him *not* to share anything about the four and our findings, but I'd tell him on Sunday when he got back. Not like it would be the sort of thing you shared when meeting your girlfriend's daughter, anyway. The last thing he'd want to do when making a first impression, was to appear crazy.

Friday night and another weekend home alone. I didn't mind actually, I had my distractions of TV and food, and I didn't have to think about anything else. What I really meant was that I wouldn't let myself think about anything else.

* * *

The weekend blurred by with short bursts of getting off the couch to shower and eat, but on Sunday afternoon I made a point to call Louise.

She'd sounded exhausted as usual, though she'd tried playing up how *good* she'd been feeling. Andre had taken the phone from her when her energy petered out, telling me, *"She's pretending she has lots of energy, but she doesn't."* I knew it, but it had been hard to hear just the same. I told Andre about Will and me. He'd been surprised and had said he'd wait until Louise was stronger to tell her the news. On a happier note he'd shared that his son was engaged and would be getting married in the spring. We'd also chatted about their plans for a Thanksgiving gathering tomorrow.

I thanked Andre for letting me talk with Louise, and for updating me on the situation and her condition. I'd had no idea she had gotten that bad. She'd kept it from me. My hope was with this wedding news, Louise would stay strong, focused on beating this and be full of energy in time for it, but I'd gotten a sense from Andre that he wasn't as optimistic. I would try to stay positive for all of them. Maybe I was in denial, but I wasn't ready to go there yet. *Too much loss*, I told myself. Before ending the call, I'd asked Andre to keep me in the loop on her condition. He'd said, *"I will—if she isn't going to."* A wave of nausea had come over me while talking with Andre, but I'd chalked it up to worry over my friend, and that it had nothing to do with my own scary worrisome thoughts.

Raven gave my hand a nudge, pulling me from my thoughts and reminding me I wasn't alone. Then he stretched out on the floor alongside the ottoman. A peaceful blanket of contentment wrapped around me, and I relaxed again for another evening of TV.

Shamsiel and Gabriel settled in on the big couch as the images from the TV flickered.

"You're going to hang out here waiting for her to what— premonition the answers?" Shamsiel asked. "It seems you've been doing a little messenger work yourself with telling the PI about her birthmother's visit—edging the information along."

Gabriel chose not to answer him. Free will or helping, he couldn't avoid it. It's not like he'd walked right up to her and said *Hey, you need to find this stuff quick.*

"The others are working on things too," Shamsiel noted. "They could always conjure up help. There's a spell for that you know."

Gabriel ignored his comments, but then said, "They've found the information about *The Guardian.*"

"What guardian? Who?" Shamsiel stared at his friend. Again, no response came to his inquiry. "The girls deflected another one of Lynn's attempts to stay involved," he added.

Gabriel said nothing again, only stared blankly at the TV, reaching out then to pat Raven's head.

"They know she started this with the journal," Shamsiel said. "It mentions The Cipher—Derek—and they feel pretty strong about him being this *fifth* they keep seeing referenced. Nothing gives any sign Lynn is involved—nothing other than her needing to bring them together. The grimoire and codex don't mention her—the letters from the Mothers don't mention her."

Gabriel sighed. "I know," he said, patting Raven again.

"When will you tell the others? They need to know about Lynn's mother—about what Armaros did to her. They think the answers are in your entry in the codex."

"I was hoping to find where she'd hid the information before having to tell them anything," Gabriel confessed.

"They need to know about the *other* four—about Zaqiel," Shamsiel said, reaching forward to touch Gabriel's extended arm.

Gabriel stopped caressing Raven's head but said nothing. Sighing again, he resumed patting the head of their canine friend.

Chapter 21

I'd overdone it with the TV watching. And I'd resigned to go to bed early before Luc arrived home, not because I'd been tired, but because I'd wanted to get up early to start with the prep and cooking for Thanksgiving.

I'd expected to be sharing this house and my first celebration in it with my husband, but I wasn't, and I wanted to make sure things resembled something close to normal. If you can call living in a big house with two roommates—one being a dog, *normal*. But perhaps this was my *new* normal.

Since it wasn't a holiday here in the US, Luc was on his usual schedule at work. In the meantime, I set up to make a big Thanksgiving meal to serve later. I spent the day tidying up, cooking, and preparing for my first gathering in my new home.

It would be me, Luc, Dunya, Mitra, plus Darius. I'd called Darius to join us last minute. He's much like Luc in the sense he's happy to get a good meal anytime. He'd also noted it would be his first visit to the new house. I'd told him the crappy news about Will and me, but I turned it around saying how I had no one now to take care of the yard work and the tree trimming, and he'd offered to help after I'd bribed him with multiple future feedings. Knowing him, he would have helped anyway.

It was my last check on the turkey, the oven door was open, and I was pushing the food thermometer into a thick part of the breast, when I heard the front door open and then shut. But no greeting followed.

It must have been the amazing aromas wafting from the kitchen that had left him speechless, because when Luc rounded through the opening to the kitchen, he let out a hunger filled, *"Groan"*, followed by an, "Oh my God that smells aaamaaaziiing!"

I shut the oven door to keep the temperature from dropping and turned to see his happy face turn to sorrow. I laughed because he looked like I'd just taken his favorite toy away. "Oh, don't worry — it's almost ready. Another 30 minutes and we can eat."

He said nothing, but his happy grin returned liked a little kid promised a cookie. I'd made cookies, homemade ginger cookies, but those were for after dinner. Then he said, "Dunya and Mitra will be over in about 20 minutes. They're bringing dessert. I tried some on the weekend — it's called Back-Lava... or Ba-clava."

I laughed at his try at what I knew as *baklava*, a deliciously rich, sweet pastry made of layers of filo filled with chopped nuts, sweetened and held together with honey. I'd had it many times back home, but the thought of *homemade* baklava made me grin like a little kid too. "I might have to eat dessert first," I told him.

"No kidding. It might be my new favorite treat," Luc added, as I finished up my prep.

When a soft *"Knock"* sounded at the door a short 20 minutes later, we both answered it. Luc took the dessert from Mitra's tiny hands and then escorted our lovely guests and their lovely dessert in for the gathering.

In the kitchen, I had the turkey out on the big island in its resting spot ready to be carved. The mashed potatoes, stuffing, and gravy were in their decorative serving bowls. My favorite, my mother's broccoli-cauliflower cheese bake, was nestled in alongside them. The dinner plates, cutlery and fresh baked dinner rolls were out in front, as I'd set things up buffet style, so everyone could serve themselves, and then gather in the dining room around the table to eat.

Darius had mentioned he had a fancy way to carve a turkey, and I promised him I'd wait for him to show off his technique once he arrived, which would be any minute now.

But before I could get the carving implements out, Luc pulled me aside. Out of ear shot of the ladies he said, "I told Dunya about everything—all of it, Lynn. The journal, the four—everything. She's cool with it—her being a seer and all." He winked.

I stood silent and stunned but freaking out on the inside. I'd been worried about this exact thing. I'd thought I was sick because I'd told him about the stuff... but now... now he would get sick... for telling. I opened my mouth to speak, but then told myself to get a grip. I needed to get a grip. My health issues were not related. In fact, I was fine, right? Merely tired. And this overreacting and the worry itself was not helping. "Okay," I managed, but I felt flushed and a bit woozy.

"Knock-Knock" boomed from the front door.

I stood there still stunned as Luc ended our conversation by disappearing around the corner from the kitchen to go answer the door. It was most likely Darius, so I tried to pull myself together. Looking back towards the kitchen sink I thought perhaps I just needed a cool glass of water. I'd been rushing around the house all day and the kitchen was warm from the hours the oven had been on. This was supposed to be a celebration for giving thanks not for worrying over a few minor health issues.

My cell phone rang.

I grabbed it from the counter. The display shown the contact name for my doctor. "Hello," I answered, as another wave of nausea hit me.

"Hi, Lynn, it's Melanie—Dr. Harris," she said correcting herself, "I have your test results and unfortunately...."

Chapter 22

At the word *unfortunately*, the blood pounding in my head seemed to drain, leaving me even more lightheaded and more stunned than before the call. But then she followed up with, "… I won't get to see you for another year. Seems all your tests came back negative and all your counts are showing as good."

A wave of relief rushed back into me along with the blood back to my head. "That's the best thing I've heard all day," I said, and let out a lengthy breath of air.

"I recommend you take a *B-complex* supplement though—with all the stress of this past year, you could use a little supplement boost. Chalk it up to stress and all the life changes you've been through—what with your Mom passing, and your Aunt, moving to a new house and now this stuff with Will." She sighed. "It's no wonder you've been feeling ill, but it's nothing to worry about. Nothing a B supplement, more rest, and some fun won't cure."

"Great, no problem," I said, relief relayed, blood back to my brain.

"Oh—that reminds me," she said, then she went on to say how she—*they*, needed volunteers at the hospital. "Know any strong guys who could help with moving the more delicate patients? We've tried to get the bigger—fit, male nurses to help, but they're too busy with their regular hospital duties."

Just then Darius rounded the corner to the kitchen.

"As a matter of fact—I do," I told her.

"Perfect—could use your help too, Lynn."

"I'll get back to you on that," I said, thankful for the good news.

"Great," she said, and hung up.

Thankful was an understatement. I wasn't sick from the telling, it was just life. Life on a rollercoaster, but still just life.

"Darius—you ready to carve?" I ask, pulling the required implements from the bottom drawer.

"At your service," he said in response, his big hands taking the carving tools from my little ones.

As Darius carved, I left the kitchen to go open the back-patio door to bring the cooler air in. At the same time, I let Raven out for a quick run-around.

I spotted a lone butterfly resting on a low-hanging branch of the oak tree nearest to the house. "Hi Mom," I whispered, "Happy Thanksgiving." At the sound of plates clinking and laughter booming from the kitchen, both Raven and I headed back in.

Luc was exiting the kitchen as I returned, his plate loaded up high heading for the dining table where the others had already seated themselves. Darius had masterfully carved the turkey, and it was now on display using the decorative platter I'd left out for him.

I loaded up my plate and then dashed to find my seat. I took the open one next to Mitra, and she caressed my hand as I sat.

Darius had taken the big chair at the far end, needing the most elbow room. Luc had taken a seat next to Dunya, but he got up then to pour wine for everyone.

"Everything looks amazing Lynn," Dunya said.

Mitra touched my hand again, then giggled.

"Thank you," I said, "and thank you for your delicious dessert contribution. I'm tempted to eat it first."

"Jadda made it," Dunya said.

Mitra giggled again. I smiled back at her and this time I couldn't help, I giggled with her.

"Thank you, Darius, for your skillful carving. You'll have to show me how you did it since I missed the demonstration."

"Feed me again—and I'll show you," he said with a grin.

"Here-here," Luc said, raising a glass. "Feed me too."

"Don't worry, I've got you both covered," I teased.

"A toast," Luc said, raising his glass higher. We all raised our glasses. "Here's to gatherings with good friends and sharing good food. Happy Thanksgiving." Glasses clinked, cheers and Happy Thanksgiving were shared by all, and my first Thanksgiving in the new house was on.

A mix of emotions flooded me, and I sucked back the tears that threatened to push out. I struggled with the fact that Will was absent for this gathering, but I realized he would have continued to be absent from lots of things in the future. He'd been away with work, traveling, working and missing out on our life together, missing out on *my* life. This gathering wasn't how I'd envisioned it, but the love I'd hoped for—was here, all around me, and it was what I was most thankful for.

"Dig in," I said as I held back the tears and released a smile.

Everyone else's smiling faces made it easier for me to get through and their continued throws of laughter made it even more so. Over the eating of Mitra's amazing dessert, and after several satisfying groans from the group, I'd relayed the info to Darius about the volunteering.

He said, "Sure thing. I need something other than just work and the gym."

"Maybe you'll meet a cute nurse or doctor too," I said.

"The kids at the hospital will think yer a real giant," Luc added, knowing Darius would love his size being for something fun—for once, rather than something to be ridiculed for.

"I'll get all the details and we can go together when you have time," I told him.

"Speaking of the gym," Darius said, "I'd better get going. I prefer training at night to avoid the crowds and the onlookers."

"Right, it's a gym day for you," I acknowledged, getting up from the table. Darius had told me before that he often felt like a freak-show when other gym patrons watched him workout. His strength and size were the things to watch apparently, but he didn't welcome the attention. He would have welcomed the women watching, but the women had their own area of the gym to workout in, away from the grunts and groans and the sweaty workouts of the men. It was a shame none of the girls took an interest, he was a great guy—shy perhaps, but a real gentleman.

"I'll be back on the weekend to look at the yard, Lynn. And the trees." he said, heading for the front door. I followed. "Thanks for a great meal and a great gathering." Then he hugged me. Not the gripping embrace he'd had on me the day he'd saved me from being mowed down by the car, this was gentle—gentle giant like. "Bye all," he called out to the other as he released me. "Bye, Lynn." Then he was out the door.

After a little cleanup and containing the leftovers, we, including Raven, moved to sit outside. Luc had another bottle of wine opened and he poured some for both Dunya and me. Dunya and he shared the *loveseat*, while Mitra sat next to me on the big patio couch across from them. Mitra had no interest in the wine and though she didn't understand much of what was being said, she sat content and smiling while we all talked.

But then she spoke, saying something to Dunya in Arabic, and she caressed my hand again as she did.

Dunya smiled at me. "You haven't asked me about Shamsiel," she said.

I swallowed my gulp of wine. I'd forgotten about him again *and* I'd forgotten Luc had spilled the beans to her too—all the beans. "Ya... been meaning to... but got a bit distracted with getting off my rollercoaster," I said. Mitra caressed my arm this time. It was her way of communicating with me I figured, and I turned to look at her. She smiled, her blue eyes sparkling at me. I smiled back at her. Without turning to Dunya, I said, "Well... you said Mitra saw him?"

"Yes, she saw him once when he was out front of our home. He's been out front of your house—on the front lawn she claims. Though she has sensed him quite a few times since then."

I was sure my eyes had widened, but I couldn't find my words. I should have been scared or at least creeped-out but I wasn't. I was intrigued. I'd seen the guy, so had Luc. But Dunya had said he was something else—not a man, an angel. My friends weren't believers in angels, but why was I been so quick to question the idea of this one? Was it because I'd never considered an angel would look like that—

like him? But what did I know? Mitra rubbed my arm again as I turned my head to focus on Dunya.

"There was something else," Dunya said, "but it was only that one time—when Jadda sensed him out on the street in front of your house. There'd been something else, something dark... evil... with him on the street, Jadda told me."

"When was that?" I asked, as if it mattered, but I was grasping here—grasping at believing they could *feel* this guy.

"The day after you and I spoke, when you told me about your abilities—your premonitions and such."

Images flashed in my mind jumping to the day she'd said—the same day I'd had that major wave of sickness and nausea, when Raven had acted all crazy, pacing in front of me and growling at the window. Had that been what he was doing—sensing Shamsiel, or was it this dark evil something? Dogs could sense bad stuff, I believed that, but was I supposed to believe Mitra could too.

"The darkness was across from him, Jadda told me. A presence she could only feel. I saw nothing, but I felt them... both the light and the dark."

"Wait—what do you mean you felt them?" I know she said that before about Shamsiel, but I was confused. Luc and I had both seen him when he came to the door. Why couldn't they see him, and only feel him?

Dunya glanced at Luc, then back to me. "Jadda said they will only show themselves when they want to be seen. But a strong seer—like Jadda, can *try* to see them. Doesn't always work if the angel is veiled."

There's that word again, *angel*. "So Shamsiel—this angel, *let* Luc and I see him?" I said, my heart speeding up.

"Yup," she gave me.

I nodded, and I was sure it was the type of nodding and facial expression like what Olivia had given me when I'd told her about Mom's journal. Dunya had told me she and her grandmother were seers, and I'd believed her. I'd liked knowing I wasn't the only person who felt freaky shit, but now I was facing more freaky shit.

"Lynn, do you want me to go on?" Dunya asked.

"Yup," I gave her back, my turn for the short answer.

"That time, with the light and dark," she continued. "Jadda and I watched from our living room window. The sky darkened, and a wild wind swirled up from the West, behind where the darkness was strongest." She paused as if checking to see I was still following. "Then the darkness was gone... as was the wind. Then Shamsiel was gone, but not truly. Jadda said she could feel him lingering still."

Mitra touched my hand giving me a little startle, and I turned to look at her again. She wrapped both of her hands around mine then. She spoke again something in Arabic, directing it to her granddaughter of course.

"Did you feel him, Lynn?" Dunya asked, relaying what I assumed Mitra had just said.

"Me? Did I feel what—him?" I couldn't feel him. At least I didn't think I could. But I wasn't feeling much of anything lately, other than nauseous. "Nope... no—I don't think so," I said.

"Have you tried?" Luc asked, adding his two cents.

"Try?" What the hell did that mean. "How?" Did I even want to know, and if I did, what would I do with that? "Who is he?" Or what is he I should have asked. A real angel or was he some kind of ghost, perhaps.

"You know the answer, Lynn," Dunya said.

Mitra took my hand she'd been holding and put it up to her soft cheek as if trying to communicate with me further. She released my hand, and I caressed her cheek in response.

"Mitra says he's an angel," Dunya shared. "I don't know how to explain it—but I believe her. I always believe what she tells me. And I believe all these things that your friends are revealing as well, even if they don't," she added.

"We think it's all real," Luc said, "That the angels... are real."

I took another sip of my wine, then tipped the glass back finishing it all. Then poured myself another.

Chapter 23

Michael was on his laptop again, sitting at the back steps of Vicki's apartment. Gabriel appeared several paces back from his fellow Angels, while the others meandered around the parking lot paying no attention to his arrival.

Michael looked up. "Well now, Gabriel—have you come to explain things?" The others redirected their attention at the sound of Michael's words.

"Yes," Gabriel said, as he came to stand next to his brethren. Then Gabriel spoke again, this time proceeding at length, making clear what had happened with his Chosen, sharing that the answers they sought were not in his entry. It had been the task of his Chosen to discover the *where* of the gathering—not him. It was part of her gift. He explained further how his Chosen had traveled to Miami days before her death. How she'd hidden the information she'd been guided to write, about her pregnancy, her role in this, and where the place for the gathering would be. He continued, giving them more, detailing why Lynn was in Miami, and how it was needed. Then he said, "But Will is not The Believer." He'd assumed—hoped, that this water-bearer, the one born under the sign of Aquarius, would be a helper—The Believer. But he wasn't. "The true Believer is still out there," he added. But where?

"What do you mean, *the Believer*," Michael questioned when Gabriel finished.

Leading with a sigh Gabriel said, "It's all part of the change I made—my request. The Cipher, The Theologian, The Guardian, and The Believer, are there in my entry."

"We know about the Cipher—he's present," Raphael said, "Luc has been functioning as a Theologian, and our Charges know about his help with all the religious items. But I presume they don't know he is needed."

"Now they have to wait for both The Believer and The Guardian to show themselves," Gabriel added.

"But how would the others—let alone this child she gave up for adoption, ever find this information? Why did she hide everything—and why Miami?" Uriel asked. "That makes no sense to keep things so far out of reach."

Gabriel bowed his head, covering his face with both hands. Through muffled hands he said, "Armaros."

Vretil gasped.

Raphael's mouth hung open, though no sound escaped him.

Uriel rubbed his hands together as if cold.

"What?" Michael shot out, slamming his laptop shut, almost knocking it off his lap.

Gabriel let down his hands from his face. "I told My Chosen *not* to speak of things, as yours were instructed—only write what she'd been told, and what she'd discovered about the gathering."

"But?" Michael said. The others only nodded as they waited for more.

"But...," Gabriel started again, "... after many years of keeping the secret, my Charge told a friend—not all of it, only some, but she told her about the child. And because of this—this *telling*, she was diagnosed with breast cancer shortly after their first meeting."

Vretil gasped again, but the others remained stoic.

"The friend was a doctor who worked at the hospital in oncology and she helped her with treatment and beating the cancer," Gabriel added.

Vretil let out a sigh of relief.

Gabriel let his friend have that happy moment before going on. "But...," Gabriel said again, only to pause another moment.

"But?" Vretil questioned, his face going grim.

Gabriel took in a breath. "...when she completed her treatment...," he said, letting out the breath, "...it was then, during the time of her recovery... that Armaros visited her—using *magic*."

This time it was Uriel who gasped, magic being his domain, but then he remained silent, listening as Gabriel continued on once again clarifying the challenges Armaros had put in place for their four Charges.

"He had manipulated my Chosen with magic," Gabriel said, "He had done it in the past before, when the lines of two of your Charges were broken." He'd known—they'd all known, Armaros had spent his time trying to disrupt things, feeding ideas to the other leaders.

They'd been watching him, but not close enough. Armaros had found a loophole in the whole *you cannot show yourself or speak to humans* command, part of the 70-generation punishment. Gabriel had only fully comprehended it after his appearance outside Lynn's home, that the loophole meant Armaros had used illusion, veils, and other means as part of his communicating with humans. The other leaders would never risk attempting such a thing, but Armaros wanted power and dominion over the humans, and now he had other leaders in his corner.

"What illusion could she believe that would make her hide the information?" Vretil asked.

"A veil to appear as one of us," Michael deduced. "I'm right—aren't I, Gabriel?"

"Yes," Gabriel agreed, "He must have come to her in an illusion, appearing as me. Influencing her decision to both speak with the adoptive mother of her child and to revisit her friend the doctor... and further influencing her to write and hide any information."

"This further impacted her mortality," Michael added, stating the obvious.

Gabriel scowled and closed his eyes tight at Michael's words. "He made sure it was as far away as possible," Gabriel said. Like the others, Gabriel had told her to make the information available, such that her child could find it, but she'd done the near opposite when Armaros had instructed her with what to do.

"But how could he know who she was—your Chosen?" Vretil asked.

"He must have been watching, knew I'd been watching over her child. He couldn't have known *why* then—wouldn't have cared. He wanted to mess with things. But he knows—figured it out, figured it all out."

"How?" Uriel questioned.

"Armaros has been watching for your Charges descendants," Shamsiel said, appearing at Gabriel's side. "Waiting for the chance to mess with the generational lines."

Flanked with support now, Gabriel said, "How could he ignore the four of yours gathering, and *my* presence? He figured it out quite fast—saw that Lynn brought yours together. Now Armaros believes if he manipulates things again he can have what he's always wanted, the power to show *Him* that the 200's interference was not wrong—that *He* is wrong about the humans, that the humans do not deserve to be free, and it is *they* who should have been enslaved."

"Well, we're on to his plan now," Raphael said, shifting to stand near Michael. "He won't be getting near our Charges again."

"Not unless he wants a taste of my wrath!" Michael roared, standing now, wind kicking up around his feet.

Uriel and Vretil stepped forward to stand by Raphael and Michael, multiple winds swirling all around them.

"We've got this, Gabriel," Michael declared.

Gabriel was quiet, but Shamsiel stepped forward and turned to face him. Gabriel knew what was coming, saw the look on Shamsiel's face. He knew it was time to share the latest in the long list of challenges the Charges would have to face... what they all had to face.

"Gabriel," Shamsiel prompted.

Not that he needed it, but Gabriel took in a long slow breath.

"Gabriel?" Michael questioned. "What aren't you telling us now?"

Turning, Gabriel walked forward towards Michael. Gabriel knew he had kept much from them, and more he would continue to keep—but this, Shamsiel was right, they needed to know.

They'd known in the beginning this time may come, but they'd done whatever was in their power to keep it from happening. It was what had kept them dedicated since the beginning. They'd asked to prove to *Him* that humanity was worth saving. In response, *He* had agreed to their request. He had told them the price, should they fail... yet they'd still accepted it.

But they hadn't suspected the time to pay the price was drawing near. Gabriel stopped in front of his friend, and said, "The Horsemen... they're here."

Chapter 24

Luc left before I woke up.

Too much wine again for me. Hell, the whole evening's discussion had been too much for me. I'd been thankful we had talked little about my girlfriends and their new endeavor, but we had talked more about this *try* thing.

Dunya had explained, did her best to explain, what it meant to *try to feel* for those unseen. She'd said you had to clear your mind, be still and relax your body so you could reach out with your senses — not your eyes, and use your other sight.

It wasn't about the normal see-hear-smell, it was about that sensation or pressure you get at the base of your neck, or that tingle across the fine hairs of your arms. That heightened sensation in your nervous system telling you someone or something is near. The "knowing" she'd called it. She'd said, *"You know those feelings you often push aside — where you tell yourself they mean nothing, your usual Lynnie creepiness, you called it."* She'd told me to open myself up to my abilities, my, *"third eye"*. I'd questioned the whole third eye thing, but she'd explained it as being a spiritual yet esoteric concept, referring to it as, *"a speculative unseen eye which provided awareness beyond ordinary sight."* Mitra had told her it was, *'the gateway that leads to inner realms of higher consciousness'*. Not sure that part helped in clearing things up for me, but she had also said that *"in certain dharmic spiritual traditions such as Hinduism, it was referred to* as the *brow chakra"*.

I'd recollected Olivia talking to Mac about chakras and how they related to body parts and how this particular one related to the pineal gland near the center of the brain. I'd found it easier to grasp it was something *in* the body that perhaps turned on when you needed more clarity, or was that intuition feeling that most people ignored.

Dunya said she'd read up on it in her youth and found that in the context of New Age spirituality, the third eye often signified, a state of enlightenment or the suggestion of mental images having deep personal, spiritual, or psychological importance. She'd added that, *it* was often associated with religious visions, clairvoyance, the ability to see chakras, and precognition. People who could utilize their third eye, were sometimes known as oracles or seers like us, and how it sometimes related to out-of-body experiences or lapses in time people experience.

That part about *lapses in time*, had sparked curiosity in me and perhaps explained or had something to do with the time warps I'd been experiencing. I'd worried it was my brain, and now I knew it was. Not that I was ill or anything, just that my inner seer switch was trying to turn on. And as the night sky had grown darker, after more wine — much more, and after more discussion and a little personal silent reflection, though still skeptical, I had agreed to entertain *trying* to feel, to sense for our unseen visitor. *Yup*, I was going to try to sense this guy I'd actually seen, the one who was now apparently an angel who only let you see him when he wanted you to.

I was still a little fuzzy on the whole concept, but I had drunkenly agreed I would try. *When* I would try, I had made no promises on that part. But what I was feeling this morning had nothing to do with any unseen beings, it was a full-on wine queasiness hangover, yet I still made the brave effort to get up.

Raven was asleep in front of the en suite bathroom door, but he woke when I attempted to step over him.

Two glasses of water and two Advil later, my furry friend followed me as I was followed the aroma of fresh brewed coffee coming from the kitchen. The clock on the wall in the kitchen showed it was 10:30 a.m.. A half pot of coffee still warmed in its holder. Luc had left me hot coffee, which was the third element in the hangover trio cure.

I'd barely swallowed my first sip when the phone rang. The display screen showed it was my doctor calling, again. Second ring in I said, "Please tell me you aren't calling to tell me I'm dying—because I feel like it this morning."

"What?" Dr. Melanie said, a touch of panic in her voice.

"Sorry—hung-over is all, nothing to worry about—unless you have something to tell me I should worry about?"

"Gosh no! I was calling to see if you could come by this evening for the orientation—bring your friend. Most of our summer volunteers are gone now—mostly students gone back to school. Could use your help."

"I'm available for this evening, but I'll have to check with Darius on his schedule." This was exactly what I needed. Distraction and something other than mysteries and notions of angels to focus on. "What time—and where?"

She gave me all the details, and I ended the call telling her I'd check back with her on the availability of my big partner in crime. I finished my coffee and then sent a text to Darius to see if he was up for the hospital adventure this evening.

A lot less queasy now, I poked my face into the fridge to scavenge for leftovers. Dunya had kindly helped with moving the Thanksgiving goodness into separate containers for further enjoyment. That enjoyment would start right now. I loaded up a plate with a huge heaping of Mom's veggie casserole, along with mashed potatoes and stuffing, and then put it in the microwave. I'd keep the nice slice of turkey I'd chosen off to the side. As a leftover, I liked it better cold.

When the microwave *"Dinged"* ready-ready, I took the plate out and moved the cold turkey on to meet its hot companions. Then I grabbed up a knife, fork, and my cell phone and moseyed into the living room to chow-down and have a little TV time.

A response text from Darius came through just as I sat down. He'd texted saying, *"I'm in,"* meaning he would join me for orientation. I sent Dr. Melanie a quick text confirmation there'd be two of us this evening.

I was thrilled I wouldn't be going alone, but for now I'd enjoy my time alone on the couch binge-watching the Food Network.

I got comfortable, stretching out on the couch and throwing a blanket over my legs. The blanket was one of my mother's. It was the one a friend had made for her during Mom's cancer treatments. I liked having it on the couch with me for those times when I needed to feel close to her, needed warmth and comfort.

It worked. Two TV shows in, the comfort I sought blanketed me, and I faded out to sleep.

Gabriel and Shamsiel sat across on the smaller couch.

"How did it go?" Shamsiel asked. He'd left the others before the last part was clarified. Hadn't wanted to be there when Gabriel explained the latest hiccup in this whole venture.

"It went," was all Gabriel gave him in return.

"Well, while you were off explaining yourself to the others last night, I was here listening in on the conversation she was having with the neighbors and The Theologian."

"And?"

"They told her they believe. That they think angels are real."

"Is that all," Gabriel commented, low in enthusiasm.

"And… that she needs to *try* to see those who are unseen," Shamsiel added.

"Yes!"

Startled awake I sat up only to realize that the afternoon had gotten away from me. It was dark except for the TV that flickered in the corner. The streetlights were coming on though Luc hadn't come home yet.

Hitting the guide button on the TV remote, the time showed 6:15 p.m.. That's when I noticed a note on the coffee table from Luc. He must have come home while I was sleeping and chosen not to wake me. The note said he'd be over at—where else, Dunya's place for dinner. I'd needed the sleep, but I wished Luc had woken me.

I only had 45 minutes to get ready before Darius would be here to pick me up to go to the hospital. But being low maintenance, I was ready in 30 minutes. Even had time to heat and eat more leftovers in time before I heard the honk of Darius's car in the driveway.

"Goodbye, Raven," I said, and was out the door.

On the drive I sat quietly as Darius shared the trials and tribulations of his day. I didn't miss working at the office one bit and definitely didn't miss dealing with drama, but I *was* looking forward to being at the children's hospital with him, contributing and hopefully making a difference in the lives of these sick kids.

Dr. Melanie had messaged me back while I was crashed on the couch. She'd stated we should park in the employee parking area and that all we needed was to give our names to the evening guard when we arrived.

As instructed, we gave the guard our names, then he pointed us in the direction of the parking space in the back far left corner of the lot. I guess volunteers got the crappy spots while the doctors got the ones closest to the doors. Made sense, but it would have been nicer not to walk what felt like the stretch of a football field to get to the door, or the fact that the wind was kicking up and showing signs of impending weather on the way.

We found Dr. Melanie inside the employee entrance, talking on her cell phone. She waved when she saw me and hung up as we got closer. "Good you're here. The other volunteers cancelled—worried about the storm," she said, maneuvering her clipboard and sliding her cell into her lab coat pocket.

"It's just us?" I questioned, staring back at her. Then I glanced up at Darius. He shrugged and gave me a smile.

"Yer it, my friend—need you both till eleven," she said, and stuck out her free hand to Darius.

He reached out a big meaty hand and wrapped it around her waiting one and shook it, then he nodded.

"Thanks for coming...," she said, glimpsing down at the huge hand shaking hers, "...can use all the *big* hands we can get." She shook his hand again and he smiled once more. "Follow me," she added, letting go then.

As we followed Dr. Melanie through the halls to the employee area, she gave us the lay of the land. She explained that the family areas and kids play areas, physio and the cafeteria, were on the main floor. The halls had lots of large bright windows with decent views. Murals with animals and cheery pictures covered the walls. She told us the wards had playrooms on each floor filled with books, DVDs, electronic games, and a kitchen for families to make tea and coffee, and even a piece of toast if they wanted. She mentioned that *child-life specialists* work in the playrooms helping the kids and families forget why they are here. I liked that part. "Our clown Molly Penny walks the halls, pulling tricks on the kids, telling them jokes and blowing bubbles. She is amazing," Dr. Melanie said.

The second floor holds the operating rooms, MRI, x-ray areas, special treatment areas, and the oncology ward. The second floor was also where the least mobile patients were and where Darius would be needed most. The third floor was for patients who were there for long-term care. It also held the NICU, a neonatal intensive care unit also known as an intensive care nursery. Here they specialized in the care of ill or premature newborn babies, and I was told this was also the floor where I would spend most of my time.

When we passed through from the employee area to the main hospital, the security guard stopped us to make ID tags with photos and our names, as part of the volunteer process. He gave us detailed maps of the floors along with a simpler one of the whole hospital. After that, Dr. Melanie explained the stats on the kids who would be *under our charge* so to speak. Then it was time to take the elevator up to meet them.

I was nervous as I stepped into the elevator, but then a wave of calmness came over me. Strange, though there was only the three of us and plenty of room, a sudden sense of being crowded, pressed against me.

Gabriel and Shamsiel road up in the elevator—not that they needed to, but purely for the fun of it. They'd visited the children's hospital before and though they loved visiting with the little ones, they detested that so many suffered. They did their utmost to ease the pains and discomforts as best they could, but they couldn't cure them.

Gabriel was fond of visiting the special nursery, as he liked the soft sounds of the new lives as they slept. He often eased those who cried out, aiding them back to sleep. Shamsiel was fascinated by the science of humankind, how far they had come and the miracles the medical community continued to make. They both liked the *hope* that these advances gave the children and their families.

Once on the second floor, Dr. Melanie brought us to the ward which housed the patients who were undergoing cancer treatments. She told us the hospital prefers to keep kids dealing with similar issues together. Keeps them from feeling like they're the only ones going through it. Also, they tended to be the weakest kids on the floor and hence the need for Darius who could easily lift and move these tiny patients from area to area when needed.

Dr. Melanie explained, "Nighttime is the roughest for them. Treatments are done during the morning followed by visits from family, and the kids often fall asleep after. But they are alone at night and are often unable to sleep. It isn't always about the need for sleeping at night, sometimes they just want someone to play with or talk with, and depending on their condition—someone to help them shift in their beds to avoid bed sores. Or worse, needing someone to help them lean forward to simply throw up."

"I've got a strong gag reflex and the throwing up and bodily fluids thing doesn't faze me," Darius said, to Dr. Melanie's delight.

I on the other hand, had a weaker constitution, just the sound of someone throwing up made me gag, so I was cool with helping on the third floor.

Before heading up, Melanie and I watched as the nurse took Darius into the room of a little girl. Six-year-old Jennifer who was being treated for cancer, that had taken not only her hair but both her legs from the knee down. A nasty kind of bone cancer I'd failed to mentally record when the nurse had said the name. Despite being ill, the little girl sat up at once when she saw Darius come into the room.

In a squeak of a voice, she said, "Fee-Fi-Fo-Fum!"

Darius quick with his response said, "I smell strawberries—want to eat some?"

The little girl giggled with delight, and said, "No-no—it's, I smell the blood of an englishmun."

Quick again, he said, "Eww gross—who wants to eat that?" Even the nurse laughed this time. Then the little girl reached out for Darius like she'd been expecting him, arms wide for a hug.

Stepping up Darius leaned down and let her wrap her tiny arms around one of his. Then he encircled his other arm around her back to cradle her. She released her arms and leaned back into his. As he lowered her to the pillows, she wrapped a tiny hand around his pinky finger.

"Time for your new tests," the nurse said, unhooking the IV bag from the machine it'd been hanging on. Then she hooked it to the travel catch of the pole on the hospital bed.

"Yer coming, aren't you my prince?" little Jenny asked.

Darius glanced over at Dr. Melanie.

She nodded, *yes.*

At the okay, Darius responded, "Yes mi-lady. At your service."

Jenny giggled some more, holding tight to his finger.

The nurse glanced over to where we were standing, and I saw Dr. Melanie give her the nod too, giving the go-ahead to let Darius accompany them. With this, the nurse then instructed Darius on how to unlock the brakes of the bed on his side. He did so all the while letting Jenny keep her little steel grip on his finger.

As they moved out of the room, Dr. Melanie gave the nurse additional instructions to pass along to Darius. "Let him know to meet us at the third-floor nurses' station once you're finished with the tests. Or at least when he can get away and out of the clutches of Jenny."

"Will do," she said. Then the nurse, the prince, and his princess rolled out into the hall.

Once they were down the hall from us, Dr. Melanie said, "Jenny's parents are never here—never visit. They're assholes who spend their free time doing drugs. And because of it, she's now a ward of the state."

"What?" I didn't know what else to say, and just shook my head in shock.

"Once she lost her legs, the parents had said, '*It got to be too hard on us*'—meaning them, and they stopped coming to see her. Their last visit they'd been higher than a kite and had to be escorted out by security."

"Well, she has a bodyguard now," I said, hoping for some light in the situation.

"Jenny tells everyone they're on a trip and very busy visiting with princes and princesses in different countries, and that she has to stay strong while they are away. She doesn't understand where they went, but she *does* understand she won't be going home with them again."

"Probably better that she's here with people who care about her," I said. Just because you give birth to a child doesn't mean you're the best person to care for them.

Surprisingly, Dr. Melanie smiled then. "This is the first time I've seen her happy in a long time. I think your gentle giant will be good for her. Looks like he's comfortable in the role of guardian prince."

There was that word again—*guardian*. "Yes, he is. She's in good hands—literally," I said, watching them roll around the corner and out of sight.

At the word guardian, Shamsiel nodded and followed alongside the rolling bed, curious to hear about these *new* tests this little one was having done. But before turning the corner, he shot a quick glance back over his shoulder.

His senses were on high alert though it was difficult to distinguish *who* was wondering about in a place like this. Angels often frequented children's hospitals and unfortunately *Death* was a regular visitor as well. There was... *something*... powerful, and comparable to the strength of the four he'd sensed outside the restaurant in Ottawa, but still lesser so, and it was a relief of sorts. Still, he kept his awareness sharp as he continued down the hall with the prince and princess.

Gabriel not needing to take the elevator, disappeared heading for the NICU.

"Okay, missy—your turn," Dr. Melanie tossed out as she turned and headed back to the elevator.

Chapter 25

There was a slight pressure at the back of my neck and shoulders, coupled with a bout of queasiness as the elevator doors closed. Though the feeling was subtle, it was there like a threat or menace of something to come. I didn't much care for it and it made the tiny hairs on my arm feel like static cling. It no longer felt crowded in the elevator, but a sense of uneasiness rode up with us to my assigned floor. The elevator doors opened then, and I got my first glimpse of the ward.

The walls were beige, not white like the floors below, but there was much more to look at. I stepped out of the elevator and surveyed all the photographs. Photos of past patients lined the service clerk's desk and ran along the physicians' desk. Moving forward past them, I spotted a room labeled *parent quiet room* as we headed down the hall to the NICU.

I rubbed my neck as we walked, listening to Dr. Melanie. "This floor has a social worker, transport nurses, nurse educator, and bedside nurses throughout the unit," she said. "This hallway leads to the unit for the transport team office and where all the transport isolettes are kept." She pointed as we passed their door. It was decorated with cartoon characters and fun pictures of all the team members.

The hallway leading to the double doors of the unit, had more photos of past patients both survivors and those who had passed, along with letters written from the families thanking the wonderful nurses and physicians. There was a ton of light and lots of multi-coloured walls, and it didn't smell or feel like a hospital compared to an adult setting. It had a joyful feel about it, and despite the circumstances that most were there for sad reasons, the staff smiled at every child as they moved about, trying to brighten both the parents' and child's day.

At the end of the hall were cheerfully coloured double doors. The windows of the double doors to the NICU were covered with big coloured construction paper flowers. The flowers left only small corners of the windows free for anyone to see in. We passed through the bright coloured double doors and... that pressure I'd had across the back of my neck and shoulders, disappeared.

Gabriel stood just inside the doors to the NICU. He'd wanted a quick glimpse and listen in on the new babies.

The *special* unit was visible through large sliding glass doors on the far side. The doors made the same soft swishing sound as the doors on the *Star Trek Enterprise*.

At the nurses' desk, Dr. Melanie pointed out the video monitor for 2-month-old twin boys who had been placed in the same bassinet. "Rylie and Finn, your new charges," she said, picking up their chart.

"Two — twin boys?" was all I could manage in response.

"They've been with us since they were born," she said. "They both suffer from neonatal abstinence syndrome and are still suffering from some side effects." She added that these two little redheads had been orphaned but were in the final stages of adoption. "Their birthmother, a heroin addict — died while in treatment after their birth." She handed me their records.

I read the first line aloud, "Methadone-exposed twin male infants, by observation were found to exhibit increased motor rigidity, dyssssregulated motor patterns and decreased activity." I continued reading in my head to avoid further embarrassment in mispronunciation,

> These motor deficits may persist into toddlerhood and be associated with less social responsivity, shorter attention spans, and poorer social engagement.

I stopped reading to look up at Dr. Melanie. She nodded when she saw my expression, the one that matched my confusion, anger, and the helplessness I was now suffering.

"Almost every drug passes from the mother's blood stream through the placenta to the fetus," she explained. "Drug dependence and addiction in the mother also causes the fetus to become addicted."

"How am I supposed to help them at this stage?" I questioned, confusion persisting and mixing with more helplessness.

"Well, at birth—for these babies, the dependence on the substance continued. But, since the drug is no longer being fed into them, their central nervous systems become over-stimulated causing withdrawal symptoms."

"Now what?" I asked. I'd seen once on one of those information TV news programs, how heroin and other opiates, including methadone, could cause significant withdrawal in a newborn, but I'd never known any kids dealing with it.

"Some symptoms can last as long as four to six months. It's the reason I have you here now."

"You're sure I can help?" I still wasn't tracking where she was going with this, nor what my role was.

"Yup. They need you—and you need them," she said, pointing again to the monitor. The smaller of the two was now experiencing some kind of shivering problem. "Hyperactive reflexes. He wakes his brother who also has sleep problems. They both suffer from tremors and seizures. What they need is to be held—and not just by each other."

I watched as the two were trying to cling to each other for comfort, but with the stress, irritability, and excessive crying, they weren't doing either of them any benefit. "I can totally do that," I said. At two months old they still resembled newborns, and cuddling them would be a huge privilege. I'd have been happier if it weren't under these circumstances, but I was eager to help, and this—I was confident I could manage.

"You'll need to help with feeding them too. They have issues with sucking on the bottles and get dehydrated if not managed properly. The nurses will show you how," she added, then waved a nurse over.

At Dr. Melanie's request, an average height middle-aged woman with short brown curly hair and kind eyes came over to us. She wore pale pink scrubs under a robe-like cover-up, made from super soft pink, yellow, and blue flower printed flannel. It was similar to the fabric I'd seen used for burping or swaddling cloth.

"This is Sarah, she's one of our angels here—she'll give you the how-to and get you a swaddling gown. Sarah—Lynn."

"Sarah—my mother's name was Sarah—but everyone called her Sally," I said, without thinking. My mother had been a nurse for almost 20 years once upon a time ago.

"Oh, only my grandmother calls me that," angel Sarah said, and then laughed. "Please to meet you, Lynn—glad you're here." She smiled and extended a gloved hand, pointing the way to a short stack of pink scrubs. "There's a changing area just outside the main doors, you'll find the swaddling robes there too." Her voice was sweet and musical in nature and would have been perfect for the narrating of children's books I thought.

"Thank you," I said. I nodded and then crossed the room to the waiting piles of scrubs. I grabbed a top and bottom in my size from the piles, and then I waved and smiled back at Dr. Melanie and nurse Sarah as I pushed through the paper flower-covered double doors.

The strange pressure I'd felt earlier, returned. Nerves again I guessed, and I continued off to the changing area.

Zaqiel was a frequent visitor to this hospital, and though he never rode the elevator, he chose to do so when he saw the doctor and her get on. Off the elevator, he'd gone to investigate Gabriel's actions. Moments ago, he'd spied on Gabriel as he leant over the side of the bassinette to caress those two small russet heads. Now he watched through a tiny opening in the flower-covered windows from outside the doors, merely listening as the tortured cries ceased. He dare not show himself to one of his own, not here—not now.

In the change room I swapped my jeans and t-shirt for the pale pink scrubs. I retied my running shoes, and then placed my clothes in one of the tiny lockers available, securing them in with a twist of the key. Each key for the lockers was affixed with a small diaper pin and I fastened mine to my nametag's lanyard. Near the exit was a fresh stack of swaddling robes and I grabbed one with a tag marked *medium*. I shook it out to open it and then slipped in my arms. I tucked my nametag in, crisscrossed the two front pieces, and then secured it closed on the left side with the attached ties.

The result was a smooth front finish. The sleeves of the robe were long and cuffed at the wrists, and it was soft and comfy to wear, and it made sense now why the robes were made of this fabric. Swaddling a baby who had tubes and monitor wires attached would be difficult to wrap in a blanket, but the sleeves and fronts of the gown would mimic that of a blanket without interfering with the medical paraphernalia. I smiled and checked myself in the mirror to make sure all was well and then I exited the room.

Three other nurses were with Sarah at their station near the sliding glass doors busily reviewing charts. I hadn't noticed before, but there was a large message board next to the glass doors that read;

> *Only medical personnel and staff beyond this point.*
> *Robes must be worn at all times.*

It made me wonder if I, like the parents, would need an escort into the nursery.

Nurse Sarah must have seen my hesitation, because she said, "Go ahead in, Lynn—use your pass. You can walk around, get familiar with the environment and I'll be in there in a minute."

"Okay," I said, reaching into my robe for my nametag. The pass part was on the backside of my nametag in the plastic carrier. Without taking it from around my neck, I leaned to swipe it over the pass reader next to the entrance. The doors star-trekked open, and I strode in.

The unit split into three pods. The pods were labeled, *Green*, *Yellow*, and *Blue*, and unlike a regular nursery with an assortment of small plastic bassinets filled with sleeping babies, the NICU contained rows of incubators or *isolettes* Dr. Melanie had called them, which looked like large clear plastic containers. Two of the areas had big windows, the third, Blue, did not. Earlier, on the monitor, the twins showed as being in the Blue area, so I headed past the barrier that divided the sections hoping to locate the boys.

There at the side of the bassinet to my soon to be charges, stood a tall blond man. I stopped to watch as he leant over the side, his arms reaching in. At first glance I thought perhaps he was a doctor or male nurse, but then noticed he wasn't wearing the proper robing, only a white shirt and pants.

He glanced up… and I froze. "You…. What are you doing here?" I questioned, recognizing his face. His expression was one of shock. No—more than shock—*fear*. And I understood, he wasn't supposed to be in there. "There's someone in the nursery," I shouted. Then I turned and ran back towards the sliding doors, through them and to the nurses' desk. "A man—I don't think he's supposed to be in there."

Nurse Sarah hit a button to open the doors again and then scooted around the side of the desk to follow me back into the room. Rounding the barrier, we found the bassinet with the twins… but no man. I turned back and wound myself through the other pods only to come up empty again. No man—nothing, nothing but sleeping babies.

"The boys are fine—are you sure you saw someone?" Sarah asked, turning and giving the thumbs up to those on the other side of the glass doors.

"Yes—there was a man in white standing over the boys' bassinet. I saw him—and he saw me."

"There's nobody here, Lynn," she said in a soothing voice, running a gentle hand up and down my arm.

"I know what I saw," I told her. *Great, she thinks I'm nuts.*

"Lynn, this room has a way of sometimes fooling the mind," Sarah said. "I know it sounds strange, but I swear I've heard voices—when I knew I was in here alone."

"It wasn't voices—I saw someone."

"Oh gosh, I believe you—I do," she said. "One of our long-time nurses, Nurse Luna, claims she's seen what she believes to be angels watching over the babies." She pointed at a grey-haired nurse coming through the sliding glass doors. The older nurse waved at us. "I find knowing this, makes the strange things we've all experienced here seem a little less peculiar, *and* a lot more calming when we think of it that way."

"Sure, okay," I gave her, but I knew what I saw. It was him—the man I'd seen on the street outside my house, the ones from my photo, the face I'd seen… or *had I dreamt that*? Maybe I was nuts.

"It's going to be a long night—why don't you go grab yourself a couple bottles of water and meet me back here. We'll go over caring for the twins then," Sarah added.

"Sure," I said again, "Sorry."

The elderly nurse, Luna, gave me a supportive smile as I crossed through the sliding doors in search of hydration.

Water bottles in hand, I headed back towards the long hall to the nursery. I stopped at the opening to a patient's room and then... *PAIN*. It clamped and twisted like a vise on my intestines and I dropped the water bottles. I bent clutching my stomach, then turned my head towards the open door.

A man stood next to the bed of the sick child. Darkness and shadows swirled around him and the child. Still bent over, I took a step forward and inadvertently kicked one of the water bottles sending it rolling down the hall. The man turned to look my way and another sharp twist of pain hit me. "I know you," I said, letting out a strangled breath. I'd never forget that face. The blips and bleeps of the child's monitors abruptly change to sounds of screaming alarms. He took a few steps in my direction.

"Again?" Shamsiel asked. He'd been watching over Darius and Jenny after her tests.

"I was alone and wanted the babies to see me—ease their cries," Gabriel explained. "I let my veil down for one second and there she was."

"Wait," Shamsiel said, turning to face the long stretch of hallway.

"What is it?"

"I sensed something earlier—*someone*... and they're back."

"Hear that? The monitors—they're going off near the nursery," Gabriel said.

Disappearing then, the two of them changed locations to the hall near the NICU.

I pushed to straighten, taking off in a strained run towards the nurses' station, but the nurses were already on their way up the hall towards me—towards the child's room. I chanced a glance back and saw the shape of that huge man emerge from the room and come my way. I turned forward just as two nurses rushed past me and I stumbled.

Down to one knee I dropped, my hands going out in front to brace my fall. A loud "*SMACK*" echoed as my palms made contact with the floor. Then that water bottle I'd previously kicked, rolled leisurely by my hand. Knee and hands stinging, I turned back to glance over my shoulder to see the nurses round the doorway into the room... but *he* was gone. I turned forward again.

There he was, about ten paces in front, standing between me and the doors to the nursery.

Gabriel took a step forward, but Shamsiel grabbed his arm. "No—wait," he said, "watch her." Neither of them moved.

I took a quick glance to the left. No one was at the nurses' station. I tried to stand but could only manage to look up. I knew I recognized him. It was the tall one from the restaurant, the largest of the four, the one with the short platinum blond Billy Idol haircut.

He stared back at me and those eyes, lurid, laser, bore a hole once again into me—into my soul. Nausea hit me so fast this time I dropped to both knees, one hand clutching my stomach the other making contact with the floor in another resonating "*SMACK*". I dropped my head and one lone bead of sweat trailed from my forehead to escape, hitting the floor next to my hand. "What is this?" I gasped out. Through a wave of nausea, I strained to glance up again.

He'd begun an unhurried stride towards me as if in slow motion, each step measured. The movement caused my vision to blur, and I dropped my head. The floor spun, and I had to close my eyes to keep from puking. I forced myself to take in a long steady breath, letting it out, and then taking in another, and then... something inside me shifted.

The coolness from the floor's surface radiated from my palms up my arms and into my chest, calming me. I took another deep breath in and the pain disappeared, the queasiness dissolving into nothing but a memory as I let the breath out. Gathering my strength, yet still on my knees, I looked up again.

He was still coming.

I closed my eyes.

Using everything I had, I threw up my hands. "Noooooooo!" I yelled, sending the word and my strength towards the approaching man. On my next breath in, the shrieking monitor alarms stopped, no longer bellowing through the hallway.

I opened my eyes again.

The screeching alarms weren't the only things gone… so was he.

"Lynn—you okay?" came a familiar voice from behind me. I turned my head to see Darius standing there. He had my other water bottle in his hand but based on his stance, he looked like he was ready to fight someone. "Where did he go?" he asked, bending to help me to my feet.

"You saw him?" I said, snagging the other water bottle from the floor on the way up.

"Ya, the huge guy," he said, pointing out in front of me. "I'm big but this guy was massive."

"Uhm, I'm not sure," I said. I wasn't sure where he'd gone or what the hell had just happened. "What are you doing here?" I asked through my confusion.

"You wouldn't believe me if I told you," he said, his expression like that of a little boy with a secret.

"Try me," I said. No need to keep secrets from me, I was full of them.

Darius cracked his knuckles and let out a long sigh. "Well… remember that day on the road—when I grabbed ya?"

"How could I forget, you saved my life."

"Well—it was like that." He paused.

Okay, I didn't need any riddles, not today—hopefully never. "Not sure I'm following," I told him.

Darius let out another sigh filled breath. "Something… something told me…." He sucked in another breath. "Something told me you were in danger." He let out the breath and sucked in another. "I needed to find ya. I came around the corner—saw you kneeling on the floor and that big guy walking towards you."

"And what—what were you going to do?" I asked.

Just then one of the young nurses passed by. "Hiii Darius," she said, poking him in the side. He blushed, even his scalp went pink. I could see it through his shortcut strawberry-blond hair. He managed a wave to the cute nurse but failed to get any words out.

"Pffff nice," I said, and poked him like the nurse had just done.

"Give me a break," he said, blushing deeper.

I smiled. I liked that the young nurses were giving him lots of attention, between work and the gym, he spent too much time *not* socializing.

"What happened—who was that guy?" he asked.

"Not sure—but he's gone now," I said. It wasn't a lie—I didn't know who he was, but I *had* seen him before. Not sure Darius would believe *me* if I told him where I'd seen him. It made little sense the guy was here. Or I didn't understand the why of it—why I'd seen him in Ottawa and again here. What about that other man I saw earlier in the nursery—or didn't see, or whatever? And what did Darius mean by *'something told me'*?

"You okay? I gotta head back to check on my Jenny," he said, giving me the once-over like he was checking for damages.

"Ya, I'm good—go check on your princess," I said. But I wasn't good. I'd forgotten what good felt like, and this shit—this disappearing stranger crap, was pushing me over the insanity edge. And other than thankful the pain was gone, I wasn't sure how I was feeling.

"Okay," he said, squeezing my shoulders with his big hands. Then he patted me where he'd squeezed, before turning to leave.

I watched as he waved to the cutie at the nurses' station and then strolled up the hall. He moved much like the other guy with those slow lengthy calculated strides of his. Must be a big-man thing. No one at the nurses' station seemed concerned about me, so I headed for the NICU's entrance.

Shamsiel and Gabriel watched as Darius continued back down the hall. Then they turned to watch as the NICU door swooshed open and closed.

"She... she did it," Gabriel said, eyes still fixed on the sliding glass door.

"Yes... she... did," Shamsiel added. He patted his friend on the back as they both continued to stare at the entrance to the nursery.

Through the doors I spotted Sarah and one of the other nurses fiddling with what they had told me were the *spare* monitors.

"Something is up with the heart monitor," Sarah said. "We're trying to swap them out with these." She turned back and gathered up the cords.

I could hear the too-fast beeping of the monitors from the different pods and one coming from the direction of the twins. "He's back," I said under my breath, then moved passed the nurses and spare monitors. I rounded the pod divider to the boys... but no one was there, only the babies and their rapidly beeping monitors. I approached the bassinette... and the beeping slowed. All the beeping noise slowed then, and sighs of relief came from the nurses on the other side of the partition. I peered into the bin.

The two were sound asleep, russet heads touching ever so slightly. I watched as the one with the wrist tag marked, *Finn*, shuddered. Almost instantly, though still asleep, the other, *Rylie*, reached out a tiny hand to touch his brother. The shuddering stopped. It was sweet yet sad to witness. I chose to stay by their bedside and not venture out of the nursery again for the rest of my shift.

The rest of the evening in the nursery was calm despite the storm outside. While Rylie and Finn slept, I meandered through the green and yellow areas of the NICU. I stopped to watch different nurses attend to the tiny patients. Each time I approached, the heightened beeping monitors seemed to slow and level out, and the discomfort the babies were experiencing seemed to lessen, as did the anguished expressions on the faces of the nurses.

"You appear to have a calming effect on these little ones," one of them said as she adjusted the feeding tube of a now sleeping baby girl. "Can you hold her while I change out her bedding?"

"Sure—yes," I said as she handed me the fragile infant who donned a pink toque. She barely weighed a thing. "Wow—so tiny," I whispered.

The nurse nodded and smiled. "It's not usually this quiet in here," she said. "And it's nice to have the extra help. Thank you."

It was my turn to smile. "I was nervous—at first," I said, "but I'm finding I really like it—didn't know I would. Didn't know I'd be working with such... *small* patients."

"Not too many people get to volunteer in here, but I see why Dr. Melanie put you with us," the nurse said, then she motioned for me to put the baby back in the isolette.

Why had Dr. Melanie put me here I wondered, as I placed the baby on the new bedding. My face must have given away my ponderings because the nurse said, "You have a way about you, Lynn. Peaceful. The babies sense it."

"Peaceful?" I questioned. Not sure I'd ever identified as peaceful before.

"Safe maybe is more like it," she corrected. "It's something—hard to explain, but from the minute you started your shift, we all felt it." She made a circle motion with her hand as if encompassing the rest of the unit.

"Well...," I started. "... if my being here helps in *any* way, I'm glad too for that."

She smiled again and gave my arm a quick rub before moving on to the next tiny patient.

I continued to move on through the rows, helping where I could and learning something new from each of the nurses. Just before the shift ended, I'd gotten word from Dr. Melanie that she wanted me to come back on Friday night, that it would be my new night for the same shift, but I was to come in Thursday morning to go over some paperwork for my role, etc.

At 11 p.m. our shifts ended, and Darius and I dropped off our scrubs and then checked out.

Darius talked the whole way as we drove, and I was good with that. Apparently, Dr. Melanie had already spoken to Darius about the forms and she had asked if he was available to work this coming Friday night as well. He told me all about the tests he'd seen and about his new charge, Jenny. Said it felt good to help, to see the little girl happy under such crappy circumstances, and that he liked being the reason she felt happy and safe. I nodded and smiled letting him go on for the length of the drive, and I was glad the subject of the big man didn't come up because I had more questions than answers to give him.

When he pulled into the driveway, I thanked him for the lift and got out of the car. I gave him the peace-sign. He waved a big hand out the window as he drove away.

The storm had stopped sometime during the night, but there were leaves, and small branches scattered around the front yard. I would tend to them in the morning, but right now I needed some solace and a little safety of my own. I was exhausted, but not from the volunteer work. It had taken no energy to watch over, cuddle, or feed the twins. It had been peaceful and gratifying, and like Darius had said, it felt good to help. The exhaustion had come from trying *not* to think about the bizarre stuff that had happened.

And now, in my bed, it was all I could think about. That sensation, the pain. Then strength. After it was the awareness of calm. The calmness that came when I searched for relief, when I'd pulled in strength and pushed back fear. It had been a peacefulness I'd experience as I tended to the babies. It had felt amazing then.

In fact, I felt amazing right now, so amazing I sat up in bed. I was *feeling*... something... or *someone* perchance.

"Are you there?" I whispered. I put my hands out but felt nothing—nothing but the air that swirled from the ceiling fan. I couldn't see anything either, well, nothing other than Raven, he too was sitting up. He, along with the foot of my bed, were bathed in the moonlight that shown through the window. I'd forgotten to close the blinds, *again*.

"Yes, I'm here... you sense me... try to see me—try harder," Gabriel whispered back from behind his veil.

Still nothing, I pushed harder, *trying* as Dunya had said... trying to see... then I called out into the night. "Shamsiel?"

Chapter 26

Wednesday morning… and feeling foolish for my pathetic attempt at *trying* to see what I thought I'd felt. I thought for sure I'd sensed something, but perhaps it was the aftermath of the night's craziness. *Or not.* But I wouldn't be telling Dunya about it anytime soon.

I grabbed my cell phone off the bedside table and padded off through the living room towards the kitchen. I stopped short to stare out the back-patio doors, then I took a few steps closer.

From the living room, the view out the back patio showed a disaster of broken and fallen tree branches. Several of the Live Oaks had sustained damage from the storm and more than a few of their appendages were scattered throughout the yard. The pool too suffered, blanketed with leaves and debris.

"Oh great," I said. After seeing the front yard I'd expected an easy cleanup today, but not this mess. "Those poor trees."

Raven, "*Woofed,*" and put his nose to the sliding door.

"Okay, buddy," I told my anxious friend. "Watch yourself—and try to avoid doing your business on any of the downed branches—would ya?" I shut the sliding door. "I need coffee," I said aloud to no one since my conversation partner was busy outside navigating the obstacle course of wreckage. I sent Darius a quick text, asking him if he could come over after work today instead of Friday. Then I continued on my way to the kitchen.

No coffee brewed in the kitchen. I was up later than normal, but still there were no sounds of Luc in the house. There were no signs he'd made himself breakfast either. I still needed coffee.

I filled up the coffee maker and then I strode to the living room's front window to see if Luc's car was in the drive. No Luc, no car. He must have spent the night at Dunya's place and left from there. When I turned back to the kitchen, I saw a large manila envelope on the front entry table. Luc must have put it there, but I hadn't noticed it when I'd come in late last night. I picked it up.

It had big colourful stamps in the corner and the envelope was addressed to me. I inspected the stamps, then flipped it over. I knew who had sent it. *Will*. The backside had the logo for his company as he must have used their stationary to send it. Reluctant, I tore it open.

Inside were travel vouchers, 50 of them, labeled, *Anywhere South Jet Goes*. There was a note attached, written by him. Seemed he'd earned them from all his travels but couldn't use them, now that he was in Asia.

He wrote;

> There are 50 return flights in here and they're yours if you want them. For you to visit your friends and family, to travel.
> See the world, Lynn.

That was all he wrote.

But I shouldn't have expected anything else, he was all about the travel wasn't he. Envelope and vouchers in hand, I wandered back to the kitchen.

The coffee maker gurgled its wonderful *I'm done* sound and then a "*Scratch-Scratch*" came from the living room. I peeked my head out and around the kitchen's opening to see that Raven was back and communicating that he was done too.

"My conversation partner is back," I said, as I slid the door open. He passed a cold nose across my outstretch hand, then padded to the kitchen. "I take it you're hungry too, eh?"

Water now topped up and kibble in my furry buddy's bowls, I made myself comfortable on one of the bar stools at the island.

Sipping my delicious coffee, I stared at the stack of vouchers.

A flash of memories zoomed across my brain, then halted at the memory of Will's mother. Why had she tried to get us together, keep us in touch? Why, when things didn't work out in the end? What was the purpose of her anguish near the end of her life over something as useless as the two of us being together? I loved her for trying, loved him, but it wasn't meant to be. Made me wonder if *meant to be* was even a thing. Could be it was just something someone coined because they had nothing else helpful to say to someone who was sad. Do things really *happen for a reason,* or are we in control of our fate? Who knows? I didn't. But as fate would have it, I was apparently supposed to travel more.

My cell phone chimed a familiar sound indicating a text, one from Darius. The message read;

I'll swing by after work, before I head to the gym. Cool?

I texted him back saying, *Cool—thank you.* I'd take whatever time he offered. Then I got dressed and headed outside.

I spent the rest of the morning and the better part of the afternoon gathering up the smaller branches and raking up the debris. Raven stayed out of my way, watching me from the sidelines, chewing on a toy that squeaked if he got it just right, and he seemed to like that.

The leaves in the pool were in thick layers and I could only scoop out a small portion at a time. If I shoveled in more, I'd end up bending the skimmer from the weight of the wet foliage.

Done now with what I could manage on my own, Raven and I finally returned inside.

Food. I hadn't eaten breakfast or lunch and that was not like me. Even with all the exertion with the yard work I still wasn't hungry, but I grabbed myself something anyhow, more coffee and a few leftover homemade cookies. Then I moved to the living room and booted up my laptop. I hadn't checked it for emails today either, again not like me. I hit the envelope icon to open my email and a few friendly emails popped in.

One was from Louise and I opened it first.

She wrote;

Hi love, Andre told me what happened. So sorry. You doing okay?

That Will, I just don't understand him. Why couldn't he take his beautiful wife with him on this adventure? Did things have to end just because he got a job on the other side of the world?

I know, too many questions. I hope you are okay, and I'm sorry I haven't been in contact. Stupid cancer treatments are like a fulltime job I hate and can't quit. Half the time I don't even know what day it is. Wish I could at least get fired from this job for that. Humor, it's all I have at the moment, but today's one of my better days. If you have time, call me.

Sending you love and a big hug, my friend.

Louise

The *sent* time on the email showed it was only 15 minutes ago. I took advantage she might still have some energy and made the call.

Andre answered. "She's up and *yes*, it is one of her better days," he said, "*and* she'd love to chat." He gave her the phone.

"Lynn, you okay?" was the first thing out of her mouth.

"Yes—fine, good actually. It's all fine." Then I told her what I'd told the girls. How it wasn't a complete shock despite how hard it had been. I explained about the offer his company had made, how I could have gotten a spousal visa to be with him yet not be able to work, but he'd still be traveling. Told her he'd been overjoyed about the opportunity, but it was the last thing I wanted to do, and that I'd told him I wasn't going. The opportunity was great for him, but he wouldn't force me to go. "It was hard enough moving here and being away from my family and friends," I ended.

"You've been left home alone too much," she agreed.

"Even when he was home—he wasn't, you know? Work has always been his first priority. He'd admitted it. And I'd let my feelings on it take a backseat."

"Did you ask him to stay—turn it down?" Louise asked, but she knew I couldn't make him stay, wouldn't make him.

"I loved him. He loved me too—just not as much as his job. I don't want to compete with that anymore." I let out a long-exhausted sigh.

Louise knew he and I had been friends a long time, and I explained that we were still friends, but we'd failed at being husband and wife. I wasn't thrilled about reliving this whole topic with her, but she needed to understand like the others. I also didn't want her to worry about me.

I wanted her focus to be on her job of getting better and kicking cancer's butt.

"Thought you two were fated."

"Well…," I said, but she cut me off.

"Joan had thought so. She had been adamant about it remember? I still wonder about the urgency she'd felt," Louise said.

"We shouldn't talk about it." Was she sick because we talked about it? "Joan said—not to—maybe that's what made you sick," I managed, but she cut me off again.

"Oh, I don't believe that. Don't be silly—I'm sick, because I am—because some spontaneous cells chose to rebel," she said. That comment reminded me of what my aunt told my mother, how they were sick because *they were* and nothing more.

"I told Andre… about Joan—what she'd said about you and Will, and about that man visiting her. Gabriel."

"You told him?" What had she done?

"He thinks we're nuts for even entertaining it. Maybe it *was* the meds Joan was taking. God knows I have my own bouts of delirium with my own meds. Last night I could have sworn that singer, Billy— what's his name—Idol was standing over my bed. Mind you he was much bigger and better looking and there was no singing involved. Not much of anything involved—just him standing over me, watching… must have been a dream."

"Wait—what?" Some big Billy Idol looking dude was in her room—standing over her bed?

"Oh ya," she said, then she went on further to describe the *big man*.

"You think you dreamt this?" How could she have dreamt or seen the guy I saw?

"I've had a few other doozies lately, *and* why I think Joan may have been hallucinating."

I wasn't so sure on that, but then I was more confused than anything lately. "Didn't she say this man came to her before she got sick?" I reminded.

"Things hadn't been all that clear for her near the end, Lynn. False memories perhaps, part of the delusions," she said as if trying to assure me.

I knew Joan's story made sense when you had all the other pieces. Still, I wasn't prepared to tell her what I—or should I say *they* have uncovered. I feared her illness may have been because of this stuff and the fact we talked about it. I couldn't be sure it wasn't. She'd shared it with me even after Joan warned her. And now… she'd told Andre. He'd be the last person to repeat a story like that but that's two people she'd told now. Was there something out in the unseen, something powerful enough to make people sick by talking about it? I hoped it was more story than fact, myth and mystery—fear based and the power of the mind, but I couldn't risk telling her the rest… I wouldn't risk her life.

"This old gal is fading, I'm sorry to say," she said, cutting my pondering short.

"I'm glad you were up for a chat," I said, wishing I could reach through the phone and hug her. I hadn't expected she'd mention Joan, and I hadn't imagined she'd be telling me about Mr. big tall and blond either. She ended the call confirming she'd try to chat later next week when she had another good day, and that she loved me. "Love you too," I told her and then hung up.

"Perhaps she's right, and it was just rebellious cells, cancer," I said aloud to Raven. "Every time I turn around someone I know has it. Can't watch the entertainment TV shows without hearing someone famous has it."

Raven, "*Chuffed,*" and then stretched out at my feet.

I hoped this part of the story wasn't true, and was just the power of suggestion, that only if you believed it, you could make yourself sick. I'd made myself sick by worrying over the possibility of being sick. And I wasn't really sick, only run down and rightly so, Dr. Melanie had said. And it was hard to disregard with the impact something like this mystery could have on you.

The other parts of the story were more believable. I understood the facts of the matriarchal line. My friends, from what they are assuming, are part of a lineage of women from before the birth of Christ. Was it possible? I liked the idea of angels being involved, but I struggled to believe they influenced things. I wanted to believe it was just human nature, a mother's nature to protect her offspring from harm, and to carry on traditions. Like Derek had told us, there were tons of secret societies out there, mostly male mind you, but it could be similar. These strange things—are just that, a strange mystery. And the deaths of these women, like my mom and Aunt Kay, must fall somewhere under one of life's coincidences.

Maybe Louise had the answer to the question. Had the cancer meds caused hallucinating effects on my birthmother, and it being why she had felt the need to write stuff down about my birth or whatever? Had the story she'd told my mom influenced my mother into thinking this secret had somehow caused her illness, her sister's illness? Perhaps she too had been lost in her own delusions.

I believe you can make yourself sick or sicker if you think what you're doing will harm you. No one ever wants to get cancer or any other illness and no one *chooses* to die—but if you think something will kill you, you may seal your own doom. Fear is a powerful emotion, it can take on a life of its own, make people do things or avoid things depending on the perceived outcome. There's power in our thoughts, positive or negative, I guess. I also think a person's fear can amplify if they're under strain or stress of medical treatments and medications.

"I believe in the power of the mind and of things unseen," I said to Raven. I'm not ignoring the idea that there's magic in the world—on the contrary, I believe in magic. Raven touched my foot with his cold wet nose. "With all the weird stuff I've seen and felt, I'd have a hard time ignoring it—hard as I might try. I've pointed out to my friends the unseen powers around us. I've felt them all my life, but a part of me— the rational part, worries about getting caught up in the possibility of this mystery and its power," I added as if Raven understood what I was saying. I wasn't sure I understood what I was saying.

There are reports and stories of unexplained events that span decades and even centuries but when one is presented with the idea that *you* may be part of something like that, the doubt seems to seep in. It's the old *that would never happen to me* fail, where you believe from a distance yet when you're in it, you struggle with it.

Another conundrum.

This whole experience, with its small steps and puzzle solutions, I feel wasn't meant for the world to know about. It's supposed to be a secret, had always been. I was happy to keep it that way, but there was another challenge here in this mystery. Could I let myself believe angels were once on earth, that they'd influenced the evolution of the earth because of their personal involvement, that God—whatever he-she-it is, punished these beings for their involvement? And these four angels, the archangels—did they exist, and had they taken it upon themselves to shift or fix the imbalance that their brethren caused, hoping to save humanity? Why, because they loved us even when their boss's love waned?

A leap—huge leap. But the world was a pretty off-balance place, how could we know if the secrets and traditions of the original four women have impacted humanity. Or was it just a lost story that is now being uncovered by the last in the line? Was what they were doing as a united group, going to have any impact? What impact, and was one needed? I had no idea, but it wasn't my concern, not anymore.

Or was it?

Was my role to get the four together? Why was it my role? Did the women in my world, my mother and aunt sacrifice themselves, so I could help these four women? Why, for what purpose? For some damn secret, a centuries old tradition… the belief that four women somehow kept the balance on earth? Really?

If Joan's story was real, then *why* did Will and I need to reunite? Not like Will had any influence on how I met Vicki. I could have even known her sooner with her living down the street from Mom. I'd lost contact with Alison and Mac, but he'd had no bearing on me reconnecting with them. I could have known Olivia sooner too since we had worked at the same company. And nothing other than my feelings for Will, had influenced my coming here to Miami. Was it another coincidence I live here now, that my birthmother had come to Miami before she died? Could be. Must be.

"I think my brain might explode, Raven." He tickled my foot again and let out a doggie sigh.

My thoughts shifted to Louise's words and the images from last night at the hospital, coupled with the memory of Darius saying, "*Something told me you were in danger.*" Derek's email with the girls had mentioned things about a guardian, and I was considering now that

Luc was right. Darius fit the description, and he'd come to my aid last night—albeit a moment too late, but he'd been ready to fight—or defend as it were.

"Maybe I should email the girls—tell them what Luc and I had discussed. Couldn't hurt—might even help them out," I said, aloud to my foot tickler. Raven once again had been resting quietly at my feet, during both my call with Louise and my internal rant. I thought I'd convinced myself that I was free of this whole thing, this whole thought process, but apparently, I was not. "Oh my gaaawd—I'm so confused!"

Raven's head came up and he touched my leg this time with his wet nose.

"What do you think, Raven—should I email the girls?"

He put a paw on my foot and touched me again with his nose. Then he put his head back down. I wasn't sure if that was a yes or a no, but I chose *yes* and sparked up a new email.

I addressed it to Alison, but in the subject line I wrote, *For The Four.*

> Hey All,
>
> Just checking in. Life is finding a new normal. Had a nice Thanksgiving here with Luc, Dunya, Darius and Mitra. Still not the same as home but it was nice not to be alone since, well—you know.
>
> I got myself a new gig too. Volunteering at the children's hospital here, in the NICU with the babies. Olivia, you know all about that. I've been assigned twin boys suffering from withdrawal symptoms due to their mother's heroin addiction. Sad case, but now they are in the process of being adopted, so happy ending for them. Darius is volunteering too with me on Friday nights. They have him working with the older kids who need assistance. He carries them to where they need to be, like out of wheelchairs to MRI machines and such.
>
> Speaking of Darius, I have something to propose to you regarding him. I saw that Derek had emailed a translation for the description of the Norse descendant. It may seem like a reach, but Luc and I think the description sounds like Darius. He's actually Norse descent as well, and it's not just the description that made us think of him. It was the fact that he'd saved my life. I think I told you guys about it but not sure, so here's the recap.
>
> It was a while back when I was still working with him and Luc. We were on our way back from lunch and were crossing the street, a busy street. Luc and I always run across, but Darius doesn't. In fact,

I'd never seen him run, ever. Anyway, Luc had crossed the whole way, and Darius and I were standing on the median in the middle of the street. When it seemed clear, I took the opening and went to run across the rest of the way. As I stepped out on to the road, I heard a screech of brakes. Before I could turn my head towards the sound, someone grabbed me and lifted me into the air, and a second later I was on the other side of the road, next to Luc, hovering above where he stood—looking down at him. Darius had grabbed me and run across the street. And that screech, it wasn't from a car, it was from a huge delivery truck, which thanks to Darius, just missed killing me. But here's the real kicker, based on the tire skid marks, it would have been near impossible for him to get across, let alone pick me up and run without getting us both killed. But he did. When Luc asked Darius what happened, Darius said he didn't know, barely remembers doing it. Said it was a reaction—instinct. Told Luc it was some kind of compulsion. He said his brain screamed, 'protect', so he ran.

I know I felt something too that day—just for a split second but I'd felt it. It was new, something different from the spidy-sense I'd felt in the past. And under normal circumstances, my heart should have been pounding through my chest, but it wasn't, I felt calm, strangely calm and safe.

We all know Derek is The Cipher. Luc and I think there's a good possibility that Darius could be The Guardian. I've been going over things and I feel confident about this. I'm not sure how it all fits, but I feel it does somehow. Maybe just like Derek, he's another friend of mine that you need.

I haven't heard from any of you about these things in a while. Guess I'm wondering how you guys are making out with everything. Have you made any more progress? Let me know what you think we should do with this new discovery, and when you'll have time to discuss it.

Miss you all. Love Lynn

I reread the email to make sure I had the facts straight and then hit send.

Darius had said he'd be here close to 4:30 p.m.. The clock on my computer read 4:10 p.m. so he would be here soon. I still hadn't eaten any *real* food, so I ventured to the kitchen to wrangle up dinner for all of us for later when Luc got home.

As I set dinner to cook on the stove, a loud *"KNOCK-KNOCK"* came from the front door, followed by a loud *"BARK"* from Raven and the sound of his paws clicking across the tile floor.

I dashed to the door and peeked through the peephole. I opened the door. It was Darius.

"Come on in," I said, swinging the door wide.

"Hey, Raven," he said as he crossed the threshold, giving the furry guy a pat on the head. "Hey to you too, Lynn." He was all smiles, still in his work clothes, gym bag in hand.

Thankful he hadn't patted my head, I said, "I've got dinner on the stove, but it won't be ready for a while. Besides, we have work to do first."

"Food—excellent. Oh, I don't want to mess up my work clothes. I gotta change first—gonna use my gym gear," he said, patting the dog again.

"Understandable," I said.

He nodded, turned and set off down the hall.

I returned to the kitchen and adjusted the burner on the stove to simmer, then put a lid on the pot. I'd made a batch of turkey chili and it was best left cooking on low and slow. While the meal cooked on the stove, I headed to the back door.

I surveyed the yard as Darius met me on the patio.

"Wow," Darius said, "Storm was worse than I thought."

"This is nothing—already cleaned up the small stuff and the debris in the pool." I pointed to the piles over to the side. "It's the large hanging tree branches I need your help on." I pointed again, this time up at the trees.

"Wow," he said again, "You got a ladder and something to cut those branches with?"

"Follow me," I said, and led him to the side of the house and the back entrance to the garage.

He spotted the items needed and scooped them up. I held the door open for him, as he passed through with an extendable ladder in one hand and a chainsaw in the other. Then he set the ladder against the side of the house and set the chainsaw next to it. "Where do you want me to start?" he asked.

Before I could answer, Mitra came through the side gate, waving a hand like always. I'd gotten used to her surprise visits and welcomed the sight of her smiling face. She tiny-stepped her way over to my side, then she glanced up at Darius. He nodded and smiled a hello. She smiled big and then turned her grin back to me. Then she followed as

Darius and I walked the yard, assessing the damage of the larger trees and their branches.

"Let's try the lower branches first—see how the chainsaw manages the cutting," Darius said. "I saw you have a can of that special brown paint stuff on the shelf in the garage—you put it on the tree after cutting. Can you get it for me?"

"Ya sure," I said, and headed back to the garage. Mitra followed me.

I returned with the can, an old brush, a cloth, and a tool to open the lid. I set it all off to the side for later.

Darius gathered up the larger of the fallen branches I'd been unable to move, while Mitra and I stood to the side under my favorite Live Oak. It was the one which often had butterflies fluttering around the trunk. I'd planted special flowers that attracted the butterflies, but there were no butterflies to be seen.

Darius cut the fallen branches into nice manageable logs and then I began stacking them next to the already cut firewood near the back patio. Mitra followed me as if she were tethered to my side. Occasionally, she looked up at Darius but then quickly resumed her back-and-forth with me to the wood pile.

Adding these to the existing pile, would make it last forever at the rate it would get used. I could wish for a few cold days come wintertime, to use the fireplace, but we'd be lucky to get weather cold enough to wear sweatshirts in December. I stood back and admired the nice neat piles I'd made.

With Mitra at my side, I moved back over to Darius who was now setting up the ladder. It was time for him to tackle the tougher stuff. He needed to reach the first of the damaged, half-hanging branches.

Darius gripped the ladder, and with chainsaw in hand, he climbed. A few steps up, just in reach of the first branch, he said, "Ready?"

"Ready," I called, and backed Mitra and myself away from the tree, directing her to sit with me on the patio couch.

The chainsaw ripped into action and made that familiar buzz-chew sound as chain met wood. Through the first branch, the broken section fell, landing on the ground with a whoosh and a bang a few yards away from us. Darius moved up the ladder further and repeated the gesture with the next two medium sized cracked limbs. They promptly met up with the first in the same manner. Then Darius descended the ladder and moved on to the next tree. This one was taller and thicker and had higher branches. Darius extended the ladder to its max of 15 feet.

Mitra and I watched as he took each step, carefully placing his huge feet on one rung after another. Up, up, up he climbed until he was at the top of the ladder and under the waiting branches. These heavier branches seemed to have become stuck in among the smaller ones. Only one branch appeared to need cutting, but the other dismembered ones would need dislodging from the clutches of the smaller overlapping limbs.

"Stand back," Darius called down to us, and then the chainsaw roared to life again.

"SNAPS," and "CRACKS," sounded, followed then by falling branch pieces, small twigs and medium branches. Finally the one large damaged and cradled limb, dislodged.

It landed harder and louder than the others had, but it was free and that meant we were finished with the dangerous stuff.

Darius made his descent down the ladder, hitting the ground just as Luc came from around the side of the fence. Dunya was at his side. "Darius! Saw your car in the drive—figured you'd be out back," Luc called.

"Hey, Luc—ya, just finishing up. What a mess the storm made," Darius said, as he shortened the ladder and lent it against the tree. He grabbed up the chainsaw again and moved to the downed branches.

Dunya called something to Mitra in Arabic, then yelled "Thought I'd find her out here with you, Lynn."

Mitra waved at her granddaughter.

"Well—this is the happening place to be," I joked as I got up. Mitra got up and followed me as I crossed the patio.

Darius started up the chainsaw.

Standing under the big tree again, I examined the broken branches that were now being cut down to size. Darius stopped his cutting then, and for the first time, Mitra stepped away from me.

"Alzzalam," she cried out, "alddaw'", then again together, "alzzalam walddaw'."

"What is it—ma hdha?" Dunya ask, running to her.

"'Innahum huna," Mitra responded.

"They are here—she says. The dark and the light," Dunya said, translating for us.

"Dark and light what?" I questioned, then grasped what it was I was asking.

In an instant Raven was up standing near the edge of the patio. He let out a deafening, "*BARK*" followed by a low protective "*Growl*" escaping his bared teeth.

Dunya let out an audible gasp. "Lynn—do you feel it?" she asked me. "I feel it—it's all around... *Darius*."

"I don't feel...," I said, just as the pain hit me. Nausea bent me in half with an overwhelming need to throw-up. I tried to speak, but thunder boomed above me cutting short my breath. I raised my head to see the sky crackle with lightning, sending a shard of blinding light into the tree above me. I shut my eyes. Then I heard... *nothing*. Nothing but a soft panting near my ear. When I opened my eyes, Raven's face and wet tongue were right there in my face. And Darius.

It appeared he'd grabbed me once again, but this time I wasn't in the air, I was on the ground with his huge body hovering over me. Past Raven and through Darius's arms I could see part of a massive multi-limbed branch. Darius had covered me, tucked me under him, allowing the weight of the rest of the branch to crash down on him. He'd saved me from getting slammed by the branch, from perhaps getting killed, *again*.

"Darius man, you okay," I heard Luc say. "Lynn?"

"I'm okay," I said, from under my protector. "Darius?"

"Sorry, Lynn—you okay?" Darius asked. "Hope I didn't crush ya." Darius loosened his grip on me and moved to stand. The branch creaked and splintered as he pushed it up off his body.

As Darius raised up, I rolled away and pushed to my knees. Raven darted to my side. Both my nausea and the stormy skies were gone. I glanced over to where Dunya and Mitra now stood and then shot a glance at the branch.

I hadn't seen this one from the ground. Evidently Darius hadn't either, possibly because of all the other branches crisscrossing in our view. He'd been focused on the limb sticking out from among the other big branches woven in with the smaller ones.

No one said a word as Darius grabbed the big end of the branch and dragged it to the side of the house where he'd been cutting the others. "Is it okay if I do this one another time?" he asked, back to business like nothing had happened, brushing away the small tree debris and grass.

"Sure, of course," I said, still stunned.

He nodded, then grabbed the ladder and chainsaw and took them back into the garage.

"Dhahab alzzalam," Mitra said, scanning the yard. "lakunnah la yazal yakhim."

"She says, the darkness is gone. But the other, he still lingers," Dunya said, translating once again.

"He—who?" I asked, checking myself for cuts and bruises. "Darius? He saved me—again, like on the street."

"No—Shamsiel," she said. "He was here."

"What are you all talking about?" Darius asked, as he stepped back through the garage door.

Luc moved to stand beside him, staring up at him. "Barely a scratch," Luc said. "Guy's barely got a scratch on him." Luc turned and looked at me.

An uncomfortable expression crossed Darius's face. "Uhm, I gotta go," he said. "I'll see you Friday, Lynn—at the hospital."

"Darius—what about dinner? Oh my gawd, the chili!" I'd left it on the stove to simmer. I turned then and ran back into the house, Raven at my heels, and Darius behind him.

"Oh crap!" The chili had bubbled over. There were burned bits dried along the edge of the pot. "Dammit," I added. I'd turned the wrong burner dial. The adjacent burner was glowing on low instead, leaving the one with the pot on high and causing it to boil over.

"Thanks—but no thanks, Lynn. I feel the need to push heavy weights around," Darius said, giving the chili a speculative look.

"I hear ya," I said. Couldn't blame him, burned chili and all. The gym was his happy place, and another taste of this weirdness was enough to make anyone seek out their refuge.

Grabbing his gym bag, he said, "Hey, did you tell Luc about what happened at the hospital?"

"What happened at the hospital?" Luc asked, as he came through the entrance to the kitchen. Mitra and Dunya trailed in behind him.

"Nope—not yet," I said, but we had way more to talk about considering what just happened.

"Crazy," Darius said, "Get her to tell ya, Luc. Just crazy."

I walked Darius to the door and left Luc to rescue what was left of our dinner.

"Thanks, Darius, for helping with the yard—and for well, you know." I hugged him, and he hugged me back.

"Hope I didn't hurt you," he said, ending the hug.

"I'm good. And I have enough firewood to last me five winters—one if this were Canada," I laughed out, as I pulled open the door. "Thanks again, Darius." He smiled and waved as he descended the steps. I waved and then shut the door.

Returning to the kitchen, I saw that Luc had bowls out and he was actually dishing out the chili.

"It was a bit burned on the bottom and around the edges, but I figured it was still edible," he said, then handed me a bowl.

"There's fresh bread—brought it from home," Dunya added, grabbing the butter dish from the cupboard.

We sat around the dinner table in silence. Mitra had none of the chili, she instead buttered a few pieces of the fresh bread and chewed it contently while we ate the burned chili. I guess none of us knew what to say, but I knew what I was thinking. Though I wasn't about to say it. Then Luc spoke.

"What happened at the hospital?" he asked.

"Oh that," I started, letting out a long exhalation. Then I trailed into the night's events, well, just the part Darius had been involved in, as I was hesitant to mention the other. I gave them a quick recap of how the night had started; tour, Darius's patient Jenny, my twin charges, scrubs, water bottles, etc. Then I went into the freaky part.

How I'd been headed back towards the long hall to the nursery, when I'd stopped at the opening to a patient's room. I told them about the excruciating pain and the man standing next to the sick kid's bed. How darkness and shadows had swirl around both. I mentioned how I recognized the guy, that I'd seen him in Ottawa, though I wasn't sure Luc believed it was the same guy. I described how the monitor alarms screamed when I'd told him I recognized him.

I explained it took all I had to get up and run towards the nursing station, but the nurses were already on their way to the room, and that I stumbled as they rushed by me. "I'd hit my knee and my hands pretty hard on the floor, but the guy was gone," I said. "Then there he was—down the hall in front of me." I couldn't explain how he'd gotten there—gotten past me, and no one was at the nurses' station to have seen how. "His eyes bore a hole into me—into my soul," I added. "The nausea hit me fast, and I dropped to both knees. I didn't know what was happening, but I strained to glance up again. He'd started walking towards me, but it seemed like in slow motion. My vision blurred, and I dropped my head. The floor spun—I closed my eyes, so I didn't puke. Had to force myself to breathe," I said, pausing before going on.

Skeptical eyes stared back at me from Luc, along with a frightened expression from Dunya. Mitra just smiled like she liked what I was telling them.

"What about Darius?" Luc asked, curious but still skeptical. And it pissed me off. He'd witnessed two incidences with Darius saving me, and it had been his idea he might be the guardian. Why the questioning tone now? "Where was he in all this?" Luc added.

"I'm getting to it," I said.

"Yer kneeling on the floor and this guy is walking over to you—then what?" Luc pushed, like the parts I'd just told him weren't interesting enough.

He didn't seem to care that this hulking guy had behaved in a threatening manner towards me. I had the mind not to tell him the rest but ignored his cynical tone. "Something changed," I said. "I'd gone from feeling boiling hot and in pain, to calm and cool. The pain and queasiness disappeared, so I looked up again. But he was still coming. I threw my hands up and yelled Nooooooo. The monitor alarms stop, I opened my eyes, and the guy was gone. That's when I heard Darius say my name and ask if I was okay. I turned to see him standing there like he was ready to fight someone. Then he'd asked me where the guy had gone."

"Where did he go?" Dunya asked, interrupting my telling of the events.

"I don't know—but Darius saw him too. He didn't know where he'd gone either—only commented on how massive the guy was. I'd asked him what he was doing here?"

"And," Luc questioned.

"He said, '*You wouldn't believe me if I told you*'," I said. But Luc was the one who'd get a beat-down if he kept up that attitude.

"What did he say?" Dunya asked.

I didn't look at her to answer, instead I stared at Luc, and said, "He asked if I remembered that day on the road—when he'd grabbed me. When I said *yes*, he said, '*it was like that*'. But I didn't quite follow and prompted him for more. Then he said, '*Something told me you were in danger*', and that he needed to find me. Said he came around the corner and saw me kneeling on the floor with this big guy walking towards me. I asked him what he would have done then, but before he could answer, one of the nurses came by and distracted him—flirting."

"Ha—good for Darius. He could use a little flirting," Luc said, disregarding what I'd just told him. "Could the guy be a doctor?"

"No," I said. I'd considered the possibility that the other one I'd seen that night could have been a doctor, only because I'd seen him in Miami before. That one I swear it was the same guy from the photo, same guy from outside my house. Too strange. "The guy Darius and I saw, looks like the same guy I'd seen in Ottawa with the other three— at the restaurant." That whole experience had been unnerving, and a bit of a freak-show and he'd disappeared then too—they all had.

"What restaurant—what are you talking about?" Luc questioned.

I'd forgot I hadn't told him about that when we talked about The Horsemen. I'd thought to but hadn't gotten into it. He'd been struggling with my idea about The Horsemen and those four leaders being one and the same. I'm not sure what he would have thought of it back then, but I wasn't interested in explaining it now, not since he wasn't even buying *this* story.

"Never mind the restaurant. What about Darius—protecting me last night—then again today? That makes three times he's come to my aid. You're the one who said he matched the description of that guardian," I ranted.

Dunya gave me a big wide-eyed look then, but I was too angry with Luc's dismissal of facts, to understand the meaning behind her expression or to care.

"What?" Mitra said.

"What-what?" I said, turning to look at her and then Dunya. It was rare to hear Mitra utter an English word, though I'd suspected she understood more than she'd let on.

"The guardian—*alharis*," Dunya said, touching her grandmother's hand. Dunya reached out to Luc and touched his arm. He'd been staring at Mitra, but he turned now to Dunya. The two of them stared at each other a few seconds, then turned back to stare at me.

"Oh—whatever," I said annoyed, slamming my cutlery down on my dinner plate. I got up from the table. I wasn't hungry, anyway.

Raven, "*Woofed.*"

They continued to stare, saying nothing.

I let out a frustrated "*Huff,*" then stomped off.

The "*SLAM*" of my bedroom door echoed when I kicked it shut.

Shamsiel had lingered in the unseen, outside the patio door to the dining room, listening. He'd understood what Dunya had detected about Darius, that she believed he was *The Guardian*. Shamsiel had known, knew it yesterday, but he'd also known Darius had needed to choose. To choose the light or the darkness himself, without hesitation, without interference. And he had.

"What did I miss?" Gabriel asked, as he appeared at Shamsiel's side.

"Mitra, she sensed the dark and light... saw it around Darius. Dunya sensed it too... and so did Lynn."

"Remarkable," was all Gabriel said.

"Why is it she falls ill around the darkness?" Shamsiel asked, still staring through the window at the three at the dinner table.

"It's that little part inside her that still struggles to believe. She fights it—it makes her sick," Gabriel said, "But when she believes—believes in herself, she can push it away. Like last night at the hospital."

"Do you think she sensed us there—at the hospital?" Shamsiel questioned.

"She sensed me, sensed that I was here last night," he said, "but she called out for you."

"Called out? For me?"

"Those women next door have her thinking that anything she might sense—is you," he clarified. "Did I miss anything else?"

"Darius saved her from an enormous falling tree limb. He saved her once before, and he was there ready to battle for her at the hospital—ran to her aid once again." He paused. "He's one of mine you know."

"Why didn't you tell me?"

"Because he needed to choose his path—no meddling."

"What does it matter? They all have to choose their paths. Choice—free will, as it were."

"You said it yourself. Just because we can influence them now—doesn't mean we should," Shamsiel stated. "I realize now, it's not what *He* wants. Like with the Charges, the others could easily step in and help them, but that won't help convince Him the humans are worthy. And this is the point—is it not?"

"The point?"

"My line... all the lines of the 20 leaders, split off—you know that. Some choosing dark while others chose the light. Darius, he is *The Guardian*, Gabriel. They have been waiting for him to show himself," Shamsiel reminded. "I hadn't known the Guardian would be here. I thought he'd be revealed to the Charges up North."

Gabriel put a hand on Shamsiel's shoulder. "But Lynn... she is not up North, now is she?"

Chapter 27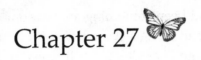

I had the weirdest dream last night about Mom.

The last time I'd dreamt about her had been a few months after she'd passed away. Will and I had still been in our old condo then. It had been morning, and I'd thought I was awake because the sun was up, and I'd been forcing my eyes closed. I'd known Will was asleep beside me—had felt his arm against me. But then, I'd felt someone else's arms come around me, a light pressure of them leaning over me, hugging me. Something soft had brushed my cheek, and I'd smelt hairspray. My mom's hairspray. I remembered breathing in deep, lifting my arms to reciprocate the hug. My first thought had been *Will is going to think I'm nuts if he sees me with my arms in the air.* But I did it— I'd lifted my arms and wrapped them around something solid. I knew it was a person, my mother, and I hugged her back. I hadn't wanted to let go, and I hadn't dared open my eyes out of fear the sensation would leave me. I'd sensed her arms release from around me, then the fragrance of her hairspray disappeared... and she was gone.

I'd had a dream about my Aunt Kay shortly after as well. In the dream I had been trying to tell her that Mom had died, then I'd recognized by her expression that she already knew. Then I recalled she had died first, and I couldn't be talking to her for real. She hadn't spoken a word in my dream, just smiled the whole time. I was sure it was a dream, well—pretty sure.

Last night's dream had been something about Mom and me, and the butterflies. We both had wings—butterfly wings, and we were flying in and out of the large Live Oak trees. It was fun, strange, and too short. I hadn't dreamt about her, or about much of anything for some time, nothing I could recall that is.

The house was quiet, thank God. I wasn't in the mood to talk about last night or anything for that matter. I was embarrassed for getting angry, but I was still disappointed by how Luc had handled the new information I'd shared. Especially after we'd have such great discussions before about these things. It had me thinking maybe Dunya had said something to dissuade him from investing in it further. He'd told her about my girlfriends and all the mysterious stuff, and they'd said they thought angels were real. But last night they'd looked at me like I was off my rocker. So much for a safe place to share.

Was I wrong to expect them to believe me? I'd shared my life's creepy shit with Dunya, and she'd had me feeling as though I wasn't the only one—that I wasn't alone. I'd expected that once I'd told them about the big guy at the hospital that I could have easily told them my suspicions about the other one, the one in white I'd seen there too—who I keep seeing. I'd also hoped I could have elaborated on what had happened at the restaurant in Ottawa too, but it seemed I had no one to tell.

Sitting in my bed, I sparked up my laptop to check my emails once again. Among a few online deal emails and a banking update was one from my trusty PI, Anthony.

It read;

> Hey, Lynn
> I got another email from your birthmother's doctor-friend. She wrote she found an old letter, a poem of some kind written by your birthmother. Said she'd found it while cleaning out the files of her home office, had it stuffed in an old appointment planner, forgotten all about it.
> Your birthmother had given it to her at their last visit, just before her passing. She thought 'my client', the one who had been looking for information, might want it. If not, she said she'd just throw it out. I figured 'yes', but you let me know what you want.
> Anthony

Ya—I wanted it, and I sent him back a quick email saying to get it for me for sure.

The only other personal email in my inbox was from the girls—via Alison.

It was a short one. And not what I'd expected. I probably shouldn't have expected a positive response to my input, but this was far from positive. She'd written back saying the same things I'd said to Luc when he first suggested the idea about Darius. Stating, *Why would he be in Miami if they were up in Ottawa?* They'd agreed that Derek was the Cipher, because he can help at a distance, but questioned how a guardian could help at a distance. She'd put, *Doesn't fit, plus we don't even know what he's supposed to do yet either.* What little else was in the email message gave me the impression again that they were bothered by my trying to be involved. Although, Alison *had* mentioned how grateful they were for my bringing them together. Her last comment had been about Will and how I must be feeling, saying she, *understood my need to connect and be part of things.* I appreciated her concern, but I wasn't seeking connection.

What I was feeling right now, was pissed off.

Every time I want to believe in all this, share my ideas, I got shot down. I could be wrong about Darius, or not, whatever. They'd thrown out my idea about Darius's role. As much as I'd wanted to argue the point, I wasn't about to share what had happened with Mitra, Darius, and the tree. And there was no way in hell I would tell them about what happened at the hospital now either.

Before reading Alison's response, I'd been ready to share the information I'd gotten from the PI. But now—*no*. They'd have thought I was trying to stay connected again, when all I was doing was relaying what was happening in my world. They didn't seem interested, and now I didn't feel like wasting my time. My earlier contributions had been overlooked and any future ones were not welcome. *Fine.* They were on their own.

I shut my laptop and finished getting myself ready for my revisit to the hospital. Showered and dressed, I stomped my way to the kitchen.

Surprise-surprise, Luc was in the kitchen standing by the coffee maker. I'd thought for sure he would have stayed at Dunya's, considering my little outburst.

I'd felt bad about it when I'd woken up, but with this morning's email response from the girls, I was no longer in the mood to apologize. Instead I said nothing and rummaged for my lunch bag.

"Lynn—Dunya thinks you're right about Darius," Luc said then.

"Oh, Dunya thinks I'm right—does she? Then I must be right. God forbid you just believe what I'm saying—but no, you need her *seer* insight to believe me."

"Look, I didn't want to say anything—and you said you didn't want to be involved, but the thing is, I've been helping Derek with some stuff for the girls—stuff they've been working on," he said, pouring himself a coffee.

"Good for you—fill yer boots."

"I think you should tell them what happened—about Darius," Luc added

"I told them—yesterday in an email."

"And?"

"And, I told them all about Darius saving me from the car—*and* about what you and I had discussed about him being this guardian person."

"And?" he threw at me again.

"And—they didn't believe me. They wrote back saying I was just trying to stay involved." That part had hurt, especially since I had brought them together. So-what if I left and came back home without telling them? "Leave me out of it," I said, continuing to pack my lunch.

"Don't you want to help your friends?" he asked.

"What I want is to not talk about it anymore."

"Lynn, you have to tell them the rest—about Darius at the hospital, and in the yard."

"Luc," I sighed, "I've been sensing strange shit all my life—why should it matter now?" I slammed the fridge door, and something toppled inside but I was too furious to care. Luc said nothing. "Even you didn't believe me when I told you about the hospital. It wasn't until Dunya said something to you—that you did." I took my travel mug out and filled it with coffee. Then I slammed the cupboard door. "Why should I—why do you, think this has anything to do with the girls? They don't." I turned and stomped out of the kitchen and headed to the front door. I grabbed my car keys from the front table and slammed the door on the way out.

At the hospital I found Dr. Melanie had left a message for me at the nurses' station, stating she wanted to speak with me about something important. I knew she wanted to review paperwork and my role, but of course I thought, *oh great now what?*

But when I found her in the doctor's lounge near the oncology wing, she greeted me with a surprisingly cheery *hello* and smile. Considering how my day had started, I'd expected something to further dampen it, but then she said, "Any chance you're interested in a fulltime gig? The NICU needs you—the nurses want you."

"Really?" I asked. I'd enjoyed the new opportunity working with these amazing women, and I hoped I'd get to continue contributing what little I could in helping the babies.

"Really," she responded. "The nurses say the unit has never been this calm and quiet before with any other volunteer. They feel more relaxed too. It's been great for them having the extra set of hands to take care of the non-medical tasks. They told me you did wonderful during your shift. They had few issues after you left. Well, not until this morning actually, they told me. Sarah asked if you'd consider working days with them."

"Wow—I hadn't thought to make this a permanent thing, but I'd love the chance to be more involved—help more, ya know." My heart was racing, this time in a good way. I hadn't felt this good about a job in a long-long time.

"Well I hope you love the shift schedule as much. It'd be ten-hour shifts, four days a week, 8 a.m. – 6 p.m. with Fridays off and a five-hour shift on Saturday, 5 p.m. – 10 p.m.. Doesn't pay much but they could really use a reliable person with them. You'd be doing the same as what you've been doing."

"I'm in—for sure," I said. I didn't even need to think about it. I knew it meant not seeing Darius for our Friday night shift, which would suck, but unfortunately, it also meant I wouldn't see much of my roommate either.

Luc had been spending most of his time with Dunya in the evenings and weekends, anyway. It was a relief I'd be busy, and he'd be preoccupied with his new relationship. I'd had enough of all this mystery-solving and to be honest, I'd had enough of my friends *not* believing in me. Luc had said he believed me this morning, said he'd been helping Derek too, but whatever. I had a new gig, a new focus, and this would be my new normal. They could all keep their stupid little mystery to themselves.

The four had chosen Olivia's house for this morning's gathering space this time, and they'd all taken the day off work. All of them, excluding Alison, sat around Olivia's big dining room table. Alison was collaborating via Skype, care of the laptop Vicki had brought.

"You know Derek has been getting help from Luc," came Alison's voice through the laptop's speaker.

"He's not directly involved, but he is helpful," Vicki responded. "Lynn told Luc everything, and she said he believes it all. He's a religious guy though—believes it really is angels. Must make for interesting back-and-forth with him and Derek," she added, laughing.

"True—but maybe Luc is this *Theologian* that's mentioned. The Cipher, The Guardian, The Theologian and The Believer, as all cited in that second entry, the one with the Enochian script," Alison said. "And don't forget the journal mentioned the Cipher—and Derek is Lynn's friend as well. Neither are in Ottawa. I'm not even there now."

"Yes, but Lynn is seriously reaching with Darius, being this Guardian. Makes little sense if he's not here to help us or guard us or whatever," Vicki followed up.

"I'm assuming Derek is this *fifth* because of all his help," Mac said. "And with Derek being such a skeptic, he needs Luc's religious insights. The Theologian role makes sense for Luc, but I agree that this Darius is a stretch."

"Yer right I suppose. Guess I just miss Lynn… wish she was here helping," Alison said, forcing a smile for the others.

"She can't help with anything now. She doesn't do magic or read languages or have any abilities we need," Mac clarified. "But I miss her too."

"Maybe she's The Believer," Olivia spouted.

"Now you're the one reaching," Vicki said.

"She believed in all of us," Olivia added. "Her mom's journal started all this too."

"Look... Lynn told Derek she didn't want to be copied on anymore emails—so we haven't. And if she wanted to stay in the loop—she wouldn't have asked him to do that," Vicki reminded. "I don't have the answer to why her mom or birthmother were involved, but it's obvious Lynn's role was to get us together. Somewhere someone orchestrated for this information to get to us—and it did. We are not responsible for what happened to the women who came before us. Mac's mom clarified that, and she suggested that Sally and Lynn must have been used by the descendants of these men—to make sure we were brought together."

"What about Will's mom and her story?" Alison tossed out from her virtual spot.

Vicki sighed. "It feels more like a coincidence, like the stuff with Lynn's new neighbors—difficult flukes I know, but the codex mentions the four originals, their descendants and these four guys. It doesn't mention the others, Gabriel or Shamsiel. I think it was only brought to our attention because of the other things we'd discovered. Just more angel references but not relevant to our task." Vicki clacked away on her laptop and then stopped to flip a page from the photocopied entries of the codex. Then she resumed typing.

"Task—what task? We don't even know what the hell we're doing," Mac threw out. "Other than translating and playing with magic, what task is there? What are we supposed to do with all this information?"

Vicki stopped typing again. "Our moms were influenced by these men to write stuff, and their mothers and grandmothers before them and so on. They were all part of whatever this is," Vicki said. "If I can get it all translated—we can figure out what our purpose is." She clacked away more on the keyboard.

"What if there is no purpose to all this?" Olivia questioned. "What if it's all just centuries old manipulation? A story that was told once-upon-a-time ago and has morphed into this, based out of ignorance and fear." Her expression grew grim. "What if it's manipulation put upon four women by four men just to control them and their offspring—what if we're falling prey to their game?"

"I saw a documentary the other day about some old codex called the *devils bible*," Mac shared, interrupting Olivia's rant.

"And?" Vicki asked, then flipped another copied page from the book of balance.

"According to one version of the story, the book was scribed by a monk in the Middle Ages. They said he'd broken his monastic vows and was sentenced to be walled up alive." Mac leaned in as if sharing something secret. "To sway the harsh ruling, he promised to make a book to praise the monastery forever and it would contain all human knowledge, *and* he'd do it in one year."

"Not seeing the reference here, and that sounds like an impossible task," Vicki interrupted.

"Well, apparently he felt that way too, because close to midnight of the same day—he realized he couldn't do it alone," Mac added.

"What did he do?" Olivia asked, eager to hear, yet afraid to find out.

Vicki stopped her typing this time to listen.

"He prayed—not to God, but to Lucifer—a fallen angel, requesting help to complete the book, and in exchange he'd give him his soul."

"That's pretty desperate... but the monk *was* sentenced to being walled up alive," Alison noted.

"No shit," Mac said. "And it seemed the devil agreed because the monk added Lucifer's likeness to the cover—as gratitude for his help. I saw the cover—scary dude." Mac made a face like she'd eaten something foul tasking. "The scientists performed tests using similar available tools to calculate how long it would take to recreate, and they estimated just the calligraphy alone would take 5 years of non-stop writing. This thing was fully illustrated too, and it had tons of embellishments."

Olivia said nothing, but her mouth hung open.

"Derek would love that part," Alison noted. "Fact guy and all."

"And how does this help? Am I to assume this story is real or something?" Vicki questioned.

"Speaking of asking for help—we need to get that spell ready. See if we can summon something or someone to help us," Mac redirected, settling back in her chair again. "I'm thinking Halloween, you know—to amp up the power."

"You need five days to prepare a spell," Olivia reminded, keen for the change in discussion. "The 31st would give us two weeks to prepare but we still need the full translation." She stared at Vicki.

Mac turned in her seat to look at Vicki as well. "Well?" Mac said, smugness oozing after her relaying of the Lucifer-monk story.

"Vicki?" Alison shot out in question.

"Okay," Vicki said, flipping back to the front of her copies. With a dash of reluctance, she said, "I'm on it," and then grabbed up Mac's grimoire.

Chapter 28

Friday—payday.

I'd spent the past two weeks fulfilling my duties and new work schedule at the hospital and not seeing anyone other than the nurses and the babies. I did happen to see Darius briefly the Friday before when I'd gone in to get my first paycheck. He'd been signing in for what used to be *our* shift, but after a quick, *"Hey Lynn"*, he'd been hurried off by that same cute nurse. I had autopay set up now, and wouldn't need to pick up my paycheck, but unfortunately it also meant I wouldn't be seeing Darius either.

The nurses on my new shift, commented regularly on how the babies always seemed to calm when I came in for my shift. I'd chalked up the positive comments to them needing my help, but they were the ones who did all the hard work. My work only involved cuddling and the occasional feeding, not even real feeding, just feedings via tummy tubes or nose feeder tubes. But they were happy to get whatever I could manage to help with off their plates.

I'd been given a few other minor responsibilities with other babies, but the twins had been my main focus. I'd gotten good at maneuvering the babies with all the tubes and wires and handling them had become second nature.

The two little guys were almost out of the woods and would go home soon with their new parents. I was looking forward to meeting their new mom and dad, but I'd been told the parents weren't allowed in to see the boys until they were fully recovered. Dr. Melanie had said early on, *"It's best. We don't want to freak them out by seeing the condition they were in."* But this morning, she'd informed me they'd be in today to see them, and that if things went well, they'd be going home in just a couple weeks.

Nothing out of the ordinary had occurred during the past two weeks' shifts this time and I was glad, but I'd still kept my eyes peeled for anything suspicious. My evenings at home after my shifts had sometimes been spent with Mitra. She'd come over and sit with me out back. Last Friday, on my day-off, she'd come and sat with me on the back patio while her granddaughter and my roomie met up for a lunch date. Understandably we didn't talk. We usually sat in quite watching a chance squirrel or butterfly clusters, ramble around the big back yard. From time to time, an occasional butterfly would come rest on the arm of Mitra's chair. Sometimes they even braved to rest on her actual arm. She always smiled a lot, I liked it, and it was enough for us.

When I'm alone out back, I sometimes hope for her to pop her head around the side of the house and come sit with me. It felt good having her near me, peaceful. And today was one of those days. Like I'd wished it, there she was, slipping through the gate, and greeting me with her cheerful smile and wave. Raven seemed to like it too because he let out a soft *"Woof"* and then stretched out leisurely near where she typically sat.

This time when she came to sit down, instead of easing into her usual cushioned wicker chair across from me, she sat next to me on the patio couch. She patted my hand, and then interlaced her tiny fingers with mine, then fixed her gaze straight ahead. She gave my hand a little squeeze, and let out a soft contented, "Sigh".

For the rest of the morning we sat watching as the butterflies came to play around the oak tree and the nectar flowers that circled it.

Closer to noon the butterflies came and danced around us and the patio furniture. Mitra still held my hand, but she extended her other hand open palm up. As if summoning it, one lone butterfly, a powder-blue one, came and landed on the thumb of her open hand.

I leaned towards the butterfly and in a soft voice, I said, "Hi, Mom." My sentiment was interrupted by my growling stomach.

Mitra giggled, letting go of my hand only to pat it again. Unexpectedly, she stood and turned to face me. Raising both hands as she'd done when I'd first met her, she gently cupped my face in her cool palms. Then she spoke something in Arabic that sounded like, "Hea tabooka." Then she smiled her little grin, dropped her hands and turned, then meandered across the lawn to the back gate.

I had no clue what she'd said, though I made a mental note to ask Dunya about the phrase the next time I saw her. What I did know, was that my stomach growl, was my cue to head inside for something to eat.

The microwave heated leftovers, while I checked my emails, but there was nothing noteworthy. I had exchanged a few random emails with Derek over these past two weeks. He'd mentioned that his help with the girls had been *infrequent* and that they were working more on their own right now. Our correspondence had been mainly about my new gig at the hospital and about how busy he was with the growth of his business. I was happier with the non-mystery stuff.

After my lunch, I made my way to check for mail in my *real* mailbox, but before going out the door I spotted a pile of mail on the front table. Since most of it was for me, Luc had gotten in the habit of putting the mail here for me to see when I got home.

There, tucked between the grocery store flyer and a pizza flyer was a brown envelope addressed to me, much like the one Will had sent with the travel voucher, but this one didn't bulge like the other had. I took it from the top of the pile.

It was much lighter, practically empty and had no return address on it to indicate the sender. I tore it open.

In contained a Halloween party flyer and two tickets attached, for what was shown to be the *Vizcaya Halloween Ball*.

There was a blue sticky note on the tickets that read;

> *Lynn, get out and have some fun. Doctor's orders.*
> *Your pal Darius and lots of the hospital staff will be there too.*
> *Giving you the night off, so hope to see you there.*
> *Trick or Treat*
> *~ Melanie*

With a *"Moan"* I turned and headed to my bedroom.

Disinterested, I dropped the envelope and its contents on my dresser, and then padded back to the kitchen to where my laptop was still set up.

I checked for anything new, only to spot one from—guess who, Darius, saying he was going to the party with a bunch of the nurses. He'd written that they were dressing him up like a warrior and they'd be going as his harem girls, *and* how could he pass that up. He'd ended it telling me I should come meet up with them and have some fun.

Have some fun, both Melanie and he had written.

I didn't write him back.

Fun, fun, fun. Ya right, so much fun—not. The party invite was for Saturday night—tomorrow.

Prior to Melanie giving me the night off, I hadn't expected going out at all after work, let alone to a Halloween party. I'd planned to stay in, order a pizza, and watch scary movies, and I was hoping Luc would be home to watch with me. Scary movies were great, but not great alone. Besides, I didn't have a costume I could wear even if I had wanted to go. And I didn't want to go.

Melanie sent *two* tickets—why? I didn't have a date to bring, and she knew that. Perhaps she'd thought I had a friend I could bring, a local girlfriend—but nope. I might have considered bringing my *best-girlfriend*, Luc, if I thought he'd go, or he'd be free—but nope again.

I did however find the location for the party an interesting choice, and out of sheer curiosity, I searched the event's website to see what the big deal was.

The site read;

VIZCAYA'S ANNUAL HALLOWEEN EVENT
SATURDAY, OCTOBER 31, 8:00 P.M. TO MIDNIGHT

Get ready to drink, dance, party and be spooked with Host Redmond Credente!

This outstanding event is held on the glorious Gilded Age estate located in Miami with 100% of proceeds supporting the preservation of Vizcaya Museum and Gardens.

Tickets are all inclusive and you must be 21 to attend. Proof of age required at entry.

This unforgettable Halloween extravaganza includes:

Outrageous Costume Contest
Live Music with SECRET SOCIETY and DJ TU-JAM
Bayfront music and dancing until midnight overlooking beautiful
Biscayne Bay
5 Full Bars
Sponsor Brewing Companies
Various Food Selections

At the bottom it read, *Tickets must be purchased by September 1st.* Under that it said, *Tickets are sold out!*

It seemed these were hard to come by tickets. I guess I should have felt grateful for the invite, but since I wasn't going, I hoped the hospital or Melanie had gotten them for free. I didn't need additional guilt for not attending.

For further amusement I browsed the gallery for last year's costume contest. The photos displayed that some guests had gone all-out for the event with elaborate costumes, but some, were just *all out,* meaning both the guys and girls wore nearly nothing but body paint. Darius and his harem would fit right in, I was sure. Me, I'd get lost in the crowd or be standing off to the side doing my impression of a wallflower. Maybe I could just dress as one and go completely unnoticed. But what did I care, I wasn't going, anyway.

At 5:30 p.m. Luc pulled into the drive.

I realized we hadn't crossed paths at all during these past two weeks. I wasn't mad anymore, but I still didn't want to talk about it. I also realized I hadn't yet gone out front to get the new mail either, and I forced myself to go face my roommate.

Luc was grabbing his lunch bag out of the backseat when I traversed the lawn to the mailbox. When he looked up and saw me, he smiled, but his smile dropped as if unsure of the greeting he might get.

"Hi," I said, and smiled back at him. I wasn't sure what else to say.

His smile returned, and he said, "Hey, Lynnie—Darius tells me you guys are going to a big Halloween shindig."

I cringed. I'd forgotten he would have seen Darius at work, *and* he would have shared all about the *fun.*

"He's going with a bunch of the nurses—but I'm sure he's told you."

"Ya, haram-warrior theme he said." Luc laughed. "I can picture it. But I have a hard time picturing Darius surrounded by girls." He laughed again.

I laughed then too thinking about our shy red-faced warrior, Darius, surrounded by harem girls.

"What are you going as?" Luc asked.

I cringed again. I thought I'd dodged that bullet with my non-reply about going, but apparently not. "Not sure I am," I said.

"Not sure you are—what? Wearing a costume?"

"Going," I said.

"Hello, Lynn," came Dunya's voice from behind me, and thankfully so before Luc could berate me for not going to the party. I turned to see her waving as she finished crossing the span of lawn that joined our two properties. Her beautiful face beamed with kindness.

"What—no hello for me?" Luc joked, mocking a pout to his girlfriend.

"And, who are you again?" she teased him back.

"Geez—I feel like that should be my line," I tossed at him. "Surprised yer home."

"Actually, we're heading up to see my sister and the family tomorrow—visit with them, do the whole kids Halloween thing." He shut the car door and strode over to Dunya for a quick kiss.

"Meeting the new girlfriend, eh?" I winked at Dunya. They were cute together.

"Just for the night—we'll be back in the morning," Dunya said. "Jadda is staying here. She told me she wanted to stay near you—watch over." She shrugged.

I shrugged. "Oh hey—Mitra said something the other day when we were out back on the patio. Obviously, I didn't understand." I rarely understood anything when she spoke—and it hadn't mattered, but I was curious about it this time, since she'd made such an effort in saying it right to me.

"Do you remember what she said—what the words sounded like?" Dunya asked, walking me to my front door.

"Uhmm, well it sounded like... *hea tabooka*," I fumbled out.

"Oh—ha," Dunya chuckled.

"What? Is it something funny?" I giggled.

"No—it's a sweet something," she said. "And it's, *she loves you*—hi tuhabbuk."

Confused I said, "Who loves me—Mitra?"

"No-no—I mean—not that Jadda doesn't love you, it's in the context of a message, that this *she* loves you," she reiterated. "Does that make sense to you?"

"Yes," I said, nodding and smiling, remembering the butterfly and how I'd said, "*Hi Mom*" when it landed on Mitra's hand. She *is* gifted in many ways, and she must have understood me then.

"Oh, by the way—I have a costume for you if you're in need," Dunya tossed out, changing the subject, and clearly in the know about the party. "Yer going right?"

I didn't cringe this time, but I threw Luc an ugly scowl. He ignored it and passed through the front door I'd left open. Raven was there to greet all of us, and I hoped once again that the talk of Halloween had abated.

No such luck.

"It's one my daughter wore in the senior play—perfectly scary and I'm sure it will fit," Dunya added.

"Uhm, sure I can try it—see if it fits," I gave her. I didn't have the spirit to tell her I wasn't going, she seemed so excited to offer me the costume. Then before I could deviate and escape into the house, she continued on with giving me the backstory on the play.

Dante's Inferno—the divine comedy, she'd called it, was based on a book. I'd never heard of it—not that I was any great reference on books or plays. She'd said it was about and how the main character goes on a journey and has to pass through Hell, Purgatory, and Paradise. Said something about his journey consisting of circles and limbo, rings and robbers and sorcerers, and stuff about regions and traders.

It sounded a lot like one of those realm-based movies like *Lord of the Rings* or that *World of Warcraft* game some people play. I tried to follow when she'd elaborated about the journey this guy Dante took through Hell to Heaven, but she'd lost me when she'd ended with how, "*It became a symbol of all human experience and an acknowledgement of life's circularity"*. Luckily for me, she had little else to add, and shortly after, she and Luc left to go over to her place for dinner.

"KNOCK KNOCK," came from the front door.

Through the peephole I saw it was Dunya. I swung open the door to find she'd returned, costume in hand for a quick drop-off.

"Oh—gee, thanks," I said, as she held out the hanger for me. I took the bag, it was heavier than I thought.

"Remember to take pictures," she said, smiling, before turning and springing happily down the front steps.

"Sure," I said, watching as she scampered back across to her house. I shut the door while staring at the garment bag.

In all honesty, I liked Halloween. I just wasn't thrilled about going alone and I hadn't wanted to admit it. And well, I was concerned that this costume of Dunya's, might turn out to be something relating to the period of the story—in the year 1300, she'd said. But when I unzipped the garment bag, I was pleasantly surprised with what I saw. Dunya had told me the theater director had opted for a more *modern* spin on things, but the term *bad-ass* was more like it. I took it with me to the bedroom and tried it on.

Despite not caring whatever this play-book-story had been about, further inspection of the costume had proven to be inspiring. And it was a perfect fit, just as she'd said

The costume comprised a black ribbed tank-top, black army fatigues, a utility belt with a flask, a plastic grenade, and a sheath with a fake plastic knife in it. At the bottom of the garment bag, there was also a pair of combat boots I could tell *wouldn't* fit, and they were what made the bag so heavy. But I did have a pair of oxblood coloured Doc Martins I could wear in place of them.

Along with the army gear was a set of three-foot-long black wings, with real feathers. They had adjustable thin black straps, you just slipped your arms through to keep them on and in place. The best part of the costume were theses realistic prosthetic horns that came with a flesh-coloured adhesive rubber to attach them. Based on the instructions attached, they're meant to go on the sides of your forehead and *not* in your hair. The charcoal grey and flesh colour scheme of the horns made it look as though they would protrude from your forehead as if pushing out through the skin. Adding to that creepiness, was the freakiest piece I'd found, attached with a note from Dunya.

Contact lenses. They were red, but not a solid red. They were just like real coloured lenses, but where you'd have shades of blue, green, or brown, there were shades of red instead. The note said, that her daughter hadn't used them, that she couldn't get past putting her finger in her eye, so they'd never been worn. I wasn't sure how keen I was on the whole put-my-finger-in-my-eye thing either, but since it would top off the whole look, I'd at least try it.

Over eating my dinner, I contemplated the idea of going to the party, alone. Then before I got into bed, I hung the costume on the back of my closet door, and I placed my Doc Martins under the hanging garment bag. Perfect.

I guess I was going to the party tomorrow after all.

Chapter 29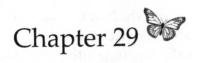

With the book of balance in her possession and her husband fast asleep upstairs, Alison sat at her dining table working feverishly to make sure all they'd discovered and continued to unearth were meticulously entered into the pages of the codex.

She'd needed to return for obvious reasons with her being pregnant, but she'd also found it difficult to keep her activities with her new girlfriends a secret now. Vicki had translated and found more information, and she continued to work into the wee hours of the night, filling each new page with more. She'd made clear references to the spells and the learning of them that Mac and Olivia were challenged with, and she also made a note of the new skills they all seemed to possess now. But the more she'd transcribed, the more she had to fight to ignore the repeating angel references and the mention of both Gabriel and this Shamsiel. She'd brought them up a few times in her video chats with Vicki, only to be dismissed because their relevance had never been mentioned in the codex. *Not yet*, she'd told herself, but she'd kept that idea quiet. She'd continued to wait for the full translations while she continued to get ready for the baby.

Olivia slept peacefully in her bed, having made great strides in her healing skill and her use of chakras. She expertly dabbled in it now with her friends, family and coworkers, but she'd had to fake that its accurate success had been due to the holistic training she'd been learning from a friend, part of which was true, but the level of intuitiveness, that was all hers. She had also helped Mac gather the items needed to prepare for the conjuring ritual, but they all knew it would be up to Mac to pull off the spell.

Vicki in her apartment alone this time, completed more of her translating, the main piece being the conjuring spell from Mac's grimoire. There were still parts of the codex that were patchy, and Vicki continued to struggle through them. Although, the one key factor they'd revealed, had been the *depth* at which these men had been involved with the first four women.

It had been along with Derek's help, that Vicki had solved yet another piece of the puzzle. An anagram from the first entry. After repeated tries on her own, she'd requested Derek's help, and together they'd found the translation for, 'harbored four guest' that the proper words were 'bore four daughters'. This confirmed in all their minds that Uriel, Vretil, Michael and Raphael must have been men, and the four original women had given birth to four daughters, the offspring of these men. Though Vicki's translation of this entry was nearly done, she had remained desperate to complete the other, the second of the Enochian script entries. This one had been entered between the entries of Alison's grandmother and mother. And though the *message* in this entry continued to be a challenge, Vicki had unraveled something new, something that referenced a *gathering*.

With only the light from her laptop to guide her, Mac tiptoed around the kitchen. She too had been up late—every night this week in fact, after her family had gone to bed. She'd needed to prepare for the spell out of sight from her husband and two young boys. Trying to run her home business and taking care of her family during the day meant she was left with little precious time to prepare.

The spell required she prepared everything five days prior, and she'd prepared the rose petals by placing them in the water with the other ingredients she and Olivia had obtained. She'd also needed to find a safe place to leave the bowl out and had opted for the same high shelf she'd kept the cookbook-slash-grimoire on. It had to be in a cool dry place *and* required that she stir the mixture for 5 minutes every couple of hours. It had been tiring to say the least, making for a lot of up and down the stepstool, and very little sleep.

She had also cleverly figures out they *didn't* need to be in the same room for this to work. She could use four element magic, tapping into Air, Fire, Water, and Earth. Spells readily require a fifth element, *Aether* or Spirit, and she'd presumed it was a given and that the Goddess was ever present. "Tomorrow's the day," Mac whispered to herself. "Halloween—*all hallows eve*. Everything is ready for the conjuring."

Chapter 30

Saturday, all hallows' morning.

I found it interesting how talk of something, especially weird things during the day, can influence your dreams at night. I'd had bizarre dreams before but thanks to Dunya's storytelling, last night's dreaming had been about being in hell or some rendition of it. She'd told me in the story, that midway in the guy's journey, he falls asleep, losing his way and when he wakes, he finds himself in the woods at night. So of course, mine did too.

In my dream it had appeared I was in the woods, and it was definitely dark because I couldn't find my way. Then it was bright, like someone had switched on an overhead light, but it must have been my brain's version of the sun. I saw a mountain, that for whatever reason, I thought I could climb, and I'd ventured forth. Part of the way up I saw a leopard, and then a lion who had both tried to keep me from climbing. Similar to the story Dunya had relayed, it wasn't until the wolf came that I'd felt frightened—which surprised me since I loved dogs, but still it had scared me, and I couldn't climb. Instead I'd cowered in some fissure in the mountain. And not that a bunch of wild animals trying to knock me off the mountain wasn't weird enough, I'd then heard a voice say, *"Until the wolf is secured, you must take another route. Let me show you."* To top up the creep-factor, I'd shifted around and saw that guy—Mr. Tall Dark'n Scary from the airport. So then my choices were to take on the wolf, or go with this guy? On some level, my mind had recognized it had been a dream, but I hadn't been impressed with my brain's imagination at that point. And of course, stupid dream-me, picked the scary guy over being eaten by a wolf. Cue images from a childhood story book. I'd realized too late that I should have chosen the wolf, because I'd found myself surrounded by—you got it, *tortured* angels. Then Mr. Dark'n Brooding said, *"Someone else will take you the rest of the way."*

My dream-self had said, *"Great."* But before I could savor the idea of getting away, four hulking men appeared, the same ones from the restaurant, led by the guy who'd come after me at the hospital. Aaaaand that's when... I woke up—thank you very much.

"Can't a girl get a nice peaceful sleep and a little sleeping-in to start her weekend?" I called out to the room *and* the universe. I hadn't expected a response, but following my outburst, Raven poked me in the cheek with a cold wet nose. "Hi buddy—I'm up." Then my cellphone rang.

The screen showed it was Alison, and I hit answer. "Yer up early," I said. It was almost 9 a.m. my time which meant 7 a.m. for her Calgary zone.

"Wanna Skype later?" she said in response.

"Sure. I haven't seen that mug of yours in a while." I liked video calls way better than chatting on the phone. I missed seeing everyone's faces, their voices were just not enough these days.

"Just for fun—with all of us," she added. "Mac wants to tell you about the boys and their Halloween costumes. The others have fun stuff coming up for tonight too, so they all liked my idea to share it in a group with you." She giggled. "I miss you, Lynn—we all do."

"Man—I miss you guys too." I sighed. "Hate missing out on all the baby prep stuff with you too, Spook."

"Ya that part'is hard for me too." She sighed. "Everyone's got lots going on today, but we thought we could try before you go to work at five," she suggested.

"Not working tonight—so I'm available anytime today," I told her. "Well after I get my coffee and breakfast that is." I was excited at the prospect of a group video chat and the fact it would be strictly Halloween related. It was my turn to giggle.

"Okay — perfect, let me check with the girls and I'll get back to you on a time. Cool?"

"Cool," I said, "Chat in a bit." We hung up, and I pushed myself up out of bed.

Raven followed me to the kitchen as usual, and since Luc was over at Dunya's place, I'd have to get the coffee going myself. I'd gotten spoiled having the coffee ready in the morning when I got up for my shift. Before, when Will was here, I'd be the one doing the morning prep, but since Luc worked earlier than me, he'd gotten in the habit of making just enough that I had a cup when I woke up. Sometimes there were even fresh homemade baked goods left for me he'd brought over from Dunya's. Bless her big sweet heart.

At 10 a.m. I received a text from Alison saying that the girls were on for 11 a.m. my time, Alison being the only one of us in a different time zone.

I took advantage of the time until the video call, to get showered and tidy up. Then at 10:55 a.m. I sat in front of my computer screen, Skype up, patiently waiting for the others to log on.

One by one the little grey dot turned to yellow and then to green as each of them logged in. Alison was first since she was hosting the call, and she had to set up in *group mode* for each of us to see one another. I'd never done a group call, but I figured they must have done it a few times now, because Alison had us all up on screen just as the clock on my laptop showed 11:01 a.m..

"Hi, Spook," she said, as our faces appeared in the grouping. "Can you see me — see us?" She typed away on her computer.

"Yup — got ya all in a square," I laughed out. "Kind of like my own mini *Brady Bunch*."

"Marsha — Marsha — Marsha," Mac belted out on cue with the sitcom's reference.

"Pfffffffffffff," Alison and I spewed in unison.

Just then Raven popped his head over my lap in view of the screen.

"Hey, Lynn — who's your friend," Vicki asked.

"My new boyfriend," I said, patting my companion's head.

Raven *"Chuffed,"* his acknowledgement, and we all laughed. He *"Chuffed,"* again and then he rested back down at my feet.

"Hello all," Olivia said followed by a high-pitched bark from her dog Bella. "Looks like you have some competition, Lynn."

We all laughed again. It felt good—really good to be seeing all those faces. The faces I loved so much, the faces of my best friends smiling back at me.

Olivia started the Halloween conversation off by saying she was hosting a party for the girls tonight at their place. Mike was doing all the cooking and she and the girls were doing all the decorating and preparing of the basement for a fun-filled spooktacular night for ten of the girls' closest friends from the barn.

Vicki was next, sharing how she would be attending a work mixer, costumes were involved, but she wasn't sure what she was going as yet. Said she'd have to whip something up, perhaps from her son's closet if need be.

Mac followed telling us that her husband was taking the boys trick-or-treating near his mom's place, that there'd be a Halloween block party going on *and* that the three of them would be staying at grandma's for the night. Apparently, there was going to be beverages available for the adults. "He felt it was best they crash there, then he could partake in the Halloween *festivities*," Mac said, using air quotes. "I'll be home aaaaaloooooooone," she added in a scary voice.

"No party for us tonight," Alison said. "Just decorating the outside of the house for the tricker-treaters. Ken suggested we paint my belly like a pumpkin, but you can imagine how well that went over." She laughed out hard at that tidbit, and we all followed suit.

"Oh, say *Hi* for me—would ya," I said, "Tell him to get pics of the house and send them so I can see the decorations."

"Sure-sure," Alison said.

Since the conversation was feeling great, I took a leap, and said, "How goes the treasure hunting?"

There was a long pause, and then Alison said, "We've stayed in contact. Me—mostly with Vicki. That way I'm able to get everything properly written down—you know."

"I copy everyone on our correspondence, so Mac and Olivia are in the loop, but not much other than that though," Vicki confirmed.

She'd cc'd everyone but me, but I was okay with that. "Mac, Liv—you guys practicing your new skills?" I asked

"Ya some," Olivia said.

"Here and there," Mac said, giving me a lot of nothing.

"Ahhh," I said. Possibly they were at a standstill I thought. "Sorry—just curious, a bit out of the loop." I had figured if they'd kept at it, stayed in touch, that whatever this mystery was, they'd find the answers.

"Feeling a bit left out too, Spook," Alison said. "Don't feel bad. It's hard not being in Ottawa with the others."

Didn't I know it. "Ya," I said. She'd have a hard time explaining the need to return again too, but knowing her—if needed, she'd find a way to travel before the baby came.

"Life had to go on," Mac said. "But the secret meetings get harder to hide from our husbands."

"We tell them it's just girl stuff—like crafts and makeup, jewelry and such," Olivia said.

"Keep the boys away stuff," Mac added with a chuckle.

"What about you, Lynn—any big plans for tonight?" Vicki tossed out, changing the subject.

"As a matter of fact…," I said, then delayed the rest for affect. They'd all seemed a tad bit anxious, possibly up to something since they'd dodged the topic, but I wasn't sure I wanted to know. I was thrilled we were doing this, I needed a pick-me-up and boost to get the nerve to even go to this gala, especially alone. "…I'm going to a big Halloween bash at this huge vintage mansion on the water." Despite Vicki asking, I knew they'd be surprised. I wasn't much for socializing, but they knew I loved all things creepy.

"Is that where you have the memorial bricks?" Olivia asked.

"No—that's the Fairchild Gardens, this is *Vizcaya*. It's a mansion-museum-gardens setup. Used to be some guy's home, but now it's a national historic landmark. The website says they host all kinds of parties and weddings, etc."

"Oh, that sounds cool, Spook. You could use a fun night out," Alison said, thrilled and envious at the same time. "Wish I could go with ya."

"Me too," I said. "A lot of the hospital staff will be there." Darius had said he'd be there, so it wouldn't be that bad. And Alison was right, I needed a night out after the long hours I'd been keeping.

"Maybe you'll meet someone," Vicki said, "I wish I could go with ya too."

Then Olivia asked, "Have you heard from Will?" She was still tender from my split with her friend Will.

"I have not," I gave her. I was tender too, but I had to move forward if I was going to heal and keep my sanity. And I'd spent too much time rehashing the demise of my marriage with everyone.

"Eat lots of treats," Mac said, changing the obvious dip in mood. "But watch out for the punch—it might pack a real punch."

"You take some pictures for me too, Spook—of you in your costume," Alison requested.

"Will do," I said, then I told them about the costume.

Both Alison and Vicki had heard of the *Dante* story, being well read and all. Mac commented on how cool and creepy it sounded while Olivia commented on just the creepiness part.

"Did you have to be one of the bad guys?" Olivia asked.

"Liv—when else do you get to be a monster in real life?" I told her. Sometimes you needed a safe means to let the devil in you—out, and Halloween was the perfect time.

"I guess," she said, halfheartedly agreeing.

I ended the call saying, that what I needed was to get them all to come down here, and for us to have fun in my new home. I had lots of room for a gathering *and* I had all those vouchers they could use too. We exchanged our goodbyes and I love yous, and then I watched as one by one their little face images blocked out and the green dot next to their images changed back to grey.

"That was great," Alison said, "we need to do that more often." They'd all stayed on the call, only blocked Lynn's profile to appear as though they'd all logged out.

"Well—*we*, do it all the time—just not with Lynn," Mac said. "Seemed like she wanted us to give her an update."

"I hated not telling her," Olivia commented.

"We have lots to discuss," Vicki said, "but it doesn't include Lynn. We need to talk about this info Derek sent us about the Enoch story."

"But why can't we include her?" Mac asked.

"You know why," Vicki followed up. "She'll want to add her own insight into what we've been working on, and we don't need the distraction."

"Is this Enoch person part of all this?" Olivia asked. "Or do you think he was just another person from back then... someone privy to the fallen 200 story?"

"What about Michael, Vretil, Uriel and Raphael, do you suppose they're named after angels or is it the other way around? Like the ancient story tellers named the angels after these first four guys?" Alison added to the inquiry. "Chicken–egg, you know?"

"Hard to say," Vicki responded. "Based on the research Derek found, the *Mountain of the Chief,* was near Sumer, and was said to have started their agricultural practices around 5000BC."

"Derek also wrote that in the book of Enoch, it stated that the Watchers came down from a mountain in 5000 BC," Alison reminded them. "He also mentions the punishment of 70 generations, their involvement on the earth, and how they could only *watch* during that time." She held up her note pad that contained the references.

"What if the 200 were an invading army, and these primitive people in Sumer thought they were gods or something?" Olivia asked. "What if this commander guy told them to *observe* theses Sumerians, but then when they found the people weren't a threat, they moved in and infiltrated the area?"

"They'd liked the daughters of this city and took some for wives," Mac said, adding to Olivia's deductions. "Most of the offspring—their sons, were stronger, more powerful and more educated than the others."

"As much as I'd like to think these 200 were a bunch of exotic charmers," Vicki answered. "There's a good chance a lot of the offspring were not a choice—if you know what I mean." She made a pained face.

"Perhaps these four men—the ones from the codex, wanted to educate the women of the area too," Alison said, trying for a lighter direction. "Not just the male offspring."

"Advanced thinking for the time," Vicki responded again. "But why was it a secret?"

"Maybe keeping it a secret, had just been for safety back then," Alison said, "and it became a tradition."

"Scary tradition," Olivia added.

"The mind is a powerful thing," Mac stated. "There's been lots of reports on people using mind over matter, regarding illness both positive and negative. It's like those old curses—if you believed it, you could make bad things happen to you."

"I prefer the idea that these four guys were angels," Olivia said, "but even if they were just men, they may have wanted to help the women—especially after the 200 invaded. Keeping the balance—not the balance of the world, just their little part of it," she added.

"They could never have expected it would carry on this long," Vicki said. "Remember the entries say a lot of the same things—not much changed in the story, other than who was telling it *and* what had happened to them."

The original four gathered outside the home of Mackenzie Miller as she once again Skyped with the rest of their Charges. It was nothing new, their Charges had been using the video chat system for weeks now. *"Cuts down on the travel"* they'd heard one of them say. Plus, with Alison being on the other side of the country, it made for an excellent coming together.

"It's safe to leave I'm sure," Vretil said. "I'd like to be with my Charge tonight, anyway. Strange things come out on Halloween, but if I'm lucky, she might have leftover candy." He grinned.

"Think I'll see what Gabriel is up too," Michael said. "He'll be watching for the *other* four I assume."

"Seems like more of the same—translating and deliberating," Raphael said, "And I'm with Michael, I want to see what Gabriel is doing about this early arrival of the Four."

"No magic and still no conjuring. Think I'll join you," Uriel said, and then they all disappeared.

"You don't think we can conjure an angel?" Olivia asked, sidestepping the idea of armies and rape.

"A spirit possibly," Mac said, "but I'm still not sold on real angels. Different cultures interpret them differently—but I believe it's probably just spirits. The grimoire sites, *conjuring angels and spirits,* so I'm sure we're covered."

"You believe in magic—but not angels?" Alison directed at Mac, but still questioning them all.

"Well, it's all a stretch for me," Vicki responded first, "but the type of magic Mac does is earth magic. I can see the elements she uses, like herbs and words. I don't have any proof angels exist, but we all experienced the other spell Mac did."

"We know Lynn has always had that weird insight thing—and she's not alone," Mac replied this time. "Tons of people claim to speak to the dead—see spirit, predict the future, etc. Perhaps our abilities were just latent ones—and hers weren't."

"Could Mac's casting of that first spell triggered something in all of us? A grounding of sorts that tuned into us having our own gifts," Vicki speculated.

"What about Lynn's help?" Alison said, continuing the theme of her missing friend.

"Well, she has her gift, it could've boosted the magic and further boosted ours," Mac surmised.

"She helped of course, but it's not like she gave us these gifts, they were passed down to us—same as hers were. Her birthmother had that *knowing* thing too—the friend had said, remember? It's hereditary," Vicki said, discounting Lynn's involvement again.

"And the journal?" Alison tossed out.

"Again—passing down stuff. Her birthmom had to find a way to get the information to her through her adoptive mother," Vicki continued, adding to the plausibility.

"How do you explain the same stories, the journal—ours, the story Will's mother told Louise—if it's not all related?" Olivia added, still having a few of her own doubts. "Mac what do you think?"

"Well, girls—I don't have all the answers," Mac said, quick in response, "But I do have a book of spells... so let's get to it."

Chapter 31

All Hallows' Eve.

I'd promised Dunya I'd bring dinner over for Mitra before I got ready and headed out for the night. Mitra and I tried a tiny bit of communication, but it was more like silent changes in expression on her part, while I rambled about my night ahead. She seemed happy to listen and happy about the food I'd brought, but when I got up to leave, she grasped my arm.

"Everything okay?" I asked, hopeful for a positive response to her now worried expression. She smiled then and like she'd done many times before, she rubbed my arm. I smiled back and patted her hand. "I'm going out for a little while… but I won't be late," I said, as though she were a worried parent and I was a teen going to my first grownup party. She smiled again and let go of my arm.

Before leaving, I showed her how to use the speed dial on the house phone set for emergencies via the alarm system in their house. She smiled again and nodded, then she put the portable phone in her cardigan sweater pocket. I smiled back, ending our imperfect communication, then set off for home.

I'd felt some relief knowing if needed, fire, ambulance and/or police, could be at a button's notice if needed, but I wasn't completely confident about leaving her alone. Her worried expression was still haunting me—no Halloween-night pun intended.

The costume.

I wasn't sure what it was, other than something from *Hell* allegedly. I'd gone to parties in the past, dressed as goofier or at least less scary things, but this year I was totally into taking it to the nasty, evil level. If I was going to go alone—well, show up alone, I might as well look like I *kicked ass*. It would keep the guys from hitting on me, as I wasn't ready for that just yet. Darius would be there if I needed him, if he wasn't too busy with his harem that is.

First things first for getting into the theme for my costume, I plaited back my hair in a long tight braid. It helped to expose my forehead for the horns. Plus, it would keep my hair from getting stuck in the glue or tangled in the wings once they were on.

Next, I applied the adhesive to both horns and pressed them to my clean forehead on each side next to my hairline. When they were dry, using the monster makeup Dunya had provided, I added a bit around the base of the horns, blending the area so it appeared as if they were protrusions *through* my skin rather than atop my skin.

Clothing was next.

Over a black sports bra, I donned the black tank-top provided as part of the get-up. Next came the black multi-pocket army pants, whose loose cuffs I tucked into my boots. I laced those up such that the pants bunched a little at mid-calf. The utility belt was easy to thread through the loops of the pants. It was lighter than I'd expected, because the army paraphernalia was only plastic.

Last were the wings.

When I slipped my arms through the adjustable loops, I got the full weight of all those feathers. In position, they were heavier than I'd expected, but the straps were comfortable despite the weight, and them being over 3 feet in length.

A brush of smoky eyeshadow and charcoal eyeliner later, I was essentially ready, and I stood in front of the full-length mirror in my bedroom to get one last look. Even at this late date, I still debated whether or not I should go. But then the anxiety I'd been experiencing abruptly dissipated, and I smiled back at myself in the mirror.

"Oh, I love those wings," Shamsiel said. "Does she remind you of anyone?" He fluttered his long thick black feathery eyelashes.

"No," Gabriel responded, scowling.

"What's the matter—you don't want her to have fun?"

"Fun—yes. Dressed like that—no." His eyebrows pinched together.

"I think she looks very warrioresque," Shamsiel tossed back. "Seems fitting—don't you think?" He leaned in and peered over her shoulder to see her reflection in the mirror and smiled. Then his smile dropped.

"Oh crap—I almost forgot the best part of this crazy costume," I said, turning and heading back to the bathroom. I'd left that tiny case beside the makeup. Cracking open the little plastic container, I leaned into the bathroom mirror. "There... *perfect*. Whataya think, Raven?" I said, turning to face my furry companion. I blinked, dabbing at the corner of my eyes with a tissue.

Raven "*Snorted*" instead of chuffing as if disapproving, then shook his head as if something had tickled his ear.

"Still like the costume, my friend?" Gabriel asked.

Shamsiel said nothing and only frowned.

"Nothing like a pair of red shaded contacts—to turn a simple angel into a demon," Gabriel added, just before disappearing.

"Come, Raven. I gotta call a cab," I said smiling one last time at my demonic self in the mirror.

Getting home might not be so easy, I thought to myself as I got out of the taxi. I'd had to carry my wings across my lap on the way, but now I was able to slip them back on again. The cabbie had left me at the front gate, though I had to show my ticket to get in at the entry booth near the start of the long driveway, anyway. Passing through the gate, I walked the long-paved road up and around the circled drive to the main house.

A half a dozen steps up, the massive white stately home, now a historical museum, loomed up in front of me, and I followed the other guests as they filed up the steps to the front entrance. At the entrance we were asked to wait our turn for our *ghoulish* tour of the main floor before being taken on to the main party.

Victor, our tour guide stepped up and introduced himself and then he ushered us into the front hall to start the journey. He was dressed in livery from the period for the mansion along with brilliantly crafted zombie makeup and oozing guts. Through a large main doorway, we shuffled to what we were told was one of several reception rooms, then we single-filed it on into the Library.

It was not a large room, but I made a note of the many references to angels the space displayed. There were paintings, sculptures and other smaller pieces of artwork on the desk and other surfaces. Despite not being able to get up close with any of the artwork due to 90 percent of the room being roped off for viewing only, there *was* something we could touch, and it was the best part of this room. It was a hidden doorway that was revealed to us from behind a tall bookshelf. It was also the way to the next room, the Living Room.

This room had a massive floor to ceiling fireplace flanked by our entrance and another door, and together they filled most of the wall. Only the first half of this space was roped off. Two large wall tapestries filled most of one wall, the larger of the two must have been a religious piece I surmised, because it had symbols representing Muslim, Christian *and* Jewish faiths. Tour guide, Victor, had said it was *"The Admiral Carpet, brought here by King Ferdinand of Spain's grandfather"*. Whatever. To the left of the door was an ornate organ with a large religious painting hanging above it. In front of the organ was a large— almost 6 foot, equally ornate bench with two red velvet cushions that stretched its length. I ran my hand over the plush red fabric and noted that the top of the sitting area was hinged. I gave a little try at opening it but managed only lifting it a couple inches when Victor instructed us to follow him through the door and on to the next room.

The East Loggia room.

This room was the largest and had elaborately painted walls and high decorative ceilings. High on the wall above the entrance was what Victor had called a, *"Caravel sailing vessel"*, and it represented the age of exploration. To the left side of the room were three expansive floor-to-ceiling arched glass entryways that were the exits to the surrounding courtyards, *and* they were also the main access to the outdoor party.

We made our way outside to the festivities, with Victor enlightening us with the last bit of his spiel. "This was originally the front of the main house," Victor explained. "The outdoor spans overlook Biscayne Bay and *the Barge*. The Barge itself is a massive 158-

foot-long water sculpture made from carved mixes of local stone." He pointed out to a large structure in the water. "Its purpose was that of a *breakwater*, to calm the proximal offshore waters. Generally a nonfunctional structure, but it remains an iconic image of the estate. The actual sculptures on the vessel were made by an artist named, *Stirling Calder*, who was born in 1870."

That DOB made those sculptures seriously old, but who would want a stone boat with giant sculpted fish on it—ancient or not? At least I thought they looked like statues of fish. All I could make out were tails that resembled something fishy.

"This way ghouls and goblins—time to get your freak on!" Victor announced, as he pointed the way and then slipped into the crowd.

I stood back and watched as the others slipped in after him, swallowed up by the crowd of mingling costumed guests. Then I glanced down at my feet. I was standing on what I assumed was an inlayed carving of a sun dial, but then swiftly realized it was a stone compass, the directions indicated by N, E, S and W. It made me think of Mac and her spell, and how she'd used her son's superhero collection as guardians to mark the directions. The memory made me smile.

When I glanced up, I swore I spotted those same four superheroes sauntering up to the closest bar. I was only partially right though, it was *Superman*, *Batman*, and *Spiderman*, but no *Wolverine*, just some chick dressed as a cowgirl. Shame, he was my favorite. There were loads of crazy costumes and crazy people wearing them, but right now I was more interested in the food options as I'd chosen not to eat dinner in anticipation of feasting when I arrived.

Pushing through the crowd, I found my way to one of the food areas. I was pleasantly surprised to find mini chicken and beef tacos, and I filled a clear plastic plate with groupings of both. Along with those were individual small bowls of guacamole and plenty of tortilla chips, so I helped myself to those as well. Content with my portable meal, I changed location to the side nearest the stage to get a look at the band. I wasn't familiar with the band name I'd read on the invite, but they sounded awesome. As I ate and continued to listen to the music, I treated the crowd as though it were a spectator sport, and I watched as the various costumed fellas try to pick-up the costumed gals.

Similar to the photos from last year's gala, there were plenty of scantily clad—albeit Halloween themed costumes of both men and women. Several large—and I mean large gym-going young males dressed in gladiator costumes shuffled by me to get to the eats. Off to the side, I glimpsed a dark figure of someone dressed like me in all black, but more reminiscent in attire to those four guys I'd seen at the restaurant in Ottawa. I searched the crowd for the person I'd glimpsed. The stage lights flashed then, illuminating the top of short russet-red hair, the hair of someone I recognized… as being dressed as *War*—the second of the four horsemen. Maybe not war, I was reaching perhaps, but then I thought it scarily appropriate for the night. That's when the nausea hit.

"Uuhh—please don't be the food," I said under my breath, catching sight of Darius as his massive body emerged from the crowd. Then the nausea fled as fast as it had come.

"Hey," I said. *It was nerves*, I let myself believe, nerves over being alone at the event. Then I caught sight of a flash above the crowd… a flash of dark red hair.

"Got everything you need there, Mac?" Olivia asked her through the video chat.

Since Mac had figured out how they could do this without having to be in the same place, they'd all logged into Skype to take part *and* watch as Mac worked her, well—magic.

"Let me run down the list—make sure I have everything," Mac said. "Let me seeee… I have…,

>   *1 black candle*
>   *1 grey candle*
>   *1 blue candle*
>   *1 white candle*
>   *1 red candle*
>   *Lavender*
>   *Matches*

A knife... and the mixture with the rose petals and thorns, and the clean water," she said. "Needed a natural source—got it from the creek behind the boys' school. And the thorns and petals, they had to be from a rose near a graveyard—max 200 meters. That was a tricky one."

"I'll say," Olivia commented. "But you got it all done ahead of time. Five days you said—right?"

"Yup. Do you all have your stones?" Mac asked, holding up hers. She'd given everyone instruction on what each of them would need, but she'd required two stones, one for herself and one for the Goddess. The one for her was a *Rhodonite*, a dark pink stone with black patches. Used to restore physical energy, calms and promotes self-confidence if used in the service of mankind. The *Rose Quartz* was for the Goddess and it was a pale pink translucent stone and was considered the *love stone*. It aids healing on an emotional level and is the symbol for unconditional love, working in conjunction with the heart chakra.

"*Moss Agate*," Olivia said, holding up a mossy-green stone. It's used to strengthen bonds with nature and the earth, and said to bring prosperity, general abundance, and success. It's also believed to help improve circulation, overcome digestive or intestinal disorders and enhance healing of all types. It's especially good for easing childbirth and is sometimes called a *Birthing Crystal*.

Alison held up a blue and white stone. "*Sodalite*. Trust in one's self and enhances truthfulness in emotions—bring it," she said, citing one of its attributes. It was also considered the stone of logic, rationality, and efficiency, good for work in groups and to stimulate thought and heal breaches in communication. It's named as the *Poet's Stone* and allied with the throat and brow chakras.

"How is this supposed to help me again?" Vicki questioned, holding up a stone that resembled compacted smoke.

"*Smoky Quartz* releases subconscious blocks," Mac said, then paused. They all knew Vicki was into this but was usually a skeptic of things she couldn't see—much like Derek. "It's a grounding stone—a protective grounding stone. It brings physical and psychic protection," Mac added. "Mentally beneficial in several ways, *and* it raises cooperation in a group—supports their efforts dynamically."

"And it works with the root chakra," Olivia shared, "Enhances survival instincts too." She smiled. She liked that *survival* part.

"Gotcha," Vicki said, then she rolled her eyes.

Mac clapped her hands twice to get their attention to refocus. "Okay girls—time to strike the match."

Another flash of red and something big moved through the crowd. Through an opening in the horde of guests, a giant of a man emerged.

He wore green medical scrubs, the top of which had blood smeared down the front. Then he hopped up on the stage.

"Hellooo, all you devils, monsters, mutants, and freaks," the giant man said. "Welcome to a night of Halloween mayhem. I'm your horror-host for this evening, Redmond Credente, and I'd like to kick off this evening of chaos by screaming out a song with tonight's amazing entertainers, *Secret Society*." The band members behind him hit a few dark notes, the keyboardist giving his version of the *Halloween* movie theme song. Then switching it up, the band led into another tune, a familiar yet darkish Irish song, and the red-haired host followed by belting out the lyrics to what I knew to be, *'Take me to church'*. The song was a soulful, smoky, bluesy sounding rendition, and that giant redhead, he was… sexy as hell.

I'd gotten passed the whole blood-smear thing to appreciate then how handsome he was. Will was handsome too, but in a clean-cut way—not like this guy, he was handsome with an edge, and downright gorgeous.

"Not bad—eh, Lynn?" Darius yelled over the boom of the music.

"I'd say," I said, referring to more than just the music.

Lifting a big arm and pointing, Darius said, "The guitarist—the guy dressed like *Beetlejuice*, he's the band's real singer."

I turned to look at him. "Soooo the other guy is what—just the host?"

"No—well—ya, but he writes music for other musicians. He has a studio here in town," Darius reiterated.

"I like this music—but it's so loud," Shamsiel said, speaking words to the world of the unseen, relocating himself a few paces back from the stage. Gabriel had entrusted him to watch over Lynn once again, but he also watched over Darius, *who* unknowingly watched over Lynn. Gabriel had stayed behind at the house, watching should Armaros show himself again. Plus, he hadn't wanted to bring attention to where Lynn specifically was tonight.

"What a wonderful night for a fright," the handsome host sang, ending their Halloween version of the song. The crowd roared and clapped. "Thank youuuu! Gentlemen," he said, addressing the band and handing the mic to the singer. Then he hopped down off the stage. Right...

... in front of me.

"Cool costume," he shot out, towering up over me.

I couldn't help but stare at the bloody mess across the front of his scrubs. It *was* at my eye level.

"It's just cherry syrup," he said, bending down to repeat the words near my ear. Then he ran a finger across the blood smear and licked it.

I laughed out just as another song boomed from the band. Then I tilted my head back to get a better look at him.

His long messy bangs were pushed back to one side, but the rest of his hair was cut short. The colour reminded me of the shade akin to someone like actors *Bryce Dallas Howard* or *Julianne Moore*, a deep fiery sherry-coloured red, and not the classic stereotypical red often imagined when people think of a redhead. His was darker still though not quite auburn. I smiled then and probably much like a fool, but I couldn't help it. I liked red hair, and I like the way he looked. He smiled back. I liked his smile too.

Then I froze. The wave of nausea was so over the top that I swayed dizzy. I sucked in a strained breath but the squeezing sensation in my throat strangled as though I were choking.

"You okay?" he asked. Then he touched my arm.

Pushing through the crowd behind him appeared a grouping of shadows. Four in fact, cutting out the light from the stage. My heart pounded in my throat, and my hands shook uncontrollably. As the figures moved closer a gasping pain cut into my chest.

Mr. Handsome must have caught my stare as I fixated on something behind him... because he turned to look.

Lighting a match, Mac set flame to the black candle. With the same match, she lit the white candle, the grey, and next the blue.

"Concentrate your thoughts. Focus them into the flame of the black candle," Mac said. Then she took a piece of the lavender, burning it first with the black candle and then with the white one. "Imagine if you will, the *spirit* of Uriel filling each of you. Draw in that energy—concentrate on the awareness of his arrival." She waved a hand over the red candle. "Celestial beings, spirits, angels, I call for your blessing," she chanted. "Harnessing darkness, we will not use it for evil. Power must *not* be abused." She lit another match and held it near the red candle. Then she held up her stone. "Everyone hold up your stones."

Olivia, Alison, and then Vicki, lifted their stones in view of their screens.

"When the match goes out," Mac said, "we have to take in its remaining energy to light the flame of the red candle."

They all watched and waited as the flame of the match crawled up its wooden path.

"Now!" Mac yelled, as the flame turned to smoke.

The others brought up their opposite hands to meet with the one holding their stone. Closing their eyes, they spoke the words in unity, "We plead to you—use the darkness as there must be darkness to appreciate light."

Taking in another breath I spun and took off for the ladies' room. I moved passed a unicorn, a fireman, and then a dragon-lady, and prayed to the Halloween sprits I didn't throw up on anyone on my way. Through the massive glass doors and across the spans of the Loggia room I staggered my way to what I hoped was the woman's bathroom. At the bathroom's entrance, I pushed past a drunk 20-something girl wearing a slutty-cop costume, and into the crowded area between the sinks and the stalls.

Shamsiel waited outside bouncing on his toes impatient like a small child who had to pee. He'd sensed the others, the four dark angels, and had been watching and awaiting their arrival. Now they were here. *Privacy* he'd thought, *give her some privacy.* "She's made herself better before," he said to the air.

The only available stall was the big handicap one, so I pulled open the door and ducked in. When my wings bumped against the side of the toilet, it was clear I wouldn't have fit in one of the regular stalls.

I didn't need to use the facilities, at least I hoped I didn't, but I did need a minute to get myself together. And since no one could see me, I put my hands up out in front of me and took in a long steady breath, pulling in all the good positive energy I could foster. In and out I breathed. Again, I took in a clean breath to defuse the nausea, letting out the bad thoughts and feelings through the exhale of another breath. I was sweating, and I had chills, but the urge to puke was now gone. Dr. Melanie had said these bouts were most likely stress related. I had to admit, going out to a party alone was definitely stressful. I took in another cleansing breath and then pushed open the stall door.

At the sink, touching up their makeup in the mirror, were two cute girls dressed in matching fairy costumes, both adorned with colourful leaves, lace and tulle, though like many of the night's costumes, not much of it covered their *parts*.

I leaned passed them to wash my hands and then got a paper towel from the dispenser above the sink. I hadn't needed to wash my hands, but I needed something to blot the sweat off my forehead.

Feeling better now, I checked myself in the mirror and blotted away any remaining dampness. I adjusted my wings, then turned to leave the same way I'd come in, just as one of the nurse-slash-harem girls pushed past me into the bathroom.

"Did yuuu see those four hotties in black," she slurred to me in the doorway. "Nice costumes, boys," she tossed back out through her inebriation.

Costumes? I turned to look, and there at the end of the hall was the huge blond man from the hospital, and again he was staring right at me.

"It worked," Mac spouted.

The others opened their eyes to see the flame was now lit on the red candle.

"Wow," Olivia said.

"Cool," came from Alison.

"Hmmmm, interesting," Vicki said, giving them all a cynical look.

Mac then took the knife and carved Uriel's name into the candle. Using the water mixture, she extinguished both the black and white candles, leaving the grey, blue and red ones still lit. Then she said, "For ours is the Air, this Fire, this Water, this Earth, Forever and Ever. Blessed Be."

Then together they said, "Uriel, we appeal to you on the words that fly, appear in our presence. You are the Air that blows, the water that swirls, the fire light, the strong earth—elements gather in this safe place, dark versus light."

Off I went, running again through the narrow halls of the mansion. I scrambled passed a group of people dressed as yellow minions, then I passed through to another room I'd not yet seen. Then I went further out the side through another set of glass doors.

I emerged to what appeared to be the formal gardens. We hadn't been shown this area, but Victor had spouted about the gardens on our tour. At the stairs, a smaller crowd of guests filled the area with their socializing. I scooted around them and descended the dozen steps down to the landing.

The dark night revealed only a sparsely lit garden dominated by low hedges in a symmetrical pattern. Beyond that I couldn't see much other than a few back-lit sculptures and mature trees, the rest of the gardens were in darkness.

Cautious, I walked forward towards the darkened foliage. My whole body was shaking now. There was a numbness in my fingers as the rest of my arms tingled. When I pressed my lips together, a prickly sensation suggestive of a sleepy-foot type feeling traveled across my mouth and cheeks. I stopped walking and took a long breath in of the night's air, then letting out the breath, I turn back around.

There, on the landing to the stairs stood four massive men dressed in all black. The largest of the four, the same one from outside the bathroom—the one I'd seen at the hospital who'd come after me then, moved forward now, taking long strides in my direction. The others followed.

"I call out to the energies and forces of nature," Mac continued alone. "Water, Fire, Wind, and Earth. I summon the power to show in sun and shade." Mac grabbed the length of her long dark hair, twirling and spinning it into position a top her head into a bun, and out of the way. Outside the house the wind beat against the living room windows. Debris swirled around the streetlights.

Armaros had waited for just this moment, he'd known this part of the spell had been translated incorrectly. He'd watch the other—*Vicki*, at her place of work as she'd translated the spell for the Witch. She'd struggled with the anagram and when she'd chanced a result, he'd caught the error. He grinned, knowing it was now the time for him to make his grand entrance.

The front door swung open letting in the wind. The strong gale filled the living room and pushed loose Mac's hair, raging it around her shoulders. Then the door slammed shut.

"Oh my gawwd—he's here," Mac cried, half excited—half panicked, turning her face towards that which approached.

Alison, "Gasped!"

Despite her skepticism, Vicki let out her own, "Gasp!"

"Wheeeerrrre?" Olivia shrieked through the monitor.

The three were glued to their screens watching as a shadow blanketed the face of their now bug-eyed Witch.

"Mac?" Alison let out.

"He's here—Uriel, and he's…. beautiful." Mac's expression shifted, and she smiled then.

Though Armaros kept himself out of full view as not to be recognized by the pregnant one, he revealed himself to the witch, dressed all in white and pretending to be one of the *good* angels.

Mac turned her laptop towards the visitor. "White suit," Mac whispered, "Like in the letters and the codex."

Only the side view of his white clothes was visible through the laptop's camera.

"You are in need of guidance, my child?" Armaros chimed, soft and sweet, hopeful of giving them no reason to fear him. Then he grinned again.

The air in my lungs caught, paining an abrupt shortness of breath. But then like I'd done at the hospital, I put my hands up. "Stoooooop!" I screamed, pushing the breath out.

And they did. More accurately, it was as if they'd been yanked back like dogs at the end of their chains. Then as if testing the unseen binds, they rushed forward again, wind kicking up the air and loose undergrowth around them.

Hands still up, I close my eyes and pushed forward with my will. "Go baaaaaack!" I yelled, straining my voice. The air stilled, and I opened my eyes.

But the four were still there. All breathing heavy now, furious expressions set like stone across their handsome unworldly faces. The one with the black hair shifted his gaze from me and glowered, fixated on something over my shoulder. I braved a turn of my head.

There was nothing there, but... I sensed something, *someone*. "Shamsiel?" I said to the night air.

"I'm here" Shamsiel said, despite knowing she couldn't hear him. He was confident he could leave to get Gabriel now. He could have left sooner, but he'd been glad he'd stayed. He wouldn't have missed this—missed her in action, for anything. Still, he was troubled why Armaros had not been here, with the *four*.

All sensations fading, I turned forward again only to catch the last glimpse of platinum blond hair as the big man and the other giants disappeared into the crowd at the top of the stairs. Taking a steady breath in, I moved forward and made my way slowly up the stone stairs.

The throng of guests close to the top resembled more a scene from the bar in *Star Wars* than a Halloween gathering. When I hit the top of the stairs, another big figure pushed through the crowd.

"Did you see those big guys?" Darius asked his expression filled with amazement. "They must be part of the show or something. Bouncers maybe—and bigger than me. Where have you been anyway—it's nearly midnight?"

"Midnight?" I checked for my watch but realized I hadn't put it on. Wasn't part of the costume. "I've seen those guys before, Darius. The bigger one is the same guy from the hospital—remember?" I took my cell phone from my pants pocket and checked the time. Darius was right, the time on my cell showed 11:50 p.m.

"That Redmond guy is big in the music bizz, he might know them. Could have been an event at the hospital too, maybe."

"But what about what you said—about coming to save me?" I attempted, just as he was grabbed by two of the harem nurses.

They'd each wrapped an arm around Darius's and were now pulling him away, leaving me standing there alone, *again*. He put his hands up as if to say *What's a guy to do.*

Awww poor helpless Darius—not.

On my own again, I set off in need of a drink this time—water preferably, and pushed through the crowd to the nearest bar setup.

At the bar they had big coolers full of soft drinks and bottled water available for guests. I grabbed the closest water bottle, cracked it open and guzzled half of it down. Then I leaned an arm on the cool stainless-steel bar rest to watch the now drunk guests mingle and dance. Glancing around I noticed that off to the other side of the bar, leaning against the stone wall, was my red-haired friend, *Mr. Redmond Credente.*

He appeared to be taking a break of his own from the craziness. I'd needed more than just the water and a break from whatever insanity I'd been experiencing. As a better distraction, I ignored the drunken guests, and instead shifted to watch *him.* He sipped from a blue plastic solo cup as he observed the drunken guests danced near the stage.

With a flush of guilt, I realized that what I needed, was to apologize to him for running off. Mortified for my earlier behavior, I nervously crossed the distance to where he stood. As I got closer, I spied a yellow butterfly on a vine that clung to the wall where he leaned.

"Hi mom," I said under my breath, pulling in a little courage.

He turned.

"Sorry?" he questioned, "I didn't catch that."

"No, I'm sorry—for taking off like that. Must have been a reaction to something I ate," I lied, giving him a more believable reason for my actions.

"You okay now?"

"Ya—yes—fine, thank you."

"Thought I might have freaked you out with the whole blood thing," he said, "Felt bad."

"No—no. It wasn't you."

"Good," he said, putting out his hand. "I'm Redmond—but everyone calls me Red."

"Red—man," one of the band members called out, as he staggered by and patted Redmond on the back.

"Or *Redman*—some of the musicians call me." He laughed

"Suits," I said, pointing to his blood-spattered clothes. Then I took his hand and shook it.

His hand was muscular yet soft with only a few rough spots that I could sense, and I noticed a smattering of freckles across the back. Up close in the light I could also see he had a few freckles on his cheeks. His eyes were dark, coffee brown… and they stared back at me.

"What colour are your eyes?" he asked me.

"Mine," I said confused, frowning, then remembered I had those contacts in. Fluttering my eyelashes, I said, "They're a lovely shade of hell-red. Wouldn't you agree?" I laughed.

"Yes—lovely indeed," he said in a deeper more sensual voice. Then he grinned an equally sensual smile. I felt the heat of a blush… and realized I still hadn't let go of his hand.

Shamsiel appeared outside Lynn's house to find Gabriel along with the other Archangels on the front lawn. They'd all wanted to discuss the halt in progress their Charges were experiencing. Even Vretil was there. He'd left Alison's side shortly after watching her husband decorate the outside of their home.

"Good—yer all together," Shamsiel said as he crossed the short spans to where they all stood. "I have something you're *all* going to want to hear."

"You're supposed to be watching over Lynn," Gabriel said, with a show of concern.

"She's fine—more than fine. And Darius is watching over her," Shamsiel said to assure his worried friend. Then he continued by sharing all that he'd witnessed.

"How is it she was able to do this?" Michael questioned.

"Is this new or has she always had this gift?" Uriel also questioned.

Raphael put his hands on his hips, and said, "Are you sure they didn't leave because of your presence?"

"No, it was all her—I'm sure of it." Shamsiel said, with confidence.

"It's true," Gabriel confirmed. "I saw it for myself before—at her job."

"But then it had been only *one*, this time had been all of them... this was much more," Shamsiel said. "What of Armaros—did he show his sinful face tonight?" he redirected.

Vretil's face paled. "Was he not at the event with the four?" he said panicked.

"With them—no. I never even sensed his presence," Shamsiel responded. "I'd assumed he must have been hovering near you, Gabriel."

Gabriel panned the face of the others. There was a collective gasp, then they all vanished before another word was said.

"I can't believe it," Mac said. "We actually conjured a spirit."

"And we got what we needed," Vicki said. "I feel confident I know the place he described, as I mentioned to you all earlier. It's the *Dominion Arboretum,* the agriculture gardens near where I live."

The sprit as Mac had called him, had answered their questions about this gathering and based on the description it resembled a place in Ottawa. He had also helped with the nagging question of who this *fifth* was. He'd said it was the one who held the answer. He'd not said who, but implied as if confirming it was this Cipher—Derek, as they had previously suspected.

"It felt like only a few minutes," Alison said. "But when I checked the clock—we'd been watching and listening for over an hour."

"I need to do a little more on that second entry," Vicki cut in. "Might be clearer now that we have this information."

"I'm exhausted," Olivia said. "Who knew chatting with spirits could be so tiring."

"I hear ya," Mac said. "Time for this witch to get some shut-eye."

"Night all," Alison said, shutting down the video chat.

Uriel stood behind Mac watching as she used the water from a decorative bowl to put out a red candle. He'd listened in on the last bit of conversation and understood now that they'd attempted to conjure him. And it sounded as though they had, but he'd *not* been summoned.

Peering over Makenzie's shoulder, he read the scratches she'd made on the description of the spirit, then realized who it had been... *Armaros*. He'd done it again, this time appearing as *him*.

His brethren understood it now, Armaros had been at Mac's home.

Vretil stood beside Alison as she jotted down her final notes about the night's events, and the additional information about the *fifth*, and that of the gathering.

Could it be the place? Vretil wondered. But how could he assume it anything but a lie, especially after what Gabriel had told them of Armaros's involvement, his interfering, his deceptions, and now this?

Michael arrived in Vicki's apartment only to find her working again on the translation from the second entry. He was furious at Gabriel for making it so difficult, and for adding yet another challenge to their journey.

Vicki typed and then hit send on an email to Derek, asking for help again on the missing pieces she'd previously sent him. He hadn't gotten back to her yet on a few of the early translations and anagrams.

Impatient, she grabbed the phone and made a frantic call to Derek. When he didn't answer, she left a tempered message demanding he work on the remaining pieces they needed. She was still frazzled after the experience with the conjuring, but now what she felt was *guilty* for the message she'd just left him.

When Derek's cell phone vibrated, he let it go to voicemail.

He'd been watching scary movies all night, and it had been the first time in a long time for him doing something non-work related. He had a life, a job, and he'd been a bit annoyed at the demands Vicki had been making lately. Luc had been helpful to him with parts, but like Luc, he too wanted to understand what the hell was going on, *and* what it was they were all supposed to do.

When the movie ended, he got up and went to his home office, choosing to return to the list of translation issues Vicki had provided in one of her emails. "Okay, let's see," he said out loud, "... *bar the fifth*," he read, checking Vicki's translation first. Then he focused on the symbols in the alphabet. "It's correct... the other piece mentions the fifth too. But those three words in this sentence don't make sense. Has to be another anagram." Jumbling the letters, he made a few attempts, writing them out on a spare piece of paper.

Breath firth... haft rebirth... and then *a herb thrift*. But none of these fit. He shook his head once, twice—stopping halfway through a third.

"Oh, man—I've been going about this all wrong. It's not a phrase—it's one word.... *Birthfather*."

* * *

IT'S NOT OVER YET

Printed in the USA
CPSIA information can be obtained
at www.ICGtesting.com
LVHW091203251123
764902LV00057B/2403